MUNICIPAL
TILT

A NOVEL

Taylor,
THANKS for All your
help At work And
continue to enjoy the
blessings of Motherhood.

ALSO BY

RICHARD
MASSEY

THE SOUTHAMPTON CHRONICLE

MUNICIPAL TILT

A NOVEL

RICHARD MASSEY

LIFFEY PRESS

AN IMPRINT OF
OGHMA CREATIVE MEDIA

ISBN: 978-978-1-63373-212-4

Interior Design by Casey W. Cowan
Editing by George "Clay" Mitchell and Gordon Bonnet

Liffey Press
Oghma Creative Media
Bentonville, AR 72712
www.oghmacreative.com

This novel is dedicated to my mother,
Mary Rensalear McClure Massey

ACKNOWLEDGEMENTS

I would like to thank the following people for helping me bring this novel to life, both in the original iteration and this one: Casey Cowan, George "Clay" Mitchell, Richard Howk, Gordon Bonnet, Greg Jellick, Vishnu Raj, Bernard Grindel, Jacquelyn Spengler, Brenda Donaloio, Albert Del Page, Sierk Braam, David Irvin, Mark Minton, Nora Novakova, and Petra Krejcova.

PLUM
BRANDY

He killed two horses and a clumsy matador in front of 45,000 people at the great bullring in Mexico City. So valiant was his performance that *El Presidente* flew the handkerchief and spared his life. To a wild chorus of *"Ole! Ole!"* and indifferent to the wounds from la corrida, he stormed across the ring's death-stained dirt to the tunnel and his corral. A retired American rodeo clown, looking for brave new blood, waited at the stinking stables.

"*Cien mil, amigo?*"

"*Vendido,*" the bull's owner said, and the deal was done.

Braggadocio recovered from the bullfight at a 6,000-acre ranch outside Oklahoma City, where he stood as the prime stud. His famous day in La Plaza de Toros Mexico had come when he was only four. Three years later, he was much bigger, much meaner, and still fond of the scent and taste of human death on his muzzle. No American rider dared mount Braggadocio, a descendant of the fierce Miura bulls of Spain. His owner tried to have him registered on the rodeo circuit, but once promoters learned of Braggadocio's violent past, they refused. He spent his days strolling across a vast, rolling pasture, lounging under a cluster of post oaks, and drinking from a pond of spring water. On occasion he toured regional rodeos and county fairs, billed as

5

the bull that managed to kill two horses and Juan Valencia "El Grito" Molina, a matador from Tijuana. A good and uneventful life, and infinitely better than dying by the sword and having his ears lopped off. Still, Braggadocio, a fighting bull from an ancient line of fighting bulls, remained restless and eager to again prove his superiority with hoof and horn.

Dominick Van Buren, a reporter with the *Scioto Times*, knew Braggadocio's story. He came to the Ohio State Fairgrounds a day before the event, to interview the one cowboy who had finally agreed to ride him. What made the event newsworthy is that Bobby Lock, a hotrod bull rider from Clarksdale, Mississippi, had agreed to do so not for the industry standard of eight seconds, but for 12, and with no Kevlar vest, no helmet and no clowns. If he completed the ride and made it out of the ring, he collected a $250,000 check. If not, he would perhaps become the second man on Braggadocio's kill list.

"I can't wait to meet the cowboy," Dominick said. "Even if he is a dumbass."

He ran a hand through his dark ringlets and sipped burnt coffee from a Styrofoam cup. Not exactly Watergate, he thought, but for $20 an hour plus benefits, he'd gladly make Bobby Lock, or Braggadocio, a star.

"I can't wait to see this fucking bull." The photographer, a hulking redhead named Big Jake Steponovich, popped in a short-range lens and set the flash. "I wanna see the bull kick the cowboy in his fucking balls. Fucking redneck piece a shit."

They pulled into the concourse between the stables and the exhibition hall, parking behind a pickup. The grounds were already open to the public, but few had yet to arrive. Dominick stepped out of the car, stretched and breathed the deep, musty scents of soil and cow manure wafting in from the stables. A middle-aged man pushed an old woman in a wheelchair down the concourse. A girl and boy accompanied them, singing, "This Little Piggy." All of them stopped and looked at the huge banner hanging from the exhibition hall—***BOBBY LOCK VS. BRAGGADOCIO! THE ULTIMATE SHOWDOWN!*** The banner portrayed a pious, heroic cowboy riding an evil bull with fire shooting out of its nose. Beneath the smoke trailing off the bull's hooves was the skyline of Columbus. By the amount of time they spent looking at the banner, Dominick figured these people were keenly interested in the outcome. Perfect candidates, he thought, for his advance article on the event.

"How are you guys doing today?" Dominick said.

All of them turned. One man noticed the notepad in Dominick's hand and the fancy camera around the photographer's neck. "You guys with the newspaper?"

"Yeah. I'm Dominick Van Buren with the *Scioto Times*. And this,"—he pointed with his thumb—"is Big Jake Steponovich."

"Are you guys here for Bobby Lock, like we are?"

"Yes, sir. He's supposed to ride that big ol' bull from Mexico. We're doing a little preview of the event. We'll be back tomorrow night, too. Would you mind doing an interview?"

"Not at all. Bobby Lock's supposed to be here in about fifteen minutes. We're here to get his autograph. You know, you might not be able to get it tomorrow night."

With a nod, Dominick opened his notebook and walked across the concourse.

"Daddy, Daddy." The girl whined and grabbed her father's hand. "Me and Josh have to go to the bathroom."

"Yeah, dad," said the son. "We have to pee."

The father looked at Dominick with cheery embarrassment and shrugged. And then his expression turned sharp with an idea.

"Look, I've got to take the kids to the bathroom, but while we're gone, why don't you interview my grandmother. She's the biggest Bobby Lock fan in the entire state of Ohio!"

"Sounds like a plan," Dominick said.

The father clicked the wheelchair brake and followed his children through the back door of the exhibition hall. Dominick bent down to introduce himself. A gray lady with pink bows in her hair looked up at Dominick and smiled.

"My name is Helen McNamara, and I love Bobby Lock."

"Mrs. McNamara, where in Ohio are you from?"

"Dayton. I've been in Columbus for a week with kin, but," and she smiled and lowered her voice, "I knew Bobby Lock was gonna be here."

"Have you ever seen him ride?"

"Two times."

The interview wound down a truncated trail of her life. The bull rider, though a stranger, reminded her of her little brother, John, who died in the Korean War. Between frantic bursts of note taking, Dominick listened as she veered from anecdote to anecdote, proud to tell a reporter of her sorrows and joys. Dominick knew he would return tomorrow night and sit with her during the big event. Her expressions, regardless of what happened in the ring, would produce great copy for the Metro Section.

"Oh, look," she gushed, and pointed toward the exhibition hall.

A man came off the roof and climbed down a long ladder next to the banner of Bobby Lock and Braggadocio.

"He's the nice young man who hung the sign," she said. "He's a roofing contractor who volunteered for the Fairground Association. We came by earlier and he wasn't done, so now we're back to see his work. He did a good job, didn't he?"

About to say something polite, a disturbing burst of shouts and curses interrupted Dominick. And then came a chilling howl of pain, and another. The man on the ladder, from his high vantage point, peered over his right shoulder. Clearly frightened by what he saw, he ran down the ladder.

"Get into the exhibition hall!" he shouted. "Now!"

In a hot wash of panic, Dominick dropped his notepad, grabbed the wheelchair's handles, and pushed toward the door. But he forgot to unlock the brake, so the wheelchair didn't budge. Grandma McNamara said something, but Dominick did not understand and kept pushing the wheelchair, its rubber tires skidding across the pavement. The man on the ladder reached the ground, hopped into the bed of his pickup and looked back at Dominick and Grandma McNamara. He dug around in the bed of his truck and then leapt to the ground wielding a crowbar.

"Save yourself!" he said to Dominick.

Clutching the crowbar with both hands, he turned to face the danger that approached, and approached fast, from around the corner of the concourse. Dominick let go of the wheelchair and darted to the safety of the exhibition hall. As he entered the back door, he bumped into Grandma McNamara's family, returning from the bathroom.

"What's going on?" the father pleaded.

"I think it's the bull. I think he's loose and headed our way!"

The roofer rolled the crowbar over his hand and retightened his grip. His chest and shoulders swelled. Dominick saw his lips move in silence, and guessed he recited a prayer.

The reckless clatter of the beast built into a crescendo. A giant, silver-black tempest of hooves and horns then came kicking and sliding around the corner. Braggadocio gained his feet, scratched his left hoof against the concrete twice, and focused on Grandma McNamara, Bobby Lock's biggest fan. She remained motionless in the wheelchair, and out of fright or out of savvy, uttered not a word. The roofer stepped between the two so that he became the target. He danced wide right, waved his arms and slammed the crowbar against the pavement. Big Jake, the camera cocked to his eye, moved in a slow arc around the perimeter of where his instincts told him the fight would occur.

Braggadocio rumbled forth like the first big rock in an avalanche. The roofer bent into a defensive crouch, the crowbar held behind his head. And he waited. When the horns were just inches from his groin, he faded to his left, bellowed, and laid a two-handed stroke across the bull's head. Braggadocio, a geyser of blood spewing from the wound, sprung four feet off the ground, wrenched his girth into a U shape and flashed his horns skyward. At the peak of his leap, hanging in the air for an improbable second, he kicked out his rear legs in an attempt to crush his opponent's skull—and missed. A large sack of testicles flapped out from between his rounds and a foul glob of dung spurted from his anus. His hooves clapped against the concourse. He lurched into a 360-degree pivot in an attempt to trample his adversary—and missed. He snapped back into the air, flaunting his virility against the backdrop of a pale February sky. When Braggadocio landed, his opponent, stepping with the speed of a wild animal that wishes to live, bellowed once more, powering the wedge end of the crowbar deep into his neck. The furious bull, snot flying from his nostrils, swiped his horns right and then left, hooking the roofer in the arm and chest. He danced on his front legs and brought his rump wheeling around, knocking the roofer off his feet and sending him sprawling over the concourse.

A metallic cadence echoed down the lane as the crowbar, matted with blood, hair and flecks of horn, fell to the ground.

Braggadocio, his back turned on his original target, savored the final moments before the kill. He snorted and scratched his left hoof against the cement. As he charged, the roofer clambered to his feet and, with one last life-saving burst of adrenaline, lumbered in retreat. Braggadocio lengthened his stride and gained on him. A whisker before the slaughter began, a platoon of rodeo men and event promoters rounded the corner. Disconcerted by their sudden appearance, all of them shouting and flailing their arms, Braggadocio wheeled to a stop, found a new target, and lunged. They ensnared him in lassos, pulling them tight about his neck, horns and legs. Tugged in six directions, and with the price of the crowbar wounds finally coming due, his strength faded. One final, soaring buck sent three men tumbling to the cement, but eight others held fast.

"What's been done to my bull!" protested the owner, a balding man in jeans and a Western shirt pulled tight across his truck-stop belly. Pointing at the gaping wounds on Braggadocio's head and neck, he stomped a boot against the ground and hollered, "Who hurt my beautiful bull?"

Dominick raced down the concourse to the roofing contractor, slumped on the ground.

"Are you okay?"

He groaned. "No. Call an ambulance."

Dominick pulled out his cell phone, dialed 911, and gave a synopsis of the event.

"You're not gonna die are you? Or are you?"

"No." He winced. "How's the old lady?"

"Fine."

"And the bull?"

"Not so good. Man, you were fantastic! What's your name?"

He coughed and dabbed a tattered edge of T-shirt at the nasty scrape across his chest.

"James O'Neal," he said at last, and then he leaned over and puked.

A champagne super-stretch limousine rolled through the gates of the fairgrounds and stopped near the spot where Braggadocio had been subdued. A chauffeur in a black suit and shades popped out of the 12-seater and went to the rear of the vehicle. He opened the door. Out stepped a lanky Southerner in elephant skin boots, skintight jeans, an oversized gold belt buckle, a burnt orange button up shirt and a black Stetson. He remained silent as he watched the rodeo men guide a tired, bleeding bull into a mobile stall with Mangold's Bovine Veterinary Service painted on the side. Bobby Lock looked at the chauffeur and shrugged as if to ask, "What the fuck's goin' on?"

"Mr. Lock," said the chauffeur, with polished decorum, "I think that's Braggadocio."

"Well shit," he said, and spit.

Ambulance sirens sounded in the distance.

—

Big Jake photographed the entire bullfight and proclaimed it worthy of front-page art. He called the city desk, which urged Dominick to follow James O'Neal through his ordeal and report the story as an award-winning spot news feature. While the medics at the scene treated the roofer, Dominick hustled for quotes from Bobby Lock, event planners and the callous owner, more concerned over Braggadocio than he was with the humans Braggadocio had tried to destroy.

"Should James O'Neal, the roofing contractor, receive the $250,000 prize?" Dominick said to the event planner. "After all, he went about 15 seconds with the bull, with no Kevlar vest, and saved a few lives."

Bobby Lock looked out from beneath the brim of his black Stetson with cold, disapproving eyes. He tucked his thumbs underneath the oversized gold belt buckle and stuck out his chest. The event planner, holding up his hands and shaking his head, glanced at Bobby Lock and said, "No event, no payout!"

Dominick jumped in the back of the ambulance and rode to the hospital with James.

"Can you call Gene Brimhall, my boss?" James groaned.

"Sure thing."

Dominick dialed the number.

"Brimhall Roofing," came a stern voice seasoned with an Appalachian twang.

"Is this Mr. Brimhall?"

"Speaking."

"This is Dominick Van Buren with the *Scioto Times*."

"I already have a subscription."

"I'm a reporter, Mr. Brimhall. I'm in the back of an ambulance with your foreman, James O'Neal. We're on our way to University Hospital."

"What?" Brimhall said. "Is he okay?"

"He just got run over by a killer Mexican bull, but otherwise he should be fine."

"Tell James to hold on! I'm coming in from Reynoldsburg!"

—

James managed to fish an insurance card from his wallet as hospital staffers wheeled him through the ER. In little time he was flat on a gurney and under the care of a confident team of nurses. Dominick stood in the corner, taking note of their medical babble.

Ten minutes later, Dominick witnessed the arrival of the boss, Gene Brimhall.

He stopped at the doorway, planted his booted feet, put his hands on his hips and smiled so wide that Dominick saw the gold cap on his bottom rear-right molar. The fierce readiness in the man's stance, the sheer horsepower in his lean frame, surprised Dominick. A tattoo of an emerald Asian dragon on his left forearm, his banner of prosperity, and the tight rear tuft of his mullet, his battle flag. The glamour of his tough persona shocked the dull hospital room with light. Trouble resided somewhere in his name, too, thought Dominick, and that hint of danger made him shine.

Dominick stood and nodded a greeting, but Brimhall paid him no heed.

"James," he said. "James O-fucking-Neal. You got trampled by a bull and lived to tell about it? I couldn't be more proud of you."

James sat up on the gurney. "If he'd killed me, I'd be out of a job."

"Yeeehaww," Brimhall cackled. He turned to Dominick and glanced at the notepad. "Are you the reporter who called me?"

"Yes, sir."

They shook hands. Brimhall sized him up with a hazel iron gaze.

"Are you gonna make my guy a hero in the papers?"

"The city desk is saying front page, above the fold, for city and state editions. I have no reason to think that'll change from now until deadline. Our photographer shot the entire thing, so the art should be choice."

"Just make sure you give him his due, okay?"

—

The brass bell on the front door jingled when Eva Havlicek left Jiri's Corner Grocery. In the paper bag under her arm was Tuesday's edition of

13

the *Scioto Times*, a pound of whole bean Colombian, two packs of Marlboro light 100s, and a sack of fresh croissants. Beneath the naked winter limbs of Mohawk Street she strolled, past foggy storefront windows, a crowded breakfast diner, and on to Schiller Park.

"Good morning, Sam," she said to the local beggar, and dropped a quarter into his jar.

"And good morning to you, Miss Eva, my Czech princess," he said, as always, and smiled through his shaggy yellow beard.

She cut across the park, its grass still gleaming with morning frost, to the row of rust-colored 19th Century brick barrelhouses lining Reinhardt Avenue. Eva peeled off her hiking boots, set them on the porch, pushed through the door and walked down the long hall to the kitchen.

She ground the coffee beans and poured enough for a nice, long morning with Oxana, who was now waking to the comforting aroma of supremo. Eva took a seat and opened the paper to a startling color photograph of a giant, airborne bull and a man armed with a crowbar. Desperate, leaning back to avoid the rear hooves that came to within inches of his face. His mouth gaping, the muscles in his arms and chest ripped with heroic exertion. The bull's head, crowned with curling gray horns, cocked skyward. Beyond the focus of the photograph, the hazy image of an old woman sitting in a wheelchair. "Man Fights Killer Bull, Saves Dayton Woman," read the headline. Eva plunged into the lead and followed the story as it jumped to the inside, to more photographs of the fight and its aftermath. One picture in particular captured the majority of Eva's attention. The roofing contractor sat in the back of an ambulance as paramedics treated his wounds. The encounter had left him disheveled, but Eva found him handsome all the same. Dark hair, a tiny mole on his right cheek, bright walnut eyes, and good shoulders. For a moment it seemed as if he peered out at her.

"James O'Neal, 24, a roofing contractor from Columbus," she read.

What a strong American name, she thought, and a working man at that.

She poured a cup of coffee. As wisps of steam rose from the porcelain cup, she lit a Marlboro. James O'Neal. She blew out a jet of smoke that crept through a shaft of morning light, and picked up the paper to take another look at the astonishing front-page photograph.

She nearly spit out her coffee when she glanced at the story's byline. Dominick Van Buren, her best American friend, had written the story. Serendipity. As she considered a plan, Oxana walked into the kitchen.

"I love our little visits, Eva, but when I leave you I'm always tired." Oxana ran a hand through her thick black hair. "You keep me up until late at night and wake me at the crack of dawn. What am I going to do with you?"

"Please. You love every minute of it."

She set the paper down. "And how can you complain? I've brought you cigarettes, coffee and croissants from Jiri's, and our favorite sausage is thawing in the microwave."

"Point made." She leaned over to give Eva a kiss on the cheek. "But I didn't eat enough yesterday, and we were drinking Becherovka—pure poison."

"Oxana, you were not talking like that last night," Eva chided.

"That was last night." Oxana looked at the empty green bottle on the counter. "A very, very long time ago."

She poured a coffee and joined Eva at the table.

Oxana and Eva had been roommates in the dorms in the spring and summer of 1993 and had been friends ever since. Eva never figured out why the university administration had put her, a Czech MBA student, with Oxana, a Kazakhstani Russian seeking a double master's in environmental engineering and environmental economics. She guessed they had been paired together because both had grown up behind the Iron Curtain. And the background yielded commonalities. Both had worn the red neckerchief of Pioneer but had shunned Komsomol. Their psyches were scarred by the hard rhetoric of Communism, and both possessed an unyielding sarcasm nurtured in a history of silence. But Eva was modern, and after the revolution cultivated her

Western proclivities in Madrid, Paris, London and Berlin. Oxana remained grounded in the gritty pragmatism seasoned in the Asian steppes of the old Soviet empire. Eva and Oxana found their friendship in the chasm between them, and agreed that at the least they were sisters in a strange and distant land, their conversations meandering through bouts of English and Russian.

Eva pulled out the Metro Section and read a story about a college student who'd been busted with 113 pounds of pot. The cops caught him doing 80 miles per hour in his Volkswagen van. A nervous demeanor invited a search, and there it sat, in five extra-large garbage bags stacked behind the driver's side seat. Eva peered over the paper's edge and noticed Oxana reading the story about the bull.

"Incredible." Oxana shook her head with disbelief. "Did you read this?"

That was the little opening Eva needed.

"Have you read the entire story?"

"Yes. It is good," Oxana said. "Listen to what the lady from Dayton said about the contractor. 'James O'Neal for president! There are plenty of devils in this world, but Mr. O'Neal's a saint.'" Oxana flashed a dark smile. She folded the A Section and looked into Eva's eyes. "Now that's American."

"Which leads me to my question. Do you think James O'Neal is handsome?"

Oxana looked at the photograph of James sitting in the ambulance and raised an eyebrow. "Yes. And I think he would look much better after a shower and some sleep. Why?"

"Well, our friend Dominick wrote the article. I was thinking Dominick could perhaps introduce me to him?"

Oxana frowned. "He is good looking, Eva, but that says nothing about who or what he is. You do not know this man."

"He risked his life to save Ms. McNamara. I think that says enough. I am just curious. There's something about him."

"What ever happened to Claus?" Oxana batted her eyes.

"Claus? He is a Saxon mule, and you know I only dated him twice." Eva's voice grew prim. "All he wanted was sex, which he never came close to getting."

"You make my point. Claus was also attractive, but it said nothing about his character. In your own words, he was a mule." Oxana paused. "But to see him was to see a bull."

"Yes," Eva conceded, "but we are not talking about Claus. We are talking about James O'Neal. His name makes him Irish, right?"

"And Catholic." Oxana sneered.

"You are just like all the rest—too godless for your own good. Should I call Dominick?"

"Go ahead, Eva." She shook her head. "Make your call."

———

The bleating of his work cell phone woke Dominick from his dream at 7:45 a.m. It had to be an editor. Muttering expletives, he picked up the phone.

"Hello?"

"Dominick, are you up?" said a female voice with an accent of heavy cream and iron ore. Only one person pronounced his name Dome-ah-nick.

At least it wasn't work. "Hey, Eva."

"I did not wake you up, did I?"

As if it really mattered now.

"No—is something wrong?"

"No. I just wanted to tell you that you did a good job on the bull story. I just finished reading it."

"Oh, well good." His voice was monotone. Eva had complimented him on plenty of stories, but never at 7:45 a.m.

"Do not get me wrong. I detest the Spanish bullfight! I saw it in Madrid— before I retched and stormed out while hooligans taunted me. But this James O'Neal, I thought he did the right thing. From your article I should assume that you know him?"

Now it was all crystal clear as to why Eva was so enthralled by the story.

17

Forget about Grandma McNamara, forget about the bull, and forget about the cowboy. Eva wanted to know about the hunk.

"Yeah, I met him—during an interview in front of a bunch of paramedics. After he fought a two thousand pound bull."

Dominick figured that the brusque qualification was enough to stave off Eva's inquiry until a more suitable time, like later that night over beers at Larry's. But Eva was not to be denied.

"Is he nice?"

"Hold on here, Eva. What about Claus?"

"What is this shit about Claus? It is not yet eight and I have already heard his awful name—twice!"

Now she was riled, and Dominick was up and eager to spar.

"Well, just a few short weeks ago Claus was your white Teutonic knight. I thought you wanted Claus to slay a dragon and build a castle in your name." He gave a caustic laugh.

"Give me a break, Dominick," she countered. "As I said earlier, Claus is a Saxon mule and it was he, not I, who had delusions of grandeur. I want to know about James O'Neal."

"Eva, you know I'm just giving you shit because you called so early."

"Yes, but now I want information."

"Okay, here's what I can tell you. He's strong, and something tells me he's pretty smart, too. I think he's also got a little bit of blue-collar philosopher in him, which is pretty cool. He seemed honest and decent. Well, you read the article. Most importantly for you, I didn't see a little gold band on his left ring finger. Don't know if he's got a girlfriend."

"These are good things to know." Eva's voice went conspiratorial. "Can you call and set up a meeting?"

"Over here it's called a blind date. And yes, I'll call him later on today."

"And I want you and Oxana to be there, too. At Larry's."

"Larry's? Are you trying to freak him out? He's a roofer, not a beat poet."

"Dominick," she pleaded.

"Okay, I'll see what I can do. And by the way, do you want me to call Claus and tell him you're no longer interested?"

"Please do." She laughed. "He does not need to build a castle if he is to sleep alone."

—

The bacchanals smoked their cigarettes, imbibed their beers, and swigged their cocktails and neat shots of liquor. The admixture of spirited talk and sharp cheer almost sounded like a foreign language to Dominick, who ogled at the unique human collage on display at Larry's, Columbus' famous university dive. He recognized Pejman, the Persian who ran the print shop, playing chess with Christos, the head cook at Apollo's Café. Beyond them, a table crammed with comrades in black-frame glasses, black turtlenecks, severe haircuts, and dour expressions. Among the students, junkies, hippies, and retro-1950s rockabilly punkers, frolicked a crew of off-duty restaurant employees in their whites and blacks. One of them drank vodka straight from the bottle as his coworkers chanted and banged on the table. Stretching down the south wall were high-backed mahogany booths, each of them elbow-to-elbow and knee-to-knee with tipsy conversationalists. Along the north wall, a long bar stretching the length of the room, where crotchety old-timers vied for the status of lush emeritus. At the far end, the bartender, Nicholas Staggs, dug into the cooler with one hand and poured mixed drinks with the other. He called out to a bald, pierced waitress who took orders from a crowd of wool-and-leather intellectuals. On the walls hung local art, academic and primitive. A galloping song blared from the jukebox, its lyrics drowned out by the crowd. A purple Mohawk bobbed amid the gentle rowdiness. Thrift-store hipsters with sideburns and pompadours pondered the fate of the world.

Dominick scanned the barroom three times but saw no sign of James.

Eva glanced at him and then at her watch. She lit a Marlboro and took a sip of beer.

"He'll be here," Dominick said. "Keep in mind that he fought a bull three days ago. Forgive him if he's a few minutes late."

Eva took a drag. "I guess bulls do have a talent for wrecking schedules."

—

James arrived confident, but that gave way to the cold feeling that a working man didn't belong here with the college crowd. He had never gone to school, and in the presence of so many students, and in the haze of history and science in which they cavorted, James felt ignorant. But that's what made this moment so intriguing. By stepping into a challenging world, he had a chance to meet Eva Havlicek, who had read about him in the papers. And from what Dominick had said about her Wednesday night over the phone, she was worth meeting.

"Have you ever heard of the Velvet Revolution?" Dominick said.

James nodded. "Yeah. When I was a senior in high school I had to write a report about it. Czechoslovakia. Intellectuals formed a government in an old theater while the people protested on the square in Prague. They stood in the freezing cold for two weeks, but no one was killed. The Communists surrendered, and now they have a democracy."

"That's right. Well, Eva was in the revolution. Do you remember the part about the labor unions?"

"Yeah."

"Well, Eva and some of her friends went to a factory up north and convinced steel workers to join the protests."

"And you're sure she wants to meet me?"

"She sure does. She's not too interested in these pompous college boys. And before you start thinking she's one of those fancy foreign exchange students, just remember she grew up under Communism. She showered in cold water, had to wait in line, in the snow, for bruised bananas. A piece of chewing gum for her was like a Star Wars figure for us. Get it?"

"So she's humble?"

Dominick grinned. "I wouldn't go that far. But she's definitely not a spoiled little rich girl from Upper Arlington, either."

"Should I consider this a blind date?"

"Uh, more like a blind round table discussion with beer. Come on down to Larry's around nine tomorrow and you'll see what I'm talking about."

"Sounds good."

"And James, Eva has blonde hair and blue eyes. And how tall are you?"

"Six feet."

"You bullfighters have all the luck," Dominick said. "Eva's five-ten."

James scanned the barroom but saw no signs of Dominick. He guessed that the "blind round table discussion with beer" was proceeding in a booth. Each time he looked into one of the dark wooden caverns, carved deep with quotes and mottos, he felt as if he barged into a private party. One group urged him to drop in for a drink, while another urged him to drop dead. A girl with doves tattooed on her wrist pinched him on the rear. James nodded and smiled, moving cautiously down the line. He waited for several musicians with guitars and bongos to finish a group hug, and dodged a waitress barreling through the crowd with a tray of tequila shots. Two small dogs fought near his feet, and a student fell to the floor as he tried to tear them apart. In one booth, a teary couple argued, while in another, lovers kissed with passion. Stoners whispered and revelers howled. "*Euchre!*" a student shouted, as he threw down the bower. And in the last booth, tucked in the most dimly lit corner of the bar, Dominick puffed on a cigarillo. His hands flailed as he told a story, but the tall booth backs concealed the people sitting across from him. In the middle of his tale, Dominick pulled the cigarillo from his mouth and dropped it in the

21

ashtray. He took a quick sip from his pint and set it back down. His eyes lit up. A warm smile tore across his face.

He stood and held out his hand. "Mr. James O'Neal! Great to see you. Are you still stiff from the other day?"

"I can barely walk," James said. "I feel like an old Irish wolfhound."

"Well get in here and rest your bones and meet the girls."

James stepped forward and peeked into the booth. The woman sitting closest to the aisle looked up at him, stunning him with the Mongolian darkness in her eyes. James had no idea where she was from, and knew that it was a place of which he'd never even dreamt.

"This is Oxana Lisakovskya," Dominick said, "from Almaty, Kazakhstan. Oxana, this is James O'Neal, from Columbus."

"Hello, James."

He smiled. "It's a pleasure to meet you."

The woman sitting next to Oxana leaned forward. A sporty grin settled in as she took the last drag from a cigarette and stamped it in the ashtray. She blew a plume of smoke into the upper reaches of the barroom, and arched her eyebrows into a playful stare.

"We know you are a saint," she said, in a metallic accent. "But the question is, are you running for president of these United States?"

The question came so quickly that it took James a moment to figure out what she meant. Then he realized she alluded to Grandma McNamara's quote in the news article. "James O'Neal for president! There are plenty of devils in this world, but Mr. O'Neal's a saint." Blushing, he looked again at the woman who had so deftly thrown him off balance. Short blonde hair tied off in a cheap plastic barrette. Bright, mildly crooked teeth. Her face rounded and plain, but sagacious blue eyes and a keen brow provided an immediate air of surety. No makeup. She wore a plaid shirt of scarlet and gray with the collar turned up. The highest three buttons of the shirt were undone, revealing an elegant cleavage topped with a diamond necklace. Part empress and part hillbilly, thought James, and absolutely splendid.

"James, meet Eva Havlicek, our resident smartass from the Czech Republic," Dominick said. "Eva, meet the bullfighter, James O'Neal."

When they shook hands a burst of warmth started in James' palm and spread through his entire body. He knew she felt it too because the heat had come from her. He managed to contain the power of that sensation as he squirmed into the other side of the booth.

"I'll be back in onnnne minute," Dominick said. "I'm gonna get us all a round of Slivovitz. It's plum brandy, James, you'll love it."

Dominick disappeared into the crowd.

"We Czechs drink Slivovitz when we greet new friends," Eva added, with a respectful nod.

"I'm sure I'll like it," he said.

And then came the awkwardness. Sitting across from him were two of the more alluring women he'd ever seen. And while the sparks were definitely flying between Eva and him, those sparks were more appropriate for a slow dance or a long walk near a lake, not conversation in a crowded bar. James fell back to what Dominick had said on the phone the night before.

"So Dominick tells me you were in the Velvet Revolution."

Eva nodded. "Yes, but from where I come from we like to call it 'November,' for the month when it started. I was on Wenceslas Square, rattling my keys with everyone else. But the Commies still got all the money."

"Oh, I didn't know that. About the money, I mean."

"Not many Americans do."

"But you guys didn't do it for money, you did it for freedom, right?"

"Of course. And I am one of the people who say we have it."

"So in that respect you succeeded."

"I suppose. But as some of them back home are fond of saying, the Velvet Revolution was too much velvet, not enough revolution. Imagine the chagrin at watching yesterday's proletarians become today's free-market millionaires."

"Still, it was a remarkable event."

"Now let us make a deal. If you get to know me, you will get to know the revolution," she said. "But surely you did not come here tonight to discuss the downfall of Communism."

"No, I didn't. I—" He paused for courage. "I came to meet you."

Eva's eyes twinkled as brightly as the diamonds around her neck. She didn't lose her poise, but it softened considerably. From the corner of his eye James saw a look of surprise, and approval, dawning in Oxana.

Dominick returned with four shots of Slivovitz and four pints of Columbus Pale Ale. "Here we are, ladies and gentlemen."

They grabbed their shots and tilted them inward so that each glass touched another.

"Here's to Mr. James O'Neal," Dominick said, holding out his shot. "May he live to be 103."

In an instant they knocked back the burning drams of plum brandy and set the empty glasses on the table.

"You like?" Eva said.

"Slivovitz, huh?" James gasped.

Eva, Dominick and Oxana burst into laughter.

His throat still ablaze, James grabbed his pint of Pale Ale and downed what would prove to be the most significant swig of beer in his adult life.

If his boss, Gene Brimhall, were looking, he'd have a hard time finding him. Tucked deep in a cozy mahogany cloister in the back corner of Larry's on a raucous Thursday night, James basked in the tender glow of Eva's smile.

—

Brakes squealing, the fume-belching Central Ohio Transit Authority bus stopped at Whittier and Mohawk at 8:07 a.m. on Friday. Eva darted out the rear door, opened her big blue umbrella, and held it against the morning drizzle. She ducked into Jiri's for a pack of Marlboros and a bagel. A few

24

minutes later she stood on the steps at her flat on Reinhart, digging in her purse for the keys. Down the hall to the bathroom, peeling off her clothes as she went, and then throwing them into the hamper. She turned on the hot and cold water, adjusted the nozzles until the temperature was perfect, then turned the lever and stepped into the shower. The warm water splashed across her face and cascaded down her slender limbs.

She hated washing off the smell of James.

ROOFING CONTRACT

James ran a hand across an Ionic column on the portico at Columbus City Hall. The heels of his black cowhide ropers skipped and clacked across the antique tile as he walked through the oaken double doors and up a curving stairwell. The stairs opened out to a wide lobby capped with an ensconced rotunda, the curvature of the dome adorned with paintings depicting the Greek agora and the Roman senate. He went to City Hall to represent the company, Brimhall Roofing Inc., in its bid for the $1 million Douglass Street roofing contract—Phase One of a four-part, city-sponsored urban renewal program on the blighted north side. An exciting moment, made even better by Eva's presence.

They had seen each other every day since meeting 10 days earlier. When he told her about Douglass Street, she asked him to take her to the restoration zone. Wide-eyed and studious, she marveled at the 90-year-old Victorian homes—five Queen Annes, four Italianates, two four-squares, two Gothic Revivals, and an Empire—pointing at the turrets, balustrades, cornices, and gables.

"So you are not just a roofing contractor," she had said to him as they drove down Douglass Street, "but a craftsman with an interest in historic preservation."

James had never thought of himself in that light, but the description sounded good, and in the back of his mind, he'd always wanted to say something like that about himself. He'd had his share of girlfriends, but none of them had ever taken an interest in his work. But here was Eva, easily the smartest and prettiest of them all, and she was as excited about the Douglass Street restoration as he was.

The roofing contract wasn't the only piece of business on James' itinerary. Just two days earlier he learned from the city clerk that the mayor would honor him with a proclamation for saving Mrs. McNamara from the bull. With so much ahead of him he felt overwhelmed, but with his hand in Eva's, he welcomed his date before the mayor and City Council.

"James, this is so exciting," Eva said. "When I was growing up, my friends and I talked about what democracy was supposed to be like. It was just an idea. We foolishly envisioned it with banners waving and music playing—a real celebration. But this is much better. The expectations and the optimism, and even the anxiety," she said, nodding toward a group of protesters.

"Eva, I have to admit. This is my first time coming to a City Council meeting."

"Are you nervous? I know this is a big day for you."

"Nervous, but confident. I'm glad you're here, Eva."

"The council will see to it that you get your way. Do not worry."

Scanning the crowd, James saw a dirty-blond mullet near the doors to council chambers and knew that his boss, Gene Brimhall, was here. He moved through the crowd so that he could huddle with his boss before the council session began. But before he reached him, a plump woman in a red skirt suit unlocked the doors to council chambers. Like cattle, the Columbus hodgepodge squeezed through. People took their seats in the long bench rows stretching from either side of the central aisle. The chatter of arrival died down when Mayor Jerry Kraus and councilmen Booker, Fromholtz, Morretti, Thomas, Kozlowski, Rinchuso, and Kerry took their seats at the long, concave table lined with microphones. City administrators sat at a subordinate table.

Without preamble, Mayor Kraus tapped his gavel and started the session. "All rise for the invocation and the Pledge of Allegiance."

And then came the collective sound of bending knees, creaking benches and the clearing of throats. An old man wearing a checkered shirt, baggy chinos and green suspenders said a prayer. He asked God to guide the City Council as it made important decisions that would affect the lives of the citizenry. After he finished, people put their hands over their hearts and recited the pledge, except for Eva. She held her head high and faced the flag nonetheless.

The first order of business was the reading of proclamations. Mayor Kraus honored the Boy Scouts for their help raising funds for the West Broad Street beautification project. A group of nurses from Methodist Memorial Hospital were thanked for their work on breast cancer awareness. Clad in floral print scrubs and high-top tennis shoes, the nurses posed for photographs with the mayor. Cindy Lane, an eighth-grader, received a proclamation for reaching the quarterfinals in a national spelling bee. And then it was James' turn. Though he'd thought about this moment from the time the city clerk had called him, he felt a spasm of disbelief when the mayor said his name. As he walked down the aisle he spotted Brimhall, who nodded his support. The mayor's hand disappeared into James' grip when the two men greeted each other at the podium. The look on the mayor's face told James he wasn't too interested in the proclamation. But he mustered a surprisingly inspired tone for the reading.

"Mayor Jerry Kraus and the Columbus City Council do hereby declare on this day, March 13, 1995, that James O'Neal is a hero and friend of the people. The mayor and the City Council grant this proclamation in honor of Mr. O'Neal, who on Feb. 24, 1995, through a selfless and courageous act, saved the life of Helen McNamara. Let it be known that Mr. O'Neal's good deed serves as a shining example for all the sons and daughters of Columbus to see. Let it also be known that from now and forever more, Mr. O'Neal is recognized as an esteemed citizen of the city. The mayor and City Council bestow this proclamation with great pride, knowing that Mr. O'Neal, in the 163rd year of the municipal charter, earned his place under the noble seal of the city of Columbus."

The applause began as polite, almost perfunctory. But Carla Stuart, a retired civics teacher who never missed a council meeting and who always sat on the front row, stood, raised her hands and clapped with vigor. One by one and then in groups, the audience rose to its feet and gave James a rousing ovation.

"Congratulations, Mr. O'Neal." The mayor beamed as he handed James the proclamation.

James turned around and saw all those wonderful people, chief among them Eva, celebrating his accomplishment. With a polite nod, he basked in the exaltation for a few glorious moments, and then returned to his seat.

He felt Eva's breath as she whispered into his ear. "You have done good."

The mayor returned to the most powerful seat in Columbus and moved on with the agenda. For the next hour, the council plodded through routine pieces of city business—bills, committee reports, budget transfers, bond issue updates, ordinances and resolutions. Finally, they arrived at James' piece of business.

"The council will now consider bids for Phase One of the Douglass Street Restoration," the mayor said. "The total grant award is $4.1 million for the renovation of 14 homes in the Douglass Street neighborhood. Phase One is the roofing contract. This is a public hearing. The grants advisor, who opened sealed bids yesterday morning at the council workshop, will make his recommendation. Then the floor will be open for public comment, but only to those who have already signed in with the city secretary. After the public hearing, the council will vote. Mr. Wade, could you please come up to the podium and give us your recommendation?"

Mr. Wade fumbled through an accordion file and pulled out a piece of paper with typed and hand-written notes. He pushed his glasses up on his nose and took a long look at the document. "There were eighteen bids for the Phase One roofing contract. For the record I should say that most of the bids were good. Two were disqualified because they did not meet deadline, and three were thrown out because the contractor did not have adequate insurance. With that said, I recommend acceptance of the bid submitted by Brimhall Roofing

Inc. of Columbus. The bid package was prepared by a licensed and bonded contractor, and meets or exceeds all grant specifications."

James and Eva held hands, trading discreet grins of victory.

"Now that we have a recommendation, I'll entertain comments from the floor," the mayor said. He looked at a list of those who had signed up to speak. "Mr. John Jim Johnson?"

James scanned the room, but saw no sign of John Jim Johnson. The council had already been in session for well over an hour. James hoped that anyone who had signed up to speak had become impatient and had already left.

But he was not to be so lucky.

John Jim Johnson, known as "Trey" because of his initials, picked his way to the end of a bench row and walked down the aisle in a quick, prancing gait. Trey hadn't made an attempt to look spiffy for the council. He wore work boots, a faded pair of jeans with the imprint of a tobacco can on the back left pocket, and an untucked flannel shirt. He owned Triple J Roofing Inc., a staunch rival of Brimhall's. Based on the history between them, James knew why Trey was here and had a good idea of what he was about to say. Trey made his way down the aisle, and Mr. Wade stepped aside, giving Trey full access to the podium.

"Could you state your name and address, please?" the mayor said.

Trey glared at Brimhall with a sly, malicious squint. "Yes. My name is John Jim Johnson and I live at 1200 Steele Avenue, on the Hilltop. The bid proposal says the council will accept the lowest and most responsible bid. But that's not what you've done. Mayor Kraus and honorable members of the council, Gene Brimhall, the owner of Brimhall Roofing, has a criminal record. I ask you, is it responsible to award a city contract to a man who spent a three months in jail?"

Trey turned around, looked straight at Brimhall, and pointed at him with a long, callused finger. "That man, Mr. Mayor, does not deserve the contract."

He turned and faced the council, which appeared to rethink Mr. Wade's recommendation. James craned his neck to gain a view of Brimhall, expecting to see his boss fuming with rage. Instead, he sat calm and composed.

"Would anyone from Brimhall like to offer a rebuttal?" the mayor asked.

Brimhall looked over at James, giving him clearance to join the fray. The mayor's tired eyes lit up as James, "an esteemed citizen of the city," inched out from the bench row and made his way to the podium, where Mr. Wade and Trey awaited.

"Could you please state your name and address for the record?" the mayor said.

"I'm James O'Neal, of 801 Oregon Avenue in Columbus. I'm here to offer my rebuttal to what Mr. Johnson said."

James and Brimhall had hoped the council vote would go smoothly and in their favor. But they knew from Hilltop sources that Trey had also bid on the job, and that he had planned an ambush. James knew all about the incident that landed Brimhall behind bars—possession of marijuana, battery, destruction of property, theft and DWI—and had prepared his defense accordingly.

"Honorable mayor and City Council, Gene Brimhall did spend time in jail, starting when he was seventeen. But he's twenty nine now and hasn't had a run-in with the law in eleven years. For the record, that conviction—eleven years ago—was on misdemeanors, not felonies."

James looked over his shoulder at Trey.

"The only reason Mr. Johnson knows about the conviction is that he knew Mr. Brimhall back when it happened."

Councilwoman Morretti wiggled in her chair and leaned into the microphone. "Mr. Wade, did you know anything about this conviction?"

"Nothing popped up on the background check." Mr. Wade's voice was confident. "And as far as the specifications are concerned, everything in the Brimhall bid was correct. In fact, the Brimhall offer was not only the lowest, but it was the most thorough. This company has never filed a bankruptcy, has no state or federal tax liens, has the proper insurance and shows a healthy cash flow and reserve." He shrugged and held out his hands for emphasis. "Brimhall is a solid company. A misdemeanor conviction from eleven years ago should have no bearing on the council's decision."

Placated, Morretti leaned back in her high-backed leather chair.

Looking at James, Councilman Kozlowski leaned into his microphone. "Mr. O'Neal, I'm a bit confused. Why are you up here?"

"I apologize for not explaining myself earlier. I wrote the bid, Councilman Kozlowski. I don't own the company, but I run it."

"I see." He coasted back in his chair and tapped his fingertips.

"Mr. Johnson, did you also bid on this contract?" Councilwoman Thomas said.

Deflated, Trey admitted that indeed, he had.

She nodded. "That's all I wanted to know."

Seeing that none of the other council members appeared eager to comment on Trey's accusation, Mayor Kraus moved to the next person on the sign-up list.

"Mr. Leon Davis?" the mayor said.

A tall, middle-aged black man dressed in a green zoot suit stood up and made his way to the podium, where Mr. Wade, Trey and James awaited. He leaned to his left, flared out his right hand, and strolled down the aisle, ostentatiously pointing and winking at the people he knew. He cinched the knot in his tie, ran the tips of his index fingers across his eyebrows, and then leaned into the microphone with an inflated gesture of self-importance.

"My name is Leon Davis, and I live at 897 East Hudson Street," he said, as if the address in and of itself made him significant. James' confidence plunged when he did the math. Leon Davis lived exactly one block north of the Douglass Street restoration zone. Leon Davis took a deep breath, looked at James and Trey, and then exhaled through his nose. The gesture conveyed anger, as did the curl of his upper lip. He grabbed both sides of the podium.

"Pardon my mood, mayor and council, but I can't help but be blown away by what I'm seeing and hearing," he said. "The contracts for urban renewal grants are supposed to be awarded to minority run businesses. At least that's what I read in the city's master plan that this council approved last year. And all the sudden, I see everyone up here fighting over two white guys who know nothing about the North Side. The way I see it, minority contractors should work on houses owned by minority residents, especially since public funds are involved. If you look down on your list, you'll see Jesse Freeman's Home Repair in bold letters, and Jesse's a minority contractor."

James could handle Trey. Now that the debate had taken on a racial flavor, he wasn't so sure he could manage the argument. He studied the council. The appeased expressions he'd seen just a few moments ago had melted into vague looks of indecision. Leon Davis glared at the council, then at the crowd behind him. James thought hard and fast. Nothing worth saying came to mind. He flushed with dread when out of the corner of his eye he saw Brimhall, scowling and with his hands on his hips, rise in protest. He said a quick prayer, asking God to help Brimhall keep his mouth shut. Council members cupped their hands over their microphones so they could whisper amongst themselves without being heard. It appeared that Councilman Booker and Councilman Fromholtz bickered without reaching a resolution. The whispering done, Mayor Kraus leaned into the microphone.

"Mr. O'Neal, would you like to offer a rebuttal?"

James met the mayor's eyes steadily. "With all due respect, I don't think race should be an issue here."

"And why not?" challenged Councilman Booker.

"Because, we followed the rules and we submitted the best bid—"

"—According to Mr. Wade," Councilman Booker interrupted.

"And Mr. Wade is an expert on grant contracts." James' voice took on an edge.

"Mr. Wade," Booker said, "can you explain to me why Jesse Freeman's bid was not accepted?"

Wade nodded. "Councilman Booker, the Freeman bid was submitted a day late, his estimate was for thirteen houses, not fourteen, and he lacks the requisite performance bond as stipulated under the grant guidelines. Acceptance of the Freeman bid, as it is, would almost certainly merit a lawsuit, and could jeopardize the entire grant program. It's been in the works for three years."

Booker appeared unimpressed. "I make a motion that we table the roofing bids and reset the deadline for submission!"

Leon Davis seized the podium. "Now that's what I'm talking about!"

"You can't make a motion until we've heard all the public comments!" countered Councilman Fromholtz. "And on my list I see that we have one more speaker. Mayor?"

"Edwina Spurlock, could you please come to the podium?" the mayor said.

In the silence of anticipation, a woman rose from a small group of what looked like her supporters, squeezed her way down the bench row, and headed to the podium, where James, Trey, Mr. Wade, and Leon Davis awaited. Just beyond petite, a brilliant copper complexion and hair as gray as slate. Her attitude wasn't aggressive, yet she radiated a smart, steady toughness. Nearing the podium, she stopped and beckoned Brimhall with an index finger. She waited until he was at her side before resuming her calm march down the aisle. When they reached the podium, she beckoned James. Thus flanked, she spoke into the microphone.

"I'm Edwina Spurlock, and I live at 831 Douglass Street. I'm president of the Douglass Street Neighborhood Homeowners Association, and I wrote the grant proposal for the restoration project, three years ago. To let Leon Davis compromise the integrity of the grant program with his trumped up race card would be a huge mistake. I would be more than proud to have an esteemed citizen of the city such as James O'Neal, who you just honored with a proclamation, working on my house and the houses of my neighbors. I strongly urge you to accept Mr. Wade's expert recommendation and hire Brimhall Roofing for the Phase One contract. Thank you, mayor, and honorable members of the City Council."

"No, thank you," Councilman Fromholtz said, as other council members nodded in agreement. Councilman Booker's motion to table the bids and reset the submission deadline died for lack of a second. Then came Councilman Fromholtz's motion. "I move that we accept Mr. Wade's bid and award the Phase One contract to Brimhall Roofing, Inc."

"I second that motion," Councilwoman Thomas said.

"We have a motion on the floor. All in favor, say aye," the mayor said.

"Aye," said councilmen Fromholtz, Rinchuso, Morretti, Thomas, Kozlowski and Kerry.

"Nay," Booker growled.

"Motion passes 6-1," the mayor said. "Now, let's move to the next order of business, a report from the public works director on the paving project on King Avenue."

———

"You were great up there!" Eva gushed, as she and James walked down the steps at City Hall.

"I didn't even know what I was saying. I just said it."

"Maybe, but you had just the right mix of passion and restraint. You were up there in your suit and you were smart and handsome and poised. And the lady, Mrs. Spurlock, she helped you and your boss immensely."

James smiled. "I know. That was awesome. Should I get her some flowers or something?"

"I think you should. Have them sent to her house. It will be a nice surprise before the work begins."

They put their arms around each other and walked across Broad Street to where James had parked his truck. Out west, the orange dome of the setting sun peeked out from behind the Hilltop. The low hanging clouds blushed crimson with the kisses of dying light.

"Look how pretty the sun is," Eva said.

"You know why it's so pretty?"

"Why?"

"Because it's trying to be you."

"Oh, James," she cooed.

———

35

Edwina and the women of Douglass Street drank cheap Merlot and celebrated the fact that they all had clean property deeds and that the roofers were on the way! Feeding Edwina's joy was her grandson, Bobby, who floated around the kitchen table in fits of clumsiness and dexterity. She didn't usually let him hover when she and the ladies talked about serious things that he didn't understand. But tonight, she told him she was happy because the council approved "the paperwork," that she had worked long and hard at something called a "grant application," and that their lives were about to get better. She told him it was time for "code red dance alert," clapping her hands when Bobby slid into the moonwalk and made a smooth orbit around the kitchen table.

"Did you see the look on Leon's face when I headed up to the podium?" Edwina laughed. "It looked like he'd swallowed a goat!"

"The way his face twisted up, it seemed more like an elephant than a goat," Mrs. Kennedy said.

Mrs. Dalrymple nodded. "Well, goats and elephants aside, that's a good looking white boy who got up there and got that contract. I mean, he stood up to all of 'em."

"Uh-huh, we got us one of the good ones," Mrs. Washington said.

Mrs. Kennedy scowled. "What did ya'll think about the peckerwood that stood up during the meeting? I mean, he might not have said nothing, but I remember him from when they came out to look at the houses. He owns the roofing company."

A long moment of silence gripped the room before they erupted with laughter. Not the kind of guffaw that follows the punch line of a joke. Rather, a collective expression of awe and uncertainty. None of the women sitting at Edwina's table quite had the words to describe a grim, tattooed, mullet-wearing millionaire like Gene Brimhall. The laugh, however, signified that he had made a significant impression.

"These little gangsters around here best stay out of his way." Mrs. Dalrymple took another drink of Merlot.

"You got that right." Mrs. Washington looked around the table. "Dang, Edwina. When he stood with you up there at the podium, it looked like he wanted to fight."

"I know." Edwina cradled her wine glass between her fingers and the palm of her hand. "I think we've got the right men for the job. Both of them are hard."

"And let's toast to that." Mrs. Kennedy raised her drink.

Bobby entertained the ladies with one of his sweet dances when the doorbell rang. A flower deliveryman. Edwina tipped him a dollar and returned to the kitchen holding a bouquet of daisies. She read the note out loud.

"'Thanks for your help, Sincerely, Gene Brimhall and James O'Neal.' They're from the contractors!"

"These guys are pretty classy," Mrs. Washington said.

Edwina shortened the stems and placed the daisies in a tall vase.

"Bobby." Mrs. Kennedy put her hand on his shoulder. "How do you feel about what happened today at City Hall?"

Bobby dropped into a man's split and held his hands up high in the "score" position.

"I feel gooooood."

Edwina bent down and kissed Bobby's forehead.

"You're my little man."

—

Leon Davis, a loser at politics. Each of the three times he had run for the District 4 City Council seat he had failed to make the runoff. With virtually no name recognition and with no credentials on his resume, he was one of those candidates who was ignored by his opponents, the press and the constituency. Each time the City Council posted a vacancy on one of the many city committees and commissions, Leon applied. He was never appointed. On a claim that Scioto Union Bank discriminated against minority homebuyers, which it did, he organized a protest. The press showed no interest in his remonstrance, and bank managers had him forcibly removed from the premises. When he balked, the police arrested him on a charge of disorderly conduct and fined him $250. Humiliated, he watched as two months later a much younger activist engineered a similar protest that yielded $500,000 in low-interest loans for minority homebuyers. The young activist made it to the state legislature on the momentum of the bank protest, but he never once thanked Leon for his pioneering efforts.

Yet if Leon was a loser, he was also resilient. He could peel himself off the pavement of defeat and start anew on nothing but the idea of an idea. Leon's resilience, not his record, sealed his reputation throughout District 4 as a useful gadfly. That's why Jesse Freeman sent him down to City Hall for the public hearing on the Douglass Street roofing contract. Freeman knew Leon would be bold in playing the race card, and that anything could happen once it was on the table. But Edwina Spurlock, known by her enemies as the Duchess of Douglass Street, had once again produced the trump.

Leon lived in Section 8 housing. A disciple of soul and rhythm and blues, he endured the perpetual pounding of hip-hop and gangster rap. He lived alone, carried a butterfly knife in his pocket, and always watched his back. He lived on a small disability pension from the railroad and couldn't afford a car. Instead, he rode a forest green British three-speed utility bike equipped with a basket, a headlight, and a rack over the back wheel. To passersby, the lone eccentric. By his own account, just living within his means. Wheeling a three-speed through the hurly burly of District 4 surely had its perils, but it also had its upside. At 54, Leon had stealth, balance, and lungs to spare. With his ability to sprint, spurt, and coast through the urban super complex, Leon was a flesh-and-bones version of a phone call, keeping people connected with gossip and news.

He parked his three-speed in front of Tony's Convenience Store and went inside for the occasional pack of menthol cigarettes.

"Did you hear about the vote today down at City Hall?" he said, speaking to Tony, the cashier.

"No," Tony said. "What happened?"

"That kowtowing City Council hired a bunch of white boys for the Douglass Street roofing contract. What do you think about that?"

Tony snorted. "What I always think about the City Council. They don't give a damn about the black community. And Councilman Booker is nothing but a tired-ass Uncle Tom."

"Hold on, now. For once I've actually got to hand it to Councilman Booker," Leon said. "He actually tried to do something. You know Jesse Freeman had a bid in on the roofing contract? The one million dollar roofing contract?"

"Yeah, I knew that."

"I went down there and told the council to take a look at Jesse's bid, and they flat looked me in the eye and didn't do a damn thing about it."

"Leon, why do you always act surprised when you get kicked to the curb?"

"Because, something's gotta change."

"When?"

"Soon. That guy they got coming down here for the roofing job—he's got that funny little haircut that some of them white boys got, you know, short in the front and long in the back. You know what that haircut says?"

"What, Leon?"

"It says, 'I'm a racist. I'm in the Klan. I don't like black people and all I want is money.' That's what that haircut says. He tried to put that pretty boy up there for the vote, thinking it was gonna fool me. But it didn't. He stood up clear as day in the middle of God and everybody and his face turned red. Uh-huh. He didn't fool me."

Tony laughed.

"Oh, guess what else happened?"

"What, Leon?"

"The Duchess of Douglass Street got up there and spoke against me—in front of all those people! White people! Edwina really put the funk on me, man. But what was so cold is that she didn't even look at me. And then she grabbed

39

that old boy with the funny haircut and brought him up to the podium with her—and then she went against me!"

"Leon, they got the big houses and the big grant, so now they think they're better than everyone down here," Tony said, and sighed. "I've seen it. Ever since they formed that neighborhood group, they've been walking down Douglass Street like they own it."

"Well, they best watch out."

"Whatcha gonna do, Leon?"

"Nothing that'll put me in jail. But when that cracker with that ugly haircut gets down here, I'll be ready for him. He'll wish he never even heard of Douglass Street."

"Whatcha gonna do, Leon?" Tony repeated, baiting him into a plan.

"I don't know yet. I'm still sniffing the wine. But you mark my words— things are about to get real tight up in here. I'm old, but I ain't dead."

Leon pedaled down Dresden Street to Joe's Café. As always, the "secret" back room behind the piece of brown velvet was alive with pool sharks hustling money and drinks. Leon walked through the main parlor to the back-back room, behind another brown velvet curtain, where the elders smoked cigars and played dominoes.

"Leon," the old men mumbled in unison.

Leon pulled up a chair, lit a menthol and ordered a soft drink.

Jesse Freeman laid down the big six for a twenty-point score, leered at the other domino players and said, "Boats!"

Leon exhaled and cleared his throat.

"Jesse, ain't nothing good happen at City Hall today."

—

Brimhall took a drink of beer and belched. He set the beer down, pulled the rear tuft of his mullet into a stub of a ponytail and tied it off with a rubber band.

For the first time in more than a year, Brimhall was in the Hilltop's signature dive, the Brown Bag Saloon. He'd wanted to take James out for a steak dinner to celebrate the contract, but the flames of young love consumed his right-hand man, who thought of the sultry Czech, Eva, and little else. Rather than sit in a restaurant alone, Brimhall devoured a drive-through burger and fries. On his way home, nostalgia overcame him, so he dropped by the Brown Bag for a beer.

The bar was out on West Broad in the heart of the Hilltop, the white ghetto where Brimhall was from. A long, dingy hole-in-the-wall lined with small tables teetering on a warped hardwood floor. Two pinball machines in the rear blinked and buzzed near the pool table and the jukebox, which hadn't been loaded with new songs since Conway Twitty topped the charts. The toilets had no stalls. Both the men's and the women's bathrooms were heavily inked with crude graffiti and stank of vomit, piss, and stale marijuana smoke. Old photographs of famous people from the Hilltop—athletes, soldiers, and politicians, as well as class portraits from the golden days—adorned the walls. On any given night straight losers could be found in the Brown Bag, drinking to their regrets under the barroom's dim, smoky light. Blood from old fights stained the floors, and everyone who worked there carried a revolver. Despite its sordid reputation as a true shithole— indeed, that was part of the charm—the Brown Bag remained the bar of choice for young Hilltoppers because it had the coldest and cheapest beer in the city. As a hard-charging contractor, Brimhall had no time for idle nights at the bar. But in his early years, the Brown Bag had been the hub of his social world.

Each evening after City Council, the public TV station played the day's meeting. People on the Hilltop knew Brimhall had been there, so for the first time in the history of the Brown Bag, the TV hanging over the steel-topped bar was turned to the public access station.

"Damn, Brimhall," Steve said. "The only time we get to see somebody from the Hilltop on TV is when they're getting hauled off to jail."

Brimhall's acquaintances crowded around the TV. They hooted and cheered when Mayor Kraus called the meeting to order.

"Now you said your employee got up there first and softened up them politicians, right?" Steve said.

"Kind of," Brimhall said.

"Well when does that happen?"

"Soon, so shut up and listen."

A few minutes later, James appeared at the podium and shook hands with the mayor.

"Is that him?" Steve said.

"That's him."

"Git 'em, James." Steve pumped his fist. "Go on and git 'em."

"Teach the mayor a thing or two, James," Rick said.

Through the noise, Brimhall heard bits and pieces of the proclamation. " ... Let it be known that Mr. O'Neal's good deed serves as a shining example ... Let it also be known that from now and forever more, Mr. O'Neal ... esteemed citizen of the city. The Mayor and city council do hereby bestow this proclamation ... in the 163rd year of the municipal charter, earned his place under the noble seal of the city of Columbus."

"Yeahhhh," Steve shouted. "You stick it to 'em, James. Now when do you come on, Brimhall?"

"I'm coming up in about thirty minutes."

"All of ya'll gather around and listen to this shit!" Steve said. "Brimhall, tell everyone in here what we just saw."

"Well, a few weeks ago, James fought this big-ass Mexican bull out at the fairgrounds." Brimhall took another swig of beer and thumped the bottle down on the bar. "While James fought the bull, the old lady who would have been trampled to death was able to escape. The story made the papers with a huge front-page photo. James became a hero to thousands of people. Right after that, we had to submit that bid for the Douglass Street contract, right? I realized that the City Council was gonna vote on the bids at the next council meeting, right? So I got my attorney to draft a proclamation, and then went down to City Hall and asked the mayor's office to put the proclamation on the agenda—for the same day that the council voted on the roofing contract! Since James wrote the bid, he represented the company. My thinking was this—they'd see him up there being honored for saving the old lady, and just minutes later, they'd see him representing Brimhall Roofing. How could they vote against him? Some shit went down and it worked like a charm."

"Hot damn, Brimhall!" Rick said. "So what you're saying is, you just pulled a slick political maneuver."

"That's exactly what I'm saying." Brimhall crossed his arms over his chest and posed in an exaggerated stance of pride.

Steve gave a sweeping gesture. "I can see it now. Gene Brimhall, the first mayor from the Hilltop."

"So, Brimhall," said his second cousin, Susie Cooper, a double gin and tonic in her hand. "Did you tell your friend, James, that you used him like a pawn for your own personal gain?"

"What?" Brimhall turned to her with a frown.

"Did James know you set up that whole scene at City Hall just so you could get a favorable vote from the council?"

James hadn't known. Brimhall was sure of that. He watched James arrive at work one morning smiling and whistling "The Bridge on the River Kwai." Brimhall figured the pleasant mood was due to Eva. But soon after James said good morning, he confided that the city secretary had told him that the mayor was reading a proclamation in his honor.

"I didn't fight the bull for glory," James had said. "But I have to admit, it feels good."

James told Brimhall that he thought the McNamaras, or someone in his own immediate family, had requested the proclamation.

"Eva will be there when it's read," James had boasted.

Brimhall couldn't bring himself to tell his foreman that he had made the request for political and financial reasons.

"Susie, don't be getting down on Brimhall," Rick said. "He's down there at City Hall with all those power players."

"That's right, Susie," Brimhall reasoned. "What I did was good business. We competed against seventeen contractors for that job. We needed every advantage we could get our hands on. And besides, the standing ovation was real. And his girlfriend was there, too."

Susie scowled. "It might've been good business, but it wasn't good friendship. I saw all that bullfighting stuff when it came out in the papers. He saved a human life, Brimhall. And you used that for yourself? You should be ashamed. And if I were James, I would sure be pissed off if I ever found out."

Steve and Rick, each on the far end of a twelve pack, scolded Susie for scolding Brimhall. And though he kept up the bravado for the sake of appearances, Brimhall knew that Susie was right. He felt a deep ache in his gut, the ache of guilt. But in a dangerous place like the Brown Bag, Brimhall would never show such a compromising emotion. Tattooed men whom Brimhall didn't know sipped whiskey and listened to the debate. Petty rivals from way back ordered more rounds and perked their ears.

"Susie, I hear what you're saying, but I still think you're wrong," Brimhall said. "And even if you are right, it doesn't matter because the ends justify the means. The Douglass Street contract gives me and James some prestige, and it puts a lot of money in our pockets, too. How can you argue against that?"

"Because friendship's more important than money and prestige," Susie countered. "And I know you, Brimhall. You need all the friends you can get."

As an exclamation point, she took a big drink from her G&T. Brimhall glared and shook his head, but offered no further rebuttal. Susie had changed more than a few of Brimhall's diapers when he was a baby, so she could say as she pleased and get away with it. Though she called him out in public, Brimhall was glad she still cared enough to tell the truth.

"Hold on, ya'll," Steve blurted. "They're about to vote on the contract."

Steve and Rick and a few others grabbed fresh beers and crowded around the TV. Steve turned up the volume. Mr. Wade stood at the podium and read the recommendation. Steve and Rick tapped their beers against the bar. They booed and hissed when Trey approached the podium.

"Damn. Trey was down there?" Rick said. "That son-of-a-bitch. Brimhall, you paid your debt to society. Why is he bringing that shit up?"

"Why does Trey do any of the things he does?" Brimhall said. "He's a jealous prick."

Steve and Rick cheered for James when he came to the rescue. And then they commented on the rest of the people involved in the bid debate.

"Look at that skinny nigger." Rick gestured at Leon Davis. "You should've beaten his coon ass right after the meeting, Brimhall."

"And look at that nigger bitch!" Steve pointed to Edwina Spurlock. "They done pulled out the whole liberal mafia on you, Brimhall. Hold on, she's on your side. You're on her side. What the hell!"

Brimhall thought about how great it had felt to stand defiant before the City Council. He had always wanted to do something like that, regardless of the issue. Edwina Spurlock had beckoned him with an index finger, and with a graceful gesture, had called James to her side. Her gumption had surprised Brimhall, but once they arrived at the podium it all made sense. The perfect spectacle of the All American, the black woman, and the wizened redneck, a triumvirate made irresistible by its improbability.

Nope, Brimhall said to himself. "Nigger bitch" just ain't gonna cut it today.

"Look, Steve, I don't give a rat's ass for Leon Davis," Brimhall said. "But uh," he added with a hiss, "you better watch what you say about my client, Mrs. Spurlock."

"Brimhall, I know business is business, but niggers are still niggers," Steve said.

"No," Brimhall said, with a harsh note of impatience, "she's a client, and she helped me get a million-dollar contract."

Though his wildest days were long behind him, Brimhall's reputation as a willing brawler with a big left hook was still very much intact. And there he stood, waiting for someone to say one more wrong thing.

Steve looked cowed. "Sorry, Brimhall. But you know, you are on the Hilltop."

Brimhall peeled two twenties from his clip, tossed them on the bar and started toward the door. He cast a sideways glance at Susie. She caught his eye, arched a brow, and sloshed her G&T.

—

Shortly after City Council adjourned, Dean Bernadette filed a Freedom of Information request at the city secretary's office. He asked for a copy of the entire Douglass Street Restoration grant program, the bid submitted by Brimhall Roofing, and a list of everyone who spoke at the public hearing. In less than ten minutes, Dean knew where Edwina Spurlock, Leon Davis, John Jim "Trey" Johnson, and James O'Neal lived. He also had all the names and addresses of the members of the Douglass Street Neighborhood Homeowners Association. The only home address he lacked was that of Gene Brimhall, but he knew where to find him. Dean tucked the records into an accordion folder inside the fat leather satchel hanging from his shoulder. "Thank you much," he said to the clerk, and slid out the door.

He had trotted down the curved stairwell and out to the broad portico overlooking Broad Street. From the top stair he looked left and right for signs of the people he'd watched in council chambers, but saw none of them. He leaned against a column, loosened his tie and made a call from his cell phone.

"Hey, uncle, it's Dean... No, nothing too terribly interesting... no they didn't. Councilman Kozlowski had a problem with the ordinance, so they sent it back to committee... I know. Kozlowski's a real puss. But what do you expect from someone who represents Victorian Village and Grandview?... The planning commission meets next Tuesday at ten... yeah, I can be there... okay. I'll see you at the office tomorrow morning."

Dean put the phone in one of the satchel's many pouches, and checked to make sure his wallet and keys were tucked away. He looked up and saw Leon

Davis streaking by on a green bike. He banked eastward on Broad Street and veered through traffic with the easy skill of a courier.

"What a wonderful freak," Dean said to himself, as Leon cut in front of a moving van and pedaled north onto Fourth Street.

Dean worked as a part-time law clerk for his uncle, Byron Bernadette, a civil defense attorney who dabbled in Columbus politics. In accordance with his uncle's wishes, and for a fee, Dean kept his thumb on the political pulse. He attended every session of the City Council, appeared at obscure committee meetings, kept tabs on the Franklin County Commissioners and, from time to time, sat in on the state legislature. In the great growth spurt of the 1990s, Columbus government hubs buzzed with activity. Those who already owned their parcels tried to expand, or at least hang on. The upstarts and the have-nots looked for new lands to conquer. Neighborhoods in decay for decades suddenly had new suitors. With urban renewal came the need for sewer bonds, enhanced police protection, amendments to old zoning laws, and tidal waves of building permits, discussion, debate, and outright conflict. And Dean, who enjoyed nothing more than a spirited meeting between the gavels, witnessed the show.

One of the most important things Dean had learned about local government was the rule of public decorum. Differences were supposed to be ironed out before the official meeting took place. If not, the language of conflict was at least supposed to be discreet. But that golden rule, Dean tartly noted, had been violated with the Douglass Street Restoration. He had watched the proposal trickle from the grants department to the community development committee, and from the planning commission to council committee, and then to the full council, and back to committee, and then back to the council where it was finally approved. Now, the city council was finally cutting checks, $4.1 million worth of checks. The mere fact that Leon Davis had appeared before the council to make a scene meant Edwina Spurlock had forgotten to close the back door on her beloved restoration deal—and now an alley cat slinked through the kitchen. Dean didn't know if he'd ever need the Douglass Street information, but if he did, he already had it in his satchel.

C H I C K E N
G I Z Z A R D

J.D. Pruitt puffed on a Dominican cigar and leaned back in a burgundy executive swivel chair. The dispersing cloud of blue smoke obscured his view of the greedy men in suits sitting at the other end of the conference table. He looked through the plate glass window of his suite on the 12th floor of the Motorists Building. From where he sat he saw the north, east and south sides of Columbus stretching outward like a giant net that had ensnared men, money, and machines. He hoped to gaze out on the sweet spring of his empire. And perhaps he was. But instead of being invigorated by the sight, he thought only of his old, weary bones. Concealing his inner doubts behind a mask of ruthless certitude, Pruitt placed the fat cigar into an ivory ashtray, leaned forward and propped his elbows on the table. He found comfort knowing that the men before him—accountants, lawyers, developers and hatchet men—would handle the dirty work. All he had to do was give orders and write checks. He cleared his throat and rubbed his protruding chin.

"Let's get down to business," he said.

—

In 1974, the year Nixon resigned, Pruitt ran for and won a seat on the Board of Aldermen in Canal Winchester, a village a few miles southeast of Columbus. He didn't run for public office to make Canal Winchester a better place to live and to do business. Pruitt was in it solely for the property deeds. His vision was to consolidate at least 3,000 acres, have it zoned to heavy industrial, and then market the vast tract as an ideal location for an industrial park. Big-city developers would pay millions for a tidy package deal like that, and Pruitt, glass of bourbon in one hand and a Dominican in the other, could sell to the highest bidder. To dupe the public into thinking that he was in office to serve the people, Pruitt hosted community cookouts, shook hands at Little League games, and made sure his smiling face appeared in the weekly *Franklin County Herald* at least two times per month. All the while he plotted with his cronies behind closed doors in the back room at Doe's Fancy Wancy.

His favorite scam he called "Land for Trash." He hired hayseeds to repeatedly dump garbage, junk cars, appliances, and furniture on property owned by absentee and elderly landlords. He then convinced the Board of Aldermen to declare the trash heap a public nuisance, and ordered town road crews to haul the debris to the dump. Pruitt would then send a garbage bill bearing the official letterhead of Canal Winchester to the landowner. Weary of the bills that kept arriving in the mail, accompanied by terse letters from the town attorney, the landowners sold out. Pruitt, smiling and with a cashier's check in hand, was there to relieve them of their burden. If the hauling bills went unpaid, Pruitt called his friend, the town attorney, who stacked the property deed with liens. The attorney would then have the liens accelerated, which meant the hauling bills came due all at once. When the landowner panicked, Pruitt, the benevolent alderman who donated coats to the needy each winter, arrived to console them with a cashier's check. The *Franklin County Herald* never picked up on the scam. To the contrary, Pruitt was hailed in an editorial as the "Garbage Czar of Canal Winchester."

"Land for Trash" was Pruitt's favorite scam, but was only one of many. He used insurance fraud, extortion, bribery, selective code enforcement, kickbacks, blackmail and frivolous lawsuits to raise the cash needed to assemble his property. Over 12 years in office, Pruitt hustled the purchase of 3,200 contiguous acres. The Canal Winchester Board of Alderman had rezoned much of Pruitt's holdings from agricultural to heavy industrial. The northern arc of Pruitt's holdings sat just a mile south of State Highway 104 and two miles east of Interstate 71, the state's busiest north-south artery. Like an exclamation point confirming Pruitt's genius, a rail spur curled in near the land's southern border. For good measure he hired a team of engineers who issued a report deeming the land ecologically insignificant, and thus, perfect for development as an industrial park.

In the management of his criminal enterprise, Pruitt exercised discipline. The same could not be said of his personal life.

Blue Bell, the femme fatale of Canal Winchester, was working at a concession stand when Pruitt first met her. He campaigned at a Little League game, goosing kids on the shoulder, shaking hands with the men and kissing women on the cheek. That was in 1978, when Pruitt still possessed the bulk and carriage of a black bear. When he approached the concession stand and asked for two hot dogs, Blue Bell said, "Would you like them with or without relish?"

Later that evening he saw her all dolled up at Doe's Fancy Wancy. "Are you the hot dog lady?" Pruitt said, appearing over her left shoulder.

"Why yes, I am." She flashed him a smile.

"Well, how do you want me—with or without relish?" he ventured.

"With—definitely."

It didn't take long for Blue Bell to figure out Pruitt was involved in numerous scams. He spent too much time in the smoky back room at Doe's, where only men were allowed. While at home he holed up in his office for hours talking on the phone. Goons, hayseeds and squinty-eyed men in cheap suits came around the house at all times of the day. Bothered at first, Cadillacs and diamonds consoled Blue Bell's conscience. She became an artist at letting things slide. The only thing she absolutely demanded was that he be a bear in bed, and loyal, too.

Alas, those standards proved elusive.

One rainy day she watched a soap opera when the phone rang.

"Blue Bell," the caller said, "Pruitt's up at a hotel in Columbus with Faye Satterfield!"

Blue Bell's eyebrows flew upward. "Who the hell is this? And how do you know?"

"This is Chuck—Faye Satterfield's husband!"

Moments later she and Chuck hurtled toward Columbus in her canary yellow ragtop Cadillac Coup Deville. Sure enough, she found J.D.'s red suburban parked in front of Room 111 at a dingy roadside dive on south High Street. Blue Bell shouldered her way into the room without knocking. And there they were, cradled in each other's arms and naked as newborns.

"Give me one hundred thousand, all the jewelry and the Cadillac, or I'm going to the prosecutor," she said.

"How dare you!" Pruitt fumbled at his underwear.

"You should have thought about all that before you fucked Faye Satterfield!"

He pulled on his pants and made a furious gesture at her. "This is blackmail!"

"And wouldn't you know." She gave a sardonic wave of her hand. "One hundred thousand, the jewelry and the Cadillac, or you're going to prison in a jumpsuit and handcuffs!"

"Okay, okay! Take it! But I don't ever wanna see hide nor hair from you, ever again!"

Blue Bell took the money, the jewelry, and the Cadillac. For spite, and to salvage her pride, she went to the prosecutor and gave a sworn statement anyway. She told all about "Land for Trash," identifying specific pieces of property and the names of the former landowners. She also told about how Pruitt made people take out insurance policies at his agency before they got their business licenses, building permits or have the utilities turned on in their homes and offices. The prosecutor called the state police for an investigation, and the dam broke. A legion of angry residents, for years paralyzed by fear of Pruitt's goons, lined up at the prosecutor's office to make sworn statements. The prosecutor charged Pruitt with one count of theft of property and one count of extortion, had him arrested, and then continued with the investigation. Defiant, Pruitt bonded out of jail in time to make the bi-weekly meeting of the Canal Winchester Board of Aldermen.

When the investigation wound down five months later, the prosecutor had enough evidence to charge Pruitt with 23 counts of aiding and abetting extortion under color of official right, 13 counts of theft of property, and three counts of bribery. If the prosecutor were to charge Pruitt, he would also have to charge the town attorney, a second alderman—his own brother-in-law— and the directors of the departments of zoning, planning, and inspections. To prosecute the case was to tear down the entire town of Canal Winchester, and his brother-in-law, which the prosecutor didn't want to do. Instead, he decided to bluff Pruitt into resigning from office and retreating from public life.

The prosecutor gave Pruitt an appraising look across an expanse of desk. "I can put you in prison for the next fifty years, or you can step down and sail quietly into the sunset."

"And you'll drop the charges?"

"Right."

Pruitt scowled. "Deal."

He fumed over Blue Bell's betrayal, but on balance, he couldn't really complain. He still had his insurance business, a savings account bloated with cash, and 3,200 contiguous acres in his name. But there remained one gigantic, deal-breaking glitch. When he was forced from office, 1,500 acres spanning the east-west trajectory of his holdings had yet to be rezoned. Pruitt owned a giant hamburger bun with no meat in the middle. By the time the statute of limitations finally expired, he learned that he had prostate cancer. The on-again off-again battle for his life lasted nearly five years. And as the war with cancer wound down, another setback. The city of Columbus annexed every acre of his property along with the entire town of Canal Winchester.

No longer the burly conniver he used to be, Pruitt was ready to rejoin the tumble of public life and finish what he'd started—the rezoning of his ill-gotten property. If the rezoning went through, Pruitt would own one of the largest pieces of undeveloped industrial real estate in the entire Midwest. Only this time, the votes wouldn't take place in the Town Hall under the authority of his gloomy gaze. Nor could deals be cut in the smoky confines of Doe's Fancy Wancy. This vote would take place in Columbus, under the watchful eyes of ace reporters and politicians with enough clout to bury him with his past.

Pruitt snapped out of his doldrums. He set his sights on the cluster of hungry men gathered at the other end of the table in his leased suite on the 12th floor of the Motorists Building. Pruitt blanched at the sight of their shiny suits and suspenders, their slick hair and clean-shaven faces. On the table in front of them sat briefcases and laptops and cell phones and pocket organizers. He'd built his empire with a gavel in one hand and bourbon in the other. Pruitt leaned back in his seat and swiveled left. As errant smoke from the smoldering cigar drifted into the upward reaches of the suite, the last 20 years of his life fluttered through his mind like a long piece of ticker tape. He exhaled and lapsed into a weary, stubborn smile. When he spoke, it was in a deep voice, the one he hadn't heard since the days of power, when he was with Blue Bell.

"We need some friends on the City Council," he said.

—

Dominick Van Buren parked on a narrow road shoulder just beyond a bridge spanning a thin, meandering creek. He grabbed his binoculars, stepped out of the car and unfolded the annexation map across the hood. He peered south and saw a sign for Gender Road. He looked back at the map and then up again, all around, turning in small half steps until he'd surveyed the land surrounding him. He stood in the middle of the annexation, one vast cornfield. Through the binoculars, he looked south across a pasture to a dense stand of trees—giant oaks bursting with the fledgling green of spring. The crowns of the trees in the middle of the stand rose high above the others. From the woods came a series of hard, repetitive knocks, a hammer tapping with the speed of a sewing machine. Woodpeckers, thought Dominick. He turned the dial on the binoculars to super power and scanned the woods. Perched on the side of a tree trunk, a huge black woodpecker with a brilliant crimson crest and a white stripe curving from the base of its beak to the bottom of its neck. It hammered relentlessly, then suddenly took to flight and careened out of view. He saw the black and red flecks of other such birds weaving through the woods. He dropped the binoculars to his chest and breathed in the thick, musty aroma of the fertile soil, which gleamed with small puddles of rain.

"What does all this mean?"

The land had been annexed about a year ago, then nothing. His editor had asked him to write a short story about the annexation, just to let the readers and the City Council know that the newspaper hadn't forgotten that Canal Winchester was now part of Columbus. The article was meant to be a baited hook, to catch a reader, a source, who might know about plans for the vast, empty acreage that surrounded the village. City leaders were mum. The best Dominick could guess was that the land would one day be cut into a sprawling maze of strip malls, cul-de-sacs and subdivisions. Predictable and tragic, thought Dominick. The urban core of Columbus was already ringed with nameless, faceless suburbs stretching for miles and miles. Did the city really need any more? He jotted a few notes and stepped back into his car. Pulling a U-turn on the vacant county road, he took one last look at the impressive stand of oaks.

"Damn," he said to himself. "That was a big fuckin' woodpecker."

He sat at his desk in the newsroom the following Monday morning, eating a bagel with cream cheese and talking with a colleague. The phone rang. The caller was a woman who said she'd read his story about the annexation, a 20-inch short that ran on the inside of the Metro Section in Saturday's edition. Dominick hadn't mentioned the woodpeckers. He saved that for a larger Sunday story later on down the road.

"That piece you had in the paper on Saturday didn't have a whole lot of meat to it," the caller said. "But I could tell by the way it was written that you actually went out to the annexation site, correct?"

"Yes, I did."

"Well, did you see anything interesting?"

Dominick frowned. "Now that you mention it, yeah. I saw a giant woodpecker on a giant tree."

The woman erupted with wise laughter.

"What's so funny?"

"Oh, you just saw the biggest lie that J.D. Pruitt's ever told, and he's told plenty of 'em."

"J.D. Pruitt? He owns a lot of land out around Canal Winchester, right?"

The woman snorted laughter again. "You bet your ass he does. And listen to this. He had a report written by some engineers who said his land was 'ecologically insignificant.' But that's not true. His land has about five hundred acres of woodlands. There's a stand of old-growth white oaks. Huge, beautiful trees. Two hundred years old, and a thriving colony of pileated woodpeckers live there. Mr. Van Buren, you ever heard of the pileated woodpecker?"

"No, I haven't."

"Well, they're the largest surviving species of woodpecker in North America, or so they say. They're the size of crows, that's why it looked gigantic to you, and they live in them woods, in monogamy, year-round. They just came off the endangered species list not too long ago, by the way."

"Wow," Dominick said.

"You bet your ass. You know why they were on the endangered species list in the first place?"

"Why?"

"Because, farmers and greedy developers cut down all the old-growth, so the birds had no place to live. And it's about to happen again. Just for kicks, go down to City Hall and take a look at the agenda for Wednesday's planning commission meeting."

"What am I going to find?"

"A little proposal to rezone about fifteen hundred acres of land from agricultural to heavy industrial. If it passes through the Planning Commission it'll go before the full City Council. If you connect the dots, I think you'll find that that's where the woodpeckers live."

"Holy shit!"

"Aha. Now I've got your attention, huh?"

"Yes, you do."

"Good. Now let me tell you why I really called."

"Please, fire away," Dominick said.

"To make a long story short, a lot of that land out there in the annexation was obtained by J.D. Pruitt through fraud, Mr. Van Buren. And there's a record to prove it!"

"How do you know?"

"'Cause I know, okay! Do you got your pen and pad out?"

"Yeah."

"Then write this down. Go to the Franklin County Courthouse and ask for the file. It's *State of Ohio vs. J.D. Pruitt*. The case number is CR-1988-003-JRM. Don't let them tell you it isn't there, because it is."

"So let me see if I've got this straight," Dominick said. "Planning commission, old-growth white-oaks, pileated woodpeckers, and a case file at the courthouse."

"Exactly."

"Wow." Dominick gave a chuckle of disbelief. "This is one helluva tip!"

"Well, Mr. Van Buren, I've been reading your articles for the last couple of years," she said. "You're a good reporter. That one about the big bullfight out at the fairgrounds comes to mind. But now, now it's time to become a star."

"Well I appreciate that, but if you don't mind me asking, who am I talking to?"

"You can't use my name in no story," she said, in a defensive tone. "I can be your seeing-eye dog, but I can't have my name in no story."

"I don't want your name for publication. But it would be nice to have it when I pitch this story to my editor. Trust me."

The line went silent. For a moment Dominick thought she had hung up. But then he heard a deep, uneasy sigh, as if a great sin was about to be confessed.

"Regina Belleview," she said at long last. "But, uh, everyone calls me Blue Bell."

———

The municipal tilt began when Councilman Fromholtz choked on a fried chicken gizzard and died.

His unexpected death shocked Columbus' political community. Though 65, as fit and spirited as a young terrier. People just knew he would live until he was 90. Dozens of politicians, including J.D. Pruitt, congregated in a flock of suits at Grandview Heights Cemetery to pay their last respects. Mayor Kraus delivered the eulogy, lauding Fromholtz for his unselfish, civic-minded commitment to the people and the institutions of democracy. Councilman Fromholtz could not be bought or cajoled. Everyone knew and respected that about him. Taking each issue on its own merits, he represented the swing vote on a city council otherwise mired in a three-three split. Nothing could pass with just three votes, so Fromholtz's "four vote" was the vote of action. And it had been like that for several years, ever since the flap over a collective bargaining agreement with the Police Department had divided the council. Fromholtz had only served four months of his third, three-year term, which meant a special election had to be called to fill the vacant post. Even before the neckties were loosened, the veils lifted, and the first glasses of bourbon poured, the plotting and scheming for Fromholtz's seat began.

Just a humble chicken gizzard, fried in a vat of grease in Ginger's Kitchen, yet it was enough to unsettle the balance of power on the Columbus City Council.

Eva buttoned her pea coat and slung the heavy backpack across her left shoulder. She pulled the faux fur ushanka over her head and glided down the long corridor leading to the lobby of University Hall. She pushed through the door and walked across the cobbled landing to the Oval, a broad lawn circled by the brick and ivy of academia. A late band of snow had blanketed Columbus with five powdery inches, leaving the Ohio State campus suspended in the lonely shine of winter. Clouds hung thick and full like a down comforter in the frigid twilight. Eva leaned into the sharp wind, and trudged across campus to the Wexner Center. She turned north on High Street, strewn with salt and lined with freshly plowed heaps of snow, and crossed at 17th Avenue. She waived to Agnes, the cashier at Buckeye Donuts, and stopped for a moment to chat with Americans she knew from the business school. A few minutes later she entered the cozy confines of Larry's. She slid into the back booth, where Oxana, wine in hand, awaited.

"How were exams?" Oxana said.

"Good," Eva replied. "And yours?"

"The same," Oxana said, which meant she had done well.

As Eva removed the ushanka and ran a hand through her hair, Nicholas Staggs, the bartender, came out from behind the bar carrying two red wines on a tray. Eva dug into her backpack for money, but Nicholas shook his head and waved her off.

"These are on the house, Eva," Nick said. "You've spent enough money in here to pay for the joint's central air and heating system."

"Thanks, Nick. I will be sure to leave a fantastic tip."

Eva leaned out from the booth, peering back toward a crowd of about 20 students gathered near the front of the bar. The excitement in their mingling signaled an important event. To Eva they looked like hippies. The women wore their long hair braided into cornrows, as did some of the men. Clothes unkempt and baggy, the guys unshaven. None of the women appeared to wear bras or makeup, but patchouli oil in plenty. Instead of greeting one another with handshakes, as was the American custom, they exchanged hugs while uttering the words "brother" and "sister." Despite their raggedy appearance and behavior as modern communards, Eva knew these college kids came from wealthy families.

"Look at the young Americans." Eva sniffed. "They act as if they are poor, but none of them ever waited in queues for toilet paper."

"I agree," Oxana said. "They are childish in their optimism. But if you look closely, you will notice that there is something smart about them."

Eva looked again. Two students in tie-dyed shirts unfurled a hemp banner emblazoned with the words Green Land and laid it across a table. More students came in from the cold and joined the gathering, which to Eva's surprise, assumed an aura of activist sincerity.

"Hmm," she grunted. "What's going on over there?"

"It is a political meeting," Oxana said. "Something about that big piece of land Dominick has been writing about. And there is an election for the town council."

"Should we listen to what they have to say?" Eva thought of that exciting day at City Hall with James, when he shook hands with the mayor and won the roofing contract in the face of opposition.

Oxana shrugged. "Sure."

They ordered another round, also on the house. They walked to the front of the bar as the rally began. A tall kid with a scruffy beard and dreadlocks stood at the end of a long table. He looked out over the crowd, frowned and shook his head.

"Brothers and sisters, my name is Peter Chancellor, and I'm here to tell you that something foul is afoot here in Columbus," he proclaimed, his face contorted with distress. "As you know, brothers and sisters, about a year ago, the City Council annexed a bunch of property south of town, including Canal Winchester. If you read the newspaper, you know that part of the annexation includes a large chunk of land owned—stolen, I should say—by J.D. Pruitt.

He's had almost all that land, our land, rezoned to heavy industrial, brothers and sisters. According to the newspaper, he wants to convert that land into an industrial park. To accomplish his goal, brothers and sisters, he needs to rezone three more tracts, or about fifteen hundred acres. As you know, the Planning Commission has already approved the zoning request, and now it's before the City Council. Three members of the council are in favor of Pruitt's proposal, and three members of the council are against it. Just a week ago, Councilman Sebastian Fromholtz died, leaving one council seat vacant. A special election has been called for May twentieth to fill the vacancy. Once the council is back to full strength, the Pruitt proposal goes before the council. Like the Campus Democrats, Green Land will endorse the honorable candidate George Beckham, who's pledged to vote against Pruitt's proposal. On the other side is candidate Byron Bernadette, who announced just yesterday that he wholeheartedly supports Pruitt's deal."

Several students booed and hissed at the mention of Byron Bernadette's name. Peter Chancellor held out his hands, motioning for silence.

"Everyone here knows what's at stake, brothers and sisters. J.D. Pruitt's property has about five hundred acres of woods. In that wooded area there's a stand of old-growth oaks, magnificent trees that are two hundred years old! An innocent colony of pileated woodpeckers— the largest surviving species of woodpecker in North America—lives there year round. Predictably, the environmental report issued by Pruitt's engineer has enough lies to fill the Grand Canyon. His engineer claims the property can't sustain a viable habitat. Pruitt's engineer claims that the trees are dying from a sylvan virus contracted back in 1985. Tell that to the pileated woodpeckers! If Pruitt gets his candidate on the council, his proposal will go through on a four to three vote. The habitat will be destroyed. If we get our candidate on the council, the proposal would get voted down four to three, and we can save a precious natural resource. Brothers and sisters, I shouldn't have to tell you how extremely important this election is for the environment."

The growing crowd of students stood and cheered. Several corralled Peter Chancellor in a group hug. Their ardor sent a surge of human electricity through the barroom. Energized, Eva grabbed fliers by Green Land and the Campus Democrats. She and Oxana returned to their booth. *Say No to Habitat Destruction. Vote for George Beckham!* read one of the leaflets. On another flier were the words, *Only YOU can make a Difference. Dryocopus pileatus Needs You!* Under the slogan was a photocopy image of the great woodpecker clinging to the side of a tree.

"This is the story Dominick has written about!" Eva said.

"He has been reading through a stack of land records for the past two weeks, and someone told him where he could find an old criminal file on Mr. Pruitt," Oxana said. "He said the election is going to be one of the biggest ever in District 4 because of the environmental issue."

Eva stared at the phone numbers listed on the fliers. "Really."

She thought about her childhood visits to Most, a soot-stained industrial town up near the borders of Germany and Poland, where her father's people were from. How could she forget the smog days, the billowing clouds of ash, the cavernous coal mines and the bleak silhouettes of the super turbines of Most? Eva set the leaflets on the table and took a sip of wine. She leaned out of the booth and studied the Green Land rally.

"Do you think they have a chance of winning?" She lit a Marlboro.

"I don't know," Oxana said. "Dominick says student reaction is huge and that Beckham should at least make a strong showing. Dominick said volunteers are crucial in local elections. But the other guy, Bernadette, is supposed to have a lot of contacts at City Hall and in the business community. He is supposed to be unbeatable."

"I know environmental standards over here are much better than they were back home when I was growing up. But still, I do not like the idea of an industrial park being built on that land. Do you?"

"No, but if there are dollars to be had, those woodpeckers will soon be flying to a new home. The environmental standards might be better here than they are back in our countries, but the American greenback is a heartless bitch. Those trees will either be bonfires or tabletops, Eva."

Eva grimaced. "Nick." She beckoned him to the booth.

Nick finished loading a case of beer into the cooler, wiped his hands on an apron and headed her way.

"Whadda ya got for me, Eva?" Nick slid in next to Oxana.

"Do you think we should join the campaign, on Beckham's side?"

"Eva, you guys are recovering Bolsheviks, right?"

She laughed. "Yes."

"There's no better way to recover from Bolshevik bullshit than to join a local election in the States."

"I think you are correct," Eva said.

"Well, then," he said resolutely, "I think you've answered your own question. Besides, you're gonna stay here in America, kiddo. You need to go ahead and start exercising your rights."

Eva's voice was curt. "I will not stay in America. But you think the election is a good idea?"

"Absolutely. Get in there and give 'em hell. And Larry's can be your lair, where you hold court with all your political cronies."

Eva liked the sound of that.

"Do you want to join the campaign?" Eva said, speaking to Oxana.

"Yeah, Oxana," Nick goaded. "Join the election."

"Eva, we cannot vote! How would we join the campaign?"

"We will be volunteers. As long as we live in America, we should do American things, right? It says here that the election is on May twentieth, and if there is a runoff, it will be on June twelfth. That is only three months, and then it will all be over."

Oxana looked doubtful.

"Do you think dear old Nazarbayev would let you do this in Almaty?"

reasoned Eva, referring to the strongman who assumed power in Kazakhstan shortly after the fall of the Soviet Union.

"You have a point," Oxana said. "A group like Green Land would be beaten and jailed in Almaty. Perhaps it is a good idea to play like I am an American before I go back home. I might not get another chance, especially if I move to Moscow."

Oxana leaned out from the booth to take another look at Green Land. "But do we have to join them?"

"No, we do not. We will call the Campus Democrats. I am sure they need all the help they can get."

Oxana raised her glass. "Then here is to our recovery from Bolshevism, may it last forever."

———

At the intersection of Indianola and Wyandotte, boisterous volunteers streamed into the Methodist Church gymnasium. Blue and green streamers hung from the rafters, the ceiling covered with like-colored helium balloons. Cool outside, but hot in the gym, where several hundred people engaged in the loud chatter that precedes an important event. Some volunteers held blue and green signs bearing the slogan, **Check 'em with Beckham**, while others toted signs reading, **Burn Bernadette**. When the candidate peaked his head out from behind the stage curtain, the crowd chanted, "Beck-um, Beck-um, Beck-um, Beck-um." Amid the collegiate giddiness stood Eva and Oxana, both of them long, lanky, and detached.

"This feels more like a pep rally for the Buckeyes than it does a political meeting," Oxana said.

The crowd erupted when Beckham pranced out to the podium. As he waited for the applause to subside, he pointed to individuals in the crowd, waving and flashing the thumbs-up sign. Diminutive in stature with wispy blond hair and large glasses that gave him owl's eyes, Beckham appeared as little more than a well-groomed gnome. Fortunately for Beckham, his reputation didn't rest on his looks, but on his sizzling record in civil court. A feared trial lawyer, he represented rank-and-file workers in massive lawsuits against large corporations. His entry into the race took the political community by surprise because he had never overtly expressed an interest in city politics. When the résumé flaunting his civic and courtroom credentials hit the streets, however, he emerged as the perfect fit for a student population eager for a good fight. And his odd appearance inspired the campus crowd. The girls thought he was "cute," whereas the guys found him to be a "cool old fart."

"I'm George Beckham, and I wanna be your District 4 representative on the Columbus City Council!" he said, raising both fists in the air. The crowd responded with a thunderclap of applause. Confetti fell from the rafters.

"I was crushed when I learned about the death of the honorable Sebastian Fromholtz. But I got over my sorrow when I heard that my opponent wanted to cut down the trees and drive the pileated woodpeckers from their home! If you elect me, I will protect the environment and represent District 4 with integrity!" He pumped his fist in the air.

The crowd cheered, the **Check 'em with Beckham** signs bounced, and a new shower of confetti poured from the rafters. The student volunteers bumped and dipped with beginner's elation, euphoric that here in front of them appeared the great defender of the birds and the trees.

"Those oaks down in Canal Winchester are more than two hundred years old! We cannot let them be destroyed! If I'm elected to the City Council, I'll immediately call for a vote on the zoning ordinance and vote it doooowwwn!" he said, bending his knees, pointing his finger to the floor and contorting his face in an expression of grief. The volunteers flew into a frenzy of shaking signs, "Beck-um" chants and chaotic swaying.

Eva and Oxana glanced at each other, half smiling at the unbridled optimism filling the church gymnasium.

Eva smiled. "I didn't think Americans got this excited about local politics.

I thought they only cared about presidential elections. I am impressed. What about you?"

"I am surprised. My only question is, will this zeal last for the next three months?"

"We shall see."

For the next five minutes Beckham shook his fists, flared his hips and scrunched his face for dramatic appeal. The volunteers rode the crescendo of his voice to the climax of his speech, erupting with angry joy when Beckham pushed out his chest and shouted, "Bernadette, bring it on!"

Beckham, his cheeks rosy from the declamation, stepped down from the stage and wandered through the crowd. Shaking hands, patting backs and telling jokes, Beckham maneuvered through the adulation toward where Eva and Oxana stood in line for District 4 campaign kits. Upon seeing them, Beckham, his face bright with laughter, stopped and stared. On the verge of ogling, he held out his hand and said, "Hello, I'm George Beckham."

Eva and Oxana smiled.

"I am Eva Havlicek, and this is Oxana Lisakovskya," Eva said, at her formal best.

"I hear an accent," Beckham said, standing at the head of his entourage. "Where are you from?"

"Prague, Czech Republic, and Oxana is from Almaty, Kazakhstan."

"Fantastic. Why did you guys join the campaign?"

"We are environmentalists," Eva said, who wasn't about to go into the whole "recovering Bolshevik" routine.

"I was in Prague in 1992 during the national election," Beckham said. "And my pocket was picked on the Charles Bridge."

"I hope that episode did not spoil your visit to my home town."

"It was a hassle, but nothing can diminish the beauty of Prague. It is truly one of Europe's finest cities. What are you doing here in the United States?"

"I am an MBA student at Ohio State."

"What's your focus?"

"International finance—direct foreign investment."

"Excellent," he gushed. "Perhaps before it's all said and done you might crunch some numbers for the campaign?"

"My numbers are right here, Mr. Beckham." She pointed to the stack of yard signs tucked under her arm.

"Well, since we have a Czech on the campaign, I will let the spirit of Vaclav Havel guide me."

"He is a worthy muse," Eva said, revealing a snippet of national pride.

Silently, she was astounded. Here in front of all these people was Beckham, and a trace of amorous yearning trickled through his owl's eyes. The salacious glint was only there for a nanosecond, but Eva detected it nonetheless. And Oxana saw it, too. As they left the church gymnasium, she looked at Eva with a suggestive grin.

"I guess democracy makes you sexy. Or more accurately, democracy makes Mr. Beckham think that he is sexy."

"Apparently," Eva said.

"He is so short." Oxana giggled. "He would need a ladder just to peck you on the cheek."

"Oh, Oxana, you are cruel."

"What? He is a short little American man who has been swept off his feet by the tall blonde from Prague. I find it rather poetic."

Oxana's laugh was infectious, and Eva couldn't resist a dig.

"If the next time we see him he is carrying a ladder, I guess we will know what is on his mind."

—

Byron Bernadette and his nephew, Dean Bernadette, sat at a long mahogany table in the wood-and-leather conference room deep inside the trust of the Bernadette and Blankovich law firm. Bernadette, whose clients included banks, insurance companies, and corporate executives, had always harbored openly secret thoughts of running for the District 4 City Council seat. He always talked himself out of it because the competition was just too tough. Councilman Fromholtz had a lock on the university elite, the rising bloc of lesbian feminists in Clintonville, and he had a strong relationship with the business community all along Morse Road. The district was Councilman Fromholtz's for as long as he wanted to stay in office. Now that Fromholtz was dead, the game had changed.

Bernadette knew Beckham would claim Fromholtz's university ties and the organized lesbian contingent. But Bernadette was convinced he could win from north Clintonville up to Morse Road, a thriving business corridor that wasn't likely to support the environmental ticket. And Bernadette would not let the south Clintonville lesbians go unchecked. To the contrary, he would plant his top operatives in their midst and make them and Beckham fight for every inch of south Clintonville soil they hoped to control. An unexpected source of hope came from the Campus Republicans, who'd had a violent reaction to the near instantaneous and widespread surge of pro-Beckham activity. The fraternity houses mobilized and had already told Bernadette that they had scheduled a series of monster keg parties in his honor. Bernadette welcomed their support, even if it came at the bottom of a beer bong.

Bernadette truly believed that his message of jobs and economic development was far superior to anything Beckham could manage to say about a stand of old trees and the pileated woodpeckers. Several prominent businessmen in District 4 had already called to say that exact thing. Bernadette doubted that the army of students who'd flocked to Beckham's banner would actually vote in a City Council election. Meanwhile, the staunch Republicans likely to support his candidacy were voting addicts. They cast ballots in elections for the School Board, City Council, judgeships, the state legislature, Congress and the presidency. Bernadette was confident. Still, he felt like he needed a little trick to confound his opponent. That's why he'd summoned his nephew Dean. Bernadette had plenty of people who could huddle with business leaders and raise cash through swanky fundraisers. His technical people could handle the press and his political advertisements. But it was Dean, his backdoor envoy, who had a willing nose for the streets.

"What's the worst thing we know about Beckham?" Bernadette said.

"Let's see." Dean dug through a pile of papers stacked in an accordion folder inside his cavernous satchel. "He has a law degree from Capital University. He did a lot of work for nonprofits. He chaired several environmental boards and won a big civil suit against Ohio Waste Management a few years back. He's currently representing a class-action lawsuit against a Dayton firm that manufactures hair dryers. He's never filed bankruptcy. He paid off his mortgage ten years ago, and he donates money to several prominent charities. Aha," he said, pulling out a stapled case file. "Here it is. Beckham is married with three kids. But he likes college girls."

Bernadette didn't say anything for a while, choosing instead to absorb what he had heard. "How do you know?" he said at last.

"This," Dean said, in a controlled burst of triumph, "is a 1988 filing for divorce: *Martha Beckham vs. George Beckham*. The suit was eventually dropped, and from what I saw on TV last night, they're still together. But at the time, she was pissed off. Listen to this: 'He repeatedly abuses the sanctity of marriage with his frequent visits to campus and the campus area,'" read Dean from a highlighted passage on page three. "Translation: He likes college chicks."

"How'd you get a hold of that?"

"A little bird at the courthouse likes to sing to me."

"Nice. Should we give it to the press?"

"I don't think the press would be too interested. This happened back in '88, and Beckham and his wife are still together. Uncle Byron, you remember that old saying, 'Zebras don't change their stripes?'"

"Yeah, why?"

"Well, I'd kind of like to see if the maxim is true."

"So we need a seductress, is what you're saying?" A smile stretched across the rustic features of Bernadette's handsome face.

"For lack of a better term, yes," he said. "And one who's not afraid to get proof."

"Don't you think it's highly unlikely that Beckham would shack up with some bimbo right in the middle of the election?"

"Oh, I don't know," Dean said, flippantly. "Poontang's a pretty powerful thing, Uncle Byron. Just ask Gary Hart."

Bernadette leaned back in his chair and tugged on his blue suspenders. At the far end of the table, under the subtle light of the conference room, his nephew looked like an alien plotting the destruction of the earth. Dean caught his gaze and gave him a mean stare.

"I'm serious," Dean said. "Let's fucking nail that little prick to the cross!"

Bernadette knew his nephew had a dark side, but he didn't know how dark it was or how deep it went. All he knew is that there was something a bit unsettling about him. With that in mind, Bernadette was on the verge of saying, "Hell, no. There's no way I'm going to try and catch Beckham with his pants down. Maybe something else, but not that." But the thought of seeing the arrogant runt humbled in front of the entire city was enticing. An easy victory for the District 4 City Council seat didn't sound so bad, either.

"Okay. Give J. D. Pruitt a call," Bernadette said.

His nephew dialed Pruitt's special private number. Staring at his uncle to heighten the drama, Dean ceremoniously pushed the speakerphone button. After a few rings, Pruitt answered.

"Hello?"

"Mr. Pruitt, this is Byron Bernadette."

"Mr. Bernadette." Pruitt's voice rose with excitement.

"I've got you on speakerphone, Mr. Pruitt. I'm sitting with one of my top campaign advisors, my nephew Dean. We're talking about how we can beat that skinny little bastard, Beckham. He had a big rally last night, and it looks like he's all but stolen the campus vote."

69

"I saw it on TV," Pruitt said, sourly.

"Anyway, we think we know how to bury Beckham in an avalanche of controversy."

"Oh, really? Please let me know how I can help."

"Here's my nephew, Dean. He'll tell you all about it."

Dean turned toward the phone with a serious expression. "Hello, Mr. Pruitt. I'm not an artful man, so I'll just come right out and say it: We want to seduce Beckham and blackmail him into dropping out of the election, and that'll cost you twenty thousand dollars."

Pruitt cleared his throat. "How much?"

"Twenty thousand. Cash!"

"Don't you think that's a little steep?"

"No," Dean said. "The same thing'll cost you two hundred in New York! This is a bargain basement Ohio deal, Mr. Pruitt. And compared to what your land's going to be worth on the back end of this election, I'd damn near say this is the deal of the century."

"When do you need the money?" Pruitt said.

"Tomorrow, no later than noon."

Dean and Uncle Byron exchanged expectant glances. Over the speakerphone they heard Pruitt sip, smoke, pace and sigh as he considered the proposition.

"Can you pull this off?" Pruitt said.

Dean looked at Uncle Byron and pumped his fist.

"Yes, Mr. Pruitt," Dean said. "It's very possible. Beckham is an old-school skirt chaser, and he's a political rookie. He'll never know it's a setup. He'll think it's just some college chick who thinks he's sexy and cool because he's running for office."

"I'll have one of my guys drop off the money tomorrow. And Byron?"

"Yes, Mr. Pruitt?"

"This better work. I really need to win this election. I've been sitting on a thirty million dollar land deal for the last ten years. I'm ready to move on to Florida. If that shit-ass Beckham gets in office, the value of my property will evaporate."

70

"Don't worry about a thing," Byron Bernadette said. "By the time the election rolls around, George Beckham will be the butt of every dirty joke at City Hall. And within a year you'll have a drink in your hand and your toes in the sand."

And they hung up with Mr. J.D. Pruitt.

"You're really into this, aren't you?" Bernadette said.

Dean smirked. "I wanna get down and dirty, Uncle Byron, but I also think we need to get out there and campaign with the people."

"We've already planned to do that."

"Not entirely true. All up and down Cleveland Road, from Fifth Avenue to Morse Road, live black people, and lots of them. If we can somehow get our hands on the black vote—jobs, jobs and *more* jobs—we can outflank Beckham and win this election—even without the blackmail."

A dark look came across Bernadette's face. He shook his head in a slow attempt to destroy Dean's notion.

"In theory, I like the idea. There are a lot of votes out there on Cleveland Road. But my core constituency wouldn't like the idea of me pandering to the blacks. I could lose the one thing I've already got locked up. And doesn't it always backfire when you get involved with blacks?"

"I would say that's an oversimplification of the situation," Dean said. "The truth is, Uncle Byron, if you don't do something unique, you could get burned in May. This is a special election, Uncle Byron. The next time around, when all the big candidates have had the time to set up their machines, the competition will be much stiffer. This is your chance. Be creative. A lot of people were at that rally last night. I mean, it was packed to the point where you could barely move. These environmental issues really strike a nerve with the campus crowd. If you wanna be on the council when all those multi-million dollar contracts come down the pike, you better start getting into the idea of black people."

Dean cracked his knuckles and shifted in his chair.

Bernadette tapped his index finger on the table as he tried to silence the uncomfortable thoughts racing through his mind. "Okay, let's say I court the black vote. How do I do that? We're all rich white people and all we know are rich white people."

Dean dug into his satchel and pulled out a notepad. He flipped through the pages to a pink sticky note. He scanned to the bottom of the page. Upon seeing the name, he scratched his chin and laughed. "Leon Davis. He's very black. And he's got balls the size of Montana. And—this is the best part—he lives in District 4, on Hudson Street."

"How do you know him?"

"I met him at City Hall about a month ago. He was bitching about a roofing contract being awarded to a white contractor. Best part is, he rides a bike, Uncle Byron. A fuckin' three-speed roadster with mirrors and a wheel-powered light."

"So this guy can cover a lot of ground in a little amount of time?"

"And 'hood-style, too."

"Can he be bought?"

"All blacks can be bought, Uncle Byron."

Bernadette took a long look at his nephew. Natty black glasses enhanced the beguilement in his brown eyes. His hair slicked back in a brunet wave of insouciance. Dressed in a starched white shirt, silk purple tie, blue wool suit, and polished Hanovers, Dean could pass for a banker, lawyer, or an upstart CEO. But Bernadette knew it was all a disguise, all of it to hide the hellion who lurked within.

"So I have my marching orders?" Dean said.

"Yeah, you do. Leave campus, Clintonville and Morse Road to the rest of us. Cleveland Road and that other thing are all yours. And Dean, don't tell a god damned soul about the little chat we've just had."

"Come on, Uncle Byron, it's me, Dean. I want this as much as you do."

NASTY
LETTERS

The century-old oak had grown up and over the Mansard home at the corner of Douglass and Medina. The swollen trunk leaned to within inches of the cornice. The limbs arching over the roof had cracked the chimney, and like the fingers of a giant hand, threatened to crumple the home like a piece of paper. James, standing in a fork high up in that tree, yanked the starter cable and the chain saw roared to life. He pushed the goggles down over his eyes and laid the blade over a crooked branch, sending saw dust spewing into the air.

A cord looped through a high crag was tied to the limb, forming a pulley, so that when the branch was severed from the tree it didn't plummet to the ground. A second cord served as the guide to control the limb's descent. On the ground, one crew worked the pulley and the other worked the guide. Under Brimhall's supervision, they lifted the massive limbs out as if they were pick-up sticks, and lowered them to the ground as if they were Ming vases.

A third cord, also looped through the high crag, was tied to the winch on Brimhall's truck on one end, and on the other, to a thick steel hoop on the leather harness around James' waist. That cord was the lifeline, and also served as the arborist's version of Tarzan's vine. James climbed out onto the limbs with

73

the patience of a predator, tying the pulley and guide knots with the flurry of a magician. Dangling by a thick rope at his waist was the chain saw, which James used to butcher the tree. Secured by the lifeline, James swung from limb to limb, above the roof and out over the street, whittling the branches down until all that remained were the trunk and the high crag holding the precious nylon cords.

The limb cutting had taken eight hours, but seemingly all at once the majestic Mansard emerged from behind the dense timber that had hidden it for the last 30 years. As the golden light of dusk washed over the crenellated stone cornice, James grooved the base of the trunk with deep, competing angles that would determine the direction of the fall. A metallic beat pierced the Douglass Street corridor as he drove steel wedges into the cuts with brute sledgehammer strikes. With the winch chain tied midway up the stump, Brimhall applied the torque of his diesel dually. The trunk budged, and budged again, and then threatened to snap and leap back against the house. James hefted the sledgehammer behind his back one last time, and with a good grunt, powered the throw spike into the heart of the crippled seam. Bark peeled back from the stump and a sharp spray of splinters glanced off James' goggles. In a symphony of slow, aching creaks the old oak dislodged from the stump and thundered to the ground. Clouds of dust rose from the gutters. An aluminum can rolled across the street.

"Yeehawwwww," cackled Brimhall, leaning out of the driver's side window.

James climbed on top of the waist-high trunk, slung the sledgehammer across his shoulder, wiped his brow with his forearm and smiled. Kids on bikes watched from behind orange pylons. Families had gathered on porches to witness the day-long tree felling. One of the neighborhood's old-timers stood on the curb, pointing at James and shouting: "He a man! He a man! Uh-huh, he a man!"

Among the onlookers was Bobby Spurlock. He had grown fearful as James and the chain saw swung from limb to limb, and had winced as he climbed out on the high branches over the street. Each time James descended to oil and sharpen the chain saw's blades, it was Bobby who approached the work perimeter with a large cup of ice water. James, who each time drank deeply from the cup, welcomed

Bobby's approach. In his blue jumper, spiked iron leg braces, leather harness and work boots, and at times wielding the mighty chain saw like a delicate carving knife, goggled James was unlike anything Bobby had ever seen. He had taken down the sprawling, 80-foot tree that made the house at the end of the block look haunted. For several decades the burly oak had lorded over the western entrance to Douglass Street, blocking out the sublime center of the spring and summer sunsets. James, in Bobby's eyes, was the bringer of light.

He darted across the street, jumped over a clump of limbs and skipped to the tree trunk where James stood. "My grandmother says ya'll are invited over for dinner."

The sound of many chain saws erupted as the crew, seven immigrants from Guadalajara, Mexico, sliced the trunk into small sections. James and Brimhall looked at each other, and then shrugged their shoulders as if to say, "Why not?"

"We'd be honored to have dinner with your grandmother," James said. "Just tell her that we're all sweaty."

"Grandma says she don't care," Bobby said.

He stood on his left foot, twisted into a full circle and then dashed down the street, saying, "Granny, Granny, Granny," as loud as his voice would allow. James and Brimhall shared a glance of sweet embarrassment as they were not accustomed to such open expressions of admiration.

"I'm glad someone loves us." Brimhall barked a few harsh commands to the crew as he and James headed toward Edwina's.

She lived in a two-story, red brick Queen Anne, the most preserved of the houses in the Douglass Street Restoration zone. Edwina's home embodied the flamboyant charm that distinguished the architecture of the Victorian era. A steeply pitched slate roof, asymmetrical, crowned with a turret, dormers, chimneys and half-timbered gables. Framed by imposing classical columns and a spindled balustrade, the wide porch wrapped around the southwest corner of the house. An American flag curled gently in the breeze, and the porch swing swayed to-and-fro. The small front yard, bounded by a wrought iron fence, featured a stone birdbath in the budding shade of a male gingko tree. The sidewalk in front of her house, the original red brick, looked like a plaid sash between the pavements. Covered with decades of grime and lined with eaves and windowsills that no longer had paint, the Queen Anne showed every minute of its 89 years of age. But like the poor school kid who wears his third-hand shirt pressed and tucked, Edwina's home, like all the others in the restoration zone, conveyed dignity in spite of its disrepair.

Before James and Brimhall reached the top of the porch steps, Bobby opened the front door and bashfully motioned for them to come inside. His round face taut with a timid grin, he sprinted down the paneled hall and disappeared into the kitchen. For a moment, James and Brimhall stood on the welcome mat, uncomfortable with the idea of entering unattended. Then Edwina appeared from the threshold of the kitchen. Smiling and drying her hands on an apron, and with Bobby peering out from behind her, she said, "Come on in. I've got some victuals for ya'll."

Faded yet neat, threadbare but surprisingly splendid, the house interior matched the exterior. James and Brimhall, both austere bachelors, immediately felt the supreme comfort of a household run by a mature woman from the old school. The tempting scents of freshly cooked food guided them down the long hall to the enormous kitchen. Running along the north wall were inlaid shelves stacked with dishes, cookbooks, pots, pans and jars of homemade preserves. The door to the pantry was ajar, revealing a larder crammed with bottled spices and large stores of dry goods. Canisters filled with sugar, flour, coffee and tea lined the tile countertop. A fresh loaf of bread sat cooling on a cutting board. Photographs and child art hung from colorful magnets on the refrigerator. A long wooden table adorned with a vase of daisies and lined with six chairs dominated the middle of the kitchen. Bobby frantically washed dishes at the deep, double-bay porcelain sink. Edwina hovered over the six-jet porcelain-plated range and stirred something in a large pot. A slow-turning fan hanging from the kitchen's 12-foot ceiling sent a soothing breeze over the deep pit of home.

James gestured at the grandeur of the kitchen. "Oh, my. This is wonderful."

"Thanks," Edwina said. "This is big part of mine and Bobby's little world."

Brimhall beamed. "It almost feels like you're in a diner. But I've never seen a diner this nice."

"I'm glad you like it," she said. "Please, take a seat."

As soon as they sat down Bobby served them with tall glasses of unsweetened iced tea.

"Mr. O'Neal, I still can't figure out how you took down that tree without destroying the house, or killing yourself," Edwina said, as she set the mixing spoon on a tray between the front burners. "Where did you learn to do that?"

With his thumb, he pointed to Brimhall.

"I was an arborist all through high school, Mrs. Spurlock," he said. "But right now I think James is the best in Columbus. I put him up in a tree about three years ago. He's been a squirrel with a chef's knife ever since."

"Mr. O'Neal," she said, "you were in that tree for eight hours. How can you do that?"

"I inherited the old Irish work gene from my grandfather."

"So you're an authentic Irish workhorse?" she said.

"Yes, ma'am."

"Everyone was watching you. It was grand theater. That whole part of the street has opened up, too."

"I love trees," James said. "But when trees and homes compete for the same space, I always side with the homes. Frankly, I'm surprised the Mansard is still there."

Bobby set the table with the quiet, studied skill of a waiter.

"You boys must be famished," Edwina said. "Dig in."

James and Brimhall piled their plates high with fried walleye, pork ribs that fell off the bone, corn casserole, lima beans and fresh cut tomatoes. They dabbed butter on thick slices of bread cut from the home-baked loaf. And when the first plates were finished, they went back for seconds. For dessert they devoured hearty slabs of pound cake. They washed the meal down with iced tea poured from a sparkling pitcher of cut glass. When the meal was done, Edwina served coffee with cream. After they'd finished, Bobby cleared the table and placed the dishes in one of the sink's bays, and then filled it with warm, soapy water. He sipped on blue Kool-Aid as the adults talked over coffee.

"So," James said, "I see where you have a Stephen Millbury campaign sign in your front yard."

The so-called "main candidates" in the District Four City Council race were George Beckham and Byron Bernadette. But there were also two "wannabe candidates" in the election, Boris Panomorov, a radical American-born Communist and a PhD student at Ohio State, and Stephen Millbury, an accountant and the only black candidate in the field.

"He's an old friend from high school," Edwina said. "He's good people. I don't know if he has a real chance of winning, but he'd be a good councilman."

James looked at Edwina and grinned. "My girlfriend Eva is a volunteer in the Beckham campaign."

"If it ends up coming down to Beckham and Bernadette in a runoff, and I think it will, I intend on voting for Beckham," Edwina said. "I think Bernadette and the landowner, Mr. Pruitt, are nothing but snakes."

"Has Millbury declared his intentions on the zoning issue?" James said.

"Not yet. The press keeps pushing him for an answer, but he hasn't said which way he'll go."

"Eva says that if a candidate wants to have a chance of winning, they have to make a choice on the zoning issue, either for or against."

"She's probably right," Edwina said. "But the fact remains that a lot of us just want to know what's going to happen in District Four, and don't care so much about Canal Winchester. The zoning issue has become so big that it overshadows the fact that whoever gets elected is going to have to represent the entire district for at least three years. Mr. Brimhall, where do you stand?"

"I don't live in District Four and I don't have a girlfriend who's a volunteer in the Beckham campaign, so I don't have a dog in the fight," he said. "But as a contractor I favored the industrial park. Then I started reading the paper, and you're right—Bernadette and Pruitt are snakes, and I ain't never liked snakes."

As James and Brimhall prepared to leave, Bobby asked them if they'd like to see him dance. James told him that they'd love to. Bobby promptly folded in his forearms, stuck his elbows out like wings and started flapping them up and down. He clicked his heels, doing what he called the Dirty Chicken. James and Brimhall laughed hysterically, not just because it was funny, but also because Bobby could really dance. He infused the Dirty Chicken with soulful dips and perfectly timed shuffles of his heels, moving with the steady zeal of a seasoned entertainer. Behind him in the hall stood Edwina, beaming with jolly abashment.

"Yes, sir," he said. "I'm Bobby Spurlock, the best dancer in Ohio."

"You sure are," James said. "What do you say, Brimhall?"

"Hmm," he mused. "I think he's the best in the United States."

"Now that's what I'm talking about," Bobby crowed.

—

Dean Bernadette peered into his beige leather satchel, the bottomless catchall of his life. Tucked between a legal pad and an accordion file stuffed with municipal records, was a brown envelope, fat with cash. The money meant autonomy, and with autonomy came decisions Dean yearned to make. He held little hope of pulling off the seduction of George Beckham. He had hatched that plan for the sake of bravado, and for the need to fleece J.D. Pruitt. Now that he had the money, he set his sights on the real target—the black vote.

Dean went looking for Leon Davis. He wasn't hard to find.

Straddling the green British three-speed with his six-foot-six-inch frame, Leon was a grand piece of pop art that had never sold. In the middle of Douglass Street, just beyond the line of pylons, watching James and the ground crews topple the oak tree. Since Dean was the only white person among the onlookers, he felt a bit intimidated. A couple of kids in baggy pants and side-cocked baseball caps eyed him with suspicion, as did a gaggle of old-time beer drinkers standing on the corner. Rather than linger in the crowd, Dean headed straight toward Leon. Seeing him here on the street, and how he commanded his little piece of the urban milieu, Dean knew he had made the right decision to seek his services. The bike, the imposing height, and the frosted hair parted meticulously down the middle, didn't set Leon apart from the neighborhood. Rather, his unique appearance accentuated the control he had over his niche. Dean congratulated himself on his good judgment. All he had to do was convince Leon to join the campaign.

He weaved through the crowd until he was close enough to smell Leon's cheap cologne.

"Good afternoon, Mr. Davis," he said.

Leon tilted his head and glowered. "How can I help you?"

"I'm Dean Bernadette, with the Bernadette campaign."

"And?"

"I saw you at City Hall a few weeks ago, when you spoke against the roofing contract."

"And?"

"I was just wondering who you're supporting in the special election."

"Don't know yet. Why do you care?"

"I want you to campaign for Bernadette, my candidate."

"Get on along!" Leon hissed, speaking to a gang of kids who'd gathered around him. Dutifully, the kids pedaled off on their low-rider bikes, leaving Dean and Leon alone at the line of pylons. Dean knew he'd been too direct about his agenda. He needed to show Leon that he supported Leon's agenda, and then merge that with his own. With that in mind, he frowned and pointed toward James, perched high in the oak.

"What do you think?" he said, with a note of gloom.

"I think the City Council screwed me. You were there, right?"

Ah, here we go, thought Dean.

"Yeah, I was there. The council should've tabled the bids and extended the application deadline so Jesse Freeman could've resubmitted his proposal. In my opinion, the guys cutting down that tree shouldn't be here, pure and simple. Let me ask you this: How'd you like to put the Douglass Street roofing contract back on the City Council agenda, and then push the contract to Jesse Freeman?"

Leon tilted his head and thought for a while.

"That would be the right thing to do." He dug into the top pocket of his overalls, plucked out a menthol cigarette and lit it. "But how could you do that?"

"Part of my strategy depends on you," Dean said. "But first, I want to know what your interest is in the contract. And don't give me that minority crap, Mr. Davis."

Dean absorbed a long, hard look from Leon. As his scrutiny developed, Dean's confidence grew. He had come to Douglass Street dressed as the power player—black Oxfords, a navy suit, suspenders and a burgundy bowtie. Across his nose, a natty pair of tortoise shell glasses. A watch, a ring, cuff links and a silver pen in the breast pocket of his starched white shirt. Dean wanted Leon to see a rich, white, arrogant dick, thinking to himself that such men had a reputation for achieving results. Dean wasn't sure of exactly what Leon found in the persona, but the sudden break in his scowl told Dean that something must have worked.

"Jesse promised me a twenty thousand dollar 'finder's fee,' and said he'd hire me at twenty dollars per hour." Leon's flat expression betrayed no shame.

"That's a pretty nice kickback, Leon," Dean said. "What would you do for twenty dollars per hour?"

"Not a whole lot." He chuckled.

"Well, here's the deal: I'll work on putting the contract back on the City Council agenda, but only if you campaign for Byron Bernadette."

"What exactly do you mean by campaign?"

"Up and down Cleveland Road—Linden Park, Huy Park, Duxberry, Northern Lights, the whole gig."

"For the black vote?"

"Absolutely." Dean raised his eyebrows. "Jobs, jobs, and more jobs."

"And how much you gonna pay me?"

"I'm offering fifteen hundred a week, for three months—that's eighteen thousand."

"That don't sound too bad," Leon said. "But how do I know you have control over the contract?"

"Oh, I do," Dean said. "Trust me."

"Now what's your name again?"

"Dean."

"Look around you, Dean." Leon gave a broad gesture. "Take a good, hard look at all these broke motherfuckers. I don't trust anybody—including you. Show me you have some control down on Douglass Street, and I'm all yours until Election Day."

"What exactly do you mean by control?"

"What I mean is that I wanna see something happen to that racist little punk down the street." Leon pointed at Brimhall. "That little peckerwood's the wheel, my friend. Show me you can make that wheel stop turning."

Dean peered down the street and studied the tattooed contractor. He had a thick rope wrapped around his waist and served as the anchorman for the team working the pulley cord. As the team labored to maneuver a giant limb from over the Mansard, Brimhall gave orders in English and Spanish, moving to and fro with the sure-footedness of a mule. Shirtless, he flaunted his deeply bronzed torso, lean and cut by manual labor. Dangling at the nape of his neck like a bundle of barbed wire, the tight rear tuft of his mullet, and on his left forearm lurked the snarling emerald dragon. He wasn't a big man—about five ten and a buck seventy. A scrap of poor white trash. But Dean saw it clean and clear. Effort. Smarts. A tough motherfucker who had already defied the odds. Taking him down would be a delight.

"I can make the wheel stop turning." Dean had to shout to be heard over the drone of the chainsaw. "But for starters, can you deal with a flat tire?"

Leon caught the gist and cracked a wicked smile. "I can deal."

"In the meantime, here's a thousand dollar advance." Dean pulled the envelope from his leather satchel. "Go buy a couple of suits and start rounding up your crew. Flash a little cash and tell them there's more from where this came from."

Leon slid the envelope into the deep front pocket of his overalls. "I sure appreciate you, Mr. Dean."

"I appreciate you. And rest assured, Gene Brimhall's gonna need a spare real soon."

Leon straightened his look, flicked his cigarette toward the gutter, and pedaled off on his shiny British three-speed.

—

Dean cruised down West Broad Street in his eggshell Mercedes Benz 600 SL. He felt like he had put himself at a disadvantage arriving on the impoverished Hilltop driving a European roadster and wearing a silk suit and bowtie. The folks on the Hilltop didn't like the downtown crowd. His accoutrements could be the source of unneeded trouble. On the other hand, reasoned Dean, the coupe and the suit would set him apart, and could perhaps give him the edge he needed to make a splash in the notorious white ghetto. He could turn around at the next block and head back to the comforts of German Village, where his glass always brimmed with Bombay and tonic. But the election demanded that he take risks, physical, mental or otherwise. And the seed of his campaign was planted here, in little Appalachia, where Gene Brimhall, and more importantly, Gene Brimhall's enemies, were born and reared.

He turned south on Hague Avenue, lined with shabby duplexes, cars on blocks and small dirt patches that once were lawns. Filthy kids without shirts and shoes fumbled with empty beer bottles and played chase with a pit bull. Toothless men and women sat on their porches in old recliners, drinking beer from cans and rolling cigarettes. Some of the women had grim blue-ink tattoos along their arms and the tops of their fingers. Hanging from the second-floor window of one of the tattered homes was a Confederate flag, and in the window next to it, a piece of plywood spray-painted with Nordic runes and a swastika. Dean marveled at the irony. One of the city's worst neighborhoods offered the best view of the glittering skyline just a few miles to the east.

He pulled into the gravel parking lot of Triple J Roofing. He took off the tie, unbuttoned the top two buttons of his shirt and slid on a pair of wayfarers. Mildly comforted by the quick change, he trudged across the lot, into the workshop and to the back office, where John Jim Johnson, otherwise known as Trey, sat at a desk watching *Wheel of Fortune*.

"Can I help you?" Trey's blue eyes squinted as if Dean were as bright as the sun.

"My name is Dean, and I'm with the Byron Bernadette campaign. I was wondering if you'd be willing to talk about a guy named Gene Brimhall?"

Trey, leaning back in the chair with his feet propped up on the desk, grabbed the remote control and turned the volume down. He took a bite out of the apple he was eating, chewed on it, and then swallowed. For a while he didn't speak. He just sat there eating the apple, whittling away at Dean with a vacant stare. Dean thought he was about to get kicked out of the workshop, or worse. But then Trey's face softened a bit as he swallowed the last bite of apple.

"Whadda you wanna know about Brimhall, other than what he can tell you to your face?"

"I saw you at City Hall a few weeks ago. You tried to talk the City Council out of giving Gene Brimhall the Douglass Street roofing contract."

"That's right. But so fuckin' what?"

"Are you guys friends?"

"Yeah, we're regular old butt buddies. Hell no! I ain't friends with that cocky son-of-a-bitch."

"Tell me what you know about him," Dean said, risking it all on one bold grab into his satchel. "I've got a thousand dollars that says I'd be very interested in what you have to say."

Trey looked at Dean and then at the neat stack of cash he set on the desk. He grabbed the brick of twenties and thumbed through them as if he were looking for a passage in the Bible. He looked up at Dean, his expression frozen in an unrighteous smirk.

"Before we go any further," Trey said, swallowing a morsel of apple that had lodged between his teeth, "I wanna ask you one question. Do you know who the fuck Gene Brimhall is?"

"Not really. I know he's a roofing contractor, and that he's got a big tattoo on his left forearm."

"Well, that ain't enough. Do you know where he grew up?"

"On the Hilltop?"

"In a shithole duplex over on Guernsey Street with his crone of a mother. He was paying all the bills by the time he was fifteen years old—with a fuckin' chainsaw and a damned piece of rope—and she still cussed him like he was the devil's child. You know what he is today?"

"What?"

"A fuckin' millionaire. Gene Brimhall's what they call a 'High-Tech Redneck.' Nope. Can't stand the bastard. But I'll give him one thing. He's worked for everything he's got. Ain't nobody given old Brimhall a damned thing. If somebody—like you, for example—were to start meddling in his affairs, well, that's a real good way to get your face rearranged. And I can see through your shades, boy. You're trying to play it cool, but inside you're scared shitless. I suggest you get on back in your little pussy mobile and head on back downtown, and leave Brimhall the fuck alone. You ain't man enough for him."

"I've got two thousand dollars that says I don't give a shit." He fetched yet another stack of bills from his satchel and plunked it on the desk.

"Well, that's all right by me." A dark cloud of collusion descended over Trey's face. "Just consider yourself duly warned."

—

Brimhall had never seen James angry until the morning he arrived at work with a nasty letter. He mashed on the brakes until his truck slid to a halt. He slammed the transmission into park, jumped out of the truck without turning off the ignition, and yelled, "We need to talk!"

James pulled a folded piece of paper from his back pocket and threw it at Brimhall's feet. "Read that."

Brimhall knelt down and plucked up the folded piece of paper. Before opening it, he looked at James. More than anger. Deflated pride. A chasm of disappointment. Brimhall feared the contents of the letter, but opened it and began reading.

Dear Mr. James O'Neal:

I write this letter to educate you on a few facts you need to know about your boss, Eugene Brimhall. Of late, he has been telling people on the Hilltop that he rigged the city council vote on the Douglass Street roofing contract. If you recall, you fought the bull, Braggadocio, on February 24. The city council approved your contract bid on March 10. In between your daring deed and the council vote, Mr. Brimhall went down to city hall and requested that a proclamation in your honor be placed on the council agenda. He said he did that to win votes from the council, not as a kind gesture for a friend. He's telling everyone how smart he was, and that you probably thought your mother had requested the proclamation. Did you? As a concerned citizen of Columbus, I thought you needed to know that the honor and applause you received at city hall was fake. It was the product of Mr. Brimhall's greed, not his appreciation for your heroism. If I was you— and thank God I'm not—I would think twice about my association with Mr. Brimhall.

P.S. You might want to ask him about a gang called the Guernsey Squares, and a cross that was burned in 1982, in the front yard of a house owned by an innocent black family.

Sincerely,
Concerned Citizen

"Fuck," he muttered, brandishing the letter in the air. "Where in the *fuck* did you get this?"

"It was on my windshield this morning. But that's not the issue," James said. "If you lie to me now we'll never be friends again. Did you burn a cross?"

To an enemy or stranger, Brimhall could lie and lie well. But not here and not now. And never to James.

"No, I didn't. But I built it for the person who did."

So once again the memory confronted him.

From an early age Brimhall was known on the Hilltop as the kid with the golden hands. He could build or fix anything, and people from throughout the neighborhood hired him for odd jobs and asked him for favors. One day he was in the garage replacing spark plugs on a friend's car when the tall kid from two blocks down on Guernsey Street pulled into the driveway. Chris Dilworth, and he had a new tattoo and something serious on his mind.

"You see them niggers moving in over on Oakley Avenue?"

"Uh-huh." Brimhall wiped his hands as he came out of the garage.

"In two years this whole neighborhood'll look like Cape Town. I ain't gonna stand for it."

Dilworth made a fist with his right hand and pounded it into the palm of his left, flexing his new tattoo, a black heart with a sword sticking through it.

"What are you gonna do?"

"That's why I'm here, Brimhall. Come out to the truck. I wanna show you something."

Peering into the truck, Brimhall saw a stack of two-by-fours and a bag of nails.

"I wanna burn a cross in their yard. And I want you to build it."

"Why me?"

"'Cause, I'm all thumbs but you got two right hands."

"How big do you want it?"

"As big as you can make it." Dilworth slipped him a ten-dollar bill.

It didn't take Brimhall long to bang out a nine-foot cross.

"That oughta scare the hell out of 'em," Brimhall boasted.

That night Brimhall sat on the porch with his friends, got drunk on Boone's Farm and let loose with a Rebel Yell when he saw the flames dancing at the end of the block. The lights came on. The man of the house stormed out into the front yard in his pajamas and started firing a pistol into the air.

"Fuck you, honkies!" he yelled. "I ain't scared!"

And then the night erupted with gunfire because all the neighbors were armed for the apocalypse.

"Nigger, you best get inside or you'll be on the woodpile pretty soon," someone warned.

"Yeeehaaa," someone howled, as the gunfire intensified.

By the time the police and firemen arrived, the cross was a smoldering ruin. The next week, a For Sale sign appeared in the front yard. Dilworth, full of swagger, strolled down Guernsey Street flashing his black heart tattoo.

Shrugging off the past, Brimhall steadied himself for the present.

"You're garbage," James said.

The immigrant roofers noticed the confrontation and ran to the scene. Unabashed in their loyalty, they crowded in behind James. Brimhall knew he had to act fast. James was about to start swinging.

Brimhall gestured toward the scaffolding surrounding Edwina's house. "What's more important to you, your present and future, or my past? If you walk out on Douglass Street, you'll regret it forever."

"Who says I'm walking out on Douglass Street?"

"If you walk out on me, or if you raise your hand against me, that's what you're doing." Brimhall cocked his chin into the position of authority. "I might be garbage, as you say, but I'm still the boss. I've always been good to you, James. That you can't deny. And there's a lot of work to be done."

James opened his mouth and moved his hand as if to speak, but said nothing. A long, angry sigh. A vein bulged in his neck.

He gave a final, searing look of reproach, turned and followed his crew to the Mansard at the end of the block. They climbed the scaffolding and went to work, just like they always did.

The hair on Brimhall's neck stood on end when he noticed Leon Davis, at the end of the block, hunched over his bike like a vulture hunches over a carcass. Next to Leon stood a shadowy figure in shades and an overcoat. His facial features were fuzzy in the pink light of dawn, but Brimhall could tell that he was young, white, and had dark hair. Leon held out his bony hands in a sarcastic shrug. The stranger patted Leon on the shoulder and they began to laugh so brazenly that Brimhall could see their teeth. His first instinct was to sprint and catch them, and then beat them to pulp. His second impulse was to grimace and endure. He looked to his left. Standing on the porch were the early risers, Edwina and Bobby. Their crushed expressions saddened him.

He promised himself that after the raw emotions had ebbed that he would apologize to James and at least try to explain why he'd done the things he'd done. Of more immediate concern was the clearing of 2,700 square feet of clay tile from the steep slopes of Edwina's Queen Anne. And, of course, there was the feud on the Hilltop, where the cross still burned after all those long, cold years.

—

Each household in the Douglass Street restoration zone received an anonymous letter from Dean Bernadette. The note was simple: In 1982, the contractor, Eugene Brimhall, burned a cross in front of a house owned by an African-American family. Edwina's phone rang for five hours straight.

"Did you get a letter?" Mrs. Washington said.

"We got us a damn Klansman down here," Mrs. Mishaw said.

"If that son-of-a-bitch even looks at me the wrong way, I'm gonna deck him," Mr. Dalrymple growled.

"One of these thugs down here is gonna shoot that old boy," Effie Kennedy said, and on and on until Edwina felt stupid for having ever sought the restoration grant. She wasn't interested in saving Brimhall's soul or in grousing herself into a civil rights lather. She wanted the roofing contract completed so that Phase Two, and ultimately Phase Three and Phase Four, could begin and end. Scaffolding was already up around her and Mr. Dalrymple's homes, and huge stacks of barrel mission tile had just arrived the day before. As president of the Douglass Street Neighborhood Homeowners Association, Edwina was responsible for the entire two-block Douglass Street enclave. In her community lived 57 people, and her job was to serve each of them to the best of her ability.

She pondered the predicament. She could march down to City Hall and tell Mayor Kraus that they didn't want a cross burner in their neighborhood. She was sure the mayor would oblige with a quick termination of the contract. But what good would that do? Little, Edwina reasoned. On the other side of the issue was Brimhall. He had a 6-1 vote from the City Council, an excellent foreman in James O'Neal, a steady crew, and all the equipment and know-how he needed. From a business standpoint, Edwina couldn't get around it. Brimhall was supposed to be here. And besides, she surmised, if Brimhall were ousted over the contents of an anonymous letter, he would likely file a restraining order against the entire grant program. In that event, Douglass Street would lose, an unacceptable outcome.

If pain were timber, she had enough to build a towering pulpit from which to denounce Brimhall. But she needed the wood to maintain her own fires, and thus could not afford to waste it on the pyres of racism and strife. She sulked for about a minute. And then she pulled rank. She called an emergency meeting of the neighborhood association and politely demanded that the letters, all 13 of them, be turned over to her for safekeeping. Association members were reluctant, but as usual, conceded.

"Whoever sent these letters wants to turn us against the contractor, and one another," Edwina reasoned. "It's a trap! Stay positive and mention this to no one!"

Her second order of business was to meet face-to-face with Brimhall. He responded with a look of surprise when she invited him to her house, but accepted the offer with only token hesitation. Guarded and wary from the moment he entered the house, it was evident he knew something was afoot. Once seated at the kitchen table, he initiated the conversation.

"Why am I here?" he said.

"Were you aware that these were circulating?" She slid one of the envelopes across the table.

"No, but if that's what I think it is, I'm not surprised."

She glanced at the stack of letters.

"It appears that you've done more than repair roofs in your lifetime," she said.

"It would appear that way."

"So you don't deny the content of the letter?"

"Does it say something about a cross?"

"Um hum." She tapped her index finger against the tabletop.

"I built that cross, Mrs. Spurlock, when I was sixteen. I'm not proud of that, but nor can I change history."

"Look, this is cheap. But as we all know, a lot of people like cheap things. As you see, there's a stack of letters. Each member of the neighborhood association received a copy. I rounded all of them up last night."

"I appreciate that, Mrs. Spurlock. Are people mad?"

"A few." She sighed. "But in the end, we held hands in a circle and said a prayer for your soul, just in case it's on its way to hell." Edwina's eyes flashed hot but quickly softened. "You don't have enemies here on Douglass Street. But there's a lot of things beyond my control."

"Well, all that happened a long time ago," Brimhall said. "I wish it wouldn't have come out. But now that it's out, what am I supposed to do?"

"Mr. Brimhall, you're on Douglass Street," Edwina warned. "If anyone confronts you about this, deny, deny, deny."

"Oh, really?"

"Yes. I'm glad you admitted the truth to me, but you could get shot over this. Let's keep the confession at the kitchen table."

"Okay. But what'd you tell the neighborhood association?"

"I told them that the letter was a sucker punch from one of your rivals—which is probably true. I also told them we have no proof to substantiate the claim—which is also true. The last thing we need is for you to open your mouth. Let's see if this thing withers on the vine."

"I can live with that."

"I was talking to one of the city planners a couple of months ago, and he said there's an old saying in the contracting business—'It takes one contract to make you, and one contract to break you.' Is that true?"

"It's very true."

"So it applies to you, too?"

"I'd survive, but it'd be a royal pain in the ass if anything were to happen down here."

"It'd be a pain in my ass, too," Edwina said.

"So I guess that makes us," and he paused, "equals and allies?"

"That's a good way of putting it."

C E N T U R Y

B

Leon woke at dawn, pedaled down to the United Dairy Farmers convenience store at the corner of Indianola and Hudson, and bought the Wednesday morning edition of the *Scioto Times*. He set the paper in the handlebar basket and pedaled back to his apartment. He put on two cups of coffee and then dug through the paper until he arrived at the classifieds. With a long, bony finger he traced down the merchandise listings until he reached the bicycle section. He saw nothing but junk and expensive mountain bikes until he arrived at the second to last entry in the column: For Sale, five used utility bikes, best offer. Leon took a sip of coffee, lit a menthol and dialed the number. A man with a high-pitched, shaky voice answered the phone.

"They were my son's, but he passed away two years ago," the man said. "I'm tired of looking at 'em."

For the price of a full tank of gas, old Zeke, Leon's friend, drove him out to the farmhouse. Stacked and leaning against the rear wall of the garage under a tarp were five British three-speeds. Leon's upper lip nearly quivered at the sight of the antique fleet. The tires dry, cracked and deflated, but the bikes appeared to be in good condition. Equipped with back racks, fenders, saddle seats and mirrors, these were the cruisers on which one could win an election. Leon slid his right hand into his pocket and felt the smooth stack of twenties given to him a few days ago by Dean Bernadette.

Leon hadn't had this kind of buying power in years. "I'll give you one hundred dollars for all five."

"Sold."

Leon hummed a happy song from his childhood as he loaded the bikes into Zeke's truck. Back at Zeke's workshop, Leon took an inventory of his purchase. With his notes cribbed onto an old receipt from his wallet, Leon hopped on his bike and headed to the North Campus Cycle Shop on Lane Avenue. And there's where it got tricky. Leon had worked there for two years but had quit in a huff about six months ago. The graduate student who owned and operated the shop, Tommy Charles, didn't give Leon the raise he had wanted. Instead of taking the smaller raise, Leon called him a "white honky racist" and stormed out.

Leon had tools and an English wrench, and was a serviceable repairman. But of the five bikes he'd bought, one was going to be used for parts. What this meant is that he needed Sutherland's Handbook—just to be sure—and he knew Tommy Charles had two editions.

"What's up, Tommy C.?" Leon said, strolling through the front door as if he and his former employer had never fallen out.

"What do you want, Leon?" Tommy glared through the spokes of the wheel he worked on.

"Oh, I just need some 26-inch tubes, some tires, hub oil and chains—and your Sutherland's manual."

"Hell, no, Leon! You blew out of here six months ago calling me a racist, and now you think I'm gonna loan you my Sutherland's manual? Forget it."

"Come on, Tommy C., you know I was just mad."

"Yeah, but customers heard that, Leon, and I lost two accounts over it."

"Sorry, man."

"Tell my bank account you're sorry. You can buy all the tires and tubes you need, but the Sutherland's manual is off limits."

94

"Come on, Tommy C., I've got four Nottingham three speeds, man," he pleaded. "I'm gonna fix 'em up and run 'em in the big City Council election. I need the manual for a measly two days."

"You're in the election?"

"Heck yeah," he boasted. "The Cleveland Road Theater."

"Who are you campaigning for?"

"Bernadette." He jutted out his chin.

"Wrong answer, Leon. I'm voting for Beckham."

"Come on, man." Leon stretched out his arms toward Tommy. "I've got to get them bikes up and running right now. Where else am I gonna get that manual? You have two!"

Tommy Charles shook his head and went back to work.

"Oh, I see. You just like everyone else."

He dug into his pocket and pulled out a clip.

"How does twenty bucks sound?" He shoved the bill in Tommy Charles' direction.

"Crappy." He snatched the money from Leon's hand. He dug behind the front counter and grabbed one of his two Sutherland's repair manuals.

"I need this back. In two days."

"You got it, Tommy C." Leon tucked the manual under his arm. "You and me are friends."

—

Eva flipped the power switch on her laptop. As the computer booted up, she sat on the porch with a cup of coffee and a Marlboro Light 100. She marveled at the fine spring morning. Clouds moved like slow boats through the sky. A shock of honeysuckle poured over a privacy fence. A bush of fragrant lilac stirred in the soft morning breeze. Squirrels scurried over the budding boughs of a young sycamore, while sparrows pecked for food in a freshly planted bed of impatiens. Tulips, about to give their scarlet kisses to the world, searched for the sun as a mocking bird yodeled from its perch on a telephone line.

Back inside she checked her email. A message from the Beckham campaign. Seniors and above, campus headquarters, 5 p.m. Eva scanned her day planner, the schedule open. She called Oxana.

"I will meet you there," Oxana said.

"And we will have drinks at Larry's afterwards?"

"Sounds good. And by the way, Dominick said he cannot be seen with us in public now that we have joined the campaign."

"Was he serious?"

"Very. I think he is kind of mad at us. He has not called you?"

"No."

Eva now spent nearly all her free time with James and hadn't talked to much of anyone since they'd met.

"When you talk to him, be prepared," Oxana warned. "He will tell you that he cannot cover an election and also hang out with people who are working for a candidate. He will tell you all about his journalism ethics and how he cannot sacrifice them—even for us."

"Reporters." Eva sighed.

She ate a bagel with lox, showered, packed her shoulder bag and headed out toward campus. She liked starting her day at James' place. He lived in an Italianate seven blocks south of campus, which meant she walked to class and didn't have to take the 20-minute bus ride from her flat in German Village. She stopped at the King Avenue Coffee House and bought two bags of Indian tea. She sat through international marketing and then international accounting and finance. She ate lunch—Caesar salad and a cup of onion soup—with two American girls from the business school. She spent the rest of the day in Main Library grading tests for the course she taught, Czech 401. At 4:35 she packed her bag and went to campus headquarters.

In the United States, the Communist witch-hunt had died in the 1950s with the downfall of McCarthy. Prague, however, still reeled from the anti-Communist fever of 1989. Now that the Politburo was no longer in power, people wanted it gone, and gone forever. Eva understood because she felt the same way. But she had grown tired of the tone in Prague, where politics were still about being, or not being, a Communist. The political parties teemed with novices, populists, and shrill demagogues. All of them claimed to know the true heart of the people and what was right for the future. Truth was, no one knew and everyone was scared. And then there was Lustrace, the government-sanctioned purge of former Communists and their sympathizers. And Cibulka's List, the 200,000-name broadsheet of butchers, shopkeepers, journalists, and teachers who allegedly served as stool pigeons for the regime. The list, recklessly published in a cheap rag, destroyed families, friendships and careers. For a while it had all been great theater. But as Czechoslovakia broke into the Czech Republic and Slovakia, and as the shysters continued sneaking out of the country with all the loot, and as former Communists became CEOs instead of legislators, public discourse in Prague soured. "Too much velvet, not enough revolution," they'd say, because the bad guys had never really been caught. In Columbus, Ohio, nobody gave a shit about Cibulka's List. And Lustrace? No one gave a shit about that, either. Birds and trees or truck depots and warehouses. Eva savored the blessing of simplicity.

She smiled at the sight of Oxana and her pupil, Frank Fuller, sitting on the steps at campus headquarters.

"You are early." Oxana hugged Eva's neck and kissed her on both cheeks.

"Aren't I always? Hi, Frank." She kissed him on both cheeks.

"Hey, Eva. How's it going?"

"Good," she replied in Russian. Frank was a junior Russian major. "Are you joining the campaign?"

"I think I am. I've got an environmental streak in me."

"Don't let him lie to you," Oxana said. "He joined because of me."

She nudged Frank in the ribs and laughed.

"Is it true?" Eva quizzed.

Frank blushed. An excellent student who had studied in Moscow for a summer, but at only 20, still awed by Eva and Oxana, seasoned 25-year-olds from the heart of the Cold War.

"I joined for Oxana," he said, admitting his crush. "So, what's all this stuff about seniors and above?"

"I think Beckham is looking for mature volunteers." Eva with a sardonic grin. "Frank, do you fit that bill?"

Along with the other volunteers, they filed into the small, two-room commercial space on 13th Avenue that served as Beckham's campus hub. The room quickly filled with juniors, seniors, and graduate students, many of whom stood because all the chairs had been taken. Beckham and two of his top campaign advisors sat at a foldout table at the head of the room. He stood and the room fell silent.

"Thanks for coming out on such short notice." He searched the crowd with his owl's eyes. "There's been a recent development. A man by the name of Leon Davis is campaigning for Byron Bernadette up on Cleveland Road. He and his electioneers are all on bikes and have already made a serious foray into that part of the district. We need to have a presence up there, if not to beat him, to at least blunt his edge. How should I say this? We need committed volunteers on Cleveland Road."

From the row behind her, Eva heard one of the volunteers whisper to another, "Cleveland Road is all black."

Eva and Frank looked over their shoulders and frowned.

Beckham explained the situation.

Long the forgotten stepchild of Columbus politics, Cleveland Road was home to one of the minor candidates, Stephen Millbury, a black accountant long on credentials but short on personality. The consensus was that he would tie up enough black votes to force a runoff between Beckham and Bernadette, neither of whom was expected to gain the 50 percent plus one needed to win the election outright on May 20. If Bernadette was allowed to lay a solid framework on Cleveland Road leading up to the election, then he would have a good chance of taking the Cleveland Road precincts in the runoff. Now that Leon Davis and his bike brigade were active, that scenario loomed like doomsday for the Beckham camp. The task of the volunteers was to campaign outright for the environment and the woodpeckers, and to also tell the voters that Beckham was the man for the entire district, not just the rezoning issue. Chief among the literature to be distributed on Cleveland Road was a list of the big civil suits that Beckham had won against major corporations. The plaintiffs in many of those suits had been minorities, thus giving Beckham an honest and relevant accolade. Once his name was out there he would hold a series of rallies at which he would introduce his "plan," which had yet to be devised, for that part of the district. The Beckham database yielded a surprisingly long list of homeowners in the Cleveland Road neighborhoods of Kenlawn, Huy Heights, Oakland Park, Aberdeen and Douglass Street. Strategists in the Beckham camp weren't sure the message of Equality and the Environment would fly in the black neighborhoods. But the message, as thin as it might prove to be, would be made directly to those who were most likely to vote, the homeowners.

"I know many of you here have already worked for me on campus and in Clintonville," Beckham said, "but now I'm asking you to volunteer for Cleveland Road. We've got to get some warm bodies up there—soon!"

Eva felt the collective discomfort of the volunteers, who until this point had frolicked through the softer sides of District 4. She felt her own discomfort, too. Though she had frowned at the whisperer behind her, Eva was in no way anxious to campaign in a black neighborhood. She had been up that way with James and had seen it with her own eyes. Bleak and blighted. No place for student volunteers. She felt like a coward, and would have remained that way were it not for a wee Asian girl on the front row who stood and said, "I will go," in a firm, steely voice. Moments later a black African stood and said, "I will go, too." From the rear of the room came a pretty voice. "I'm only a sophomore, but I'll go." Eva turned to see a plump, cherubic student, her hair in cornrows, standing near the door with her hand raised. She caught Eva's eye, and with a smile and a nod, said, "Stand up." In an uncontrollable instant, Eva stood and blurted out for all to hear, "I will go." Oxana stood, and so did Frank Fuller. As Beckham continued to probe the crowd with his owl's eyes, four more volunteers, all of them white Americans, stood and pledged themselves to the Cleveland Road campaign.

"Ten hearty souls." Beckham pumped his fist and nodded his head in a gesture of deep gratitude. "All you guys stay. For everyone else, this meeting is adjourned."

—

Eva shook hands and introduced herself to the other volunteers. Mingmei Yang of Beijing, Alphonso Anku of Luanda, Angola. Barbara Thurman of Columbus, and the other Americans—Donna Rosenbaum, Davita Mitchell, Mike Jones, and Kristin Booker. As the volunteers mingled, Eva turned her attention to the African.

Anku wore Birkenstocks with white socks, khaki shorts and a three-button pullover. Dangling from his neck, a small silver crucifix. He might have dressed like a Catholic preppy, thought Eva, but he had the balanced, spiritual demeanor of a warrior king.

"I felt a bit strange volunteering when I do not have a vote," Eva said. "Did you?"

"At first," Anku said. "But the woodpeckers need us, regardless of our immigration status."

"True enough. I have read our opponent's quotes in the paper. As the Americans say, he is a real horse's ass."

Anku nodded. "Judging him by his own words I would have to agree."

As their conversation progressed, several volunteers introduced themselves to

Anku, who was like a magnet to the young Americans. Many features made him compelling, including his age. Easily in his mid-30s, by far the senior member of the group. Eva looked to her left and met the stoic gaze of Mingmei. Eva stood nearly a full foot taller than her Chinese colleague, and must have outweighed her by a good 30 pounds. But Mingmei showed no signs of timidity. Deliberate as an army ant, she conveyed authority.

"I will feel much better when we are out on the campaign trail," she said.

"So you are excited?" Eva said.

"Yes," she said, without showing any excitement. "I am tired of the shouting matches on campus. I want to campaign."

"So do I. The hard left and the hard right are trying to turn this election into a family feud, but I am not related to any of them."

"Nor am I," Mingmei said.

One of the oddest vocal sounds Eva had ever heard wrecked the gentle hum of conversation.

"Whatsuuuuuuup?"

It was Barbara, flashing peace signs with both hands.

"Whatsuuuuuuup?" she repeated.

Frank Fuller pumped his fist.

"Yeahhhhhhhhh," he roared.

"Whatsuuuuuuup?"

"Yeahhhhhhhhh," replied the undergraduates.

"Are we up in here?" Barbara planted her hands on her hips and stood out-bowed as the Mojo Princess.

"Yeahhhhhhhhh," the Americans cried.

"Are we up in here?"

And this time, everyone but Mingmei raised their fists and roared, "Yeahhhhhhhhh."

"Give it up!"

"Yeahhhhhhhhh."

Before the bonding resumed at a higher decibel, Mingmei gestured for silence.

"Are we done acting like drunk freshmen?" she said. "Mr. Beckham says we need to elect a president—and I nominate Eva."

Mingmei searched the volunteers for agreement or dissent. Most of them were still coming down from the shouts and cheers and had not yet digested the import of the recommendation. When her eyes finally met with Anku's, he said, "I think Eva would be a good president."

"Yes," Oxana said.

"I agree," Frank said.

"I don't have a problem with that," Barbara said.

And the rest of the Americans nodded in concurrence.

"Eva, do you accept?" Mingmei said.

"Uh, yes, I accept. But why me?"

"Give me three good reasons why it should not be you?" Mingmei challenged.

"I am not American, I cannot vote, and I have never been president of anything."

"I asked for three good reasons," Mingmei said.

"If I am president, then who is going to be vice president?"

Eight voices came quick, confident, and in unison: "Mingmei."

"Do you accept?" Eva said.

"I accept."

"What are we gonna call ourselves?" Barbara said. "I mean, we've gotta have a title. We're worth that much."

A lot of mumbling and loud thinking ensued before Davita Mitchell raised her voice. "Diversity Team. Let's call ourselves Diversity Team."

"Diversity Team." Frank moaned. "That's pretty cheesy."

"Maybe," Kristin Booker said, "but it's true, and it's politically correct, and do you have a better suggestion?"

"Not yet, but give me a minute and I probably will."

"We should first do an audit of our diversity, and then think of a name," Eva said, in her first act as president. "If we come up with something we like better than Diversity Team, then we will use it. If not, Diversity Team it is. And let us be quick about it."

"And remember," Barbara said, "we need something that's gonna sound fresh and clean up on Cleveland Road, not just here in campaign headquarters."

Everyone agreed on that point. The auditing began. Five minutes later Eva had all the important facts neatly written and quantified in her notepad.

Religion: Methodist, Catholic, Episcopal, Atheist, Judaism: 5

Language: English, Czech, German, Russian, Portuguese, French, Spanish, Yiddish, Chinese, Bantu: 10

Country of origin: United States, Czech Republic, China, Angola, Kazakhstan: 5

States: Pennsylvania, Ohio, Maryland: 3

Continents: Asia, North America, Africa, Europe: 4

Men: Three

Women: Seven

Field of study: MBA, chemistry, environmental economics, environmental engineering, Russian, landscape architecture, English literature, history, journalism: 9

Eva totaled the "diversity elements" and arrived at 46. She added 4 and 6 to arrive at 10, and then multiplied that by the number of original volunteers, 10, to reach the nice healthy number of 100.

"Barbara, since you are up in here," Eva said, awkwardly, "work with one hundred and see what you come up with."

Barbara paced across the room, mumbling to herself. Everyone watched in hopeful silence as she nodded her head to a secret beat. Her face went bright with a grin as she turned and pointed at Eva.

"We're Century B! Century represents one hundred—our diversity—and B stands for Beckham: Century B, and it's gonna pop up there on Cleveland Road."

It took a few moments, but the laughter of acceptance came once the name had sunk into the collective psyche of the volunteers.

"Century B," Eva said. "Barbara, that is outstanding. And Davita, at heart we will always be Diversity Team. I appreciate your input."

Eva turned to Mingmei.

"Can Century B win the Cleveland Road precincts and save the woodpeckers?"

"Absolutely," Mingmei said, without jest or hyperbole.

—

"Hello?"

"Mr. Beckham, this is Eva Havlicek," she said, and lit a Marlboro.

Standing on James' front porch, she gazed into an amber sunset.

"Oh, Eva," Beckham crooned, "it's good to hear from you."

"I just wanted to let you know that they named me president of the Cleveland Road volunteers, and Mingmei Yang is vice president. We call ourselves Century B, which is slang for Diversity Team. We are deploying in Duxberry tomorrow from 3 to 6 p.m. I have already called the shuttle driver. We are bringing forty campaign signs, twenty T-shirts, a stack of handbills, and a box full of caps. All ten of us will be there."

"Excellent. So you're calling me from the cell phone we left with you guys?"

"Yes, sir."

"And the pager is up and running?"

"Yes, sir."

"Great. How does it feel to be president?"

"Ask me later, when I know." Eva exhaled smoke through her nose. She waved to two students racing down the street on skateboards. "Can I tell you our big news?"

"Sure."

"We went ahead and formed our own political action committee. We filed the paperwork at City Hall. Yesterday, we went to Canal Winchester and knocked on every door. It is a nice village. Anyway, we know that they cannot vote because they do not live in District 4, but get this. We asked them if they wanted a factory in their own backyard. To a man, they all said no. We asked them to contribute to our committee so that we could win the election for them. And guess what?"

"What?" Beckham said.

"We raised six thousand five hundred dollars and sixty cents! Americans are so rich!"

"Great." There was a sour note in Beckham's voice. "Are you running your own campaign?"

"Yes and no. Our political action committee is called Century B for the Election of George Beckham to District Four City Council. We are clearly on your side. And we are distributing your campaign materials. But we will pay our own expenses and keep our own receipts. However, we still need the shuttle van and an extra thousand dollars."

"A thousand bucks?"

"For sundries."

"I wish you guys would've asked me before you formed that PAC. Whose idea was that?"

"Mingmei's. She has studied American elections for seven years."

"Okay," Beckham said, cheering a bit. "We'll have the money down at campus headquarters first thing tomorrow morning."

"Very good."

"... So what part of town do you live in?"

"I keep a flat in German Village, near Schiller Park. But for now I stay with a friend in Victorian Village."

"Hmm. Can I come by later and pick you up? I know of a great little café in New Albany with pasta and an excellent wine list. A guy named Luigi plays the violin on Thursday nights."

Eva already had plans for marinated, grilled chicken breasts and white burgundy with James.

105

"I have prior obligations," she said, with a proper touch of diffidence. "But thanks for the offer."

"Maybe later, then." Eva heard the chime of disappointment in his voice.

"Perhaps," she replied, but just because she didn't want to anger the candidate. "Thanks for allowing us to campaign on your behalf, Mr. Beckham. Cleveland Road will be a challenge, but we think there are rewards there."

"Don't thank me, Eva. I owe all of you guys. And please, call me George. Mr. Beckham was my father."

"Well—George—have a nice evening."

"You, too."

Eva sat on the porch swing, took a sip of wine and waited for James to come downstairs from his shower. She sang a song by Karel Gott, the Wayne Newton of the Czech Republic, and laughed at herself for having done so.

James peeped through the screen door. "Are you ready?"

"Yes." She walked with him to the kitchen.

"I am president of the volunteers, and we call ourselves Century B," she said to James, effecting a playful air of self-importance.

"I know." He reached out to hold her. "Elected by unanimous vote."

James gave her a little hug and pecked her on the cheek. When their embrace ended, he pulled the chicken breasts from the marinade and set them on a plate. On the patio, flames flickered in the grill. A bottle of white burgundy chilled in a cooler. It was supposed to rain in sheets all through the night and morning, which meant James didn't have to crawl up on the roofs tomorrow, and that he could stay up late and sleep in. Eva knew this and it made her happy.

"So, you are a boss, right?" she asked.

"I've been a foreman for three years."

"How many men work for you?"

"At least seven, but sometimes as many as ten."

"And how do you lead? I have nine people."

"It's real easy." James looked her straight in the eye. "Be firm and fair and honest. Work longer and smarter than them. And sometimes you have to be hard."

"What do you mean, hard?"

"Sometimes you just have to make a tough decision. But you rely on your wisdom first, so that the tough decision is still the right one, regardless of what people think."

"Do you like being hard?"

He shook his head. "No. I absolutely hate it. But when you're out there making money—or if you're in a political campaign up on Cleveland Road— it's gonna come up."

"So as president, I have some hard decisions ahead of me?"

"If this election is gonna be as hot as some people think, I know so, Eva. You're about to be tested."

"Will you be there for me if I fail?"

"Yeah, but if I can help you succeed, I'd rather do that."

Eva smiled.

James headed out to the patio with the chicken breasts and a pair of tongs. Eva remained in the kitchen to slice baguette, Roma tomatoes and mozzarella. She took a sip of wine and breathed the delicious scent wafting in from outside, the sizzle from the grill reaching her ears like a whisper. She stacked the slices of cheese and tomato on top of the wheels of baguette, and then drizzled and dashed them with olive oil and freshly ground black pepper. Eva floated out to the patio with the plate of appetizers in one hand and a glass of wine in the other.

After dinner and dishes they curled up in bed, came together, and listened to the rain as it danced in from the north. Eva draped a leg over James' legs, and rested her head on his chest.

"James? What is it that got you so agitated the other day?"

Last week James had come home from work in a foul mood, which was unusual. Eva had asked what was wrong, but all James said is that he'd had a bad day. Eva knew there was more to the story than that, but did not want to pry. Now, she hoped, James would be ready to talk.

"Eva, you don't need to get mixed up in all that stuff. Believe me."

"But you are wrong." She shifted her head so that she looked into his eyes. "You have been wounded, I can tell. I am already your lover and your friend. Tell me what it is that hurts you. Please."

James remained silent for a long while. Eva's eyes did not stop beseeching.

"Well," he began, "I got a letter the other day, and it was all about my boss, Gene Brimhall."

As the story progressed, Eva nestled in deep and shivered.

T I T A N I U M
PISTON

Dean and Trey barreled westward on I-70 in Trey's lazy pickup truck. As the skyline faded from the rearview mirror, Trey flicked on the blinker and veered onto the off ramp near the Madison County line. They turned into a rural area with winding country roads, billowing hardwoods, and sagging red barns. They crossed Darby Creek on a rickety two-lane bridge, Trey's old truck somehow hugging the road as he took several sharp turns at speed. Dean didn't mind that Trey was drunk and driving recklessly. He was on an adventure. The only thing that mattered was that he receive a thrill. And if the day's promise was fulfilled, then beyond thrilled he would be.

Trey turned down a bumpy dirt road and curved left at the fork near an abandoned farmhouse. A few dusty minutes later he pulled into a large lot with a ramshackle trailer home surrounded by debris and the rusting hulks of cars. A crimson flag emblazoned with the Nazi swastika flew high atop a pole. Beneath that flew the Stars and Bars of the Confederacy, and beneath that the American flag turned upside down.

"Where in the fuck are we?" Dean said.

"In Madison County. You said you wanted to stick it to Brimhall, right?"

"Yeah."

"Well, this is the guy who can do it," Trey said.

He pulled a warm tallboy from between his legs and took a big swallow.

"What makes this guy so great?" Dean gestured toward the mobile home.

Trey shrugged. "Well, he just got out of prison. And he hates Brimhall."

"Why was he in prison?"

"Manslaughter. But it was really first-degree murder. The prosecutor had some tricky evidence, so Dilworth took a plea on the lesser charge. He was in the joint for seven years."

"Dilworth?"

"Chris Dilworth. You know, the cross burner. And about four years ago he sent a message to Brimhall. He wanted him to deposit money into his commissary account. Brimhall said, and I quote, 'Not no, but hell no.' And Dilworth's sworn vengeance ever since."

"How much money was it?"

"Don't recall, but it was enough to chap his ass real bad. Brimhall done known the man all his life. He turned his back on his own people."

"Is this guy really a Nazi?"

Trey nodded. "Uh-huh. And he's got a little gang now. Ever last one of 'em is meaner than a snake, too. If you really wanna get Brimhall, you've arrived."

"And I take it Dilworth would be pretty upset that Brimhall's fucking a black chick named Edwina Spurlock?"

"Oh yeah." Trey's voice was thick with cunning. "Edwina—now don't that just sound like a dirty nigger?"

Dean grinned. "It sounds nice and disgusting. So, am I in danger right now?"

"Of course. You're on Dilworth's radar now, and if you cross him, he'll fuck you up."

Trey lowered his head and peered at Dean with a long, baleful stare.

"If you want out, this is your last chance, 'cause once you get out of this truck and Dilworth sees you—well, you know what I mean."

"I want in," Dean said.

"Then let's do it."

They got out of the truck, and just as they reached the trailer, the front door flew open. An oily teenage girl came out to the screened-in porch. At her side stood a brindle pit bull with cropped ears and a spiked collar.

"Who is it?" she snarled.

"It's Trey, from Guernsey Street."

"What do you want?"

"Is Chris here? I need to talk to him about some stuff."

She pointed at Dean. "Who's that dork?"

"This is Dean. Dean from Downtown."

A voice came from deep within the mobile home.

"Stacy, who's out there?"

"Trey from Guernsey Street and Dean from Downtown," she yelled over her shoulder.

"Tell 'em to meet me over at the tree," he bellowed.

The girl pointed to a junk car beneath a sycamore tree. They went to the spot and waited. After a while, Dilworth, shirtless and in blue jeans, came out to the porch. Dean took a good look, transfixed by what he saw. In an arc across Dilworth's chest, tattoos of the shamrock, the iron cross, and Nordic runes. On his right forearm, a big black swastika on a field of red. A true lug, a living pile of excrement wizened by hard prison years. Eyes of old blue peered out from beneath his meaty brow, and a ray of setting sun skidded across his skinhead. He carried himself with the pop and click of a soldier, his combat boots crunching the ground beneath him.

"What do you want, Trey?" he said, glaring at Dean.

"Brimhall's up to no good," Trey began.

"Is he?" he said, still staring at Dean.

"He's balls deep in a nigger chick," Dean said, as if Brimhall had committed the greatest sin in the history of mankind.

"Tell me more," Dilworth said.

Trey and Dean spun an elaborate tale about Brimhall and his new life as an infidel and race mixer. Dilworth didn't drink, but Dean pulled a bottle from his satchel. He and Trey got drunk and happy as they spilled their lies and provocations.

—

Brimhall stood on the ridge of Edwina's Queen Anne, watching his crews break down for the day. He peeled off his T-shirt, folded it and stuffed it snuggly under his belt at the small of his back. He loved to stand on the ridge at the end of a long day. Being at eye level with the trees, the chimneys and the sunset made him feel like he had accomplished something. At the other end of the block James was in total control at Mrs. Dalrymple's Mansard. From where Brimhall stood, James and his crew looked like an entirely different roofing company that could compete for its own contracts. And maybe at heart they were, and maybe one day they would. Brimhall and James used to speak each day, both business and personal. Those moments were priceless for Brimhall. But silence had come between them since the letter arrived a week ago, and Brimhall couldn't shake the feeling that the loss was permanent, and thus, devastating. I don't have the answers right now, he thought, but I'll eventually figure it out.

Down below, Edwina and Bobby pulled into the driveway. The back of the station wagon loaded with brown sacks of groceries. Bobby, trailing his grandmother with steady steps, carried a sack under each arm. Brimhall chuckled to himself because he could tell that it wasn't the first time Bobby had carried a sack under each arm. Going to the grocery store with Grandma Edwina must have been one of his dedicated chores. Back and forth they went until they'd emptied the car. Brimhall thought back to the day when he and James had eaten dinner with Edwina. Though attentive and extremely well mannered, Bobby had still managed to be a little kid. He'd danced the Dirty Chicken, but only after he'd cleared the dishes from the table.

At the other end of the block, James and his crew piled into their trucks and pulled out from Douglass Street. Brimhall looked down the asymmetric line of Victorian turrets, spires and chimneys stretching out on either side and across the street. He envisioned the value of the rooftops once they were dressed with slate and tile, and looked ahead forty years into the future, when his stamp of excellence would still be seen in this neighborhood. Snapping his finger, he summoned a bit of swagger. "Fuckin' A," he said, and felt better.

From the street came a pretty voice he'd wanted to hear.

"Whatcha doing up there? Everyone else is gone."

Edwina, standing out in the front yard, arms akimbo. The hem of her floral print dress danced at her knees. A cautious smile showed in her face. Brimhall gave a tentative wave and returned a smile as cautious as hers.

"Just thinking," he said.

"Can I come up?"

Brimhall scratched his chin as he studied her expression. Not the stern look from City Council. And not the dour lines that had creased her face when they had discussed the letters. She seemed relaxed, almost playful. The look became her, and Brimhall couldn't resist.

"Only through the hatch," he said, doing his best to be firm.

She walked toward the house and out of view. Brimhall heard the front door close. He shimmied down the steep slope to the scaffolding next to the eaves and grabbed a safety harness and two stout lengths of nylon cord. Veteran roofers like Brimhall didn't use safety harnesses because they slowed the pace of work. But since this was a public contract he at least had to have them on the premises. Rather than wear them, he and the crews left them on the scaffolding in case a city inspector dropped by to check on their progress. But Edwina Spurlock? She wasn't putting so much as one big toe on top of this roof without being tied in to at least two anchors. Brimhall ran one cord around the very bottom of the chimney and looped the other cord to the top rung of the ladder leading up to the roof hatch. As soon as he'd tied the last knot Edwina appeared in the attic.

"Are you sure I can come up?"

"Yeah, but you'll be tied in nice and tight."

"That's fine."

She climbed to the top of the ladder. Brimhall cinched the harness around her waist and fastened the cords to the big steel hoops now hanging from her hips.

"Now." Brimhall helped her out to the rooftop.

"Wonderful." She stood at full height and looked this way and that. "I've lived in this house for sixteen years and I've never once been up here."

"It is a nice view, huh?" He pointed toward the gleaming skyline.

Hugging the east side of the Scioto River along High Street, the clean peaks of downtown Columbus were a portrait of optimism and prosperity. LeVeque Tower, standing like a petrified rocket, was the city's architectural centerpiece. But the Huntington, with its bold plates of glass, and the geometric Nationwide Plaza, vied for ascendancy along the horizon.

"It's beautiful, Gene. Everything looks so different. Look at all the other roofs."

"These are some serious houses." Brimhall nodded his head for emphasis. "I wouldn't be here if they weren't worth working on."

"How high up are we?"

"About thirty-five, forty feet."

"Is that high?"

"It ain't the Empire State Building, but it ain't a one-story ranch, either. We're up here, Edwina, and it would be a long, hard fall."

"Just by being here I have an entirely new respect for what you do. This is real work."

Brimhall laughed. "That's what they say. It's not necessarily molecular biology, but you have to think like water and compete with gravity—two of the most powerful forces in our universe."

"So tell me what all you're doing."

"I'm gonna strip off all the tile and replace the decking. If memory serves me well, you need five rafters replaced. The rest is healthy virgin timber. When all the carpentry is done—gutters and eaves—I'll start laying the tile from side to side and from the bottom up with blind nailing. All the flashing will be replaced, and I'll lay a crown across the ridge. I'm gonna wrap the turret with Vermont slate. It'll take me about a month, and you can stay in your house the entire time. And after I'm done and it rains, I dare you to stand in the attic."

"I'm so excited," she said. "It's been a while since I liked the rain."

"You should be excited. This is a big moment for the neighborhood."

Edwina's face grew sour. "The taxes are gonna go up, aren't they?"

"You knew that, Mrs. Spurlock."

"Yes. I just keep thinking of the day when we get our new assessments."

"Death and taxes, Mrs. Spurlock. Death and taxes. But once these houses are done, you'll save enough money on utilities to pay the new tax bill. If I were you, I'd lay your fears to rest."

Side by side, they watched in silence as the LeVeque Tower turned hot orange in the dusk. Suspended in a soothing spell, Brimhall did not want this moment to end.

"Getting dark," Edwina said at last. "We probably need to get on down, huh?"

"That's fine. I'm glad you came up."

"So am I."

Downstairs they sat at the kitchen table. Bobby sang a Motown song, "My Girl," as he set the table with cream, sugar and a pair of coffee mugs.

"Can I go watch Teenage Mutant Ninja Turtles now?" he pleaded.

"Yes, but what do you say to Mr. Brimhall?"

"Goodnight, Mr. Brimhall," he said.

"Goodnight, Bobby."

Bobby cut into a spin move before disappearing into the din, leaving a smile on Brimhall's face.

"I've noticed Bobby is kind of like your right-hand man," Brimhall said.

"That he is. He's fairly reliable."

Edwina poured two cups.

"You and Bobby kind of remind me of me and my mom," he said, blowing on his coffee. "We didn't have a whole lot but we at least tried to take care of what we had. And if I didn't do my chores I had hell to pay, let me tell you."

"Me and Bobby have had our moments," she said, with a terse nod and a smile, "but on the whole he's been an excellent homemaker."

"For the longest time I just thought my mom was being mean, but I got my work ethic from her, and for that I'll always be thankful. But she was tough, Edwina. I still make the bed and wash the dishes thinking mom's gonna rise from her grave and come look at how I live. I still don't wanna make her mad."

"What was your mother's name?"

"Betty Jo McClain, and she was from Hazard, Kentucky. Remember those tornados that hit around Cincinnati back in 1984?"

"Vaguely."

"Well, I knew they were coming, or at least I anticipated that some would come—some big ones. I had watched the weatherman and he said a cold front and a hot front were gonna collide. So I got me a pile of ropes and chainsaws and a sledgehammer. When them tornados hit, like the weatherman said they would, I jumped in my truck and headed out. I stayed down there for four days and slept in a fleabag hotel. I peeled trees off of churches, houses and a bank. I pulled 'em off of telephone lines and cleared 'em from the streets. I made me a bunch of knots and pulleys that week, Edwina, knots I didn't even know I could tie. So anyway, I never called mom, and she got pissed. When I got home she was waiting for me at the kitchen table. She smacked me so hard I saw stars. And then I pulled out a money clip with eight thousand five hundred and sixty seven dollars in it, and I threw that clip on the table, and I said, 'Mom, don't ever hit me again.'"

"And what did she do?"

"She started crying, and then she apologized. And I accepted. And then I apologized and she accepted. That's when we became friends. I was in high school at the time."

"How old are you now?"

"Twenty-nine—going on fifty." He grinned.

"And how'd your mother die?"

"She passed about eleven years ago, suddenly. She was diagnosed with lung cancer and died just a few weeks later."

"I'm sorry to hear that. And your father?"

"Killed in Vietnam. I never met the man. Eugene Wheaton Brimhall Senior. But from what I heard it was best he died in the jungle. Me and my mom raised me."

"And now you're a roofing contractor and you make big money because of your mother?"

"Yes, m'am. So I told you a story. Can I ask you a question?"

"Sure."

"How'd you get Bobby?"

Edwina sighed. She took a long sip of coffee.

"My only child, Valencia, died in a car crash in Cleveland."

"Well, I know you have loss, but Bobby's incredible." Brimhall's voice was soft and stern.

"Not a day goes by that I don't think about Valencia, but not a day goes by that I don't thank God I've got Bobby. Obviously I wish I had both of them. But if one is all I have then one is all I get, right?"

"That's right," Brimhall said. "You're still blessed."

"I had Valencia when I was twenty, and she had Bobby when she was sixteen."

"How old's Bobby?"

"Nine."

"Which makes you—"

"—Old enough to be your mother."

"But not my grandmother."

Edwina and Brimhall looked at one another in silence, and suddenly shook with the kind of laughter that embraces the anguish of loss yet heralds the resilience of the survivor. Not everyone owned that laugh, but Edwina and Brimhall held permanent deeds.

—

Brimhall pulled out from Edwina's house feeling good about life. For the third night in a row they had sat and talked after work. Practical and mature, she had just enough regret in her soul to make him feel comfortable. He was uneasy around people who hadn't seen hardship, and wasn't too interested in what they had to say. He had told her that and she confessed to him that she felt the same way. What he couldn't quite figure out is why she was being so nice to him. He figured she had a motive. He was the boss of work. She was the boss of the neighborhood. If the bosses got along, then everyone else would follow. A lot was at stake, so Brimhall understood why she would offer the olive branch. But he sensed that she sought more than a pragmatic peace. And whatever it was she was after, Brimhall was convinced she was getting it. Despite the rift with James, and despite the simmering shame of the cross, Brimhall felt new and decent. Her grandson Bobby coaxed from him a tender laugh he had never heard before. And when he talked to Edwina, he talked casually of things that he kept secret from others.

Brimhall owned three roofing companies. Grocery stores, apartment complexes, subdivisions, office buildings, and strip malls. He roofed anything and everything and he did it for the money. But a strange new mission had come into his life. A shiny tile roof on Edwina's Queen Anne, his gift to her.

He downshifted into third and rumbled up the on ramp at I-71 and Hudson Street. A few minutes later, as he eased into the fast lane at the I-70 interchange, his cell phone rang. He didn't recognize the number that appeared in the message window. Thinking it was a potential client, he answered the call in his well-rehearsed business voice.

"Brimhall Roofing."

"Is this Gene Brimhall?" came the voice on the other end of the line.

"This is he. Can I help you?"

Based on the volume and proximity of the background noise, Brimhall guessed that the call came from a pay phone.

"Do you know who this is?" came the voice, and in it Brimhall detected something sinister.

The hair on Brimhall's arms and neck stood on end, and in an instant he knew who was on the phone.

"Yeah. You're the punk who sent those letters to Douglass Street."

"Your instincts serve you well. How'd you know?"

"Because you called from a pay phone, and you sound how you look—like a dick suckin' queer."

"Damn. It sounds like I've pissed you off."

"You're fuckin' with my friends and my money. And when I find you—"

"—Well lookie here you nigger-loving piece of shit, I won't be too hard to find. I'll be having a beer—at the Brown Bag Saloon."

"Then you're gonna get hurt tonight," Brimhall said.

"Fuck you!" Dean's voice held a sneer. "I'd even be so kind as to buy you a drink, but I don't think you have the balls to come down."

Brimhall hung up and mashed down on the gas pedal. The diesel dually lurched from the fast lane to the off ramp at West Broad Street. He blew through the red light at Schultz Avenue, banking left as the transmission howled from third gear. A minivan screeched to a stop to avoid sideswiping him, and a Toyota, its horn bleating, veered out of a head-on collision. Minutes later he slid into the gravel lot outside the Brown Bag Saloon. He popped out of the truck and stormed through a cloud of dust toward the door.

The first thing Brimhall saw was the concern in the eyes of his second cousin, Susie Cooper. She took a sip of whiskey and warned him with her eyes. Plunging through his mind went the unsettling thought that he'd stepped into a trap, a simple trap that should have been beneath him. Edwina had implored him several times not to go looking for the man who had written those letters. But here he was, driven by a mix of selfish pride and foolish curiosity. From the jukebox came a slow, dreary song with a steel guitar. The grim joy of conflict pervaded the room. Brimhall knew he had one chance to turn around and either grab his revolver from the glove box and return, or fire up the diesel dually and haul ass. He let that chance pass, stepping deeper into the mosaic of the Brown Bag Saloon. None of the familiar faces smiled. To the contrary, they greeted him with hostile stares. In a far, dark corner sat Trey, talking and drinking at a candlelit table with Joe and Jinx—and a tattooed man in a cowboy hat who Brimhall didn't recognize. People murmured as he walked to Trey's table. They saw the fury in his face and the mettle in his eyes, knowing that the emerald dragon on his left forearm was about to take flight.

Never fond of empty preambles, Brimhall planted his feet, cocked his chin to the right and glared down at Trey, his old foe.

"Who sent them goddamned letters to Douglass Street?"

"I don't know nothing about no letters, Brimhall." Trey's face contorted in a baleful smile.

"Yeah you fuckin' do. Just tell me who sent them and how I can find him, and me and you'll be fine."

"Brimhall, I don't know what you're talking about."

Before Brimhall responded, his world stopped turning, as he recognized the man seated at the table. Chris Dilworth, looking up at him. Had he known he was here, Brimhall definitely would have left when he had the chance. But beneath his cowboy hat, a shadow had hung over his face when Brimhall had scanned the bar for his enemies. Candlelight danced in his vacant blue eyes as he tilted back the brim.

"What's going on—big, bad roofer man?" he said, in a malevolent baritone twang.

The goad drew a few laughs from Trey and the others.

"Nothing that concerns you."

Brimhall swallowed hard to steady his nerves. A shooting star of certainty soared through his mind. If Dilworth puts me down, he thought, I'll never get back up.

"Brimhall," Dilworth said, carefully taking off his hat, "you keep asking about these letters, but what people really wanna know is what's up with you, getting all that pussy up in nigger town."

"What the fuck are you talking about?"

"I hear you been getting some monkey ass named Edwina Spurlock." He served a dreadful glare that showed neither remorse nor pity.

"I don't ever wanna hear that name come out of your mouth again."

His calm, quiet voice rang loud and pure in the kinetic silence of the barroom. No longer hesitant, he ached for a fight. He welcomed the chance to stand for Edwina. Dilworth rose, peeled off his shirt and unfurled his cellblock frame. The prison-ink shamrock, Iron Cross and Nordic runes embellished the swells of his chest. Dingy bar light shone on his skinhead and sparkled in the spiked buckles of his combat boots. In keeping with Brown Bag tradition, the onlookers pulled back the chairs and tables to create a pit in the back of the bar near the pool table. Brimhall backpedaled, peeled off his T-shirt, and flashed the life and labor in his physique.

"Come and get you some."

He put up his defense and bounced on the balls of his feet. As Dilworth lumbered into the pit, the crowd grew fierce with shouts and jeers, dousing Brimhall with spit and beer. Dilworth opened with a slow barrage of hooks, jabs and upper cuts, but Brimhall ducked, weaved to his right and bounced outside Dilworth's reach. Having collected himself, Brimhall sprang forward with a haymaker but was badly off the mark. The opening complete, the combatants backed away and sized each other up.

"I've been waiting for a long time." Dilworth's tattooed chest heaved with adrenaline.

"You'll wait forever," Brimhall hissed.

Holding up his defense, and flashing the big black swastika on his forearm,

Dilworth inched his way forward. Mindful of Dilworth's advantages, Brimhall resorted to his greatest asset—his quickness. He circled smooth and swift, closing in with each rotation. To keep from being outflanked, Dilworth pivoted. During the turn his right heel came down on an errant beer bottle that had rolled into the pit. The misstep broke Dilworth's rhythm and defense for a nanosecond. Brimhall slid through the gap in time, his overhand right pumping like a hot titanium piston.

And then, Brimhall uncoiled with the dragon.

His aim was true, too, as angle, trajectory, velocity and momentum met in an arc of power to unleash a fantastic left hook that shook Dilworth down to his rectum. Before Dilworth could even utter a yelp of pain, Brimhall brought a boot-shod heel crashing down on a kneecap. Groaning, Dilworth wobbled and fell. As he did, Brimhall clinched Dilworth's right wrist so that when he hit the ground his arm hung like a dead snake from Brimhall's hand. He flashed the big black swastika to make sure everyone in the Brown Bag Saloon saw the defeated flag before he let it drop to the warped hardwood floor. Brimhall spit in Dilworth's face and stepped over him. He dripped with swagger as he planted his feet and put his hands on his hips.

"Now," he said, with aggressive finality, "are there any more questions about my friend, Edwina Spurlock?"

The men with mullets who had gathered outside the pit stared at Brimhall in silent disbelief. Trey couldn't even look Brimhall in the eye. Instead he stuffed his hands in his pockets and stared at the floor. Still crumpled in a hideous heap, Dilworth moaned and flinched. Brimhall knew that by beating Dilworth with his bare hands he had earned a first-class ticket out of the Brown Bag Saloon. And indeed, he wanted to redeem that ticket immediately because he knew it would soon expire. But Brimhall wasn't done fighting. Not even close. Just as it appeared that the crowd would part and let Brimhall walk off into Hilltop legend, a new band of demons appeared. Dilworth's gang—skinheads in boots, jeans, white Ts and suspenders—and Dean Bernadette among them.

"You came for me, but they came for you," Dean said.

"Fuck all ya'll." Brimhall calmly stepped to the rack holding the pool cues. He grabbed the one whose butt end he knew to be weighted with lead. He cracked it over his knee, dropped the shaft but clutched the weighted remainder flush in his palm. To Brimhall's surprise, Tim Pfeiffer and Danny Wise broke from the crowd and rallied at his side. Then came a new sliding of tables and chairs as the fight was about to spill well beyond the confines of the pit. Dean pulled a four-inch buck knife from his back pocket. Trey fished out a pair of brass knuckles. One skinhead armed himself with a blackjack, while another carried a two-foot length of tree chain. A handful of people scurried out of the bar while others peeled off their shirts and filed in behind Trey, Joe, Jinx, Dean and Dilworth's supporters. Emboldened by the show of what appeared to be overwhelming force, Trey felt obliged to launch the final verbal salvo.

"You fightin' for the nigger, Brimhall?"

Dean bent with laughter.

Like a starving cur guarding a bloody bone, Brimhall flashed his teeth. He cocked the butt end of the pool cue over his shoulder, and lunged forward hacking and cleaving. The barroom grew cacophonous with wrenching shrieks of pain, wads of blood and snot hurtling from broken noses, teeth rolling as thrown sets of dice. Talented at carnage, Brimhall pumped his knees into groins and broke faces with his elbows. He growled and bit and gouged and flailed and told them all to go fuck their mothers and their sisters. He ignored the chain that whipped against his chest, and the harrowing boot swipe across his shin. He shrugged off the blind punch to his temple, and absorbed the uppercut across his chin. He kicked in a ribcage and thumbed out an eye, split a lip and shattered the hand at his throat.

Three Nazis soon lay in limp, leaking piles at his feet. Tim and Danny overtook the fourth and drove him to the floor. Shocked by the results of Brimhall's crude offensive, Joe, Jinx and the others finally fought back. They rushed Tim and Danny, all of them tumbling across the floor in a dense tangle, the struggle cruel and personal.

Brimhall focused on Trey and Dean, the mad architects of the struggle.

A Nazi tried to get up but Brimhall sent him back down with a stroke of the pool cue, which finally shattered. And that's when Trey, his right fist braced with the brass knuckles, stepped into the fray. He came with a combination of ineffective swings. Brimhall backpedaled, then countered with another terrific hook, sending Trey reeling toward the bar. Brimhall shielded himself with his left forearm, and suffered a deep gash there, as Dean closed with his buck knife. Once inside the crescent of his attack, Brimhall's right jab erupted, peppering Dean until he dropped his knife and fled.

Brimhall leaned back, held his arms out, bent his head to the heavens and let loose with a Celtic yell.

"Brimhall!" Susie Cooper yelled.

He turned to where she pointed, only to see Trey closing in. He clocked him with the brass knuckles. Brimhall staggered across the floor, his hand cupped over his eye. Trey picked up Dean's knife, and with a triumphant howl of his own, stuck it into Brimhall's gut. Brimhall twisted and fell to the floor, where other men laid and bled. Susie Cooper stormed out from behind the bar with the house revolver aimed at Trey.

"I'll blow your fuckin' head off!" She cocked the gun.

Trey grimaced, pocketed the knife, and surveyed the destruction. Then he ran. As people limped and hobbled out of the bar, Susie Cooper called 911 and told them she needed ambulances at 2201 West Broad Street. She grabbed a few rags from the bar, knelt at Brimhall's side, and stanched his wounds.

"Eugene Wheaton Brimhall Jr.," she said, tears rolling down her cheeks, "I won't let you die."

And then she prayed, asking God and Christ and Mary to fly down from the rooftops and hold him in their healing hands.

—

The landline rang, and then the cell phone, and then the pager. Convinced that something terrible had happened, James rolled out of bed. He exchanged somber looks with Eva as he put the receiver to his ear.

"Hello?"

"Is this Mr. O'Neal?"

"Yes."

"This is Betty Jellick, a nurse at Mt. Carmel West. Do you know Mr. Gene Brimhall?"

"Yes. What's wrong?"

"There's been an emergency. Mr. Brimhall's been stabbed."

"Is he alive?"

"Yes. But you need to get down here as soon as you can."

He and Eva jumped into the truck and sped to the hospital. She slid across the bench seat, like a country girl, and held his free hand in hers.

James could barely contain himself as the elevator climbed to the fifth floor. When the doors slid open he bounded down the corridor, Eva at his heels, to the nurse's station. Room 515, they told him. He took a deep breath before easing into the room. Brimhall, an IV in his arm. His face brownish purple like a swollen fig. A big white bandage over his left eye and brow. His left arm wrapped in gauze and three fingers on his right hand set in an aluminum splint. Somewhere beneath the hospital gown was the stab wound. Though the sight disheartened him, James had ample reason for hope.

Brimhall lived.

A tall, husky women with broad shoulders, an auburn ponytail, a missing front tooth and a blue-ink tattoo—Baby Boom—running the length of her right forearm, stood watch over Brimhall's sick bed. Her fierceness subsided when she realized that it was James who had just walked into the room. Susie Cooper wept when she saw the grief in James' pretty walnut eyes.

"They said," she began, quavering, "that if the knife would've been a half-inch over—" She fell into his arms and cried on his shoulder. "He's been such a cocky son-of-a-bitch the last few years, but he's my son-of-a-bitch."

James drew strength from her anguish. Denying tears, he squared his shoulders, kissed her on the forehead and cradled her neck in his palm. Wiping tears from her eyes, she looked up with a meek yet stubborn smile. They inquired of the nurses, who promised them that Brimhall was in stable condition and that he would live. With that assurance, James, Eva and Susie went down to the front entrance of the hospital. Eva stopped along the way and purchased three stale cafeteria coffees.

They sipped from Styrofoam cups as Susie relayed her side of the story.

"There's this guy," she said, "and he's a real dickhead, too. From what I heard he's backing one of the candidates in that election they're having downtown."

"The Beckham-Bernadette election?" James said. "For City Council?"

"Uh-huh."

James and Eva exchanged puzzled, sidelong glances. Eva lit a Marlboro and stepped closer to the conversation. Susie flashed a warning glance, as if she didn't approve of Eva's proximity, but Eva didn't budge.

"What campaign is he with?" James said.

"Bernadette. He came out to the Hilltop a couple of weeks ago. Trey was bragging about it."

"Why?"

Susie bummed a cigarette from Eva, who also gave her a light.

"Because, that little prick from the Bernadette campaign paid him a lot of money. Trey said he was gonna put Brimhall in his place."

"Why?"

"Oh, James, you're not from where we're from. Brimhall's supposed to be a piece of shit from the Hilltop—like the rest of us—but he's not. Motherfuckers up on Guernsey Street are fuckin' jealous of him. And that guy from the election came out of fuckin' nowhere and set that jealousy to spinning like a goddamned top."

"But why?"

"I don't know," she said. "But he must've known what he was doing because all the sudden Chris Dilworth's involved!"

"Who's Chris Dilworth?"

"A fuckin' Nazi," she said. "He's from Guernsey Street, where Brimhall's from, and he's been in prison since God knows when. He's had it in for Brimhall for years, too. A while back Brimhall won that big settlement with the insurance company. Remember that?"

"Of course," James said. "I was in the judge's chambers when the terms were announced."

"Well then, you know Brimhall made some money, right?"

"A lot, plus attorney's fees."

"Well, Dilworth got word of the settlement and asked Brimhall to start putting money in his commissary account. Brimhall told him to fuck off. Dilworth felt betrayed and vowed revenge. From what I hear, that guy from the election sent out some letters, knowing that Brimhall would come looking for whoever bought the stamps, so to speak. And when he did, Dilworth was waiting for him."

Susie took a drag from her cigarette and blew out a long, comforting plume of smoke.

"What was in those letters?" James said.

"It was something about that cross."

"What about the cross?"

"You ain't gonna tell nobody what I'm saying to you, right?"

"No."

"And her." She looked over at Eva.

"Your secrets are safe with me," Eva replied, and lit chain cigarettes for both of them.

"Everybody from the old neighborhood knows the story. Brimhall built the cross, and Dilworth burned it. Some blacks moved into the neighborhood and nobody wanted them there, so Dilworth volunteered to scare them off."

"And?"

"Dilworth's dumb as rocks, so he went to Brimhall, who had been building shit and fixing shit since he was a kid. Dilworth asked him to build the cross, and sooner rather than later Brimhall had it all straightened out. And it was huge. Dilworth loaded it up in a truck, and the rest, they say, is civil rights history. All that's old news, James. But it's a modern world—and Brimhall's got a big contract up in a black neighborhood—so all the sudden it becomes new news."

"And that's when the fight broke out?"

"Aw, man." She turned in a circle and pumped her fist. "Brimhall looked like fuckin' Zeus. I mean, he put Dilworth on the ground, James. That fucker is big, too. He was in the joint for years, but he couldn't beat my cousin."

She bowed out her chest with the grim pride that comes with winning a point in the feud. "But do you wanna know the weird part?"

"It's all weird," James said. "But yes. Tell me."

"It all ended up being over a black lady."

"What?"

"Brimhall's from the Hilltop," she said, *sotto voce*. "He's one of us. But he started making money, you know, and his mind started moving to new places. Brimhall would never build another cross, James! Everyone knows that! Or at least they should! That's why it pissed him off so bad when it got brought up— especially so long after the fact. So when he went looking for answers, Dilworth was there, fresh from prison. The guy from the election said Brimhall was hot and heavy with some black chick up on Douglass Street. I love Brimhall, so he can pretty much do anything he wants and I'm cool with it. But Dilworth's a Nazi, James. If someone from the neighborhood is making time with the blacks, especially someone like Brimhall, Dilworth's gonna be interested. That guy from the election saw two stars heading in different directions, and he made sure they collided. At first it was about money and jealousy, but by the time those two tied in tonight, it was a real fuckin' race war."

"What was the lady's name?"

"Ummmm, Edna something," she said. "Edna Sherwood?"

"Edwina Spurlock?"

"Um-huh," she purred, and batted her brow. "Edwina Spurlock. And she must be one helluva lady 'cause I've known Brimhall all his life, and he ain't never fought for a woman's honor until tonight. Is she pretty?"

"She's beautiful," James said, "and I'll fight for her, too."

After a long embrace, Susie turned and headed toward the parking garage, but not before giving James her number in case there was another emergency. "Brimhall's still got some friends back home, and a lot of enemies. Don't let him go back to the Hilltop until he can fend for himself. Will you make me that promise?"

"Absolutely," he said. Eva gave Susie her pack of cigarettes and her lighter, and kissed her on the cheek.

"Thanks." Susie gave Eva an awkward hug. "And James, don't worry about the cops. They've heard five conflicting stories by now, and to be honest, nobody died. That's the only time the pigs really care. In a few weeks they'll get busy with something else and forget about what happened tonight. Just know that what I told you is the truth and be content with that."

James and Eva returned to the hospital room where they kept vigil for the rest of the night. While Eva napped on his shoulder, James thought about his friendship with Brimhall and how important it had become.

He had just dropped out of Ohio State after only two quarters. Nineteen, ashamed of himself, and living in a drab apartment on Morse Road. Flipping through the *Scioto Times* one morning, he saw a want ad in the classifieds: Roofers Needed. Since he was no longer in school James had been dropped from the "parental plan" and needed a full-time job. He drove out to the Hilltop to a shabby little workshop on West Broad Street with the words Brimhall Roofing Inc. hand painted in green letters above the front door. The guy sitting behind the desk with his feet propped up looked venomous. This was before Brimhall had gotten his braces and before the lion's mane of a mullet had been sheared into the tight rear tuft he now wore. The ugly blue-ink dragon slithering down his left forearm had yet to be covered with the expensive pigments of emerald and gold that now adorned his skin. The crude exuberance in his face hadn't yet been tamed somewhat by middle-class comforts. James couldn't see himself working for a man with crooked teeth, a tattoo and a mullet. He nearly turned and walked out without even speaking. But even in the hungry years, Brimhall commanded an odd, powerful charisma. James decided to stay.

"I just dropped out of Ohio State," he confessed.

Brimhall stood up, strutted out from behind the desk and studied the lanky kid from head to toe.

"Good." He laughed. "You're hired."

And that's when the work began.

Brimhall drove James like a mule and taunted him with the refrain, "college boy wannabe," or "college boy dropout." When a client called back two days after the completion of a job and said the roof still leaked, Brimhall scolded James and then looked over his shoulder as he found the problem and fixed it. He would also make him explain to the customer in minute detail exactly what had gone wrong and what had been done to remedy the problem. James remembered crying one Saturday, at the end of a 72-hour week in July, his bones dry, his skin roasted. But he was at the work site Monday morning at 6:30. That was the routine for three years, and Brimhall, who held himself and the other crew members to the same rigid standard, never budged. In those three years James was the only one to survive. Everyone else had come and gone and had been replaced by fresh faces who flourished for a few weeks, or maybe a few months, before withering under Brimhall's brutal regimen. "Go on back home and suck your mama's tit, son, and get the fuck off my work site," he had said to a roofer who showed up drunk and stoned one morning. When the roofer appeared to buck Brimhall's command, he leveled a Godless stare and peeled off his t-shirt. Without a word the fired roofer turned and scampered away.

"Why don't we hire Mexicans?" James had said. "I hear they work hard."

Brimhall frowned, but relented. "Go ahead. The white boys sure as hell ain't working out."

That's when James first began to feel pride in hanging slate on an old mansion or laying a metal roof across a 40,000 square foot industrial building. His coworkers, immigrants from Guadalajara who had families to feed, were people he had hired.

One year when business was seasonally slow, James thought he didn't have to work one morning, but Brimhall rousted him at 6 a.m. to tell him to be at the steps of the Franklin County Courthouse at 8 a.m. sharp. He didn't explain, but the surprisingly soft note in his voice intrigued James. They met on the steps of the courthouse, and in the freezing cold, drank coffee from Styrofoam cups. Brimhall smoked a cigarette and then led James into the real estate office.

He handed James a list of twenty addresses that he recognized as former work sites. "I want you to pull the cards on all these properties." Once he had pulled the cards Brimhall asked him to write down the 1993 appraisals and the 1994 appraisals, and then compare the two totals. The 1994 appraisals came in just over $4 million more than the year before.

"That's the tax base, James, which you helped to improve. Now a lot of these people had a lot of other stuff done to their property, so it ain't all us, but ain't none of it worth a hill of beans without a new roof. That's the tax base, James. That's schools and cops and trash collection and all that good shit. The city you love."

"We did that?" James beamed at Brimhall with a pupil's smile.

"That's right, James." He grinned. "You're a lot more important now than when you walked into my office a few years back—college boy wannabe."

They laughed so loudly that a clerk glared at them and put an index finger to her lips.

Later that day Brimhall introduced him to Steve Greenberg, the Bexley attorney who handled all of Brimhall's big contracts. Also in the room was Amanda Snow, the accountant.

"Meet the team," Brimhall said, with the easy wave of a hand.

And still later Brimhall took him to the City Center Mall and bought him a worsted navy suit, a cotton shirt, a red silk tie, black socks and black leather broughams.

"I don't wear suits, 'cause everyone knows me," he said, alight with one of his hazel iron gazes. "But James O'Neal? He's up and coming and he wears a suit."

On the way back to the truck James noticed that Brimhall wore new jeans, a crisp flannel shirt and a snazzy Russian stadium coat. On his feet weren't the scuffed work boots he always wore, but a pair of shiny lizard skin ropers. On his left pinky, a gold baguette encrusted with diamonds and emeralds, and around his neck, a rope of gold. He took a long look at Brimhall, his teeth still tethered by braces, and marveled at the self-made man.

A few weeks later Brimhall asked him to write a bid for the Sacred Heart Catholic Basilica in Italian Village, which needed 20,000 square feet of Spanish barrel mission tile.

"Sacred Heart?" James said, "That's a $300,000 bid. Maybe more."

"And?"

"You trust me with that?"

"Yeah. But as you do the bid, start looking around for a piece of property. Ain't nobody gonna write contracts for me if they don't own a home. Just find something affordable and let me know."

"A house?" James said, incredulous.

Brimhall shrugged. "What, you have to be married with kids to own a home? See if you can find something in the range of $60,000. Have some fun with it, man."

He wrote the bid, won the contract, and found a cozy, long-neglected Italianate on Oregon Avenue, a shady, porch-lined street in Victorian Village just south of campus. Brimhall cosigned on a $59,000 mortgage a few weeks later.

Those memories made James cry. He felt guilty that he hadn't been at Brimhall's side during the fight, and disappointed with himself for letting a rude letter from a stranger come between him and his friend. He felt he should have shown patience and maturity, not anger and indignation. His mind raced back to the bullfight and to the jolt of joy he had felt when Brimhall arrived at his gurney with such bravado, saying, "James O-fucking-Neal."

Pondering the circumstances in the heavy silence of the hospital room, James found peace in his hardening sense of purpose. He couldn't figure out why somebody from the Bernadette campaign had targeted his boss. What he did know is that he and Brimhall had been conscripted into the rough and tumble game of local politics.

He looked at Eva, who had recently awoken from her slumber. A melancholy twinkle danced in her eyes.

"I guess I'm in the election now," he said.

She kissed him on the cheek.

"You are on the right side," she whispered, and caressed his shoulder.

O R T O N
H A L L

Century B canvassed Duxberry for three days straight. Relative to expectations, the initial foray into the Cleveland Road theater was a success. According to Mingmei's records, Century B had placed 43 *BECKHAM!* signs in front of 35 residential addresses, had handed out 22 *BECKHAM!* T-shirts and had placed small stacks of *BECKHAM!* fliers in the storefronts of five small businesses on Cleveland Road. According to Mingmei's notes, Century B had made direct contact with 61 registered voters and had been asked to speak at two small Baptist churches on Dresden Street the following Wednesday. According to Mingmei's schedule, which ran right up to 7:30 p.m. on Election Day, Century B had two more days in Duxberry before crossing Hudson Street into Linden Park.

Nobody in Century B really knew how to campaign except Mingmei, and even her experience was meager. But she had been wise enough to put Barbara and Eva up front to handle all the introductions and the handshaking. Warm and gregarious, Barbara spoke to the residents in a language they understood. "Hey, ya'll," she'd begin, and work her magic from there. She made people laugh, and with laughter came a comfortable atmosphere in which to deliver the campaign spiel. Eva, speaking staid English and presenting herself formally—*Please, we need your vote for Beckham*—was the ideal foil. Frank and Anku carried the stakes and yard signs, while Mike, Davita and Kristin drove the signs into the ground and handed out woodpecker T-shirts and fliers. Oxana, exotic underneath the brim of Frank's big floppy planter's hat, was Century B's mystery mascot. Donna Rosenbaum, at Mingmei's request, served the campaign from her North Campus apartment, where she dug through reams of 1990 census data on a high-powered desktop computer. Donna, a junior journalism major, also filed Freedom of Information requests at City Hall seeking 20 years of records on the council's appointments to the city's many commissions and committees.

Mingmei had a hunch that the information would serve the campaign well, when and if Beckham made the runoff.

Each volunteer had his or her own campaign T-shirt. On the front of the shirt was the image of a pileated woodpecker with the word **BECKHAM!** beneath it. Sewn across the back shoulder in blue satin was the volunteer's last name, compliments of Mingmei's speedy skill on a sewing machine. Though abundantly clumsy and with more rebuffs to its credit than successful entreaties, Century B was organized and asserting itself. Mingmei allowed a tiny, internal smile before leading Century B to the next block, and to the next chance to rally support for the woodpeckers and the trees.

—

Eva enjoyed campaigning, but an ember of fear smoldered in her heart.

She had grown up in Prague, among the safest capitals on the planet. Regardless of the time of day a person could walk the streets with a reasonable presumption that he or she would not be a victim of crime. That was not the case on Cleveland Road. Aimless kids, some of them presumably armed with unregistered guns, cruised through the days and nights in long cars with tinted windows. Eva considered herself cordial, but didn't have the nerve to smile or wave to the youngsters, even when one stopped, rolled down the window and said, "Damn, white girl, you sure is looking fine today."

Through sidelong glances, Eva saw that on the corners drugs were sold, and in the alleys, abused. During backyard barbeques, dice rolled and dominoes flipped. Bets were made. Gin flowed. Life unfolded beneath the heavy domes of bass that rumbled up from the trunks of old Buicks and Fords. In Prague's post-revolution discos, Eva had welcomed rhythmic Hip Hop thunder as part of the soundtrack of freedom. But on the American streets, where rap was born, the raucous beats arrived with an unsettling edge. Eva had been in the United States for two years, and almost all that time was spent on campus or in the quaint quarters of German Village. People were happy. They had money and hope and the ability to chase their dreams. Cleveland Road was the flipside of that utopia.

Women, young women with braided hair and diva attitudes, huddled at the bus stops with their children. Vagabonds hustled in and out of alleys and nameless lounges. Men guarded street corners as if they were forts, and they rode bikes for transportation, not exercise and sport. Everything looked cheap and mean. Buildings and people leaned. Gunshots rang out—pop, pop, pop, pop, pop—on a notorious block where Century B dared not tread. Still, Eva recognized a certain vibrancy peaking through Cleveland Road's surface of decay. Taxis and buses roared past the storefronts lined with diners, hair salons and boutiques. Colorfully clad vendors from Somalia sold their wares from vacant lots or from patchwork stalls along the sidewalk. People on the streets laughed and called out each other's names. Lovers kissed while old men danced. Youngsters at the car wash polished their vehicles as if they were the crown jewels of the kingdom. Banners emblazoned with the tri-colored seal of Africa hung in the windows and dangled from storefront flagpoles.

Culture, Eva concluded. American culture.

Walking these streets was a grand adventure, one she could not duplicate in Europe. Smiling, she looked over at Barbara, who was almost as tall as Eva and a good twenty pounds heavier. Thick and solid. Her hair in an afro. A true hometown girl, too, as much a part of Ohio as cow corn, a golden autumn moon, and a dusting of March snow. Eva tried to imitate her easy, cheerful stroll, but only succeeded in looking awkward and wooden. Barbara glanced at her out of the corner of her eye.

"Sista, you got a long way to go."

"I will learn one day," Eva said.

She went back to her normal walk, moving with the dour grace of a proud cat.

"I know I have asked you before, but I will ask it again," she said to Barbara. "What do we need to do to make it on these streets?"

The other volunteers gathered around so that Barbara was no longer talking only to Eva, but to the entire membership of Century B.

"Be decent and have an open mind." She arched her brows and scanned the faces of the volunteers. "If we play it cool, people will know that we're down here for an election and folks'll respect that. And since Eva's the president, we need to treat her like the president. Eva, it's key that you remain confident. That's the law of the streets: Walk like you own it. Everything else will follow. I know all ya'll have heard of the new philosophy called Political Correctness. Up here people play by an older set of rules. They say what they think and ain't about to apologize for saying it. You'll hear the truth, especially if we screw up, so we can't get caught slipping. And Anku," she added, with an expectant, worried smile, "please watch our backs."

All eyes turned to Anku. He responded with a slow gesture of approval. Sunlight glinted off his crucifix. The solemnity in his manner suggested that he already thought of himself as the guardian. He allowed the trappings of civilization to fall away so his colleagues could see the third-world soldier he once was, and to an extent, would always be. A vacant, remorseless calm settled in his eyes. His muscles went taut as he morphed into the Black Roster at Dawn. Cautious and subtle, positioning himself so that none but Century B could see, Anku pulled back his shirt to reveal the well-worn hilt of a U.S. Marine issue K-Bar—a true killing blade—tucked inside his shorts at his hip. He shrugged as if to offer an apology, but it wasn't needed. The members of Century B, peaceniks to a man, found reluctant comfort in the fact that Anku was armed. He tucked away his past and was once again the polite, pleasant electioneer in Birkenstocks and khakis.

"And Frank will also watch our backs," he said, bestowing status on the scrawny kid from Pittsburgh, who to this point was known only as the cute guy who was lovesick over Oxana. Anku and Frank shared a deep handshake, the kind that seals an oath.

"Are we ready, then?" Eva said.

She pushed the shades down from her forehead, adjusted the collar of her *BECKHAM!* shirt, took the last drag off her cigarette and stamped it out. Century B, stretching shoulder to shoulder across the entire width of a backstreet, trudged deeper into the campaign.

—

A lanky blonde standing on a porch stared at Leon with candid curiosity. She pushed the shades up over her forehead and stepped out into the front yard as her cohorts tapped campaign signs into the ground and chatted with residents. Leon didn't hear what she said, but from the movement of her mouth and hands it was clear she had issued a command. In a matter of seconds, a hard knot of electioneers in garish *BECKHAM!* woodpecker T-shirts formed in the middle of the street. At their center was the blonde, and the left corner of her upper lip was curled into an imperious smirk.

Leon was impressed. He and the four men rolling with him had heard that a band of college kids was in the area campaigning for Beckham. Ever since hearing the news, Leon had yearned to see them. Details were sketchy as to who they were, but of one fact everyone was sure—their leader was a sight to behold. And here she was, as advertised, proud of face and built of handsome timber. Leon chuckled as he and his men pulled to a stop ten feet in front of them, standing over their bikes.

"So this is Century B, huh?" Leon said, effecting nonchalance.

"That is correct," she said.

Leon's sources had mentioned a foreign accent—English stamped with steel rivets—but he hadn't believed them until now. He had expected a bubbly American from the suburbs, but this was a serious girl from some sad corner of Europe. Leon could tell that she had lived through trouble.

"Have you come to join us," she said, "or have you come to surrender?"

"Neither," Leon said.

"Then you must be training for the Tour de France." She gestured toward Leon's Nottingham three-speed. "And if you are, do not count on me for a sponsorship." Century B laughed.

In an attempt to gain footing in the conversation, Leon injected a bit of venom into his voice. "I don't need the Tour de France. I've got the election. Bernadette!"

"But you have already lost." She gave him a devilish wink.

"I don't think so. The way I see it, you guys are going nowhere up on Cleveland Road. You're a bunch of misfits."

Leon's men responded with sharp murmurs of support, and Leon glowed with the sheen of an antique cello.

"I agree," she said, ruefully. "We are short and tall and of different colors. And we come from different parts of the world. But people have a way of finding their places. And are we not people?"

"Oh, yeah." Leon gave her a gaping, sarcastic smile. "You're peoples, all right. But you're up in the hood, sweetheart. And people up in the hood don't vote for woodpeckers. Black folks vote for two things: Other black folks and money, honey."

Eva turned and glanced at the modest row of **BECKHAM!** signs lining the yards of McGuffy Avenue. She turned back to Leon and shrugged.

"Perhaps you do not know 'the hood' as well as you think you do."

"I guess we'll find out on Election Day," he said.

Leon knew he wasn't going to crack the nut this day, thinking it best to move along before she got his goat.

"Look, sweetheart, I'd love to stay and chat but I've got an election to win."

"And so do we—Leon Davis."

"How do you know my name?"

"What do you mean?" she said, her eyes sardonically wide. "You are a famous cyclist on your way to the Tour de France to take Miguel Indurain's crown. All the world knows you!"

Century B convulsed with laughter as Leon and his bike brigade curled away and turned the corner.

At a stop light, one of Leon's men, Bingo, looked at him and frowned. "That's a bad bitch, huh Leon?"

"Not as bad as she thinks she is, Bingo. And definitely not as bad as me."

———

Dean rolled over and pushed the snooze button, hoping a few more minutes of sleep would numb the pain. He was wrong. The knots on his face throbbed with each breath he took. He downed a sprinkling of painkillers and stumbled out of bed. He hadn't expected to fight the other night. He thought he'd walk into the Brown Bag Saloon just in time to see Brimhall begging for mercy. Instead, the roofing contractor was at the pinnacle of triumph, with Dilworth, touted as Mr. Invincible, slumped at his feet.

"Shit," he muttered, looking into the bathroom mirror.

The concavity of skin beneath his left bloodshot eye was as dark as a grape. His nose a swollen gourd of flesh. His lower lip a nasty red protuberance. Rubbing the crick in his neck, Dean flipped the hot and cold nozzles, let the water mix until it was nice and warm, and then stepped into the shower.

As he toweled himself dry, the cell phone rang. Groggy in spite of the shower, Dean ambled down the hall and answered the call.

"Well, well, well, you're a man of your word," Leon twittered.

"What do you mean?"

"I'm here at the corner of Douglass Street and it's seven-thirty in the morning and for the second day in a row I don't see no redneck. The kid's down here with them Mexicans, but the big shot's gone."

Dean allowed himself a grim chuckle of success. "Yeah, well, Mr. Brimhall got into a little trouble the other night. I don't think he'll be coming down to Douglass Street anytime soon."

"What happened, man?"

"I'll spare you the details, Leon. Suffice it to say, Mr. Brimhall owed somebody some money, and the bill finally came due."

"Damn! So it looks like you've made some inroads on that contract?"

"Uh, I'd say that's correct. Which leads me to the next topic. How's the campaign going?"

"Fine. Me and my men have rolled hard for the last week. We've hit every nook and cranny from Seventeenth to Hudson. People are into it, brother. And that little crew of college kids, Century B, well, to tell you the truth they're pretty tough, but they ain't got nothing on me."

"Where all have they been?"

"All through Duxberry. And now they're up in Linden Park."

"How's the money holding up?"

"I could always use some more," Leon said. "I wanna throw a 'Get out the Vote' barbeque at the VFW coming up here in the next week or so. That'll cost some cabbage, but it'll get you some votes."

"Sounds great." Dean dabbed at the raw lump on his lip. "So, tell me a little more about this Century B, our competition."

"There's ten of them, and most are Americans. But they got some foreigners in there, too. There's this chick named Eva. She's the leader. Gotta smart-ass mouth, too. She's tall, and from what I hear on the streets, she's from Czechoslovakia. You know, where the Communists come from."

"No shit?" Dean sounded puzzled. "What's a Czech doing in the campaign?"

"Beats me. She's probably trying to live some kind of 'American dream.' You know how them European people are. They all wanna wear blue jeans, chew bubble gum and vote."

"Well, is this 'American dream' gonna cost us some numbers up on Cleveland Road?" Dean was a tad concerned with the slight note of respect that he heard in Leon's voice.

"Some, I'm afraid, but not enough," Leon said.

"Well, what if someone threw the fear of God into this Czechoslovakian girl. Do you think that might slow them down?"

Leon howled with laughter.

"What's so funny?"

"Even I know this. Communists are atheists! They can't be afraid of God!"

He kept laughing until Dean was annoyed. Then he became angry that Leon, of all people, had used an historical tidbit to poke fun at him.

"Okay," Dean continued, heavily so as to convey that he had been peeved. "Do we need to scare her?"

"Uh, I don't think so. They got this African guy with them. Name is Alfonso Anku. Up in the 'hood he's what's known as a hard nigga. He dresses like a college boy, but he don't fool me. If you look real close, he kind of looks like one of the warlords you see on TV. You know, one of them guys who rebels against the government in some hell hole like Sierra Leone or the Congo. You go messing with the Czech chick and you'll end up in the hospital or the morgue. Shit, you'd need a machete and an AK to get to her. I've pulled up a few yard signs and I've told people not to listen to them, but as far as confronting Century B—you best just let them go. Believe me."

—

Inside the phone booth at the south end of Douglass Street, Leon cocked the receiver between his ear and shoulder, and with his free hands flicked a menthol from the pack and lit it. He scanned the block and saw James, one of his roofers, and Edwina standing on her porch. Judging from their body language and animated gestures, Leon knew that the conversation was heated. The three of them stepped down from the porch and walked in Leon's direction. He and James made eye contact, and that's when a bright light shone in Leon's warehouse of memories. James. James O'Neal. James from City Hall. James the bullfighter—who had sat next to Eva, the leader of Century B.

Leon's mood soared to euphoria.

"Dean! Let me call you back in about five minutes!"

Leon stood on the pedals and pulled out of Douglass Street. He wound through the alleys to Hudson Street, turned north on Republic and coasted into the back parking lot at Joe's. Once seated in the back room with a cup of coffee and the day's edition of the *Scioto Times* in front of him, Leon dialed Dean's number from a long-corded rotary phone. He propped his feet across the bench.

"Leon?"

"It's me."

"What's up?"

From the first moment he'd met him Leon had known that something was wrong with Dean Bernadette. He had seen the freakish piss in his eyes the morning of the letter, and just moments ago, he clearly heard the bellowing accordion of hell—"Do we need to scare her?" Dean wasn't fit to be free and in possession of cash. But as long as he was, Leon was more than willing to be one of the takers. First, however, he needed to give.

"You know who James O'Neal is? The foreman down on Douglass Street?"

"Yeah. Why?"

"Well," Leon said, ramping up his voice with conspiratorial relish, "guess who he's dating?"

—

When Dean first talked about the election with his uncle he had promised to do two things, turn out the black vote on Cleveland Road and somehow manage to damage, or destroy, Beckham's election hopes with an affair. Dean was the campaign darling for having transformed Cleveland Road from an election backwater to a slush pile of votes. Leon and his bike brigade had exploded into the Cleveland Road extravaganza, stumping at gas stations, car washes, barbershops, pool halls and bars. The tenants at the old folks home on Huy Avenue had agreed to vote for Bernadette if they were given rides to the polls. Leon had already made arrangements with a nearby funeral home to provide transportation. The "black" VFW was gearing up for beer and barbeque in Bernadette's honor. Fliers were stacked neatly in fellowship halls and tacked to bulletin boards at day care centers. Drooping in the windows of storefronts, hanging from walls and stapled to telephone polls from Eleventh to Hudson Street was the name ***BERNADETTE!***

While Dean rightfully claimed the credit for Cleveland Road, his elation was tempered by the obvious failure of his other plan.

On the strength of a few introductions by an ex-girlfriend with whom he still had cordial relations, Dean was able to scour several sorority houses looking for the ideal vixen for the Beckham seduction. A few girls were interested in the money—$8,000 for pictures of a nude candidate sprawled out in a bed that wasn't his own—but ultimately, there were no takers. Dean concluded that the plan was at best impractical, and at worst, impossible. All effort to perpetuate the scheme died, until Leon told him that the leader of Century B was dating the foreman at the Douglass Street Restoration. His second plan had suddenly risen from the grave, alive and well.

He called down to Beckham's campus headquarters and pretended to be a volunteer.

"Is Century B out campaigning today?" he said to the girl who answered the phone.

"Yeah." From the background noise Dean could tell she was flipping through a schedule. "They're heading out at two p.m. and are due back here at five. Did you want to volunteer?"

"Yeah," he gushed, affecting an undergraduate's naïve ebullience.

Later that day he sat on the patio at Insomnia Coffee House, across the street from campus headquarters, sipping espresso and reading The Lantern as he waited for Century B. A few minutes past 5 p.m. the weary electioneers poured out of the cargo van and straggled into campus headquarters and said their goodbyes with hugs and handshakes. Eva and two others headed up High Street. Dean gulped down the last drop of his third espresso and fell in behind them. From his leather satchel he pulled out a pen and pad and jotted down the names embroidered across the shoulders of their woodpecker T-shirts— *HAVLICEK, FULLER*. He had a hard time reading the third person's name because the brim of a ridiculously large planter's hat covered the letters. But her head tilted forward momentarily and Dean was able to decipher the name. *LISAKOVSKYA*.

FULLER was one of those skinny kids who never quite grows into his frame. Somewhere between sophomoric and handsome, he carried himself with the confidence of a liberal patrician, and thus did not seem entirely out of place with the older, foreign women on either side of him. And from what Dean could hear, he spoke their language—Czech?—and spoke it fairly well. He glided out in front of them in a series of comedic ballroom steps. He made a silly face, leapt and clicked the heels of his fine hiking boots. In short, he did the foolish things that a young American dandy might do when he is trying to coax smiles and laughter from hard-boiled women of the Cold War. And though Dean found the whole thing annoying, it worked well for *HAVLICEK* and *LISAKOVSKYA*. Their laughter came and went in fits like the songs of warblers, and their heads bobbed and tilted with delight. In such leisurely fashion they passed Apollo's Greek Café, the pizzeria, Long's Bookstore, and Bernie's basement pub. Traversing 15th Avenue, *FULLER* pretended to be a crossing guard even though the green light was theirs and no traffic was coming.

When they reached Buckeye Donuts, the trio stopped and began their farewells. **HAVLICEK** hugged **LISAKOVSKYA** and kissed her on both cheeks. She did likewise with **FULLER**. Dean crossed High Street with **HAVLICEK** and stood within a few feet of her as she waited for a southbound bus.

"Bye, Eva!" called **FULLER**.

"Bye, Frank."

Eva dipped into an elegant curtsy. Her eyes, as blue as a robin's egg, caught the afternoon light and sparkled, and for a grand moment she stood as a prim duchess of the Old Regime. And then she grinned. Dean noticed her crooked teeth. The imperfection made her smile rather gawky, but in no way detracted from her beauty as the flaw was a mark of authenticity.

Eva flashed a monthly pass as she stepped onto the Neal Avenue bus. Dean fumbled through the folds of his satchel for $1.25. By the time he found a seat the bus was already passing Mershon Auditorium, and Eva had already buried her head in a book. She pulled the stop cord when the bus reached Fourth and Neal, stood with one hand clutching the balance bar, and trotted off when the back door folded open. Dean exited from the front and fell in behind her.

After two hours of lurking, he at last was alone with Eva, who, in his opinion, was a perfect piece of man-catching bait.

—

Eva stepped off the bus. She sighed with relief when the cab pulled up to the corner and Frank got out. He joined her in front of the Romanesque church, and that's when she sprung her trap. She whipped around, made a false gesture of hospitality, and to the man behind her said, "Welcome to Victorian Village."

Eva shook a Marlboro from the pack, cupped her hand over the flame and lit it. She tilted her head and spewed out a confident plume. It was all a show. Eva was terrified, and had Frank not met her here as planned, she would have fled. But with Frank at her side, it was time to start figuring everything out.

"Why did you follow me?" she said to the man who had trailed her from campus headquarters, onto the bus, and now to the corner of Fourth and Neal.

"Why do you think I followed you?" he said. He pointed to an elderly woman who had gotten off at the same stop and was walking north on Neal Avenue. "All kinds of people ride the bus."

"Bullshit," Eva retorted. "You followed me down High Street. Had Frank gotten on the bus with me, you wouldn't have followed. That's why he hailed a cab. We lured you to this spot. The least you can do, now that you have been caught, is answer a simple question: Why did you follow me?"

"I wanted to talk to you—alone." He gave Frank a toxic look. "I have a proposition."

"If you are who I think you are, then your propositions are dangerous."

"What do you mean?"

"I know what happened to Gene Brimhall the other night, and why it happened. Are you the jerk who paid the Nazis to jump my friend?"

Dean smiled.

"Answer her, you creep," Frank said.

"Don't get on my bad side—*Fuller.*"

He turned to Eva. "I was wondering if you'd like to switch sides and come to work for the Bernadette campaign."

"No thanks," she said.

"It's a paid position." He fished a neat stack of $20 bills from his satchel.

"And what would I be paid to do?"

"I need a pretty lady like yourself to, uh, how should I say this: Catch George Beckham with his pants down."

"So you want me to fuck him?"

"Uh-huh."

She snorted with laughter. "Fuck you! There is a saying in my country: 'Fish stink from the head down.' You, sir, are a fish."

Dean wagged his index finger and shook his head.

147

"Not so fast, Eva. I know who James O'Neal is."

"So what? Many people know James."

"Yeah, well, I know he also happens to be your boyfriend. I'm sure you'd hate to see him get hurt."

"Like his boss?"

She flicked her cigarette at Dean's feet.

"Kind of, but with a twist."

"What makes you think you can hurt James? If you didn't hear the news, he fought a killer bull from Mexico—and won. How could you or any of your goons do any better?"

"I read the news, Eva. The bullfight was a fluke. What you need to know is that there's powerful forces at play up on Douglass Street where your boyfriend works. Those forces are already swirling."

"So if I don't sleep with Beckham, then you send someone, or some people, against James?"

"You're damn right. I did it to Gene Brimhall, and I can do it again."

"You are bluffing," Eva said.

"Eva's right," added Frank. "You're talking out of your ass. A white guy like you can't have any pull up on Douglass Street."

"I'm not bluffing, Eva. In fact, I'll up the ante. Dismantle Century B, or else. The Nazis aren't the only ones who have their eyes on Mr. Brimhall and your little fuck buddy. There's blacks, Eva. Black people with guns and knives and four hundred years of hate and anger churning inside of them. If you don't think at least one of them isn't capable of putting a bullet in James' head while he's digging in his truck for a tool, then you're as stupid as I think you are. You're from a little piss-ant country in the middle of fucking nowhere. Czecho-Who-Gives-A-Fuck-Slovakia. But you're in the United States now, Eva, and if you piss off the wrong people over here then you get hurt—I mean hurt. I want you to dismantle your election gang and come to work for me, the easy way."

Eva was speechless.

"You thought you were so fucking smart getting off that bus a few minutes ago." Dean looked at her contemptuously from head to toe. "But now I'm going to tell you what it's really all about. Kill the Cleveland Road campaign and come to work for me—or else."

Dean stepped on the burning cigarette stub and ground it out.

———

Eva called her first emergency meeting, summoning all members of Century B to the back table at Larry's. While waiting for her cohorts to arrive, she called George Beckham.

"From here on out I do not want you to look at me with yearning eyes," she said. "And for that matter, look at no one in that fashion. The Bernadette campaign is onto you, George. Your desires are obvious."

"But—"

"—There is no time for buts, Mr. Beckham. What is more important, your political career or your libido?"

"Now wait just a minute," he complained. "I have a wife and kids."

"And a roving eye, Mr. Beckham. Why would a greasy little volunteer from the Bernadette campaign speculate as to your proclivities? He must have known something."

"Well, there's some divorce documents down at the courthouse," he confessed. "But the case was dismissed ten years ago. The documents are supposed to be sealed."

"Seals are like rules, Mr. Beckham, meant to be broken. Your past indiscretions have already cost me some grief. But I will continue to campaign for you because I believe in your word. I can believe in your word, can't I, Mr. Beckham?"

"Yes, Eva, yes."

"Good. Let us keep this conversation between us and only us. Deal?"

"Deal."

She pushed two tables together and ordered a pilsner. A few sips later, Mike, Davita, Kristin, and Donna came in through the back door, where the regulars stood in circles and smoked pot. Oxana and Frank appeared a few minutes later, as did Anku and Mingmei. Barbara, lugging her Art 101 portfolio, was the last to arrive.

Eva looked at Frank.

"Should I tell the story or should you?"

"Why don't we both tell it," Frank said. "We can fill in details for each other."

"Fair enough," she said.

As president of Century B, she positioned herself at the head of the table.

"Thank you all for coming here on such short notice," she said. "I have a story to tell. It all started when we got back to campaign headquarters earlier today."

She and Frank told them about their encounter with an operative from the Bernadette campaign. Eva provided a whitewashed background on Brimhall's fight at the Brown Bag Saloon. She gave them details about the Douglass Street restoration and how her boyfriend James was the foreman over a $1 million contract. Intrigued by the tale, members of Century B interrupted Eva to ask questions, or to offer their own interpretation of events, or to say nasty things about Bernadette and his volunteers. Through it all, Eva showed poise. She would hold out a hand to delay someone's comment, while gesturing with a forefinger to solicit another. She repeated herself, moved back and forth, opened up her vocabulary and conversed fluently with nine people at once. She ended by giving them three choices—continue campaigning as Century B in the Cleveland Road Theater, campaign on campus or in Clintonville, or disband and drop out of the election altogether.

"I have already made my decision," she said. "But I want you guys to discuss this amongst yourselves."

Mingmei slammed her fist against the table. "I will *not* cancel the Cleveland Road campaign! I will go it alone if I have to, but I will not bow to a threat from one of Bernadette's thugs!"

At Mingmei's declamation, Century B erupted with discussion and debate.

Eva stepped outside and smoked a cigarette and waited for James. She grew anxious when she saw his truck pull into the parking lot. She ran to him and they embraced.

"Are you all right?" He kissed her on the forehead.

"Yes." She buried her head in the curve of his neck. "Come on inside. I want you to meet my friends."

The roofers in the back of James' truck poured out and followed their boss.

Eva had not bragged of James ad nauseam, but everyone in Century B had heard a lot of "My boyfriend this" and "My boyfriend that." Now that they were finally seeing him in person, Century B stood courteously and extended their hands in greeting. Eva, prideful and beaming, stepped aside so that James had enough space for a dignified arrival. He possessed the artist's exquisite mix of ruggedness and refinement. His smile was capable of shining, but at this moment it was subdued. He retained the full pleasantness of youth, yet it was evident he had embraced an adult's life. He and Anku shared a lengthy handshake, hugging and clapping each other over the shoulder. They whispered an oath into each other's ears and nodded stiffly with concurrences. After he had greeted the electioneers, he rejoined his roofers, and for a split second the lot of them looked like a gang.

"Don't worry about us," James said. "We can handle ourselves, and Century B has an election to win."

And then came the unanimous vote: Century B, all 10 members intact, would stay in the Cleveland Road theater until the election was over. Mike Jones touched his beer to Barbara's Shirley Temple.

"To Century B," they said.

"To Century B," came the collective reply.

———

Orlando Cruz dumped a bag of ice over a cooler full of Budweisers. He pulled one out, popped the top and took a drink. Fidel, Caesar, Reuben, Jose, Enrique, and Julio did the same. They sat in Orlando's backyard in old lawn chairs under a billowing sycamore tree. The crescent moon peeked at them through the branches. The scent of pork al pastor and hot corn tortillas wafted from the grill while a wild bolero sprang from the boom box.

Orlando went to the grill and turned the meat a few times before closing the lid. He took a long drink of beer and then set his gaze on Julio. "Let's talk about this now, Julio, so we can get it over with. Because when I wake up tomorrow morning, I'm not dealing with it anymore."

Orlando referred to an incident that had occurred the night before at Larry's, when the Guadalajara crew had gone with James to the campus bar to meet Century B. They had greeted the electioneers, and using James as an interpreter, told them not to heed the threat made by the Bernadette campaign. The salutations were going extremely well, too. Eva, James' girlfriend, had even addressed them in fluent Spanish. She introduced herself, shook their hands and thanked them for all the hard work they did for James and Brimhall. But the situation plummeted into chaos when Eva met Julio.

"I love your man James," Julio had said. "And if anyone touches him, I've got a Smith and Wesson for them."

In a flash, Eva's smile vanished.

"Excuse me," she said in Spanish, and arched her right brow. "I love James, too, but somehow love, in my mind, does not equate to death."

She then spoke in rifle shots of English that were too fast for Julio and Orlando to digest, but not for James. The boss shot a reproving look at Orlando, the undisputed leader of the Guadalajara crew.

"Orlando," James had said, and by so doing made him responsible for dealing with Julio.

And now he was. He took another drink of beer, assumed the swagger of a *patrón*, and spoke to Julio again.

"What do you have to say for yourself, Julio, now that the boss man thinks we are bloodthirsty *cholos*?"

"Fuck that Eva bitch!" Julio jumped up and pushed out his chest. "I don't take orders from no bitch like that!"

"But the boss does," Fidel said. "And before you opened your big mouth, she was treating us like kings."

"That's right," Orlando said. "We are already in deep shit. The last thing we need is more shit. We don't need a gun."

"But all the negroes have guns, Orlando. If they come to pop us, then we pop them. You know the rules."

Indeed, Orlando did know the rules. And if Eva—and as a result, James—had not made an objection, Orlando would have let it slide. The members of the Guadalajara crew knew Julio was their loco strong man. If scores needed to be settled, Julio was the guy. But Orlando had been in the United States for seven years, and the last five of them had been his best, and they had been under James. If he couldn't settle this issue for the boss right now, then he didn't deserve to be on Douglass Street making $17 an hour.

"If it comes down to it, we'll throw knuckles and pile on, and if we do, we'll win," Orlando said. "But no gun."

Julio drained his beer, crushed the can and flung it across the yard.

"You take a risk being on this crew," Orlando said. "But we don't kill, we work."

"What's gonna happen when those motherfuckers come looking for us?"

"We don't know for a fact that they will. Some threats are idle." Orlando looked to the other members of the crew for support, and he received it through reluctant, yet confirming nods of unity. "Come on, Julio. James likes you. He gets you plenty of work and pays you well so you can put food on your table and diapers on your son's ass. You've listened to him in the past, so listen now. No gun at the worksite."

Julio grabbed another beer and took a drink so long and hard that his Adam's apple slid up and down. He glared at Orlando and the other members of the crew. "Fuck you, you stupid motherfuckers, but I will abide by James."

"Good," Orlando said. "Now that we've settled this thing like men, let's eat."

—

The next morning Eva and Oxana stepped on the bus at Frambes and High Street and headed south to downtown. They got off at the central terminus at City Center Mall and walked past the statehouse to the *Scioto Times* newsroom a few blocks east on Broad Street. The squat, stone edifice conveyed the might and magnitude of the print press, the Fourth Estate, the watchdog of democracy. As morning traffic thundered south on Summit Street, Eva and Oxana stood at the corner, gazing up at the Roman frieze girdling the top of the building.

"If we can't find it here, we can't find it anywhere," Eva said.

When the light turned green, they scampered across the street, trudged up the stairs and pulled themselves through the heavy wooden doors. A plump, balding security guard confronted them once inside the tiled lobby. He made them sign their names, show their identification, and state their business with the newspaper.

"We need to see the March editions of the paper," Eva said, repeating what Dominick had told her to say the night before.

"Hav-li-cek," he mumbled, peering up from Eva's student identification.

"Yes."

The security guard turned a probing look at Oxana.

"Li-sa-kov-sky-a," he said, as he read her ID.

"Correct."

An expression of wonderment shot through the security guard's sleepy eyes as he beheld the stately Czech and the exotic Russian, both of them crowding over him as he wrote their names on the visitor's log.

He made a phone call and spoke discreetly into the receiver. A mousy clerk appeared from the elevator and motioned for Eva and Oxana to follow her. As they walked into a cluttered room at the end of the hall, the clerk turned and rather rudely said, "You know, you could've gotten online and used the electronic archives."

"No." Eva wagged her finger. "We already tried, but what we are looking for does not exist on your incomplete data base. But thanks for the advice."

Oxana laughed inwardly. She loved it when the Americans threw slights at Eva, who always caught the barbs and flung them back in an instant. How could the clerk, stressed out and disheveled as she was, know that Eva was on a mission and had no time for paltry attitudes? The clerk turned to Oxana with pleading eyes, as if seeking some type of support. But Oxana pursed her lips and looked askance.

"We always keep two months of hard copies bound and available to the public," the clerk said. "If you need a copy of anything, just let me know." She gestured toward two tomes sitting on a rickety table. "I'll be in the lobby. Let me know when you're done."

Eva and Oxana went to the beginning of March, when news of Councilman Fromholtz's death and the special election first hit the papers. They thumbed through the A and B sections, day by day, week by week, until they arrived at what they were looking for—***Byron Bernadette Enters Race for Vacant Council Seat.*** The candidate, flanked by his wife and campaign advisors, stood in front of his law firm. Radiant with confidence, the photograph of Bernadette had definitely been taken before Beckham and his army of volunteers had entered the race. Eva and Oxana studied the six faces in the photograph, and then read the caption. Realizing they had found what they had come looking for, they exchanged excited glances and began to laugh. Standing three people to the right of Byron Bernadette was a young, handsome man identified in the caption as Dean Bernadette. Looking smart in a bowtie and a pretentious pair of glasses, he was on a cell phone and looking into the distance.

"Is that the wolf who threatened you?" Oxana said.

"Indeed. He must somehow be kin to the candidate. Son or nephew."

"Or bothersome stepchild."

Eva pointed at the photograph. "Look how sure he is of himself. He is standing to the right, but he thinks he should be front and center."

"No doubt he is smug, but only because he had yet to see the trouble in his future."

"Mrs. Clerk," Eva called.

The clerk bent her face with frustration and sauntered down the hallway and into the room.

"Does the paper have any extra copies of the March 21 edition?"

"Maybe." She rolled her eyes. "They'd be upstairs."

"If you could, please retrieve as many as this will buy." Eva pulled a billfold from her backpack and flicked out a $5 bill. The clerk let out a sigh of disgruntlement, shambled down the hall and disappeared into the elevator.

"I do not think the clerk likes you," Oxana said.

"I do not give a shit what the clerk thinks of me. Just as long as she does as I say."

Oxana leaned back and shook with laughter.

"Eva, dear, I love you more and more each day."

Five minutes later the clerk appeared in the lobby with ten March 21 editions of the *Scioto Times* draped over her arms. Huffing and puffing, the clerk plodded across the lobby as if the newspapers were a fifty-pound sack of potatoes. Eva took the papers, skillfully rolled them up and slid them into her backpack.

"Thanks for all your hard work," she said with a fine blade of sarcasm.

—

The light turned green. The bus sputtered forward. Eva, scurrying to an afternoon class, was soon out of view. Oxana turned from the window and leaned back in her seat, thinking of a sweet moment two years ago. She was in the dorm room unpacking from her trip from Kazakhstan when a pretty face appeared in the door.

"I hope your trip from Almaty was better than my trip from Prague," Eva had said in rolling Russian. "My luggage was lost in New York City."

Oxana's trip had been miserable. The train out of Almaty had broken down halfway to Moscow so she had to stay in Novgorod for three days with a cousin she didn't like. The man next to her on the flight over the Atlantic had gotten drunk and puked in her lap. Customs officers at LaGuardia rifled through her bags and called out the drug dogs. She stepped onto the wrong subway line and wound up in a nightmare—Brownsville, Brooklyn. The Greyhound from New York to Cleveland got stuck behind a three-car pileup, so she missed the connecting route to Columbus and had to spend the night in the Cleveland bus station. She accidentally gave a beggar on High Street a ruble. She hadn't spoken Russian in a week. It was enough to make her scream, and when she finally arrived at the dorm room, she did.

"My trip was fine," Oxana said, swallowing the lie. "And you are?"

"Eva Havlicek, your roommate for spring quarter here at Ohio State. Welcome to Columbus."

"I'm Oxana Lisakovskya." She hugged Eva's neck. "And I'm glad you speak Russian."

And they had been close friends ever since.

For the first few months Eva talked about the revolution and how the communists had thrown her uncle, a dissident, in prison for five years. She railed against her hometown, Prague, and complained that her friends would disown her if she went back "too American." She also praised her country for its long history with the United States, and bragged about how an Americanized democracy had been installed in old Czechoslovakia between the world wars. The Czechs, Eva gloated, considered themselves true Westerners. Hence, their revulsion to the manufactured economy, rigged elections and militarism of Russian socialism. With the exception of Dominick, whom she had known from Prague, Eva was reticent around the locals to the point of being standoffish. Oxana didn't mind because in her own way she was much the same. She talked incessantly of her life in the squalid tenement of Soviet times. Her people, Oxana would say, had never known freedom, only various forms of tyranny. Their destiny, she would say with grim pleasure, was to endure any and all hardships. Even in the United States, the tattered red cloak with the star and sickle clung tightly to their shoulders.

All that changed the night Eva convinced Oxana to shave her legs and arm pits. While ashamed at having shed the Old World, she could not deny the thrill of modernity. They dressed in skirts and halters and went dancing at the Garage, the largest club in the city. Men whistled and jealous women sneered. The DJ goaded them on as the disco ball went round and round and round. From then on they remained as close as sisters but branched out into the greater world, leaving the dorms behind. Eva went south to a flat in German Village, while Oxana went north to Clintonville. Both of them began to move with measured steps, largely free of the nagging weight of history.

Oxana didn't find it hard to believe that an anonymous foreign student from the dorm had risen to become the leader of Century B. She wouldn't be surprised if the misfit band of electioneers actually made a difference in the vote. But regardless of who was involved, and regardless of how things turned out, Oxana knew that this was Eva's game. The degree. The election. Brimhall. James. All of it adding up to the biggest moment in her life. The image of Dean Bernadette's picture in the newspaper burned in Oxana's mind. She told herself she would not let him bully Eva back to the dorm. If he were to come too close to Eva, then something bad would happen to him. That, Oxana could guarantee.

The bus creaked to a stop. The back doors folded open. Oxana stepped out and turned north, and then east down the wooded, garbage-strewn alley behind Northwood. Once inside her flat on Indianola, she tossed her backpack on the couch and went to the mantle. She picked up a framed snapshot Dominick had taken of her and Eva standing in front of the bell tower at Orton Hall. Oxana in a green sundress, Eva's crooked grin shining warm and true.

"Don't worry, dear friend," she said to herself. "This war will be won at all cost."

Y O ′
G R I L L

J.D. Pruitt rifled a ring of cigar smoke through puckered lips and leaned back in his tan swivel chair. As the dense ring floated over the oak expanse of the executive table, Pruitt laughed the dim, sardonic laugh of a man who knows he's in trouble. In between the time he'd hatched his plan twenty years ago and now, tantalized by thoughts of fruition, birds and trees had become as important as industry and labor. What was supposed to be a smooth, triumphant procession to the steps of City Hall had become a harried, rearguard maneuver through a mountain pass.

"The little bastard," Pruitt muttered, referring to George Beckham.

The candidate canvassed District 4 with an army of volunteers that could very well put him into office, where he would quash the zoning proposal. Beckham had already vowed to repeal the zoning ordinance on referendum should it somehow be approved by the council. And if that failed, head to court.

"That little four-eyed bastard." Pruitt puffed out another ring.

Money didn't grow on trees, nor did it last forever. To bankroll his campaign and his posh suite on the 12th floor of the Motorists Building, Pruitt had taken out a huge loan against one of his properties, the amount inflated to reflect the parcel's future value when it was part of a 3,200-acre tract zoned for heavy industrial use. Without victory and the subsequent rush of capital it would produce, the property loan would dangle, perhaps into foreclosure, and he would lose a keystone of his empire. He survived on a modest portfolio of stocks, bonds, and savings accounts. But Pruitt didn't have the resources to retire serious debt, which is exactly what he'd have to do if Beckham won the election. Every permit, every variance, every plat approval—even if he switched his focus to high-end, low-impact residential development—would be contested by the council if Beckham triumphed in District 4. New men with new ideas, and with decidedly less money, would circle his boundaries and call for a new deal. Pruitt longed for Florida—bourbon with a brunette as he pulled out from the boat launch behind his canal-side condo. With each passing day, however, Pruitt had visions of a beach cabin and a bass boat in South Carolina, swilling beer with an old scold as they skimmed through the salt marsh.

"That bastard." He puffed out yet another ring.

Pruitt might have enjoyed the election if he didn't have so much at stake. The campaign generated a steady stream of newspaper and television stories, radio soundbites and vicious color ads in the *Scioto Times*. Campaign rallies looked like protests. And then there were the candidates. Beckham's persona, urbane and effeminate. Buckled shoes, silver watch, large glasses hanging at the bottom of his nose. Bernadette, the barrel-chested man's man and former college athlete. Beckham, a plaintiff's attorney who represented workers and consumers. Bernadette, a corporate lawyer aligned with insurance companies, banks, and manufacturers. The obvious differences between the two boiled over into the campaign rhetoric, transforming the election into a bitter personal feud.

Beckham and Bernadette had to be forcibly removed from each other during a candidate forum hosted by the League of Concerned Voters. Beckham's glasses were broken during the fray, while one of Bernadette's loafers flew from his foot during an unsuccessful attempt to kick Beckham in the shin. The candidates and the people who stopped the fight went tumbling over a table, sending plastic pitchers filled with ice water spilling and bouncing across the floor. Amidst the cacophony of cheers and jeers, the forum was abruptly cancelled. For diehard political junkies, the scene was a mess. But for the casual observer, and for Pruitt, the fight between Beckham and Bernadette was great entertainment.

Bernadette's nephew, Dean, told Pruitt that blacks were campaigning for him all along Cleveland Road. He didn't believe him—even though he'd peeled off $20,000 for that very purpose—until he saw an 11 o'clock news report. Pruitt poured himself a glass of bourbon, neat, and relit his cigar. The camera panned in on a very tall black man, his graying hair oiled and meticulously parted down the middle. He straddled a green utility bike yet was dressed in a black suit, cuff links, and a red power tie. At the top of a long piece of thin PVC pipe fixed to the bike's back rack flew a **BERNADETTE!** flag.

"Why do you support Bernadette?" the TV reporter said.

"Because," he replied, looking straight into the camera, "black people in Columbus need jobs and money."

His supporters, some of them on bikes, punctuated his comments with words of encouragement.

"Ain't nobody ever put no food on no table standing around looking at no woodpeckers."

—Amen!

"As a concerned citizen, I can't sit idly by and let Mr. George Beckham sacrifice this city to a nature trail—not when black folk got bills to pay."

—Go on, Leon!

"Columbus has a chance to put people, good black people, to work making livable wages. Damn straight. If Mr. George Beckham cared about black folk as much as he say he do, he'd quit worrying about the woodpeckers and concede the election to Bernadette!"

—Uh-huh! You know that's right!

Pruitt liked the campaign spiel even if it came from the mouth of what appeared to be a black radical.

"I own him," Pruitt thought, and his hopes soared.

And then came the rebuttal.

"Why do you support Beckham?" the TV reporter said.

"Mr. Beckham has a vision for District 4 as well as the city," said a blonde with a foreign accent. Backed by a formidable group of supporters wearing woodpecker T-shirts, they underscored her remarks with commentary of their own.

"Mr. Beckham wants to issue bonds for sewer and street repairs."

—That's right, girl.

"He supports equal representation on all city commissions."

—Come on!

"Preservation of the last stand of privately owned old growth oaks in the entire state of Ohio."

—Excellent!

"And clemency for the woodpeckers living there."

—Sho 'nuff!

"If you are out there listening, Mr. Bernadette, know this," she said, wagging an index finger high above her head. "We will beat you at the polls!"

—You right about that, sista!

"I'm Christina Wells, and we're live on Cleveland Road," the TV reporter said.

Pruitt gulped down a stinging swig of bourbon. "Where in the hell did all these weirdoes come from?"

—

Dominick Van Buren picked his way through the election minefield under the constant crunch of deadline. Special meetings, raucous campaign rallies, hot tips from readers and the filing of open records requests. Dominick could only shake his head and laugh. A dull, for-the-record story on an annexation had become the backbone of what the pundits were calling the hottest City Council election in decades.

"Thank God for Blue Bell," Dominick would say, each time one of his stories landed "out front" on A-1 with the national news.

During contentious elections every syllable of every story is read ten times by the candidates and their staffs. What they look for is the tiniest hint that the reporter favors one side over the other. Neither Beckham nor Bernadette had found anything that could impugn Dominick's objectivity. But they sure tried.

When an article appeared describing how one of Bernadette's big supporters had lost a civil rights lawsuit just a year earlier, Bernadette flew into a rage.

"The worst thing to ever happen to this town is the *Scioto Times*," he said, speaking during a TV interview. "I can't believe that the editors of that fish wrapper would send a cub reporter like Dominick Van Buren out to smear me and my supporters during such an important election."

Beckham took issue with Dominick's description of the brawl at the candidate forum. Dominick—and he still didn't know how it had slipped by the copy desk—wrote, "It looked as if Beckham learned how to wrestle in ballet class."

Like Bernadette, Beckham delivered his criticism on the eleven o'clock news.

"Dominick Van Buren of the *Scioto Times* obviously prefers useless violence over the civil process that is at the heart of our democracy. I have a sneaking suspicion that if I had a black belt in jujitsu, I'd be the toast of the news columns."

Bernadette backers—accountants, bankers, insurance brokers, contractors, corporate executives and union bosses—formed a political action committee called Bernadette for City Council, its sole purpose to slam Beckham with savage ads. The first one showed a picture of Beckham, altered so that his nose was a beak, alongside a pileated woodpecker. The caption read, *No Head Bangers on the Council*. It played in the middle of the Metro Section in black and white for a week, concluding with a color, double-truck haymaker on Sunday.

The Beckham campaign rallied with an ad of its own. It featured an unflattering photo of Bernadette on a hunting trip, clad in orange and camouflage, a rifle in one hand an open can of beer in the other. The caption read, *Can We Trust This Man?* It ran only one day, but was in color and appeared in the News, Metro, Sports and Business sections on a Sunday. On the editorial pages, Letters to the Editor revealed the polarization triggered by the election. One writer described Beckham as a "liberal, tree-hugging scum bag," while another called Bernadette a "mean-spirited robber baron that would sell his own mother if he thought it would turn a profit."

On campus, the Republican frat houses hosted a well-attended "Burn Beckham" keg party, the climax of which was the burning of Beckham's effigy on the Kappa Sig lawn. In response, Beckham supporters clogged Bernadette's law office with mass faxes and junk emails. The tit for tat was what instigated the candidate brawl at the forum hosted by the League of Concerned Voters.

"This is fucking crazy," Dominick said, speaking to a colleague.

He knew he wouldn't make it to Election Day without receiving at least one angry phone call from Pruitt. But would Pruitt be drunk or sober when he called?

He was drunk.

The call came shortly after publication of a news feature describing the woodpeckers and the trees. The article was an open confession that Dominick had trespassed on Pruitt's land.

"... The knotted oaks are topped with billowing crowns that tower 100 feet into the air. The bark on these massive trees is thick with lichen, and skinks dart through the deep grooves lining the trunks. The tops of the roots bulge from beneath the ground like the knuckles of great wrinkled fingers. One tree even bears the inscription of a pair of initials inside a heart, a memento carved by a lover years ago. Among the living oaks are the dead ones, called snags, standing in defiance of ice, wind, and time. It is in these dead hulks where the pileated woodpeckers raise their young, roost through the frigid winter, and forage for food. Before the settlers arrived, about 98 percent of the state was covered with trees. An old saying in Ohio was that a gray squirrel could walk from the Pennsylvania line to the Indiana border without ever touching the ground. But then came the settlers and the lumberjacks and the mining companies, which leveled what farmers hadn't already cleared. A few other stands of old growth still exist on the Appalachian Plateau, and all of it is owned by the state. Indeed, Pruitt's property is unique."

Brilliant photographs taken by Big Jake Steponovich accompanied the story.

"Well, well, well," Pruitt said, "it looks like you've been on my land without my permission. In America, that's called trespassing."

"It does appear that way, Mr. Pruitt," Dominick said. "How can I help you?"

"Stop writing articles about my land, and stop putting my name in the paper."

"You know I can't do that, Mr. Pruitt. For the next couple of months, you're the news."

Dominick heard Pruitt breathing on the other end of the line. He heard him take a sip of something. Pruitt sighed and took another sip.

"I've got my eye on you, you little son-of-a-bitch!" he said at last. "You print one word about me that's not true and I'll sue you and your lousy paper for libel. You hear that?"

"Loud and clear." Dominick tried his best to keep from laughing. "Is that all you have to say?"

"Not even close, you little rodent. You're costing me money."

"You should have thought about that a long time ago, Mr. Pruitt. You're news now, and I'm a reporter."

"I called the police chief today."

"Oh, yeah?"

"Yeah. The little coward said he's not gonna write you a ticket for trespassing."

"Thank God," Dominick said. "On a reporter's salary, I don't know if I could afford a citation."

He heard Pruitt take another sip.

"Did Blue Bell tell you where that file was?"

Dominick had waited for that question for the last month.

"I don't reveal my sources, Mr. Pruitt," Dominick said, with relish.

"Tell me!"

"Not in this lifetime."

"Tell me!"

"Mr. Pruitt, you're drunk and you're yelling. I'm also on deadline. Maybe we can talk later?"

"You, you, you shitass!"

"Thanks for reading the *Scioto Times*, sir."

Dominick hung up.

—

Brimhall had no idea how long he'd floated in and out of sleep. He couldn't tell the difference between reality and dreams. The searching pain in his gut was real, he knew, in spite of the happy drugs dripping through the IV. The words he heard were murmurs, his name a chain of dreary syllables. Through his right eye he saw the dim silhouettes of people standing near the bed. He tried to speak, but his bloated tongue would not let him. His feeble groans and the twitch of his body heightened the attention of those standing over him. Their faces came alive with somber smiles. His waking efforts summoned a piercing stab of pain and stars shot through his vision. Before drifting back into the boundless ether, where he would face his agony alone, the handsome lines of a familiar face became vaguely clear.

"James?"

"That's right, Brimhall. It's James, and Eva and Edwina are with me."

A warm caress came over his hand. To his right he saw a hint of blonde hair and the glint and gleam of diamonds and blue eyes. Struggling to keep from tumbling into slumber, he noticed another kind face, framed by hair as leaden as a Southern storm cloud. Brimhall's eyes eased shut, but the darkness didn't envelop him.

The stab wound near the right pelvis throbbed, and his face was still swollen and splotched with purple stains of blood that had formed under his eyes. A large wad of gauze covered the bruised left eye socket and the crooked lash of stitches over his brow. His left arm was wrapped in bandages from wrist to elbow. Brimhall had yet to shake the grogginess of the concussion, but clarity of thought was dawning. He'd lost one tooth, an upper left second bicuspid, and had broken two fingers on his right hand. What was originally feared to be torn ligaments was only a deep sprain in his right ankle. Ribs bruised but not broken, the scrapes across his elbows and knees superficial. Though expected to make a full recovery, Brimhall would always carry the scars from the brawl. He wouldn't be up on the rooftops making money anytime soon, and in the middle of a big contract, that was cause for concern. His grounding wouldn't be permanent, however, and for that he thanked God.

He hadn't yet pieced together the entire fight, but bits and pieces of it flashed through his mind. The breaking of bones and the splash of blood, Dilworth in a grisly heap at his feet. Macabre shrieks and the shrill drone of ambulance sirens. Brimhall felt that he had won the fight for the simple fact that he had made it out of the Brown Bag Saloon alive. And his honor was burnished because he had fought for something special, the dignity of Edwina Spurlock's name. Still, Brimhall boiled with the urge for revenge, not against his rivals from the Hilltop, but against Dean Bernadette, the stranger who had recklessly rekindled the old fire.

Waking quietly, Brimhall looked to his left. Edwina, as on prior occasions, sat next to the bed, humming a gentle tune as she knitted. At first she didn't notice him, so he took the chance to study the woman as she appeared in private. Bent over the loom, her face shaped by the strain of concentration. Her hands fluttered as fleetly as the wings of sparrows as she looped the yarn, and her lips pursed and parted as she reached a high note in the song she sang. Brimhall found her beauty in the placid, stubborn cast of her cheeks and brow. Her silky, amber complexion suggested youth, but wary eyes and a distinctive thatch of elder's hair were ample proof that she was no doll. She wore the lightest trace of makeup, silver stud earrings and a crisp tuxedo shirt. Her hair, pulled back tight and tied off with a black ribbon, which meant she had come to the hospital directly from work. On several occasions before the fight, Gene had seen her, dressed in a tuxedo skirt and with a briefcase in her hand, darting out to her little station wagon. One day he finally asked her where she was going. "I'm heading down to the shop and then I'm going to the Westerville Country Club for a wedding. I'm a chauffeur with Crown Limousines." Edwina was also a maid, Brimhall discovered, and a cook, a baker, a vending machine owner, a grassroots politician, a grandmother, and more.

In a curl of pain, he coughed. Edwina set the needles and yarn on the bedside table and stood.

"Can I get you anything?"

"Water would be nice, and," he added with a sheepish note of embarrassment, "I need the pee bottle."

Edwina turned her back while he peed, even though everything happened underneath the sheets. Brimhall handed her the bottle, warm with his urine. She took it without the trace of a grimace and emptied it in the toilet. She washed her hands and returned with a cup of cool tap water.

"Thanks."

He gulped down the water in a vain attempt to wash the foul taste from his mouth. He forced his right eye wide open and licked his lips.

"Did you just get off work?"

"Yeah. I had four Japanese businessmen who came in for the day. They're doing some stuff with Bank One."

"Interesting. Where all'd you go?"

"From the airport to Bank One, then to Hyatt on Regency Square for lunch, back to Bank One, then to Lindy's for dinner, and then back to the airport. One of our regular clients flew in on the 7:30 from Atlanta, and I drove him to his house in Dublin."

"Sounds like a full day."

"Eleven hours." She stretched her arms and shoulders.

"Do the Japanese tip well?"

Edwina smiled. "Oh, yeah. The Japanese who come to Columbus on business are all from Tokyo, and they're real high rollers."

"So among other things, you're also an ambassador to the city?"

"Absolutely. That's one of my favorite parts of the job. You'd be surprised at who all comes here for business. The Dutch, lots of Germans, the Swedes and the British. And New Yorkers all the time."

"It always comes down to New York, huh?"

"If there's money involved, always."

"So, what are you knitting?"

"A scarf for Bobby. I know he can't wear it until fall, but this'll be one of his birthday gifts. He turns ten next month, you know."

"I see. So will Bobby have a big birthday party with a lot of friends?"

"Um, a few friends. But it'll be nice. I always bake him a chocolate cake with extra icing."

"I bet he loves that."

"You're telling me." She laughed. "He starts asking for the cake about a week before the party. It's like clockwork."

"In my mind's eye I can see him prowlin' through the kitchen, maybe even doing a little high kick."

Brimhall grinned. Then came a long pause.

An immense swell of appreciation overcame him. The hospital room sunk into the silence of night. He had frequently envisioned a day when he would lie wounded and helpless in a hospital bed, the victim of a bad fall from a roof. Alone in a dank room and nobody would know he was there. That dreaded day had finally come. But he wasn't alone, and the modest collection of vases and flowers on display at the other end of the room proved that at least some people knew, and cared, of his whereabouts and condition.

The warmth of Edwina's presence chased away the steely chill of the unhealed stab wound.

"Edwina, thanks for being here."

"You're welcome," she said, and held his hand.

Finished with his sentimental musings, Gene wanted to get back to the rooftops, the job site, and the Douglass Street contract.

"So how's James?"

"Good. He's been on Douglass Street at sunup for the last three days. He told me to tell you that he's cleared the deck on the Mansard and that Orlando Cruz is pointing the chimney. James and three others have moved over to my house and have made a lot of progress. The Hispanics work hard."

"So it sounds like James is taking care of business, then?"

"Just like his boss taught him."

"How long have I been in the hospital?"

"Three days. The stab wound is deep, Gene, and the knife was contaminated with some type of bacteria. They're keeping you here so you don't get a staph infection. Those things can kill you."

"So James is going good, huh?" Brimhall said, not wanting to dwell on his misfortunes.

Edwina unexpectedly giggled. "Can I tell you something?"

"Sure."

"All the women on Douglass Street, young and old, have a crush on James."

"They do?"

"Uh-huh. They say he's 'One good lookin' white boy.' And the men like him, too, because he's 'straight up' and shows respect."

"That's exactly why I like him."

"You know what he did? He asked me to call a special meeting of the neighborhood association. He spoke to all of us, and assured us that everything was under control. He also asked for our support. You should have seen him. I mean, I had said some things to the neighborhood, but he really set everyone's mind at ease. He's special."

Gene mashed his thumb down on the automatic bed switch until he was in a sitting position.

"Remember the other night when I told you that I'd built a cross that I knew would be burned in someone's yard?"

"Yeah." Edwina showed surprise at Gene's willingness to revisit that conversation.

"You kept a stiff upper lip, but I knew you were disappointed. You sacrificed your own feelings so that the contract would go on for the entire neighborhood."

"That's right."

"And in the process, you probably raised more than a few eyebrows."

"Probably."

"And there's a strong possibility that something could happen up on Douglass Street."

"I'd say that's possible."

"I guess I'm just wondering why, or how, you thought we could go through all this trouble together and survive. And why would you want to? You could have called me the racist redneck and been done with it."

"But you're more than that, Gene. You're a man, right? And sometimes a man has to confront the consequences created by the life he's lived."

"I agree. But it also sounds like you're purposely testing me."

"I'm testing all of us, Gene. We all need to get over that. Not just you, and not just me, and not just James, and not just the neighborhood. But all of us. And thus far, it's been tough, but we're still ahead of the curve."

"How so?"

"For starters, how does your heart feel?"

He didn't answer for a moment. "My body hurts like hell, but inside, I feel better than ever. The other night I looked at all the people lined up against me, Edwina, and realized that they represented everything I've tried to leave behind—ignorance, self-hatred, and bullshit pride. For the first time in my life I was on the ugly end of the racial stick, and I was glad to be there."

"And please believe me," she said, clutching his right hand in hers. "I had no idea you'd end up fighting a gang of Nazis."

"Edwina, my fight had been in the making for years. I can't necessarily say I'm glad it happened, but it needed to happen. I'm just glad it's over."

"I am, too. And I'm honored that you fought for my name."

"Once Dilworth opened his mouth, there was never a doubt."

She graced his forehead with a tender kiss.

"I'm gonna spread some information of my own," she said, pulling back.

"What do you have in mind?"

"We went to the courthouse yesterday and found Chris Dilworth's file."

"What'd you come up with?"

"His crime, his time, and an updated physical description, the one listing all his nasty tattoos."

"Why'd you dig all that up?"

"The knucklehead who sent out all those letters against you got that stuff from the Hilltop, right?"

"Right."

"So I'm basically doing the same thing. Only this time, it's not ancient history but piping hot news. And instead of it being against you, it's actually for you. Gene, you fought the black man's worst nightmare, a prison Nazi, and from what James told me, you put him down pretty good. You can bet I'm gonna sell that story to whoever'll buy it."

"Almost sounds like we're jumping into this election." Gene felt a surge of hope and confidence.

Edwina smiled.

"Honey, we've been in the election for quite some time."

—

Dean wanted to be at the helm when the big contractors came to City Hall needing construction permits, tax breaks, zoning variances and plat approvals. Uncle Byron's vote would be worth a mint as it pertained to the sprawling landscape of a 3,200-acre industrial park. As his uncle's back-room aide de camp, Dean would determine the black-market value of something as routine as a logging permit or a temporary easement to haul dirt over city streets. What Dean knew is that corruption was universal. From the pits of the former Soviet Union to the slums of Sierra Leonee, and from the teeming cities of India to the sleepy courthouses in western Indiana, corruption was rife. Bribery, extortion, and blackmail were tools, as far as Dean was concerned, not crimes. Most contractors viewed extortion as a business expense and would gladly play the game if they knew they could score. State prosecutors were set up to combat violent street crime, not the complicit dealings of payola. And at the level where Dean planned to conduct his hustle, federal prosecutors would have little interest. All he had to do was win the election, help Uncle Byron push through the zoning ordinance, and then position himself in the web of city politics.

With an eye toward keeping his place in his uncle's hierarchy, Dean had started keeping meticulous notes, all hand-written in tidy script, on plush Byron Bernadette letterhead he had stolen from the firm. Each page was rubber-stamped with his uncle's signature. If down the road Uncle Byron tried to cut him loose for any reason, Dean would simply blackmail him with the notes and keep his place through threats if not good graces.

Dean had chronicled the campaign from the first phone call with Pruitt to the brawl at the Brown Bag Saloon. Diligent as an accountant, he had recorded every illegal cent funneled into the campaign by Pruitt—$20,000—and had logged all of the cash payments he'd made to Leon, Trey, and Chris Dilworth. Knowing that the documents might one day have to be used, he made sure that the writing was legible and appropriately lurid. He spelled names correctly, and entered times, dates and locations with the accuracy of a conscientious reporter. When there were public documents that corroborated the notes, he obtained copies from the courthouse or City Hall and included them in the file. In just a few short weeks he had penned enough notes to sink his uncle's political career, yet the campaign had just begun.

"De-fucking-licious," he said.

Indeed, he had grown fond of sitting in silence at the large desk in his room to create the documents that could one day be the source of his uncle's downfall. There were times when he felt guilty about what he was doing. He assuaged that emotion by reminding himself that Uncle Byron was, after all, his father's brother. How could anyone be so closely related to that prick, thought Dean, and not be a prick himself?

"This is gonna be fun," he said, and kept at his notes.

Around 11 p.m. he went downstairs, poured a glass of Pinot Noir, flopped on the couch and turned the channel to the local news. A dainty red head, clutching a microphone in one hand and a notepad in the other, stood in front of the camera. Dean took a sip of wine and turned up the volume.

"I'm Kristina Mulholland with Channel 7, reporting from Columbus City Hall," she said. "Earlier today the Columbus Civil Service Commission upheld the termination of police Corporal Todd Blackburn, who was fired two weeks ago for neglecting to turn in a piece of evidence seized from a drug raid in a timely manner. According to one of the commissioners, the evidence was a crack pipe. Corporal Blackburn maintains that he should have been punished but not terminated, and also says that the Civil Service Commission upheld his termination because he is black. All three of the commissioners who voted in support of the termination are white, while the two who voted to overturn the termination are black. Meanwhile, community activist Clovis Whitfield appeared today before the commission and in Mayor Kraus' office to protest Blackburn's termination. Whitfield has agreed to talk exclusively with Channel 7."

The camera then focused on a young, angry black man dressed in a metallic blue suit, aqua blue bowtie and black bowler. Diamond studs in his ears, the platinum necklace draped over his shirt a row of gnashed teeth. Though his expression was partially hidden behind an oversized pair of gold-plated, rose-tinted glasses, his immense presence was unmistakably sinister. Behind him stood his entourage, all of them in combat boots, camouflage jumpsuits, black berets, and gangster shades. Posing on the steps of City Hall, Clovis Whitfield spoke into the microphone with mad charisma.

Dean sat up, took another sip of wine and turned the volume higher.

"Mayor Kraus, I'ma be up in yo' grill each and every day until you overturn the commission's termination of Corporal Blackburn. This city administration is racist, it supports Americanized apartheid, and until you reinstate Corporal Blackburn—with back pay, a promotion and a raise—I'ma crash yo' cotillion."

"Mr. Whitfield, the mayor said he doesn't have the authority to overturn the commission's vote," Kristina Mulholland said.

Clovis's face grew pained with disbelief.

"Oh yeah he do," he shouted. "Or how 'bout this. Terminate the commission! Mayor Kraus don't want no black man on the police force 'cause he a sick racist. Mr. Mayor, I'ma be up in yo' grill until you do the right thing!"

In a ceremony of defiance, Clovis folded his arms across his chest, and through the huge pair of rose-tinted glasses, filled the camera with his menace. His crew, a platoon of the aggrieved, crowded in behind him. Kristina Mulholland went on to explain that Corporal Blackburn's only recourse was to appeal the commission's decision to the courts. And that's when Clovis Whitfield and his crew pumped their fists and chanted, "Jus-tice! Jus-tice! Jus-tice! Jus-tice!"

Dean guzzled the last drink of wine, fetched the cordless phone from the kitchen counter, and called Leon. On the fifth ring, he answered.

"Hey, Leon. This is Dean. You ever heard of a guy named Clovis Whitfield?"

"Clovis? Yeah. He's out on the east side—Livingston Avenue. Thinks he's Malcolm X one day and Jesse Jackson the next."

"Do you know him?"

"Not really," Leon said. "I try and stay away from them kids, you know. All they wanna do is take drugs and shoot guns. I ain't with that."

"I don't think Clovis is into guns and drugs, Leon. I think he's into social justice."

"I don't know 'bout all that. But continue."

"Well, think about this. Shouldn't Clovis know that Gene Brimhall, our little cross burner, has got the contract up on Douglass Street?"

Leon's chuckle rolled into a rooster's crow. "Clovis Whitfield and Gene Brimhall? Now that's something I'd pay to see."

"Can you meet with this guy, ASAP?"

"I'll call you before noon tomorrow with an update—if it's worth something for me."

"Of course it is, Leon. Don't worry about that."

Dean poured himself another glass of pinot, took an aristocratic sip, and sauntered to the mirror in the hallway. With an index finger he traced the perimeter of his sore, yellowing black eye, and the deep cut across his nose. He could still see and feel the knuckle marks on his forehead. He licked the long hedge of stitches on the inside of his swollen lower lip.

"Brimhall," he said, imitating Clovis Whitfield, "I'ma be up in yo' grill."

R E G A L
C L O V I S

Clovis Whitfield came out of prison with an unblemished reputation as a tough independent. The most important thing he'd learned to say in prison was, "I ain't got nothin' for ya." Clovis stood his ground rather than align himself with a crew. He had paid for his recalcitrance, too. On three occasions beaten and stabbed. Each time he returned from the infirmary with his lip curled in defiance and his fists clenched in preparation for the next encounter. The blacks had come after him first. And when he didn't succumb to their entreaties, they unleashed the whites. Through the turmoil, Clovis established himself as a man who couldn't be had. The last two years of his sentence, quiet and trouble free. During the long and lonely days in his cell he plowed through the history of Western Civilization, the Bible, the dictionary, and piles of novels. Through the unsuccessful process of trying to gain his freedom on appeal, he had become the equivalent of a paralegal. His jailhouse education is what gave him hope for the future. He figured out what the white man knew, and when he returned to the neighborhood they lauded him as a martyr who had survived the tortures of the white man's prison.

In the penitentiary he learned that Clovis was the fifth century Frankish warlord regarded as the "first king of France." Clovis was the old root of Louis, one of the most important names in Western history. All through his childhood and adolescence, Clovis had hated his name because it wasn't cool enough. He wanted to be a D'Angelo, a JaMarcus, or a Tayshawn. An Afrocentric name. A black name. At an early age he started calling himself C-Note and would become violent at the mere mention of Clovis. To find out that he in fact was named after a Merovingian king as well as an entire line of French royalty was a watershed in his self-realization. He was no longer Clovis, a man who would rather be known as something else. He was Clovis, a leader of armies, a conqueror of worlds.

Clovis had entertained notions of doing the "right thing" when he returned to the free world. But Clovis's pride, indeed, his common sense, wouldn't allow him to work for a poor-man's wage, which is what black convicts did when they tried to do the "right thing." Instead, Clovis traded on his profile as a hardened ex-inmate who had served time on a violent crime. He met with the local drug dealers and agreed to be their mule. He would take a Greyhound bus to New York and buy a few kilograms of high-grade Colombian cocaine from a gang of black Dominicans in the Bronx. He brought the cocaine back to the distributors in Columbus, where it was converted into crack and sold on the streets. He made enough cash, laundered at a liquor store owned by a friend, to take out a mortgage on a modest storefront office at the intersection of Livingston and Miller. He bought a mint Chevy Suburban painted flat black with aluminum rims and limo-tinted windows. He went to the swap meets and loaded up on shoes, suits and jewelry. In the meantime, the drug dealers were busted and sent to federal prison, which meant Clovis was able to make a clean break with his criminal employers without being killed. His name never came up during the investigation, so he'd never even been subpoenaed as a witness.

With his drug smuggling days behind him, he concentrated on his new career as a civil rights operative. Clovis felt that if you were black and angry and yelled loud enough, guilty, frightened white people would give you just about anything you asked for. And he was right. Subsidies for blacks had started in the 1960s and had dripped into a mine of corruption, ineptitude and neglect. Inside the world of grants, sub-prime loans, public housing, minority contracts, Equal Employment, and "community programs" was a great opportunity for aggressive race mongers like Clovis. Having read the histories of slavery and segregation, he was of the firm belief that government and the private sector owed a debt to all blacks. Clovis's philosophy could be summed up in the short phrase, "I'ma get mines, and you gon git yo's, too."

Clovis had little trouble asserting his will. An all-state linebacker in high school, he was six-foot-one and ripped with muscle. His face, a padlock, his shoulders, diorite. And underneath the flashy suits, gaudy eyewear and immaculate black bowler burned the dreadful sheen of the felon. The thought of Clovis Whitfield staging a protest was enough to make white business owners cringe in fear, and then empty their wallets. He liked to ease into the nice restaurants right before the dinner rush and peer into the kitchen. If he saw nothing but white chefs on the food line and nothing but poor blacks manning the dishwasher, he'd ask for the owner. "I'ma camp out'n front a yo' joint," he'd say. "And when Miss Priss get up'n here with Sugar Daddy, they ain't gon see nothin but pissed off gorillas." That line was always worth $1,000, and he had recited it to restaurant owners across the city.

Clovis realized that in the liberal age, the media rarely criticized minority activists. For instance, a reporter had dug into his court record and published an article on his conviction and ten-year sentence on three counts of aggravated robbery. Instead of condemning Clovis, the reporter quoted a sociologist who blamed society, not Clovis, for his crimes. Clovis, the sociologist had said, suffered from "post-civil rights malaise" and was powerless against his criminal impulses because the "arc of disenfranchisement had damaged his ability to think and function as a law-abiding citizen." Clovis liked that conclusion, and even chuckled at the phrase "post-civil rights malaise." But he knew it wasn't true. By his own account, he wanted money without having to work for it, plain and simple. On Christmas Eve in 1980, he stuck a revolver in a woman's face and robbed her, her sister and their mother of cash, checks and jewelry in the parking lot of a shopping mall. His only regret is that he had been caught.

While the press naively made excuses for his criminality, Clovis took care of all the rest. He didn't drink, smoke or do drugs, worked out five days a week, and surrounded himself with loyal convicts in need of a productive leader. To avoid going back to prison on felony gun possession, Clovis never carried a firearm. Instead, one of his bodyguards toted the Glock 9mm when they were out on the streets doing their thing.

Five years into his career as a civil rights hustler, Clovis didn't have as much to show for his efforts as he would have liked. His name was out there and he had plenty of "work." He and his men were minor celebrities in their neighborhood and none of them had to worry about going hungry. But compared to the Black Muslims and the Baptist preachers, who flourished on the collection plate, Clovis and his crew were the poor men on the block. Plus, he had envisioned his name, his medieval, regal name—Clovis—being at the forefront of "the struggle." Clovis, however, was still a foot soldier among many foot soldiers.

Hungry for something a little more fulfilling than simple success, he had jumped at the opportunity to represent Corporal Blackburn, the cop who had been fired for not turning in a crack pipe in a timely manner. It was simple. If Corporal Blackburn were to be reinstated, all the "back pay" would go to Clovis. A covert political action committee on the east side had paid him to instigate the protest, and thus start the cycle of negative publicity for Mayor Kraus, who would face a black candidate in his bid for re-election next year. The Blackburn job placed Clovis in front of the cameras on the steps of City Hall, and put him in the mix for next year's mayor's race. Clovis, however, wasn't so sure that the Blackburn job would prove fruitful. Mayor Kraus wasn't going to terminate the Civil Service Commission, and he had no authority to overturn the commission's vote. Everyone who followed local politics knew that Clovis's demands were impossible to meet. The longer Clovis protested, the more and more he looked like a fool. Blackburn, Clovis concluded, needed to cut his losses and start looking for a new job.

"All this bullshit about Corporal Blackburn is weak-ass," he said to Rasheed, his top lieutenant. "Blackburn's a fuckin' crack head who don't need to be no cop. And he for damn sure don't deserve my services. We need sumpin new, Rasheed."

He and Rasheed sat at the desk in his office, sipping on Cokes and eating plate lunches of fried walleye, greens, and yams. These were the simple times that Clovis craved, when it was just he and Rasheed talking tactics and strategy. Rasheed sopped up some juice from the greens with a crumb of cornbread and plopped it into his mouth.

"What about Cornell X," Rasheed said. "He needs help with that car dealership out in White Hall."

"Naw, naw, naw. Cornell X don't pay nothin', and he always wants to convert me to fuckin' Islam. You know I ain't with that."

"I understand, but maybe we need to strengthen our ties with him," reasoned Rasheed. "He could be a valuable ally."

"He'll call us allies one day and vassals the next? Fuck that."

Clovis squirted lemon juice over the filet of walleye, sprinkled it with hot sauce and laid a piece of onion over the top. He took a big bite. As he dipped his spoon into the yams, a peculiar figure pulled up to the storefront on a green utility bike. He parked it on the sidewalk and dismounted. On the bike's back rack, a bulging manila envelope beneath a bungee cord. The man straightened his suit, ran his fingertips across his eyebrows, grabbed the envelope and made his way to the door.

"Can I help you?" Rasheed said, as the man entered.

"I'm Leon Davis," he said. "Is Clovis D. Whitfield here?"

"It depends on what you want," Rasheed said.

Leon presented the envelope. "Believe me. I'm the man you wanna meet."

—

Leon stood outside and smoked a menthol as Clovis and Rasheed read over the grant program for the $4.1 million Douglass Street Restoration. Looking east and then west, Leon spied a group of gangbangers lounging on the stoop of one of the mean brick row houses of East Livingston Avenue. Women and children huddled at the bus stops, and men from nearby apartments carried their clothes in plastic sacks to the coin laundry. An Arab swept up a pile of broken glass near the front door of his convenience store, while a car with bass pumping so hard that the windows rattled sat idling at the red light. Livingston Avenue looked like Cleveland Road. Only out here on the east side, folk were tougher, the atmosphere more tense, and the sense of desperation much more pervasive. It had been a while since Leon was out this way, and he knew the reason why. In Columbus, north side and east side didn't mix. An invisible line down the middle of Broad Street made them strangers, competitors, and oftentimes enemies, even though race, creed, history, culture and class united them. Leon had plenty of theories as to why that was the case, but for now, none of those theories were on his mind. He was an old-timer from the north who was trying to do business with a young blood from the east. With a serious wad of cash tucked in his pocket and a grand plan in his head, he was content to watch his back and play it cool.

Rasheed motioned for him to come back inside. He stubbed out his cigarette, blew a plume into the wind, and stepped into Clovis's office. Once inside, Rasheed drew the shades over the storefront windows and motioned for Leon to take a seat. Clovis, dressed casually in sneakers and a beige jump suit, beckoned with a foreboding nod of his bald, shiny head. He wasn't wearing the thick platinum chain, the diamond earrings, the flashy shades, zoot suit and black bowler. This was the stripped down, bedrock ghetto Clovis, the part of him that inspired fear in those he targeted for exploitation.

"You know I don't typically take meetings without an appointment, right?"

He glared at Leon, who had been glared at so many times in his life that he wasn't easily shaken.

"Uh-huh," Leon said. "But you ain't listed in no phone book."

"Even with the impropriety, I'm glad you came by today."

He picked up the copy of the Douglass Street grant program and flipped to the page where the grant total was listed. "This a big grant. Has it started?"

"About a month ago. The roofing contract, that is."

"Why'd you bring this to me?"

"I saw you on TV and I thought you might wanna get in on this. As you see, money's gonna be pouring into Douglass Street for about a year."

"What's the hook?"

"Whadda ya mean?"

"Why do I need to go to Douglass Street—besides the money? We all grownups here. What's my moral justification?"

"Flip to the final page. The addendum."

Clovis did as instructed.

"Tell me what you see," Leon said.

"*On Feb. 24, the City Council voted 6-1 to hire Brimhall Roofing Incorporated to complete the Phase One roofing contract of the Douglass Street Restoration.*"

Leon looked Clovis straight in the eye. "Well, Gene Brimhall, the owner of the roofing company—get this—he a cross burner."

Clovis popped up from his chair and looked down at Leon with eyes so full of passion that Leon could barely hold his gaze. He thrust out his arms in victory. "God works in mysterious ways."

Rasheed studied Leon with the unnerving skill of a predator. The temperature in the room seemed to rise by 10 degrees.

A bead of sweat rolled down Leon's forehead. He nearly went limp with fatigue. He knew he had made a mistake by coming here. Clovis would not only take what he wanted out of the grant monies, but would start a war on Douglass Street as well. Leon still saw the dollar signs, only now they had asterisks behind them. Shrugging off internal doubts, the old-timer from the north started doing business with the young blood from the east.

"How you know about this cross?" Clovis said.

"A very reliable source," Leon said.

"Naw, naw, naw. How you know about this cross?"

"I know a white boy in the Bernadette campaign. He went to the Hilltop, where the contractor stay, and talked to his enemies."

Clovis searched Leon's eyes for the tiniest trace of a lie. Under such scrutiny, Leon proved legitimate enough to square his jaw and match Clovis's intensity. Satisfied with what he saw, Clovis continued.

"So this guy from the Bernadette campaign told you about the cross?"

"And everyone on Douglass Street, too."

Clovis and Rasheed exchanged looks of elation.

"And how'd they react?"

"They sticking with the contractor." Leon shook his head in disbelief.

"Why?"

"'Cause a Edwina Spurlock. She's the president of the neighborhood association."

"So it sounds like I need to have a chat with Mrs. Spurlock."

"Watch out, Clovis," Leon said. "I don't call her the Duchess of Douglass Street for nothing. She tough."

"She ain't shit to me," Clovis said. "So back to the beginning. Why me?"

"'Cause, you got what it takes to flush the contractor outta there. When he out, the City Council puts the contract back up for bid, and that's when my guy Jesse Freeman come in. He'll 'hire' all of us for big money. And we can do the same damn thing for Phase Two, Phase Three and Phase Four. That's a four-point-one million dollar grant program, Clovis. And you get to have your 'moral justification.'"

"How I know you for real?"

"This is why."

Leon dug into his breast pocket, pulled out the envelope stuffed with twenty-dollar bills, and tossed it onto the desk.

"That's one thousand dollars." Leon winked. "It's what the white folk call a 'token of appreciation.'"

Clovis took the money, handed it to Rasheed, and shook Leon's hand.

"How'd I miss the Douglass Street Restoration?" Clovis said.

"You didn't," Leon said. "You right on time."

—

Edwina dabbed her neck with subtle perfume. She clipped on a pair of daisy-pendant earrings, wrapped her hair into a tight occipital bun and slid into a modest pastel dress that hung to just below her knees. From her neck hung a string of cheap pearls, and on her wrist a dainty silver watch. She stepped into a pair of pumps, checked her look in the mirror, and then went downstairs to the kitchen, where her first cousin, Darren Bell, waited at the table.

"You ready?" He looked up from the classifieds.

"Yeah."

The dour look between them vanished into confidence as Edwina grabbed her keys and headed toward the door.

Bobby appeared from the den and hugged her at the waist. "When are you coming back?"

"Soon." She kissed him on the forehead. "Now you be nice to Miss Kennedy, and when I get back, I'll make you some cinnamon toast, okay?"

"Okay." He darted back to the den, where Miss Kennedy, his great aunt, sat working a crossword puzzle.

Darren Bell wheeled out from Douglass Street and turned right on Cleveland Road. He gunned the accelerator and glided through a yellow light.

"So what's this all about?" he said, keeping his eyes on the road.

"If Clovis Whitfield's involved, nothing good. But he's like cancer. If you ignore him, he'll spread and kill you."

"You think he knows who he's dealing with?"

"I don't think he has a clue. But all that's about to change."

"That's my girl."

Darren Bell leaned back in his seat, propped his hand on top of the steering wheel and weaved through the southbound traffic. Once the metallic blue Monte Carlo with spinning aluminum rims reached the off ramp at Parsons Avenue, Darren and Edwina were officially on the east side.

Two days ago, Edwina had received yet another odd letter in the mail. Only this one wasn't anonymous. It was from Clovis D. Whitfield, who had requested a meeting. Since the letter was addressed to her as president of the Douglass Street Neighborhood Homeowners Association, she called an emergency meeting of the board. Normally there were certain actions she could take without permission. But in light of the current controversy with Brimhall, and since this was Clovis Whitfield, Edwina felt it prudent to seek the board's input. After an hour of heated debate, the board voted 4-3 in favor of her meeting Clovis at his office on Livingston Avenue. She was to report the results of that meeting posthaste.

Edwina didn't know Clovis personally, but she knew of him through his sporadic appearances in the newspaper and on TV. She had also seen him on several occasions at City Hall, the courthouse, and on past campaign trails. She didn't like him because he used phrases like "white devil," "legacy of slavery," and "honky-tonk turbo power." While explaining his causes, he spoke of "po' black brothas and sistas," "disenfranchised descendants of the African Diaspora." He used the latest claptrap, saying, "A black ghetto ain't nothin but a white man's dirty bathroom." Edwina didn't necessarily disagree with everything she'd heard Clovis say. There were plenty of "white devils" and a "legacy of slavery," millions of poor blacks and many "disenfranchised descendants of the African Diaspora." Those were core facts encrusted along the underbelly of American history. But Edwina could not justify Clovis's reckless, opportunistic use of the phrases, or how he adorned his verbiage with a gangster's mix of savagery and style. For Edwina, people like Clovis cheapened "the struggle," and thus, cheapened the quest for simple peace and dignity.

Two bodyguards in combat boots, army fatigues, and wearing dark wraparound sunglasses, stood at either side of the entrance to Clovis's office. Curling in the breeze above the door flew the green and white Nigerian flag.

Darren pulled into a parking lot across the street. "What the fuck?"

"Are you up for this?" Edwina looked at him, arching her brows.

"I'm up. Everything just looks so formal."

"He's trying to impress us. I see it's already worked on you."

"I'm cool. But this meeting—we have Leon to thank for this, don't we?"

"I'm afraid so." She sighed.

Edwina had a good idea why Clovis had asked for the meeting. In all likelihood, Leon had told Clovis about Brimhall, and now Clovis was using that as an excuse to stick his nose into Douglass Street's business. Convinced that she couldn't arrive unarmed at the meeting with Clovis, Edwina had pondered her options. And then it came to her. She remembered reading a news article about the fact that Clovis had spent time in prison on a violent crime. The morning after her meeting with the neighborhood association, Edwina went to the courthouse and pulled Clovis's record from the circuit clerk's office, much as she had done with Chris Dilworth. She then went to the prosecutor and requested transcripts of Clovis's court hearings. She waited two hours and endured sour looks from the assistant who retrieved the material from the vault, but nonetheless, Edwina found what she went looking for. She stayed up late that night reading through the court documents, and probably knew Clovis's case as good as anyone. Indeed, if Clovis were to attack Brimhall, Edwina would attack Clovis.

She and Darren crossed the street. One of the bodyguards held out his right hand as they approached the door.

"Stop!" The second bodyguard stepped forward.

"You can't go in until I've frisked you."

"You ain't touchin me," Darren said. He stepped back and pulled up his New York Knicks jersey to reveal the 9 mm tucked snugly in his waistband. "And you for damn sure ain't touchin her." The sudden presence of a gun heightened the stakes, but Clovis's guards remained cool. "I ain't gotta go in," Darren continued, "but if anyone messes with this woman here, I'ma be blazin'."

"She's safe," said one of the guards, who with a jerk of his head indicated that Edwina was cleared to enter. She exchanged a look with Darren and then followed one of the guards into Clovis's office. He instructed her to sit at a chair in front of a large wooden desk adorned with neat stacks of paperwork, a laptop, and a bronze bust of the Honorable Elijah Muhammad. On the walls were black-and-white photographs of prominent blacks. MLK. Eldridge Cleaver. Marcus Garvey. Malcolm X. The Blackstone Rangers. Bobby Seale. Muhammad Ali. Curiously, one portrait was of a white man with a groomed beard and bejeweled crown, who appeared to be a medieval king. Behind the desk hung the red, black and green flag of Black Liberation. With the exception of the white king, thought Edwina, Clovis had all the props a man of his position would be expected to have.

Edwina wasn't impressed.

And then came Clovis, sweeping in from a back room. Wrapped in a broad-shouldered, canary yellow suit, a metallic purple tie and a powder blue shirt—his plumage in full. He sat down, propped his elbows on the desk and leaned forward with his chin resting on his clinched fists, twinkling with rings. Light from the ceiling fixture danced off his dark, shiny cheeks, the pair of large, gold-plated shades resting just below the bridge of his nose. His neck as thick as a gorging python, his face as square as a floor safe, he glared at Edwina from beneath the cocked brim of his bowler.

"Mrs. Spurlock," he said, in a voice of unctuous false amity. "I'm so glad you could meet with me on such short notice."

"Well," Edwina said, with a pinch of dry sarcasm, "since I was summoned by the honorable Clovis D. Whitfield, I came as quickly as possible."

Clovis tried to rattle her with his penitentiary stare, but Edwina did not wane.

"I want you to implore the City Council to terminate Mr. Brimhall from the

Douglass Street contract." He locked his fingers and placed his hands on the desk. "You're harboring a racist, Mrs. Spurlock. If you don't do as I say, there could be real trouble up in yo' hood."

"I don't cave in to threats, Mr. Clovis. And I don't trust your motives. Something tells me that with Mr. Brimhall gone, the next roofing contractor— and all the contractors that come after him—might have important ties to you and Leon Davis. And the last time I checked, Leon was a bike mechanic, and you were nothing but an opportunistic thug."

Clovis fidgeted and sighed. "Mrs. Spurlock, it don't have to be war. In fact, if you work with me, I'll make sure your house gets dolled up like a Rockefeller mansion. And who knows, you might even have some stack left over for a few dresses and some nice jewelry."

"And what if I say no?"

"Then I'ma scream *RACISM* from here to Jerusalem and irreparably tarnish Mr. Brimhall's image in the press and among his peers. And then I'ma piss all over yo' hood and still be in control of the Douglass Street grant! I'm trying to be nice, Mrs. Spurlock. Are you gonna work with me or not?"

Clovis leaned back in his chair with the brash confidence of a man who thinks he has won the battle.

"You said I was harboring a racist. Can you explain that?"

"He burned a cross, Mrs. Spurlock, and you refuse to punish him for his sin. You should at least be asking him for hush money. But you're not. That not only makes you a weak, boot-licking Uncle Tom, but it also makes you an accomplice in the ongoing emasculation of the black man."

"Where's your proof that Mr. Brimhall burned a cross? Oh, let me guess. Leon Davis told you."

"Leon Davis is not the issue."

"Oh, yes he is. You're using information, questionable information, from Leon as an excuse to come up to my neighborhood and start trouble. Again, where's your proof that Mr. Brimhall did what you said he did?"

"My instincts."

"Did Leon tell you that Mr. Brimhall was jumped the other night by a gang of skinheads?"

Clovis didn't respond.

"To be specific, Chris Dilworth. Do you know him? You and him were in prison at the same time a few years back—up in Mansfield."

"No one by the name of Chris Dilworth comes to mind."

"Well let me tell you about him. He's six-foot-four with a big black swastika on his forearm and a shamrock on his chest. He did nearly ten years on a watered down charge of manslaughter. You didn't know Mr. Brimhall took him out with a big left hook? You didn't know that Mr. Brimhall fought for me? Leon must be behind the times."

"I fought skinheads in the joint, Mrs. Spurlock. Lots of them."

"Then that makes you and Mr. Brimhall even then, doesn't it?"

"Good try, but it ain't gonna work."

"What if Mr. Brimhall is working on our houses with the hopes of finding his own brand of redemption—if, of course, he did what you say he did. Shouldn't he be allowed to at least search for atonement?"

"Nope," Clovis said. "Not at the expense of the black man."

Edwina peered through his rose-colored shades and into Clovis's bright brown eyes. She found brilliance and bitterness, competence and courage, but not one shred of compromise. She and Clovis had known each other for five minutes, and they were already blood enemies. Since there was no friendship to lose, Edwina decided to piss him off. When and if she won this street fight, she wanted him to smell the full stink of defeat.

"I went down to the courthouse," she said. "Unlike Mr. Brimhall, you actually have a record."

"Oh yeah?"

"Absolutely. I read the transcript of your plea bargain. You pleaded no contest to three counts of armed robbery and agreed to serve your sentences concurrently. The judge asked if you had anything to say to the court—the victims were there—and you said, 'Nothing comes to mind.' Don't you think you could've at least apologized?"

"Why? I got caught and I did my time. Ain't nobody got killed."

"But you robbed three innocent people—on Christmas Eve. You had no remorse over that?"

"None. Next question?"

Edwina cleared her throat and dipped into some of the hearsay that had surfaced at the emergency meeting of the neighborhood association.

"I hear you keep life insurance policies on your sister, your mother, and your grandparents. Is that true?"

"Who told you that?" Clovis said, losing his swagger.

"A bird, Clovis. A pretty little bird that knows all kinds of nasty little things about you and your past."

Clovis exhaled through his nose.

"Is it true? Because if it is, that's pretty low—pimping out your own family like that." The fighter's shine burned in her eyes.

"What makes you think I won't jump over this desk right now and pop you like a bitch?" He stood up from the chair.

"Because you know I'm not afraid of you. And because you know that whatever you do to me doesn't change who you are and what you think about yourself."

"You about to bring out the nigga in me," he warned.

"I've got a little bit of that myself. If that's all you have, Mr. Clovis, I'd say you don't have enough."

Edwina stood and prepared to leave.

"If you come up to Douglass Street, you'll be in the wrong neighborhood." She turned on her heel and headed toward the door.

"Mrs. Spurlock," Clovis said.

Edwina stopped but did not look back.

"Tell that racist redneck Boss Hog little punk bitch I'ma comin for him."

"Don't worry, Mr. Clovis. I'll tell everyone." Edwina walked out.

—

"Hello," Leon said, answering the phone.

"This is Clovis. Edwina Spurlock's a boot-liking, ass-kissing, kowtowing Oreo cookie who don't deserve to live inside that suit of beautiful black skin!"

Leon leaned back and laughed so hard his gut hurt. "I see you two have met."

"Uh-huh, and she way up on my shit list."

"And you on hers, no doubt."

"No doubt," Clovis said. "And as much as I wanna march up to her doorstep with a bunch a pissed off gorillas, I don't think that's the right thing to do. At least not yet."

"You ain't scared are you, Clovis?"

"I ain't scared a nothin, but I just don't think it's in my best interest to cause a ruckus. How bout doin something stealthy?"

"Didn't know that was your style."

"You don't know me too well. I'm a gorilla and a panther."

"So what do you wanna do?"

"You know Douglass Street better than me. Think a something and gimme a call."

"I can do that, brother."

Leon was still laughing—"a bunch of pissed off gorillas"—as he poured a coffee with cream and sugar. Stirring his caffeine cocktail, Leon pondered the situation.

Clovis might not have wanted to admit it, but he was right to be cautious. Storming down Douglass Street was a good way to get hurt. Darren Bell was Edwina's right-hand man, and everyone knew he packed heat. And if Darren was ever in a pinch, all he had to do was call Wayne McFadden, Richard

Porter, and Eric "The Eric" Johnson, and things could get mob ugly real quick. Stealth? Absolutely.

The City Council vote on the Douglass Street roofing contract was not unanimous. Councilman Booker of District 1 voted against it. Based on his vote, Leon believed that Councilman Booker would entertain the idea of terminating Brimhall from the contract. All he had to do was place the item on the agenda, gain a majority vote and Brimhall was gone. Leon felt confident that he could at least gain an audience with Councilman Booker because he was black. And the hook—that Brimhall was a cross burner—would surely galvanize Councilman Booker's resolve. But to make this thing happen in a hurry, and to gain an advantageous position in Councilman Booker's world, Leon knew he would need money and muscle, to be provided by Dean and Clovis respectively. He thought it over again and again but couldn't find any major holes in his plan. The worst thing Councilman Booker could do was say no, and if that were the case, then he and Clovis would simply move on with "Plan C," whatever that may be. He lit a menthol, poured another coffee and called Dean.

"I need two grand, Mr. Dean."

"Two grand! What now?"

"The roofing contract."

"That doesn't sound like my campaign on Cleveland Road."

"You've got your campaign, Dean. My men are up in Linden Park as we speak, puttin out yard signs. But Douglass Street is my campaign, and as long as my men are out working for you, you need to be helping me."

He heard grousing, so Leon was quick to sooth the nerves of his financier. "Clovis Whitfield's now on your payroll."

Leon told Dean about his meeting with Clovis.

"You clean up well," Dean said. "Where do you want to meet?"

"Joe's Café at Hudson and Cleveland."

"I'll be there in an hour."

Leon arrived at Joe's early. He slid into a booth, opened up the newspaper to the Metro Section, and scanned the page for headlines. ***Lead Council Candidates Under Fire***, by Dominick Van Buren. Leon dove into the story. The Communist candidate, a PhD student named Boris Panomorov, called both Beckham and Bernadette "capitalist pigs" and derided them for trying to "squeeze cheap political points out of the woodpecker issue." The real questions, said Panomorov, dealt with the poor and homeless in District 4. He also advocated for the "revocation of tax-exempt status for all churches and faith-based houses of corruption." Candidate Stephen Millbury criticized Beckham and Bernadette for basing the election on a "two-dimensional question of the environment versus industry. It's a false dichotomy. With today's technology and environmental laws, we can address the concerns on both sides of the debate, and thus, explore the third dimension." Beckham took aim at Millbury. "He doesn't understand how the world works. If you give corporate America an inch, they'll take a mile. Environmental laws are gutted each and every day in this country. What we're talking about is the preservation of land, not the appeasement of big money." Bernadette scolded Panomorov. "Pardon my French, but I'd rather be a capitalist pig than a brain-dead Communist ideologue. And didn't we win the Cold War back in 1989? Boris Panomorov needs to grow up and get real." The jump page featured a photograph of all four candidates at a political forum. A scowling Panomorov pounded his fist against the podium as Beckham and Bernadette pointed accusing fingers at each other. Millbury, reserved as always, appeared pious in comparison.

Ah, local politics, thought Leon. He hadn't had this much fun in years. Wearing suits and Polo cologne. Doling out twenties as if they were dimes. The neighborhood folk who used to ignore him now looked and waved as he and his bike brigade glided by. And his tilted ghetto stroll, shelved long ago, had returned to such form that even the young girls did a double take when he entered the diners, hair salons, and community halls of Cleveland Road. "Yes, indeed, ladies. I'm as tall as a tree and eager to please," he'd tell them. If Leon's plans came to fruition he could get rich, cement his place in the vast hierarchy of municipal life, and perhaps keep the revenue stream flowing for years to come. Failure, on the other hand, would drop him to below where he started, with new enemies and yet another defeat on his record.

He mulled the prospect of failure. His opponent, Century B, had proved itself formidable and capable of victory. The first time he'd seen them, Eva Havlicek had chided him with a humorous remark about the Tour de France. Leon left that encounter impressed, but confident the group was out of its league and that the ardor of its members would diminish as the harsh realities of Cleveland Road emerged. But that hadn't happened yet. Century B besieged the streets of District 4. When they came upon residents who were open to the woodpecker pitch, they talked and shook hands with everyone in the household, including the children. Before leaving, they ceremoniously planted a campaign sign deep in the front yard. When the gangsters rolled slowly by with the bass beats pounding, Century B held their heads high and kept moving, allowing no opportunity for easy mischief. Leon enjoyed watching them huddle at the street corners while they studied maps, checked notes, made calls from their cell phones and plotted their next moves. Intriguing were the tidbits of information leaking out all along Cleveland Road. Eva and the Velvet Revolution. The Chinese girl and Tiananmen Square. A Russian and the downfall of the Soviet Empire. Anku, the African, said to be a veteran of the Angola Civil War. As much as he wanted to think of them as kids, and thus to dismiss them, Leon knew better.

He flipped to the obituaries. Since he saw no familiar names, he set the paper down. When he did, he saw Dean pushing through the front door of the café.

"Damn, he's white," Leon said to himself.

"What's going on?" Dean said, as he slid into the Formica booth.

"Waiting on you, money man." Leon ordered a cup of coffee for Dean.

"Anything good in the papers today?"

"Just your uncle ripping the Communist a new asshole."

"Did you read the latest poll numbers?"

"Uh-huh," Leon said. "Your uncle is ahead by three points, which is in the margin of error."

"Exactly, which means we have a lot of work to do."

"We're doing it. You know I got that big fish fry coming up at the VFW. And I'ma be at the Shiloh Baptist Church on Sunday morning telling everyone how great your uncle is."

"Good," Dean said. "But today we're doing your deal, right?"

"Exacta-mundo, my friend."

Dean dug into his leather satchel, pulled out a brown envelope, and slid it across the table.

"It's all there. In denominations of twenty."

"*Merci beaucoup.*"

He grabbed the envelope and slid it into his breast pocket. He didn't want to say anything, but Dean was a wreck. He wore a snazzy, navy suit and sporty red bowtie. He smelled of the finest cologne. His hair thick and wavy with gel. But the yellow sack of blood under his left eye hung beneath the curvature of his sun glasses. His lip was swollen. A scab meandered up the left side of his nose, and a bruise, like a rotten grape, blemished his forehead. From Dean's aura, Leon could tell that this kid was brooding over a dark vortex of regret and shame. Leon decided right then and there that he would dump Dean as soon as he could, but until that time came, he needed those brown envelopes stuffed with bribes.

"When you get done with your deal, gimme a call," Dean said. "I've got some ideas about that fish fry you've got going on. I think my Uncle Byron wants to give a speech there."

"Sure thing."

To Leon's relief, Dean took one gulp of coffee and left.

Leon went to the phone booth outside on the corner and called Clovis.

"You know Councilman Booker?"

"I live in his district," Clovis said. "Of course I do."

"Then call'm up and make an appointment. I have our stealthy plan all mapped out."

"You a good man," Clovis said.

—

When Councilman Booker pulled up in front of Clovis's office, Leon and Clovis looked at each other and smiled. He stepped out of his silver Cadillac Coupe Deville, popped a mint into his mouth and entered. He breezed through the door with an affected pomposity meant to imply that his arrival marked the beginning of an important occasion. A radiant smile, a worsted pin stripped suit, two-tone Bally shoes and an abundance of gold jewelry. He stopped, held out his arms, and in a round and soaring voice, said, "Leon Davis! Clovis Whitfield! It's great to see you two!" Leon and Clovis stood and greeted him as on old friend, even though neither knew the man personally. Clovis, in a rare act of subservience, fetched a soft drink for Councilman Booker.

He took a long drink, wiped his lips with a crimson handkerchief and smiled. He took a seat at Clovis's desk. "Gentleman, as a proud representative of District One, what can I do for you today?"

"We have a delicate situation up in District 4," Leon began. "Do you remember the Douglass Street grant program that came before the City Council on February 24th?"

Booker leaned back in the chair and thought for a while.

"Nothing comes to mind."

"It was a roofing contract for Douglass Street," Leon said. "I spoke against it, remember? There was a bunch of white folks up there arguing about it."

"Oh, yes. Now I remember. A little roofing contract. I voted to extend the bid deadline, right?"

"Yeah. And it was the right thing to do. Anyway, we recently found out that the man who got the contract, Gene Brimhall, has some dirty secrets in his past."

"Like what."

"Mr. Brimhall is a cross burner," Clovis said. "And we don't think it's right that a white racist is making money off the backs of poor black folks. Do you?"

"That's horrible." The councilman's eyes glittered with the spirit of collusion.

Leon pulled the brown envelope from his chest pocket and slid it across the table toward Booker.

"We were hoping you could bring a resolution to the City Council asking that Mr. Brimhall be terminated from the contract, for 'unspecified transgressions against the integrity of the Douglass Street grant program,'" Clovis said.

"And what's this?" Booker pointed at the envelope.

"Gas money," Leon said. "We didn't expect you to come all the way out to East Livingston Avenue without paying for your gas."

"Thank you." The older man tucked the envelope away. "Gas prices have been on the rise these days."

"Now you know what I'ma do if you back out and don't sponsor the resolution, right?" Clovis said.

"No," Councilman Booker said. "What?"

"I'ma campaign against you like a motherfucker when you run for re-election next year." He pointed his finger to within inches of Councilman Booker's face. "And before you ask, yes, I know about yo' 'assistant,' and yes, I'm up in yo' district. And yes, I know yo' wife got a job but don't do nothin' down at the DMV. It'll be me and a bunch of pissed off gorillas getting up in yo' grill if you don't put this resolution on the agenda. Got it?"

"Don't worry, Mr. Whitfield. It'll be on the agenda before the week is out. But please, dear God, when the council convenes, I don't want either one of you there."

Two bodyguards dressed in black fatigues and combat boots escorted Councilman Booker out of Clovis's office.

Leon watched the councilman's sedan drive away. "You think he'll do it?"

"If he knows what's best for him he will."

L A S T
M U L L E T

At the break of dawn on a Sunday, Brimhall, James and Orlando Cruz drove out to Brimhall's house on the Hilltop, packed his clothes, cleaned out the refrigerator, and secured the windows. The next day Brimhall shut off the utilities, forwarded the mail to the roofing company's P.O. Box, and routed home calls to his cell phone. He hadn't wanted to leave and seek shelter with James, but he couldn't ignore reality. Defenseless against his enemies, the Hilltop just wasn't a safe place to be. While Brimhall sorely missed his recliner and his big-screen TV, he enjoyed his time away from home, James keeping him sane as he bobbed through the straits of self-reflection.

Eva had appeared at James' doorstep three weeks before Brimhall's arrival, and it showed. His household was no longer a clean yet spare and colorless bachelor pad, but a home infused with a touch of domestic sophistication. Eva brought over piles of books and an authentic Persian rug, and placed them in the den, which she had commandeered as her study. The presence of a thinker's lair revived the aesthetics of the old house. She dressed the dining room table with an expanse of Amish lace, hung ferns on the front porch, and eggshell drapes across the windows. Above the mantle she placed a framed, five-foot-by-five-foot, sepia tone photograph of the Manhattan skyline circa 1946. She stocked the kitchen with porcelain plates and real silverware, pots and pans, a coffee grinder, wine glasses, towels and hot mitts, a ladle and an ancient soup spoon. She stuffed the refrigerator with market-quality condiments, hunks of cheese, butcher meats and brown bags of whole-bean Arabica coffee. Brimhall complimented her on her efforts to brighten James's homestead, but asked her why she had gone to so much trouble.

Eva lit a cigarette. "I grew up under Communism. In those days, true comfort could only be found in the home, so we Czechs work hard at where we live."

He wasn't sexually attracted to Eva. Too European for his taste. Besides, Brimhall couldn't harbor desire for a woman involved with James. But Brimhall found her beautiful, and he was happy that such an alluring woman had walked into his friend's life. And since he was part of the makeshift family at the rustic Italianate on Oregon Avenue, Brimhall had seen Eva's many faces. While studying, a monk in the scriptorium. Returning from the campaign, the sun-soaked electioneer. On her way out the door for a symphony date with James, the silk and diamond princess. And when out on the front porch drinking wine and speaking Russian with Oxana—chain smoking and laughing like a horse—the bawdy lass from far, far away. And then there was the time when her hair was up in a dew rag and she walked through the house with a broom in her hand and a basket of dirty laundry on her hip. "I worked at a pension back in Prague," she said, and grunted. "I can cook and clean for ten at a time."

Brimhall even heard her bitching someone out over the phone one day and laughed to tears when she told him it was her candidate, George Beckham, and that he had pissed her off by speaking ill of the press.

"A candidate should never pick a fight with someone who buys ink by the barrel," she had said.

What Brimhall enjoyed about her most, and what gave her and James the best chance of surviving as a couple, is that she was no automaton. Even in play her deeds were acts of passion, not of hollow presentation. Eva Havlicek, and Brimhall was proud to know her.

—

On a damp spring morning, a Midwestern Saturday morning when fleeces and flannels are worn, Brimhall sat on the porch drinking coffee with his new roommates. Gentle tears of rain pattered in the twinkling leaves as blooms of lilac and dogwood tried to find the sun. Between James and Eva fluttered the vibrant, merry chatter of new lovers. They rocked back and forth on the porch swing. Up and down the street people on their porches drank their morning cups of brew. Brimhall couldn't help but appreciate the meaning of the word "community."

On the empty chair beside him was a folded white towel and a spray bottle. A black backpack that seemed as if it had been carried across continents leaned against one of the chair's legs. Brimhall looked up from the backpack and noticed that James eyed him with suspicion.

"What's up, man?" Brimhall said, taken by James' surprise change in demeanor.

James's face grew dark, and Eva turned away as if she didn't want to hear the words that were about to be spoken.

"Brimhall," James said, in a low, serious tone, "there's something I have to say."

Alarmed, Brimhall maintained a calm exterior.

"Go ahead." He set his coffee down.

James stood and paced across the porch. He looked down the street, as if in deep thought, and sighed.

"This is hard for me to say," he said, heading back toward the porch swing, "but I think it's time to get rid of the mullet."

"What?" Brimhall's voice rose an octave.

"I thought about it long and hard, and Eva and I talked about it."

Eva shook her head, looking down at her coffee.

Peeved, Brimhall served a sour look.

James continued. "It just seems like you're about to enter a new phase of your life, and, well, I think the mullet is a relic of your past and that it has nothing to do with your future. And Eva agrees."

Eva nodded with concurrence, but dared not make eye contact with Brimhall.

"I've had a mullet since I was in the seventh grade, James. It's who I am."

"A few months ago I met with Amanda and went back through the books, Brimhall, like you told me to. In the last five years, we—you—have grossed millions of dollars. Not once have we—you—missed an insurance payment, or workers comp, or taxes, or loan payments. And we won that lawsuit. What I'm trying to say is, you're an up and coming contractor in this town, and that's what people need to see. The mullet?" James grimaced and shrugged. "It conjures up too many images of the Hilltop and redneckism and ignorance and all that stuff. Some of the people who put you in the hospital have mullets, Brimhall. I don't think it's fair for you to lump yourself in with those people."

"Are you asking me to be a conformist asshole rather than a hell raiser?"

"No, I'm not. The hell raiser is the man I grew to love and respect. You'd still have your tattoo. But the mullet? I'm not gonna give you some big explanation, Brimhall. All I'm saying is that I think it's time for a haircut, because it's more than just a haircut."

"That's all you're sayin', huh?"

"Yes, sir."

Brimhall didn't have a grotesque mullet that flowed in thick, greasy curls to the middle of his back. He had worn one like that years ago. But as his stature as a roofing contractor had grown, the mullet had shrunk proportionally. Now, it was tapered into its final form as a tuft that dangled like a wad of barbed wire. When he turned quickly or laughed heartily, the mullet jiggled. When it was tightly pulled and tied off with a rubber band, it poked out like the short blade of a pocketknife. He wore the mullet with such reverence that it was like a sacred flag of liberty, and it had flown in various incarnations for the last seventeen years. It was important for Brimhall to not only be tough, but to look tough. While he knew plenty of people made fun of the mullet, he also knew that none of them had made fun of it to his face.

He pursed his lips and set his hazel iron gaze. James matched his intensity.

"You know James, there was a time when I would've told you to fuck off. And I almost just did. But that time has come and gone."

He and James looked at each other for a long while. What began as an exchange of reticent smiles grew into the warm, meandering laughter that exists only between the truest of friends.

"You bastard." Brimhall filed the word with a tone of admiration. "So you're gonna cut my mullet off right here?"

"No." James grinned. "Eva is."

Brimhall fixed a concerned look on Eva.

"Do not fear," she said, and stepped to the well-traveled backpack.

She pulled back the zipper and fetched a fold-over case of butternut leather. She set it on the porch ledge, opening it to reveal a set of shiny antique hair scissors with long, curving finger props. She grabbed the spray bottle and the towel and set them on the ledge.

"Back in the dark days before the revolution, everyone made money on the side. This is how mother and I made ours. We cut hair for all our neighbors in the 'rabbit hutches' out near the cemetery on Vinohradska, where we lived. We did it for crowns and used that money to bribe the postman for letters from our cousins here in America. You would not believe the stories these scissors could tell you. Come now," she urged, gesturing toward the chair. Once comfortably situated, Eva draped the white towel over his shoulders. She dampened his hair, and then ran a brand new comb over his scalp until his locks were dark and soft. James disappeared into the house but soon returned with a bowl of hot water, shaving cream and a bag of plastic razors.

"Ya'll ain't gonna make me bald, are ya?"

"What, and ruin all this beautiful blond hair of yours? Never," Eva said.

"Just relax," James said. "She's gonna make you look like a male super model."

"Ya'll planned this," he said, in a mock tone of warning, taking a sip of his now-cold coffee.

With a few snips Eva cut off the tail of the Last Mullet and let it drop to the porch floor.

"Wooowhooo!" howled Brimhall, and that was the end of that.

—

Brimhall inched down Oakley Avenue, a thin street lined with steep shanties infested with the unemployed, the drunk, the hopeless, and the insane. The ghetto of the Hilltop ghetto, a place where white trash spawned year after year. Brimhall wondered why a black family would ever want to live in a mean place like Oakley Avenue. Alas, the blacks had come and the cross had burned.

When he approached the 700 block, he eased on the brakes. This was definitely the house, and it was in livable shambles. He jotted down the address on a debit card receipt and moved on. He took West Broad Street all the way into downtown and parked at the courthouse. Swift yet awkward on his crutches, he managed to catch the elevator before it closed. He hobbled down the hall to the real estate office, where all the clerks knew his name.

"What happened, Gene?" one of the clerks said.

"I finally slipped and fell," he said. "But I'm fine."

"Are you sure?" She frowned at the wicked row of stitches around his left eye.

"I'm fine."

The clerk shook her head. "Okay. How can I help you today?"

"I was hoping you could pull the property card for 720 S. Oakley Avenue."

"Sure thing."

She tapped on the keyboard and a few seconds later the property card slid out from the printer. She handed it to Brimhall, who handed her 50 cents. With his index finger Brimhall went down the list of people who had owned the 1932 house. He found what he was looking for. On June 21, 1982, a man named Zebulon Reed and his wife, Mercy Reed, bought the house for $39,500—and sold it to a slumlord for just $31,000 two months later. Brimhall checked a courthouse phone book for a listing for Zebulon Reed. Convenient. Zebulon and Mercy Reed lived at 3820 Plymouth Street in east Columbus near White Hall. Confident that the Zebulon and Mercy Reed on Plymouth Street were the same Zebulon and Mercy Reed who had bought the house on Oakley Avenue, Brimhall jotted down the number on the back of the property card and left the courthouse.

He knew he couldn't just show up at Zebulon Reed's home and say, "Hi, I'm Gene Brimhall. I'm one of the dirty white punks that burned a cross in your front yard when you lived on the Hilltop. I'm sorry." Brimhall didn't even know if apologizing was feasible, but lately, he felt like it was the right thing to do. He needed to show the Reeds his knife wound and the nasty gash above his eye so that they would know that he also bore the wounds of hatred. He knew of only one person with the ability to broach such a delicate topic. He put the truck in drive and headed to Edwina's.

Bobby skipped down the hall as he and Brimhall made their way to the kitchen, where Edwina stirred two pots of homemade spaghetti sauce with a giant wooden spoon. The lingering joy of fresh garlic, tomatoes and deftly measured seasonings lifted Brimhall's sunken spirits. A flash of Edwina's big brown eyes caused a ripple in the shimmering fjord of his soul. Uttering a brief greeting, he took a seat at the kitchen table. She set the spoon on the stovetop and joined him.

"It smells wonderful in here."

"Thanks," she said. "It's like this every Wednesday."

"Who are you cooking for?"

"I do the Thursday special for my church. I've done spaghetti for the last eight years."

"Nice."

She smiled. "That's what they say. I perfected the recipe about ten years ago and haven't changed a thing since."

Edwina put on a pot of coffee. She and Brimhall sat at the table and talked for a couple of hours. They discussed the roofing contract and how James and his Guadalajara crew were four days ahead of schedule. Edwina told him about her meeting with Clovis Whitfield and reassured Brimhall that she had the full support of the neighborhood association. She complimented him on his new haircut, too, and Brimhall told her the story about how James and Eva had bamboozled him on the front porch.

She stirred the giant pots of spaghetti sauce.

Brimhall told her about the night that Eva's political team, Century B, met at James' house to discuss the campaign and to have a few drinks. Before the night was over, all of them danced in the living room to the "Grease" soundtrack. Brimhall told Edwina that he was impressed that people from all over the world could come together for that kind of moment. Edwina laughed and told him about the time she took six Japanese executives to a business reception at the Franklin Park Conservatory. When they didn't come out on time, Edwina went inside to tell them that if they wanted to stay, fine, but that they'd have to pay for an extra hour in the limo. All six of the Japanese men were in a circle out on the banquet floor, dancing, and dancing hard, to Snoop Doggy Dog. As Edwina and Brimhall talked, Bobby fluttered around the periphery, sometimes jigging, sometimes serving coffee, and at other times showing Brimhall the latest picture he'd painted at school.

Brimhall was having a great time, and the last thing he wanted was to break the happy spell of fellowship by steering the conversation toward the dreaded cross. Still, he reasoned, part of Edwina's appeal was that she handled the serious stuff. Edwina must have read the subtle change in his demeanor because she asked Bobby to go fold the towels, and when he was finished with that, to sweep the hall. Bobby responded with mild resistance, but one sharp look from his grandmother sent him scurrying to the laundry room.

"What's on your mind, Gene?" she said, once Bobby was gone.

"Well, I've been thinking about a lot of things lately. You know, I'm on the other side of the fight, and things are different now. That cross is nagging at me, Edwina. It's still burning."

"You're finally coming to grips with what you did. You're starting to draw inspiration from new places, and that's making you re-evaluate the old times, correct?"

"Indeed."

"The question becomes, what do you want to do about it?"

"I wanna apologize, if not for Chris Dilworth, then at least for myself."

"You know that's gonna be tricky, and even dangerous."

"Yes ma'am. But that's why I'm here."

He pulled the property card from his wallet, unfolded it and set it on the table.

"This is the address and phone number of Zebulon and Mercy Reed," he said, in a near whisper. "This is the family that lived in the house when the cross was burned."

—

Edwina looked at the property card and shuddered. Zebulon and Mercy Reed. Old-school decent folk. Family folk. Church-going Christian folk who did not deserve the horror brought to them. For a dark, visceral moment the sorrow of centuries bubbled up inside Edwina and she wanted to hate Gene Brimhall. *Get the hell out of my house and stay gone!* Because of him, members of the neighborhood association gave her odd looks. Because of him, Leon Davis and Clovis Whitfield plotted against her. His sin, her obligation. In deference to him she had abandoned her concrete set of morals and was instead pondering a nebulous notion of forgiveness. By building a cross he knew would be burned, Brimhall had attached himself to the legacy of ignorance that would forever stain the pages of the American story. Oh, how she wanted to hate him. But here he was, scared and vulnerable. Here he was, offering her a chance to be larger than history, to be greater than the sum total of bigotry and racism. He flinched with uncertainty as he awaited her answer.

"I'll help you," she said.

"Thanks, Edwina," and they clasped hands.

Edwina served both Gene and Bobby a bowl of spaghetti and meatballs and then sent them to Graeter's Ice Cream in Bexley for desert. She told Gene to take his time because she didn't know how long this phone call would take. Edwina didn't want to rush into this, but she also didn't want to let it linger. Despite the anxiety gripping her as she picked up the phone, she was also curious. How would the Reed family react? How deep was the wound? Dear God, bless us all, she said, and dialed the number.

An older man picked up the phone. "Hello?"

"Yes," Edwina said, "is Mercy Reed there?"

"Hold on."

Edwina heard Zebulon calling for his wife, and soon she was on the phone.

"This is Mercy," came a husky, beautiful voice as thick and creamy as the petal of a magnolia bloom.

"Hi, Mrs. Reed, you don't know me but my name is Edwina Spurlock," she said, in the most polite, deferential tone she could muster.

"How can I help you Mrs. Spurlock?"

"Well, back in 1982, did you live on the Hilltop at 702 S. Oakley Avenue?"

"Briefly." Edwina heard a distinct note of alarm in that one word. "Why?"

"I know what happened."

"Oh, you do?" Now the tone was accusatory.

"Yes, I do."

Edwina already had her answer. The wound extremely deep. She regretted having made the phone call, but it was too late to just hang up. Edwina felt the palpable fury on the other end of the line and knew that she was about to be skinned, tanned, and hung out to dry.

"So you called me up out of the blue to tell me that you know what happened back in 1982?"

"I know one of the men who was involved, Mrs. Reed, and he wants to apologize."

"Come again?"

"I said I know one of the men involved, and he wants to apologize."

What came next was a low, angry laugh that Edwina barely endured. It rolled and rolled for what seemed like eternity before culminating in a broad sigh of warning.

"You know what my husband and my two sons would do if they ever got their hands on that man? Think about it, Mrs. Spurlock."

"I understand that it must've been traumatic."

"Oh, you understand. Let me ask you, Mrs. Spurlock, has anyone ever burned a cross in your front yard. Tell me?"

"No."

"Now you listen up little lady and you listen up real good. I've got your name written down and I'ma keep that name in a real safe place, where nobody can find it but me. But if you ever, ever call me again I'ma come looking for you, Mrs. Spurlock. And when I find you, I'ma make you tell me who this man is, and then somebody gonna come looking for him, too. You hear me? You hear me Mrs. Spurlock?"

"Yes, m'am," Edwina said. "I hear you."

Mercy Reed slammed down the receiver, jarring Edwina's composure. Her ears still ringing with rejection, Edwina crumpled up the property card and tossed it into the garbage can. She stirred the pots of spaghetti sauce and then took a seat at the kitchen table. She wiped a tear from her eye, cold silence creeping over her.

She wasn't angry with Mercy Reed, who had every right to be upset, even after thirteen years. Indeed, the nature of the crime, eternal, and so too, the pain. Still, she couldn't help but think that Mercy Reed had seized the chance to finally take her revenge. As the matriarch of the Reed family—"my husband and my two sons"—she was the only person who could truly give Gene the redemption he sought. By denying it, she knew she could damn him to a lifetime of regret. Perhaps that's what Gene deserved. Edwina said a little prayer for the

Reed family and for Gene. Who knows, she thought, if Mercy keeps my name, then maybe one day she'll change her mind and call.

Edwina heard footsteps on the porch. She chased away her countenance of dejection and donned a simple smile for her darling little Bobby. He burst into the kitchen, a big grin on his face.

"Grandma, Grandma, Mr. Brimhall got me a banana split, and then we went to the dollar store and he got me this" he said, showing her a baseball cap with the slogan, "I'm the Man."

"That's good," she said, as Bobby gave her a hug. "Did you say, 'Thank you?'"

"Yes, ma'am. Twice."

Gene looked at her from across the kitchen.

"No go, Gene," she said, with finality.

Brimhall nodded with disappointment.

"Well, I guess I should go."

"No, you don't have to go," she said, revealing sympathy. "Mercy Reed ain't the only person in the world, now is she?"

CRUSHED
COUP

Dominick plopped into his chair, kicked his feet up on the desk, and breathed the long, dramatic breath of a reporter who is exhausted. He had just finished a weekend story highlighting the results of an opinion poll commissioned by Ohio State, The Associated Press, and the *Scioto Times*. According to the poll, Bernadette led Beckham by four points—42.5 to 38.5 percent—with a margin of error of plus or minus four. Stephen Millbury was a distant third with 15 percent of the poll, while Boris Panomorov, the fiery Communist, barely registered with just 4 percent. What the poll showed, however, is that Millbury and Panomorov had garnered enough support to keep Bernadette and Beckham from claiming the 50-percent-plus-one majority needed to win the election outright. Based on the results of the poll, Dominick wrote a piece about the strong likelihood that Bernadette and Beckham would have to fight it out in a runoff for the honor of being the next District 4 representative. Dominick recounted their spirited campaigns through the first six weeks of the race. He knew the story by heart, so he had no problem writing a 45-inch piece. Now that he was done, all he had to do was sit at his desk until 4 p.m. and pretend like he was working. If nothing blew up, or if Mayor Kraus didn't get shot by a disgruntled former municipal employee, then he was free to leave for the weekend.

A cold, sweating beer at the Short North Tavern loomed at the center of his thoughts. And then he saw one of the clerks, Kelly Crenshaw, walking through the newsroom with a small stack of papers. He groaned. Kelly Crenshaw checked the fax machine at the middle of every hour and delivered the various faxes to employees throughout the newsroom. If Dominick received a fax, he might have more work to do. He groaned again. After a brief stop at the Style editor's desk, Kelly Crenshaw headed his way.

"Go away," he said.

But Kelly, her red bob bouncing, was undeterred. She gave him a vicious smile. "Sorry, Van Buren, but it looks like you're headed to City Hall, at four-thirty on a Friday."

Dominick snatched the fax from her hand and started to read. She snickered under her breath and continued on her way.

"Hell's bells and a bottle of rum," he said, and twisted a ringlet of hair around his left index finger. He read the fax for a second time.

Councilman Tom Booker has called an emergency meeting for 4:30 to discuss the following agenda item: Termination of Brimhall Roofing from the Douglass Street Restoration, due to unspecified transgressions against the integrity of the grant program.

This wasn't something that the paper had to have from a news perspective, but for Dominick, it was personal. He knew that James O'Neal was the foreman for that company, and that he was also Eva's boyfriend. Dominick could no longer be seen in public with Eva because he was covering the election and she was a volunteer in the Beckham campaign. But they still talked on the phone and he had gone to James' house on a couple of occasions for drinks and chitchat. He knew weird things were going on in the Cleveland Road Theater, where Douglass Street was located. Looking at the fax, an old newsroom adage came to mind—this didn't pass the smell test.

He flipped through the "O" section of his Rolodex and dialed a number.

The other end of the line went live, but for a few seconds all he heard was the whispering wind and the tapping of hammers. At last James answered.

"Hello?" he said.

"James?"

"Yeah, who is this?"

"It's me, Dominick. Did I catch you at a bad time?"

"Uh, no. What's up?"

"Man, I'm sorry to call you while you're up on a roof, but I've got some news you definitely need to hear."

"What's that?"

"Councilman Booker's called an emergency meeting of the City Council, and it's scheduled for four-thirty today. There's only one thing on the agenda."

"Which is?"

"The City Council is convening to discuss the termination of Brimhall Roofing from the Douglass Street Restoration—Councilman Booker's trying to fire you, man."

"How do you know this?"

"I cover City Hall. I just got a fax from the city secretary's office, just like I do for every meeting."

"Can they call a public hearing on such short notice?"

"They can if they declare an emergency. They've already notified the press, so their ass is covered. If you have any plans for later on, I suggest you cancel them. James, if you're not there, I guarantee you you'll get fired. I know these guys."

"Did Councilman Booker say why?"

"Get this—*due to unspecified transgressions against the integrity of the Douglass Street grant program.*"

"Jesus," James said. "I'll be there."

"Give 'em hell, James. Councilman Booker is the weakest link in that chain. And by the way, do you want me to call Eva?"

"Why would you call her?"

"Because, you're about to fight City Hall. You're gonna need all the firepower you can get. And these days, Eva and her gang can bring the heat."

"Call her," James said at last, "and tell her to meet me on the steps of City Hall at 4:15. Are you going to be there?"

"I wouldn't miss it for the world. But when you see me, act like you don't know me."

—

James slid the cell phone into its holster, shimmied down the scaffolding and jogged down Douglass Street to Edwina's house. He banged on the door. Edwina answered with all the urgency that the loud knocking implied.

"What is it, James?"

He looked at his watch. It was 2:40.

"Councilman Booker's trying to terminate me from the roofing contract at four thirty! He's called a special meeting of the City Council!"

Edwina folded her arms across her chest. She made no pretense to decency.

"That shit ain't gonna fly. I'll start working the phones. We'll be there, James, and there's gonna be hell to pay."

They gave each other a short, fortifying hug and exchanged hasty kisses on the cheek. James ran into the middle of the street, planted his feet and cupped his hands into a megaphone. His voice echoed down the brick Victorian canyon.

"Orlando! Fidel! Caesar! Reuben! Jose! Enrique! Julio! *Vamanos!*"

—

Eva could kill for a cigarette. It was always like this when her students took their exams. Teaching made the time go fast, so the craving for nicotine never became acute. But when all she had to do was sit at her desk and read the papers, she felt like sipping on an espresso and smoking. She plunged into an editorial in the *Scioto Times* officially endorsing George Beckham as the top candidate in the City Council election. "George Beckham has the right ideas for District 4," read the editorial. She heard the vibration of her pager from inside her backpack. She fished it out of a side pocket and looked at the number. *672-4912-911-911.* She looked at her students, hunched over their blue books, immersed in the composition portion of the exam. She looked back at the pager—911-911, the code for emergency. She headed toward the door, her backpack slung across her shoulder.

"I will be just outside in the hall," she said to her students, who nodded and went back to their exams.

She leaned against the wall, pulled the campaign cell phone from her backpack and called the number on the pager. It was Dominick, calling from work.

"Why did you call with a 911?" she said.

"The City Council's trying to fire your boyfriend from the Douglass Street Restoration."

"What?"

"The city council is trying to fire your boyfriend from the contract at four-thirty this afternoon. I figured you needed to know."

"Have you told James?"

"Of course. I told him I was going to call you. Thought you might want to round up your army and storm the gates of City Hall. It's a very American thing to do. And today, I think it's important for James and that entire neighborhood that you be there."

She gazed through the door window at her students. "I will."

"And so will I. You know the routine, right?"

"Yes. I shall act like I have never met you."

"Good luck."

"Thank you, Dominick. You are a good friend."

She called Mingmei and told her what she had heard from Dominick.

"But we are scheduled to campaign on Cleveland Road this afternoon," Mingmei said. "If we do not go there today, we will have to do double duty tomorrow."

"That is fine." Eva waved glumly at a colleague down the hall. "And if Beckham finds out and is angry, I will handle him."

"I will tell Century B what you have told me. But I will not try and force anyone to come with me."

"I understand. This is not their fight."

She slid the pager and the cell phone into her backpack and re-entered the classroom. Several students watched as she returned to her seat.

Eva knew that the Czech language had no real practical use for a young American, but these students were all of Czech and Slovak ancestry. They studied the language and history to get back in touch with their "roots." Most of these students had been under Eva's instruction since she arrived in the United States two years ago. All of them had butchered her mother tongue through sections 101, 102, 103 and 104. But now that they were juniors with two years of intense, earnest effort under their belts, she could converse with all of them in brittle, yet endearingly conversational Czech. All of them had been to Prague, could do the Polka and knew Antonin Dvorak's "From the New World" symphony by heart. Her students were among the best in the Slavic Studies department, and Eva loved each and every one of them. Seeing them crouched over their blue books was gratifying, and in the context of a looming emergency, heartening.

One of the students must have sensed her emotions because he looked up from his test and smiled before returning to his work. With the exception of Dominick and Oxana, she had known these students longer than anyone else in the United States, and she needed to have them at her side when she made her entrance at City Hall. Gulping down her trepidation, she said to each of them as they turned in their tests, "Wait for me downstairs at the bench under the tree." As usual, Eva had to wait until the final minute of class for Abbey Vandra, her brightest pupil, to finish her test. She slid the blue books into her backpack, turned out all the lights, locked the door and made her way downstairs with Abbey at her side.

All eight students were there. From the collective look of curiosity, Eva knew each of them had detected a hint of urgency in her voice. She guessed that they had even discussed this impromptu meeting while she waited for Abbey to finish her test. Eva lit a Marlboro and blew out a long, conspiratorial jet of smoke. When her words finally came, they sounded old and grave.

"I am storming the gates of City Hall," she said, and looked each of her students in the eye.

Eva couldn't believe such bravado had spilled from her mouth. Waiting for her at City Hall would be the most powerful elected body in Columbus. Would they laugh in her face and tell her to move on along, or would she be punished for her belligerence? Eva cared little. James would be there, and she needed to fight for her man. He had accepted her into his house without laying down his rule as the price of entry. James, rugged yet gentle James, at night would hold her in his arms, whisper dearly in her ear, and mine her warm spots for affection. The stubborn chill at the bottom of her heart always lifted when he was near. If someone were trying to take something from him, she felt duty bound to stand in the way.

Eva's students bent into convulsions of incredulity as they asked, in fitful bursts of English, to repeat what she had just said.

"I am storming the gates of City Hall, and I want you guys with me. The City Council is trying to terminate my boyfriend from an important contract, and I intend on stopping them."

"But you can't do that!" protested one student.

"Why not?" asked another.

"Because, the councilmen will kick her out."

"Eva's too mild mannered to do something like that!" said a third.

"What, you think that just because she's a woman she can't cause a ruckus?" asked a fourth.

217

"Hold on, hold on," Eva pleaded, raising her hands for silence. "This will not influence the way I score your exams. It is just that I need you—now!"

She squared her shoulders and tightened the timber of her lanky, five-foot-ten-inch frame. She leveled her chin and flashed the wary ghetto gaze she'd perfected up on Cleveland Road. She flicked the cigarette to the ground. Her lip curled into a potent grin. Street fever burned in her cheeks. For the first time in two years Eva wasn't the exacting, reserved Czech instructor with the mists of Communism hanging in her eyes. A volatile, reckless creature beckoned the students with the promise of devilment. Yet underneath the keen demeanor was the Eva they knew, the one who had taught them the language of their ancestors. The students remained silent. A gentle breeze rustled through the tree. Eva didn't blink.

"I'm parked at the stadium," one student said, in a spasm of excitement.

"So am I," said another.

Eva checked her watch.

"It is three forty five. We have to be there by four thirty!"

They darted to the stadium parking lot and piled into the cars. They arrived at the steps of City Hall at 4:10. With Mingmei, Barbara Thurman, and James standing at its center, Century B awaited.

—

Mayor Kraus saw them rallying on the steps. He didn't know why they were there until he overheard one of them say, "special meeting," and another one say, "dirty trick." That's when he put the pieces together—they had come to oppose Councilman Booker's proposal to terminate the roofing contract. Councilman Booker had called him the night before and told him today's meeting would be an "in and out" and that the vote itself would be a "slam dunk." Mayor Kraus reminded himself to never again believe Councilman Booker.

At last count, 39 people had signed up to speak—at 4:30 on a Friday—on the lone agenda item. Worse still was the look and feel of the crowd, smart, diverse, and palpably angry. Some of them were also Beckham volunteers, which added a dimension of political high jinks to what was shaping up as an old-fashioned showdown at City Hall. Mayor Kraus had arrived somewhat perturbed because he'd cancelled a golf outing to accommodate Booker. Now, he was curious as to what these people had to say.

The long blonde who appeared to be their leader breezed into council chambers with the brusque momentum of a budding populist. A loud column of people followed her as she stepped to the podium and signed up to speak. She read a copy of the resolution terminating Brimhall Roofing from the contract, and shook her head in dismay. She studied the council while her cohorts signed the comment registry, or read a copy of the resolution. Mayor Kraus chuckled to himself when out of the corner of his eye he saw Councilman Booker, his face contorted with embarrassment, explaining himself to councilmen Kozlowski and Rinchuso.

"A real slam dunk, huh Book?" chided the mayor.

"It ain't over yet," Councilman Booker said. "Let's get this show on the road."

Mayor Kraus tapped the gavel.

"A special meeting has been called to consider a resolution to terminate Brimhall Roofing from Phase One of the Douglass Street Restoration. We have a lengthy list of speakers, so please, try and limit your remarks to two minutes. And you are only to address the agenda item. Our first speaker is Eva Havlicek."

She slid out from a bench row and made her way to the podium. She grabbed both sides of the lectern and leaned over the microphone as if she were a doe dipping to drink. She peered out from over the rim of her eyeglasses, and like a schoolmarm on the brink of administering punishment, hoisted an index finger above her head.

"I am Eva Havlicek," she said, "and I am here to crush the coup!"

She picked up the resolution and flailed it above her head.

"As proffered, this resolution is poorly conceived, and if approved, poorly executed. We did not come here late on Friday to watch the honorable City Council commit a dubious deed. But if that is the case, then the deed will not be forgotten." She glared at Councilman Booker. "I beg you, vote 'No' to the resolution."

Her supporters stood and cheered. This was not the pitter-patter of adulation, but the roar of defiance. Eva Havlicek had used the word "coup," a strong noun rarely, if ever, heard inside council chambers. The mayor surmised that she knew much more about what was going on than he did. Her thick European accent had not detracted from her address, either. If anything, it had enhanced the seeming importance of the moment, while also setting an irreversible tone of confrontation. Mayor Kraus settled in, anxious to witness what would happen next.

After the applause died down, he called the next speaker. "Edwina Spurlock."

Once she arrived at the microphone, she turned around and beckoned toward the gallery. A man stood and moved in her direction. Mayor Kraus recognized him as the bullfighter who had saved the senior citizen down at the fairgrounds. Mayor Kraus still remembered his name. James Joseph O'Neal, "an esteemed citizen of the city." Two months ago when he was here to collect his proclamation he had been a pretty kid. Now he was grim, tanned, and fiercely handsome. Clutched under his forearm was a thick, neat file of paperwork contained in a big black binder. He let it plop to the podium so that the council could sense its weight. Pleased to the point of almost being smug, Edwina Spurlock turned her sights on the council.

"Mayor and honorable members of the City Council. I'm Edwina Spurlock, president of the Douglass Street Neighborhood Homeowners Association. And this is James O'Neal, the contractor." He nodded but said nothing. Edwina continued. "I must say that I was quite surprised to hear that the roofing contract was up for termination. I understand that Councilman Booker called today's meeting and placed the item on the agenda, and as an elected official, that's his prerogative. However, he never even consulted me about this resolution. If he had, I would have strongly urged him not to do it."

"Well, I heard there were problems," Councilman Booker said.

"Nothing we on Douglass Street can't handle."

"Are you sure? I hear a storm's coming."

"Hold on here," Councilman Kozlowski interjected. "What storm?"

"I'll let Mrs. Spurlock tell you about it, since she knows so much."

"If you're talking about the work that's being done, then there is no problem." She picked up James' binder. "Everything is here, Councilman Booker. And the men are four days ahead of schedule."

She set the binder back down.

"That's not what I'm talking about," Councilman Booker said, the smirk of victory in his eyes.

"Then tell us," Edwina demanded. "You're the one who called this meeting, not me. And since we're on the record, speak freely."

Edwina gestured toward the assistant city secretary who manned the tape recorder. Councilman Booker leaned back in his chair and laced his fingers across his chest. He made a show of being in a moment of deep thought. Then he leaned into his microphone.

"I hear there's gonna be a race war down there," he said, as if he were indicting Edwina.

"And who, might I ask, told you that?"

"They shall remain unnamed."

Council chambers went silent. Councilman Booker's words hung in the air like the smoke from burning tires. Eva stood, arms akimbo, and gestured for her supporters to rise. One by one and then in groups they stood with her. And there, in an instant, they charged the room with the intensity of a protest.

"So hold on here, let me get this straight," Councilman Kozlowski said. "You drug us down here—on a Friday—to have us terminate a one million dollar contract based on information told to you by an anonymous source?"

"Yes, I did."

Councilman Kozlowski shook his head in disgust.

"I make a motion that we reject the resolution as presented, and adjourn," he said.

"No, no, no, no, no," Mayor Kraus urged. "Councilman Booker called this meeting, so he should have to listen to everyone who signed up to speak. And there are thirty-seven more speakers. Mr. O'Neal, you're next."

James' fierceness dissipated into humility.

"I invite everyone on the City Council to come to Douglass Street and see the good work we're doing. The Douglass Street Restoration is a great program and I think it enhances not only the neighborhood, but all of Columbus. Me and my men enjoy the full support of Edwina Spurlock and the neighborhood association, and meeting the residents has been a great experience for me—and vote 'No' to the resolution."

And so it went.

Six Hispanics in work-worn T-shirts approached the podium one by one and asked the council to vote 'No.' Members of the neighborhood association, all of them black, middle-aged or elderly, respectfully stood before the council and asked it to reject Councilman Booker's proposal. Interspersed with the Douglass Street residents were students and Beckham's electioneers, some sporting exotic names like Alfonso Anku, Mingmei Yang, and Oxana Lisakovskya, while others bore American names such as Mike Jones, Frank Fuller, and Barbara Thurman. They all said the same thing—*Reject the resolution*! As each person came and went, Mayor Kraus grew more and more pleased that he had come to the meeting. With the exception of James and Edwina, he had never seen any of these people at City Hall. These were the real people, the ones who were too busy in their regular lives to attend public functions but who still cared about what went on in their city.

It was unspoken among council members that each of them had what was called a "gimme," a rare instant in municipal life when one elected official could look at another and say, "Do this for me," and it would be done without question. This was supposed to be Councilman Booker's "gimme," but somewhere between 2:30 and 4:30 things had drastically changed. And was Mayor Kraus relieved. If these people hadn't appeared, then the council would have voted "Aye" to the resolution and been back in their cars in five minutes flat. It was a roofing contract, for Christ's sake. Despite all the gushy rhetoric about cleaning up the city and making Columbus the centerpiece of Ohio, nobody on the council really cared about the Douglass Street Restoration. Approve the bids and listen to the final report from Mr. Wade, the grant's director. That was it. The duty of the constituency was to make their elected officials care, or at least make them fearful. Eva, Edwina and their supporters had done both today. Mayor Kraus glanced to his left and then to his right. With the exception of Councilman Booker, it appeared that this unlikely band of citizens had charmed everyone on the council.

At 5:36 the last speaker, a thick, slow-moving man in denim overalls and work boots approached the podium. A shimmering gold tooth showed in his mouth. His plump belly connoted the comfort and status of an elder. He chewed on a toothpick and walked with a limp.

"My name is John Dalrymple, and I live at 1021 Douglass Street. I'm retired military. Marines. Vietnam." He held his head high and cocked his chin with pride. "Councilman Booker, I know who you been talking to. But if you ain't man enough to say their names, then I ain't gonna say them for you. If you play around with fools you end up looking like a fool. We all know that." He held out his hands in a gesture of honor. "Now Mr. James O'Neal, the contractor, he a good man, and Miss Edwina, she a good lady. Anything infringe on them infringe on me. Vote 'No' to the resolution."

"Thanks, Mr. Dalrymple," Mayor Kraus said. "That concludes the public hearing."

And then it came time for Booker to make his move, thought Kraus. He needed four votes. If he got them, the bullfighter and his gang of roofers were out of a job, and the Douglass Street contract was back up for grabs. But before he could call for a vote, Booker had to rescue his embattled resolution.

"I appreciate all the comments," Councilman Booker said. "I wish all the issues that came before this body generated such passion. But before I call for a vote on this resolution, I would like to ask one question of you all." He paused for a few moments and took a sidelong glance at Mayor Kraus. He refocused on the gallery. "Of all the people who just came up to protest, who can actually vote in a Columbus city election? Don't be shy, now. Please, stand and let it be known."

Mayor Kraus saw that the number standing was far fewer than the 39 who had signed up to speak. Eva Havlicek, the brazen leader of the protest, remained seated and sullen, as did most of the electioneers, all the Hispanics, and some of the blacks. But Edwina Spurlock and the cluster around her stood, as did James and a few electioneers. Not quite the crew that it had been in the beginning, but formidable nonetheless. Councilman Booker had hoped for spades, thought Mayor Kraus, but had only managed to garner hearts.

Still, he had proven a point.

"That's what I thought. This protest was a stunt, organized by a lady who can't even vote." He pointed at Eva. "Little lady, I suggest you keep your nose out of city business and do whatever else it is you do. This here is for citizens, not for visitors. I make a motion that we accept the resolution and terminate Brimhall Roofing from Phase One of the Douglass Street Restoration, 'Due to unspecified transgressions against the integrity of the Douglass Street grant program.'"

"We have a motion on the floor, do we have a second?" Mayor Kraus said.

"I second the motion," Councilman Rinchuso said.

"Now that we have a second, are there any comments from the council?" Mayor Kraus said.

"Yes, I have a question," Councilwoman Thomas said. "I still haven't heard an explanation as to why there will be a 'race war' on Douglass Street. Mr. Booker, can you please elaborate?"

"I have a source."

"That's obvious," Councilwoman Thomas said, "but I want to know who that source is before I cast my note. Surely you can tell us where you got your information, since this is, after all, your meeting."

Booker remained silent. He straightened his tie and cleared his throat in an aggressive manner, implying that he was not about to honor the request. The Mayor, to his surprise, watched as Eva walked over to Edwina and huddled with her in whispered conversation. When the secretive discussion was done, she turned to face the council. "Councilwoman Thomas. I can tell you who his source is."

"So who is this person?" Thomas asked, "and what proof do they have that a race war is in the offing?"

"There is no proof. It is something Councilman Booker and his 'sources' want to create." Eva turned her sights on the Mayor. "Your friend is the instigator of this mess."

"What friend?" For Kraus, the pages of time were turning. In front of him was an important person, the likes of whom he'd never seen until today. The rigidity in her speech and movement betrayed apprehension, yet she also radiated certainty. Perhaps she had already seen herself in this situation and knew that victory was hers. She made a fist and her breast swelled. Impressed with her poise and mesmerized by the barbed wit of her tongue, he craved to hear the words she was about to speak.

"Clovis Whitfield, Mr. Mayor, is the man who speaks of a race war."

"Clovis Whitfield? The one who accused me of supporting apartheid?"

"Indeed."

"The one who called me a racist because I won't overturn a decision by the Civil Service Commission?"

"That would be him," Eva said. "He wants to sink his teeth into the Douglass Street grant, and is using trickery to do so."

Kraus, with an expression of rotten meat and burnt gravy, turned to Councilman Booker. "Did Clovis Whitfield ask you to sponsor this resolution?"

"Yes, he did!" Booker snarled. "We have to dissolve this contract before people start fighting in the streets!"

"Do not believe him, mayor. The people you see here are the ones who count." Eva gestured to her supporters. "Please, kill the resolution."

Mayor Kraus shook his head and sighed. The last thing he wanted was a racially charged, recorded public brawl over a mere roofing contract. He had too much to lose across all aspects of his life. And from the hardened looks of Eva and her supporters, and the recalcitrance of Councilman Booker, it seemed that this conversation could go on extant. Under authority of the city code, Mayor Kraus had the power to "call for the question," meaning he could end all discussion and go immediately to the vote. He chose to exercise that option.

"I move that we consider the motion as stated. All in favor of terminating the Brimhall Roofing contract, say aye?"

"Aye," Councilman Booker said, quickly and with confidence.

"Aye," followed Councilman Rinchuso.

Eva put her hands on her hips and turned her focus on Councilwoman Thomas. She motioned for her supporters to stand, and once more, they did. A hot, anticipatory hush settled in.

"All opposed, say nay," the mayor said.

"Nay," Councilwoman Thomas said, who was followed by three of her cohorts.

"This motion dies for lack of support," Mayor Kraus proclaimed. "I move that we adjourn."

"I second that motion," Councilman Kozlowski said.

"All in favor say, 'aye?'"

"Aye!" came the majority voice.

"This meeting is adjourned!"

Mayor Kraus slapped the gavel.

The crowd erupted with cheers, laughter and applause. Councilman Booker grabbed his keys and fled through the side door. But before he disappeared, he turned to Mayor Kraus. "You got hoodwinked by that foreign broad, and it'll cost you."

"It's better than being hoodwinked by Clovis Whitfield," the mayor said, dismissing him with the wave of a hand.

—

Leon sat with Clovis at his desk and waited for the phone call from Councilman Booker. He buffed his nails while Clovis leafed through a wrinkled, three-day-old edition of The New York Times. This was clearly the most important phone call in Leon's political career. With Brimhall ousted from Douglass Street, little could prevent him and Clovis from bilking thousands out of the remainder of the grant program. What charged this moment with such excitement was the fact that this was his plan. He had taken a modest pile of money, mixed it with a dash of street politics, and for good measure, sprinkled it with a show of force. If the scheme developed in accordance with Leon's dreams, he would have enough money to lay down eight percent on a one-bedroom ranch in White Hall. If only, he thought.

He peeled a stubborn hangnail from his left pinky and let it fall into the trashcan next to Clovis's desk.

Peering over the top of the paper, Clovis knit his brow and made eye contact with Leon.

"It's already five thirty," he complained. "I thought this was supposed to be a five-minute meeting."

Leon feigned nonchalance.

"No worries, brother. He's probably just taking his time."

Clovis caught the hint and returned to the paper.

Leon put his nail file away, crossed his hands over his stomach, and closed his eyes. For the thousandth time he asked himself if he was in over his head. Things had moved quickly since Dean appeared out of nowhere with an intriguing proposition and a pile of cash. Leon didn't think of himself as an utter fool. Still, he couldn't shake the notion that he was somehow "in the loop" while also being "out of the loop," and that frightened him. Here he was working for Dean, a man he didn't know, and working with Clovis, a man he didn't know, while waiting on Councilman Booker, yet another man he didn't know. The only thing that united them was the dollar bill, and that, Leon knew, was not enough to foster healthy relationships. His ultimate goal, domination of the Douglass Street Restoration, had taken him away from what was familiar. New faces greeted him with deference, or defiance, while old faces simply frowned and turned away. He was now in cahoots with Dean, a shady law school dropout, and Clovis, an ex-convict who used intimidation like a credit card.

Lordy, how he wished he was back at the bike shop with Tommy Charles.

And then the phone rang.

Clovis folded the paper, slid it onto the desk, and let the phone ring three more times. He mashed the speakerphone button. "Clovis Whitfield."

"Did you know I was headed into an ambush?" Councilman Booker said. His voice was so loud over the speakerphone that Clovis and Leon both grimaced. They exchanged sinking glances. Leon pointed to himself, intimating that he would be the first to respond. He cleared his throat.

"No, I didn't." Leon's voice was conciliatory.

"Are you sure, 'cause I ended up looking as silly as a preacher with an empty plate on Sunday!"

"I apologize, Councilman Booker. But hey, at least you got paid."

"Yeah, but it for damn sure wasn't worth it!"

"It's politics," Clovis said. "You win some and you lose some."

"Uh-huh. But I lost a battle that wasn't even mine. And I didn't just lose. I got my black ass kicked by a big 'ol white girl who can't even speak English."

Despite his disappointment, Leon grinned. Though he was surprised at what he had just heard, he knew what Booker was talking about.

Eva Havlicek had caused a scene at City Hall.

"Don't get down on yourself, Councilman Booker," Leon consoled. "That white girl speaks great English."

"The next time you two clowns come around wanting something from me, the price is gonna be high, or we don't have no deal. You hear that?"

"Loud and clear," Leon said.

Councilman Booker hung up.

"I don't know who that nigga think he talking to," Clovis said.

"He just mad because he don't have as much juice down at City Hall as he think he do."

Clovis stood up, stretched his thick shoulders and paced across the office. "So who's this white girl?"

He turned and caught Leon's eye with a terrible penitentiary gaze.

"She's a volunteer for the Beckham campaign."

"Then why was she down at City Hall fuckin' with my money?"

"Her boyfriend works for the roofing company."

Clovis nodded. "What's up with the way she talk?"

"She's from Europe. Czechoslovakia."

Clovis cupped his hand over his mouth and coughed. "If that commie chick get in my way one more time I'ma show her how we do things on the east side." He arched his brows and scowled.

Leon thought not of Eva, but of Anku, the warlord from Angola.

"Clovis, I'm only gonna tell you this one time, so you need to listen up. Be careful what you wish for."

—

Oxana grabbed a beer from the refrigerator and retreated to the relative quiet of James' front porch. She sat on the steps, wiped sweat from the back of her neck and took a refreshing drink. Inside in the living room, Century B, Eva's students and James danced to the "Saturday Night Fever" soundtrack as they celebrated the day's win at City Hall. Through the screen door, Oxana saw Barbara, clapping her hands above her head, leading a Conga line that inched forward with the juicy rhythm of a fat caterpillar. Eva, shoving herself against James, brought up the rear. They shouted and cheered and laughed and sang and stomped clumsily and drunkenly, but somehow kept time with the beat. Hips swung to and fro and heads bobbed, their spirits soaring through a super galaxy of exultation.

Oxana had been a part of that Conga line and had enjoyed her time inside its steamy links. But unlike the others, she wasn't blind with the joy of triumph. She felt that the stand at City Hall had undoubtedly been a great moment. Still, only a battle, not a war, had been won. The prevailing thought on Oxana's mind—what was next? Mindful that blood had already been shed, she took a drink of beer and grew sullen with speculation.

Inside, the revelers issued a concluding cheer as the last song from the soundtrack, "Disco Inferno," came to an end. A louder cheer arose when the pop elegance of ABBA sounded in the speakers. As "Dancing Queen" rolled into the first refrain, Brimhall pulled into the driveway in his teal diesel dually. As he approached the porch, a curious look came across his face.

"What's going on in there?"

"We are having a party to celebrate our victory at City Hall today," Oxana said. "You and James still have a contract."

"I know." He smiled. "I just came from Edwina's. She told me all about it. Thanks."

"You were not there today. Why not?"

"I was at the hospital getting my stitches taken out," he said, pointing toward the jagged pink line above his left eye, and a similar one across his left forearm. "I didn't know what was going on until it was over."

Oxana took a drink of beer. She gave Brimhall a warm smile and asked him to sit next to her on the steps. Eva had told Oxana everything she knew about Brimhall, which meant Oxana knew of the cross, the fight with the Nazis, his rooftop tutelage of James, and his hardscrabble upbringing in a white ghetto known as the Hilltop. Oxana could feel his toughness and liked that about him.

She had only met him a couple of times in passing, but felt an affinity for him. He sat next to her and propped his arms on his knees.

"So why aren't you in there with the others?"

"I was, but I thought I would come out here and think about life for a while."

As Oxana had hoped, he recognized the opening she had given him.

"What part of life?"

"All this mess that we find ourselves in."

From inside came several voices, Eva's chief among them, imploring Oxana to come dance. The music selection had shifted to reggae, while the shouts and cheers remained the same.

"I will be there in a minute," Oxana called, and then turned to Gene. "Tell me the truth. Do you think they would be in there dancing if the City Council had fired you and James? And if you say yes, I would like to hear your justification."

"No, you're right," he conceded. "If the City Council had done what it was supposed to do, I reckon things would be downright gloomy around here."

"And Eva would have taken the blame. Remember, we had a chance to quit the election, but we voted to move forward. And when we did, something almost happened to James—Dean Bernadette's threat nearly came to fruition."

A loud thud sounded in the living room, and then came silence. "I'm all right, I'm all right," someone exclaimed, and then came applause and wild shouts. The music returned, and with it, the jolly flow of celebration. Oxana and Gene exchanged glances but did not comment on what they had heard.

"But if we would've gotten fired by the City Council, how would it have been Eva's fault?" Brimhall said. "From what I heard, James told you guys to keep moving forward in the election and to not worry about us. He did the right thing."

"True, but Eva is a bit self-centered. She would have pointed the finger at herself. And if that were to happen it would not be good."

"I can understand," he said. "But how bad would it be?"

"I know Eva better than anyone in the United States, and since I have watched her bloom in the last two years, I like to think that I know her better than anyone except her family and all but the closest of her friends back home. If something were to go wrong, she would not forgive herself. She would flee from James and never look back. The shame would be too much for her to confront. She puts on a strong show—and it is true—but still, she is not invulnerable."

"So what are you trying to say, Oxana?"

"That if it is in my power, I will not let her lose. When she first got here the little university boys would come calling. They would brag to her about how many languages they could speak, but Eva speaks six languages, so she is not impressed. They would brag to her about all the places they have lived. But Eva has lived in five countries, I think, so travel does not make her swoon. But then she meets James, and he is a workingman who has no university education. Yet he is brave and strong and kind and generous, and in his own way, extremely intelligent. She has not said so, but I think she loves him."

"Already?"

"From the moment they met," Oxana said, batting her eyes. "Then came the election and the roofing contract and Century B and this jackrabbit named Dean Bernadette. Eva finds herself far away from where she was just a month ago, and she is clinging to James as if he were a life raft. Now tell me, what would happen if the life raft were to sink?"

"Figuratively speaking, Eva would drown, and her time here in the states would be ruined."

"You see my point," Oxana said. "The stakes are high, much higher for her than they are for me. I am not in love, and this game of democracy? I am not yet sure I like the rules. But if Eva wants to play, she should play and win."

Oxana drained her beer and stood. "Are you going inside to dance?"

"It's not my kind of music. I'm a two-stepper, not an ass-shaker. And you?"

"When duty calls, I can shake my ass with the best of them," she said, and went inside.

A chorus of praise and encouragement greeted her entry. Barbara reimplemented the Conga line. Oxana slid in, wrapped her arms around Eva's slender hips, and held on for the ride.

———

Leon leaned back in the Formica bench and took the first delicious sip of morning coffee. He pulled out the Metro Section of Saturday's edition of the *Scioto Times*, spread it across the table and scanned the headlines. Nothing interested him. He flipped through the inside pages, but saw no familiar names in the obituaries. He arrived at the Back Page, and to his amazement, saw a large, color photograph of Eva Havlicek crouched over the podium at City Hall. Beneath the photograph ran a crisp, 20-inch story written by Dominick Van Buren—***Residents Rally for Housing Contract***. Reading the article, Leon grew uneasy with the thought of his name appearing alongside Clovis Whitfield's in the largest newspaper in central Ohio. In victory, an alliance with Clovis could prove beneficial, but in defeat, embarrassing. Relieved that he was never mentioned, Leon returned to what he now recognized as a telling portrait of his archrival.

The photograph was a panorama, as if the photographer had stood on something and shot downward with a wide-angle lens. Eva's sharp profile, caught inside the narrow confines of a wide aperture, stood in dramatic contrast to the fuzzy faces of the large group of supporters behind her. The arm held above her head. Her mouth wide open yet stately in her grievance. This, Leon thought, must have been the moment when she had said, "I am Eva Havlicek, and I am here to crush the coup!" Beyond the focus on Eva was the City Council, a series of fuzzy blobs behind the most important dais in Columbus. Leon looked at the photograph for a long time as he drank his coffee and finished his menthol. Joe, the owner of the café, came to the table and poured another cup.

Leon pointed to the photograph. "What do you think about her?"

"She look like a baaaad mamma jamma," Joe said.

Leon smiled and silently agreed. He looked through the storefront window and saw his crew arrive on the fleet of British cruisers. Blue and white Bernadette banners fixed to makeshift flagpoles curled in the breeze. The back racks loaded with yard signs. Stacks of handbills bound in rubber bands rested in the baskets. His men appeared as they should, early and dressed in suits. Leon rolled up the newspaper, tucked it under his arm, and dropped a two-dollar tip on the Formica table. He slid his left hand into his pant pocket, leaned slightly and let his right arm dangle. In his finest north-side stroll, he walked across the café and through the front door. With a histrionic sense of importance playing in his face, Leon looked north and then south. Cleveland Road roared with early morning traffic. He plucked a pair of shades from his breast pocket and slid them over his nose, then grabbed his crotch and clicked his heels three times. His men laughed at the bravado.

"We got work to do, gentlemen."

They pedaled off into the campaign.

C U B I C
Z I R C O N I U M

Oxana stood at a German Village bus stop at dusk on Sunday. She and Eva had just eaten dinner at Café Barcelona. Sated by salad, broiled walleye, fried soft shell crab in cream sauce, steamed vegetables, cheesecake, and three glasses of Pouilly Fuisse, Oxana was eager to return to her north campus flat, curl up in front of the TV, and watch reruns of her favorite show of all time, "Dallas." She kissed Eva on both cheeks, said goodbye, and watched her friend until she reached the end of the block and turned out of view, en route to a rendezvous at her flat with James.

As the bus crept slowly toward the stop, Oxana looked across the street and was amazed at what she saw. Standing on the sidewalk by the side kitchen door with several restaurant employees was Dean Bernadette, the guy who was causing trouble for Eva and Century B. Oxana read the small wooden sign hanging over the front door—The Mohawk Grill. Dean must have gone there often, thought Oxana, because the way he gestured and laughed with the employees suggested that he knew them well. Had she not known him for the scoundrel that he was, she could have mistaken him for a regular guy. He wore spiffy eyeglasses, a dark suit with a white shirt, black suspenders and a yellow bow tie. His dark hair combed and gelled. Hanging from his shoulder, the brown leather satchel that he'd carried on the one occasion she'd seen him. If anything, Dean looked like a banker who had just gotten out of church.

Oxana knew better.

She was the only person in Columbus who recognized Dean for what he truly was, a wannabe Mafioso. A native of Kazakhstan, Oxana was an expert on the mob. They had controlled the country since shortly after the fall of the Soviet Union in 1991. Dean, Oxana believed, was driven by the same eternal greed that motivated the crime syndicates back home. If the election and the big zoning vote went in Dean's favor, millions of new dollars would flood into Columbus. Using threats of violence and promises of political ruin, like they did in Kazakhstan, Dean could manipulate the sale of special-use variances, plat approvals and construction permits. He could extort money from contractors in exchange for favorable government votes, like they did in Kazakhstan. If Dean were an authentic gangster, however, Brimhall would be dead, James would be out of a job, and Eva would be sleeping with George Beckham. None of those things had happened because Dean didn't have the requisite apparatus to be a real mobster. True, violent and shrewd. And in time, perhaps, he would assemble the gang he'd need for a career in crime. At this point, though, Dean was still a wannabe.

Oxana could have hopped on the bus and gone on with her business—a quiet night of reruns with J.R. and Bobby Ewing. But the election was still in the balance, and Dean needed to be punished for his wicked deeds. In an instant of clarity, perhaps fueled by the Pouilly Fuisse, Oxana knew how to tear the guts out of this election while also avenging the wrongs inflicted on Eva, Brimhall and James. The bus pulled up to the stop and the door folded open. "No," said Oxana, and waved the bus driver away. After the bus cleared her path, she strolled across the street and walked straight toward Dean and the group of employees from The Mohawk Grill. Dean approached the punch line of a story, talking excitedly and flailing his arms. "And then I said, 'Screw you, Johnson, I drank all the wine, and I'm from Texas!'" The employees howled and slapped him on the back. Dean doled out high-fives and did a jig, and then he noticed Oxana. He straightened his stance and watched her cross the street.

Dean has only seen me once, thought Oxana, when I was wearing Frank's big hat and sunglasses. She wondered if he knew who she was.

"Can I have a cigarette?" she said to Dean.

"Yes you can," he said, in a playboy's voice. He shook a cigarette from the pack. Oxana fumbled in her purse for a lighter.

"Allow me."

He pulled a Zippo from one of the satchel's front pouches and lit it for her.

"Thank you."

"The pleasure's all mine."

For several seconds their eyes locked. Oxana saw nothing but a kindling of lust, and as it applied to her plan, kindling lust was a good thing. Oxana gave him a polite nod and left for the bus stop on High Street four blocks away. From behind she heard the nasty laughter that follows a dirty comment, but Oxana was too excited about her new plan to be offended. She would remain with Century B, but the campaign, at least for her, would no longer be waged on the dirty asphalt of Cleveland Road. She was moving her operation to the cobbled, shady lanes of German Village, and to what was now her favorite bar, The Mohawk Grill.

"What a wannabe," she said to herself as the bus rumbled northward on High Street. "He doesn't even recognize me, yet I am his greatest enemy."

—

She appeared from nowhere, gazed straight into his eyes, and gave him a salacious wink. The boys from The Mohawk Grill had witnessed the event, giving Dean proper cause to gloat over his virility. Dean was good at talking women into bed. He'd heckle them with a fake Southern twang, and then it was off to the duplex he rented on Bruck Street. Every bar had a lecher, and Dean filled that designated spot at The Mohawk Grill. Conquest of the woman he'd met Sunday could only enhance the prurient legend he liked to perpetuate. Tall with shiny black hair, voluptuous curves, and eyes as enchanting as a train ride through the mist. A trophy of a woman. She also had an accent, and that made Dean skeptical. After the hot carnal thoughts had died down, he pondered Eva and Century B.

Was it possible that Eva had dispatched one of her lieutenants down to The Mohawk to spy on him? Would she do something like that, or was she too much of a prude? He hated to admit that the Czech had gotten into his head, especially since he'd only spoken to her once, but here he was, wondering if she knew about his deals with Leon and Trey, and the illegal cash contributions from J.D. Pruitt. After a long internal debate, he ruled out the possibility that the woman he'd met Sunday was one of Eva's minions. Still, he looked through his notes for a name—and he found one. *LISAKOVSKYA*. He had written it down the day he followed Eva to Neal Avenue. *Lisakovskya*. A name like that didn't come without an accent. "Can I have a cigarette?" she'd said. Lisakovskya. Dean was no internationalist, but the name, and thus the accent, he presumed to be Russian.

Monday morning he made a call to Beckham's campus headquarters.

"Hello," said the receptionist.

"Hi, my name is John Jones and I'm a reporter with the *Scioto Times*," Dean said. "I'm writing a feature story about the volunteers who call themselves Century B."

"Great. How can I help you?"

"I need to make sure I've got a name spelled correctly. Lisakovskya?"

"Hold on for a second."

Dean heard her shuffling through papers.

"Here we are," she said. "Oxana Lisakovskya. L-I-S-A-K-O-V-S-K-Y-A."

"And how do you spell that first name again?"

"Oxana. O-X-A-N-A."

"And she's from Moscow, right?"

"No. It says here she's from Almaty, Kazakhstan."

"Great. You just kept me from making three errors. I appreciate it."

"No problem. Just write a good story. She's a great girl."

Oxana Lisakovskya from Almaty, Kazakhstan. Dean poured a victory drink and took a big gulp. He jumped on the Internet. He paused at the keys before typing "Soviet Union." He clicked the subject bar. He soon had the information he needed. Kyrgyzstan, Tajikistan, Turkmenistan, Uzbekistan and Kazakhstan—all former constituent republics in the former U.S.S.R.—where Russians live.

Dean grinned. He was anxious to meet Oxana again.

—

Salenka Stepanova Bolinskya's house teemed with life. Counting extended family, husbands, wives, and their children, the four-bedroom Italianate at 853 Dennison Ave. was itself a Russian enclave of 23 people. Clothes always hung from lines in the backyard. A baby always cried. The feet of so many children had trampled the front yard so that grass no longer grew there. Before heading to the early shift, the second shift, or the graveyard shift, workers smoked and drank coffee in the kitchen. Ancient women who remembered the Russian Revolution sat like stones on the front porch. The scents of disinfectant and bleach used to fend off the filth and stench of life lingered throughout the cavernous house. The TV in the living room constantly blared with Russian sitcoms and soap operas beamed in by satellite. The Russians who lived at Salenka's Place were not double-masters students like Oxana, but real immigrants who worked for pennies as bakers, dry cleaners, maids, and garbage men. Oxana knew them because she was a Russian from Kazakhstan, and if you were a Russian from Kazakhstan and you lived in Columbus, you knew all the other Russians from Kazakhstan who lived in Columbus. Like Oxana, the residents at Salenka's place were South Ural Russians with a dark drop of Tartar.

Salenka, known as Anka, was an unreconstructed Red Bolshevik who presided over the house as if she were secretary of the politburo. The Star and Sickle flew proudly at Anka's place. English, the language of survival and of commerce. Russian, the language of the soul, and it was spoken around the clock at Anka's place. Quick to scold yet reluctant with praise, Anka was the master matriarch, the iron dame on the capitalist frontier. She poked, pried and jested at failings. She was sober 99.9 percent of the time, but when .01 came around, she got sloppy drunk on Vodka and screamed like a banshee. Mired in the tough bravura of her rule, Anka was bitterly disdainful of those she thought lived lives of meaningless leisure. Oxana was no Bolshevik, and at times she grew weary of Anka's caustic wit. Still, Anka's loyalty sustained Oxana as she journeyed down the American road, and her name was writ large on the short list of the people she loved.

They were in the top bedroom near a window that overlooked the brick row houses across the street. On one porch, students played acoustic guitars and sang. On the next a knot of friends joked and laughed as they huddled around a keg. A third porch was crowded with artsy types who smoked pot as they reclined in lawn chairs and hammocks. On the last, two intellectuals hoisted bottled beers and debated the origins of the French Revolution. From the window Oxana could see the handsome stone columns that marked the entrance to the emerald, oak-studded expanse of Goodale Park. The scene bathed in the golden hue of Friday twilight. A somber smile came to her face. She knew she would never again live in a town blessed with such easy charms.

Oxana sat in a chair, painting her fingernails red, while Anka stood behind her and trimmed her hair. Tatiana and Dimitri, two of Anka's six children, slept on the bed.

"I don't understand why you dishonor yourself by dressing up like a *suka*," Anka said. "And you do all this for Eva?"

"I'm doing this for a lot of people," Oxana said. "But yes, mostly for Eva."

"The Czechs," Salenka said, and sighed. "They think too much. All a woman needs is food on the table, a sturdy roof over her head, obedient children, and a strong man, like my Stepan, who likes to hang his pants on the bedpost. Eva has led you astray by making you think that a woman needs more than that. And now this?"

"Anka, you're jealous of Eva," Oxana said, speaking into the mirror.

"Perhaps," Anka said. "But still I speak the truth. Eva has poisoned your brain."

Anka rubbed oil into Oxana's scalp and hair, and then combed the shiny locks into a fine satin coat. She pulled the hair back tight, and interlaced pieces of red and gold silk into a single Slavic braid that fell between Oxana's shoulder blades. She traced Oxana's eyes with liner and painted her lips with soft cherry. Around her neck a strand of cubic zirconium, on her ears a pair of silver studs, and around her wrist a dollar-store bracelet of faux silver hearts. Having dabbed sampler perfume on her wrists and neck, Oxana slid into a black sheath and stepped into a pair of black pumps. And there in the mirror she stood, Oxana Petrovna Lisakovskya, a *suka* from the steppes.

"When he sees your braid he will want to unlock it, and when he does he will be yours for as long as you'll have him," whispered Anka.

From deep within her dresser drawer Anka fetched a peculiar amber vial. When she opened it, the stink of cat urine assaulted Oxana's nostrils. Suddenly, the room went sweet with the scent of yearning roses.

"What's that?" Oxana said.

"Oh," Anka said, as a few drops dripped into the palm of her hand, "just an old trick from back home."

She rubbed the liquid in her hands and grabbed the top of Oxana's braid. She worked her hands from the top down until the thick rope of hair was coated with the potion. Oxana felt a warm tingling in her crotch.

"Is there black magic in the braid?" she said.

"But of course," Anka hissed. "Go and claim what it is you seek."

From a dresser drawer Anka grabbed a thin stack of documents wrapped in a blue, ink-stained rubber band. With a deep breath and a grave expression,

Oxana took the documents and stuffed them into her purse. From the window she saw the dusty cab pull up to the curb. Oxana and Anka kissed each other on both cheeks and shared a brief embrace.

Oxana dashed down the stairs. She slid into the back seat of the Acme cab.

"Where to, miss?"

She pulled a cigarette from her clutch. "The Mohawk Grill."

———

If Oxana Lisakovskya from Almaty, Kazakhstan looked for him, then Dean intended to be found. After the Sunday encounter, he made sure he went to The Mohawk Grill everyday instead of appearing spontaneously, as was his custom. Monday, Tuesday, Wednesday, Thursday—and then Friday. She entered with the grace and distinction of an empress. Compared to Oxana, the other women in the bar were wilted dandelions. Dean watched her with an air of nonchalance. Seated at the bar, she ordered a shot of vodka. She lit a cigarette. Through the smoke she glanced at Dean, sitting at the far end of the L-shaped bar. The left corner of her mouth bent into a seductive smile. She beckoned with the raising of an eyebrow. Dean considered the colossal question of what might happen tonight. If this actually was Oxana, and if she were acting as an agent for the Beckham campaign, then she was going to get hurt, and badly, before the sun came up Saturday morning. But what if she was just an easy rider out looking for action on a Friday night? Dean swallowed his paranoia, grabbed his Bombay and tonic, and meandered through the crowd, her immense beauty steering him with the force of an ocean tide. Before speaking, he took note of the steep cheekbones and gazed into the twinkling universe in her eyes. Breathing in the scent of her perfume, he gawked at the exquisite, ribbon-laced braid. His pulse quickened. The steel hit the flint and the fuse was lit.

"I'm Dean," he said.

"I am Alexandra."

"Nice to meet you," he said, slowly. "So I hear an accent. Where are you from?"
"Russia." She stamped out her cigarette. "Chelyabinsk."

———

At 4:14 a.m. on Saturday, Dean slid out from underneath the covers and tiptoed into the den. Her purse sat on the coffee table next to a half-empty bottle of Vodka and an ashtray crammed with cigarette butts. He unzipped the purse and rifled through the contents. Lipstick, Marlboros, a small wad of cash, chewing gum, a bus pass—and a small stack of documents tied off with a blue, ink-stained rubber band. He removed the rubber band and set the passport, the student I.D., and the visa on the table. He tiptoed into the living room and grabbed the Russian-English dictionary he'd purchased at Long's Book Store just for this very occasion. The student I.D. listed Alexandra Mikhailovicha Vitkovskya as a student at Ohio State. The visa listed the same person as qualified to work in the U.S. And then he turned his attention to the Russian passport, which was written in Cyrillic. Flipping through the passport's back pages he saw five stamps—Poland, Germany, Denmark, England, and the United States, but not Kazakhstan. Using the dictionary's English-Cyrillic alphabet, he deciphered the vital information in the passport. Name, Alexandra Mikhailovicha Vitkovskya. Date of a birth, July 10, 1971. The birthplace, Chelyabinsk. The documents were current. The photographs on the student I.D. and the passport looked a lot like the woman curled up in his bed.

He took one last look at the passport. Dean just couldn't believe that Eva Havlicek would violate international law by sending in an operative with a fake, borrowed, or stolen passport. Eva was formidable, he admitted, but she was too much of a twat to do something like that. Was this a friend of Oxana's? An act of violence hung in the balance. "Stop being so goddamned paranoid," Dean said to himself. He carefully rewrapped the documents with the rubber band and put them back in the purse—just as Oxana and Anka had hoped. He peed, drank a handful of water, and returned to the bedroom. He slid under the sheets and snuggled up close to Alexandra.

He couldn't wait to tell the boys back at the Mohawk that he'd bagged an authentic Russian snow leopard from Chelyabinsk. As the clock hit 4:34, Dean leaned back on the pillow and yawned. Alexandra kissed him on the neck and whispered something sweet and Russian in his ear. Drained of energy and with his faculties fleeting, Dean fell into a deep, unrelenting sleep. On the wings of dreams, he arrived triumphant at the shining gates of utopia.

—

At 8:03 a.m. Saturday the cab arrived at Ankas's place. From the bedroom window, Anka watched Oxana, disheveled and dull with fatigue, step out from the rear passenger-side door. A bulging leather satchel hung from her shoulder. Anka raced down the steps and met her at the door. It didn't appear that Oxana had been injured, but Anka could tell that she had been crying. In grave silence, Oxana handed the passport, Visa and student I.D. to Anka and headed upstairs.

Anka looked at the young girl pictured in the passport and shook her head. Outside of having black hair and dark eyes, Alexandra Mikhailovicha Vitkovskya looked nothing like Oxana. Perhaps the potion in the ponytail had worked, or maybe Oxana's adversary was not as clever as once imagined. Regardless, Anka gazed long and dolefully at her friend's smiling face in the passport, and allowed herself a rare moment of grief.

Alexandra Mikhailovicha Vitkovskya came to the United States in the last wave of 20th Century Russian immigration. Alexandra soon met a young American, fell in love and made plans for a wedding. A few months before the nuptials, doctors told Alexandra that she would never have children. The radioactive waste she'd inadvertently ingested all her life in a village outside Chelyabinsk had ruined her reproductive system. Rather than face the ignominy of life as a barren woman, she went to the top of the parking tower near University Hospital and jumped. Before the suicide she paid a visit to Anka, who had no idea of Alexandra's intentions, and secretly dropped off her passport, visa and student ID. Anka found the documents a week later while cleaning out the hallway closet. Anka never turned the documents over to the consulate because she always knew Alexandra's credentials would be important. Until now she didn't know why. She went upstairs to her bedroom and stashed the documents deep inside the top dresser drawer.

"What is done is done," Anka said. "Now we await the storm."

———

Oxana awoke at 6 p.m. Sunday from a deep slumber. She rubbed her eyes, walked through a cloud of guilt to the bathroom and peed. She washed her mouth out with cold water but dared not look in the mirror. Yawning, she walked downstairs to the kitchen. Stepan sat at the table drinking coffee and smoking cigarettes with Yevgeny. A pot of beef stew simmered on the stove. Young Tatiana stood on a stool and washed dishes. Oxana poured a cup of coffee, grabbed a cigarette from Stepan's pack, and took a seat at the table.

"Where's Anka?" She yawned.

"At the grocery store with Mita," Stepan said, as two jets of smoke curled from his nostrils. "The stew is ready."

Oxana ate and listened to Stepan and Yevgeny complain about their jobs unloading cargo during the third shift at a warehouse on the south side. They hated their boss because he laughed as he called them "Rooskies" or "Reds." She liked the fact that Stepan did not poke and pry about the weekend's activities. The cadence of pure Russian soothed her aching conscience. Oxana finished the stew and poured another cup of coffee. She took the cordless phone and went out back to the ramshackle courtyard. She called Eva. James answered.

"Hello, James," she said. "It is Oxana. Is Eva there?"

"Hey, Oxana. She's here. I'll see if I can peel her off the couch. Sometimes

I think she's addicted to C-Span." James called Eva's name. Moments later she was on the phone.

"Oxana?"

"How's my favorite electioneer?" she said in Russian.

"I haven't heard from you all weekend." Eva's voice was husky with concern. "I left messages at your house but you never returned my calls. Are you okay?"

"I'm fine. I was with Anka."

"Oh." Eva sounded miffed. "You missed the campaign. We went out Friday and Saturday. Frank and the others asked about you."

"How is Frank?"

"Fine, but he's always better when you're around." Oxana chuckled, but her laughter was stale and empty.

"What are you doing later?"

"Studying," Eva said.

"Can I come over before you start?"

"Of course. Is there something wrong?"

"I wouldn't necessarily say wrong. You'll understand when I get there."

"Do you need a ride?"

"No, I'm walking. I'm going to take a quick shower and then I'll come over."

"I'll be waiting on the porch."

Oxana showered. She slid into a blouse, a tight pair of third-hand Jordache jeans and a pair of sneakers. She grabbed Dean's satchel, and with a woeful stirring in her soul, threw it over her shoulder and made her way to James' house. Stepan and Yevgeny walked with her.

The first thing Oxana saw when she rounded the corner at Third and Oregon was Eva, standing on the porch, bright with curiosity. Oxana nearly lost her nerve, yet she kept walking, showing nothing but her usual confidence. Stepan and Yevgeny had no idea of what was happening, but Oxana had hinted that she was frightened and needed their protection. They stayed with her until she reached the steps of James' house. Oxana and Eva hugged and kissed on each cheek. Stepan and Yevgeny remained in the background, smoking in silence beneath a tree. Oxana glanced over her shoulder. She wished she was still with them.

"So," Eva said, with a huff, "you are here."

She propped her hands on her hips like a peeved grandmother. Oxana gave her a cold stare and dropped Dean's satchel at her feet.

"What is this?" Eva gave her a sharp, disapproving glance.

"A key to the election, perhaps."

"No, no, no," Eva protested. "What is it?"

The speed and focus of Eva's anger surprised Oxana. She realized that Eva intuitively knew that this was Dean Bernadette's satchel. The hard inquiry was more an expression of disbelief than it was a question. Oxana remained defiant, absorbing every liquid ounce of Eva's dissatisfaction.

"How did you get this?" she demanded.

Oxana said nothing. Pointing to the satchel and stomping her foot, Eva asked again.

"How did you get this?"

Oxana walked across the porch and grabbed one of the glasses of red wine Eva had poured before she arrived. She took a long pull and set the glass back down.

"I stole it," she said.

The bold confession refreshed her nerves. Now she was ready for Eva's scorn. But before Eva could grouse, Oxana continued.

"Must you know the source of every river you cross?"

"At the least I must try. Where did you get Dean Bernadette's satchel?"

"From his house Saturday morning. I fucked him for it. Twice. He was sleeping and I stole it. I met him at The Mohawk Grill on Friday night. I was dressed like a *suka* and I seduced him. Eva, I will not apologize."

"The reason why you didn't return my calls is because you were fucking Dean Bernadette at his house?"

"Correct."

"That's disgusting, Oxana. Leave this porch." Her voice sunk into a slow alto. "And take the satchel with you."

"I'll leave, but I'm not taking this with me." She pointed to the bulging leather sack. "It's up to you to decide the next step."

Eva didn't like the outright challenge to her authority. Oxana had always been pleasingly obedient.

"Do you think that this is an expression of friendship?"

"Among other things, yes. This election is important to you."

"It's not more important than my propriety."

"Don't worry about your propriety, Eva. I've taken care of all that. Keep the satchel. I'm sure there's something in there that you can use against your rival. Smear him! *Win!*"

"You Russians play by different rules."

"That's right." A baleful grin danced in Oxana's eyes. "Just don't forget that there are Russians on your side."

—

Brimhall couldn't believe his eyes. In front of him on James' kitchen table sat Dean Bernadette's beige satchel. The supple bag clearly played a significant role in Dean's life. The leather's rich patina and the many folds and creases were proof that the satchel had been on his hip-and-shoulder for years. The sheer volume of material that appeared to be inside suggested that Dean used this bag for all his needs. Brimhall salivated at the prospect of sorting through the contents. Indeed, that is what he would do—once he and James had convinced Eva to tell them exactly how the satchel came to be here.

"Eva, this is very, very serious," James coaxed. "We need to know how Oxana got this thing."

Up until this point, all Eva would say is that Oxana had somehow gained possession of the bag. Her countenance, however, betrayed that she knew much more. James and Brimhall were keen to her reticence and continued to press for information and news.

"Eva," said Brimhall, "we won't repeat what you tell us."

She looked at James, who nodded his agreement. Eva stood from her chair, paced across the dining room and drained her glass of wine.

"She seduced Dean Bernadette and stole it while he slept," she blurted. "This weekend—in his own house!"

James and Brimhall turned toward one another and exchanged the dusky looks of conspirators. Brimhall's hazel eyes lit up like pilfered diamonds. "Damn. I didn't see that one coming."

"Nor did I," Eva said. "What should we do?"

"For now we're keeping it," Brimhall said. "He pulled an episode out of my life and used it against me. I'ma do the same thing to him."

"We cannot keep this, can we?"

"Why not?"

"Because, it is not ours."

"Yeah it is," Brimhall said. "Look, it's right here. Right, James?"

Eva turned and burrowed into her boyfriend with a powerful stare that said, "Side with me, lover."

But James had already made his decision. "Brimhall's right. We're keeping it."

Eva breathed the heavy sigh of disappointment. Brimhall felt the need to explain what was about to happen so that she would be at ease. Brimhall liked Eva and James as a couple. If he didn't step in and take charge right now, this situation could spiral out of control and spell lasting trouble for their young relationship.

"First off, you did nothing wrong," he said. "Second, I'm gonna turn this bag and its contents over to my attorney. Your name will never be mentioned. This is my deal now. Does that make you feel any better?"

Eva wrapped her arms around James and put her head on his shoulder. "Somewhat," she conceded. "But I am still at odds with Oxana."

"If she's a real friend, and if you're a real friend, you'll get over your differences and move on. Eva, it's about time we started fighting back. Something tells me Oxana knew that. I know the whole thing is kind of over the top. But look! We've got Dean's life in our hands!"

She looked at the satchel for a long time.

"I must study," she said at last, and retired to her books.

"Come on, James." Brimhall rubbed his hands together with gleeful anticipation. "This motherfucker took me off the rooftops and put me in the hospital. He cussed your girlfriend. He's trying to get us fired from the contract and he's using the race card to do it. If there's any revenge to be had, my friend, I'll have it."

James took a seat. Brimhall unbuttoned the top flap and dug into the satchel with both hands. He pulled out spiral pads, legal pads, and manila folders packed with documents. He rifled through the pockets and among the standard trifles found a little black book, a brand new buck knife, and a half-empty vile of cocaine. Brimhall made two stacks, one for himself and the other for James. They commenced to digging. What they found did not disappoint them. More than two hours into their task, reading through page after page of blackmail notes, Eva peeped into the dining room. Brimhall looked up from a document and laughed.

"I knew it," he said. "I knew you'd come around."

Eva feigned embarrassment as she took a seat at the dining room table.

"Read this." James shoved a stack of documents in her direction.

WINDSOR TERRACE

Dean fell into a serious fit of paranoia soon after he realized that "Alexandra" had disappeared with his satchel. The sheer pleasure of the sexual experience didn't compensate for the monumental sense of impotence at having been duped by the oldest trick in the book. "Hell," Dean said to himself, "I'm a sad sack of shit just like all those losers on 'Jerry Springer.'" The information in the leather bag could sink his uncle's election bid and his practice. But he thought he'd been prepared. Before heading out to the Mohawk in search of "Alexandra," he'd taken the damning blackmail notes from his desk and put them inside the satchel and then hid the satchel in the kitchen pantry right next to the bag of campaign money. That the cash was still there told him that she had come for the satchel and nothing else.

"Fuck, man."

Unable to find solace in his sober head, Dean turned to other sources of comfort.

He bought an ounce of hydroponic pot and a liter of gin and locked himself inside his house. He turned off his landline, pager and cell phone, and smoked marijuana with the zeal of the addict who finally returns to his one true love. He tilted back a frightening gulp of gin and nearly fell down from the double punch of drink and pot. His anxiety evaporated in the toxic rush. But once the surge had subsided, he was again fretting over the fate of the satchel and its contents. He returned to the glass pipe again and again, and drank the gin in monstrous swigs. In just an hour Dean lie spread-eagle on the kitchen floor. When he woke up, he did it all over again. He lived like that for three days, leaving the house once when he needed more alcohol.

On the fourth day, famished and reeking, he realized that the world still turned. He nursed himself back to health with two gallons of Gatorade, a baguette, and a crock-pot of chicken spaghetti. By the fifth day Dean was nowhere near 100 percent but was well enough to get out of bed and face the day. He shaved for the first time in a week, took a long hot shower, and masturbated to "Alexandra." Refreshed, he turned on his landline, pager and cell phone, and started the laundry. He didn't answer the 51 messages left on his cell phone. He didn't call the numbers left on his pager or return the messages on his answering machine. He knew his uncle and Leon had made most of those calls. Both of them were probably pissed that he had fallen off the face of the earth for nearly a week. But Dean wasn't worried. A ticker running on the bottom of the TV news had a glorious headline—***Bernadette and Beckham to Duel in Runoff.***

Dean poured himself a cup of coffee. He put on a pair of sweats and a T-shirt and stepped out to the front porch, where a bright and cheerful sun greeted him.

"Now," he thought to himself, as he reached down and grabbed the newspaper, "where was I?"

It didn't take long to find his bearings. Inside, the cell phone rang. He apprehensively glared at the message window. It was Leon. Dean returned to the porch before he clicked the receive button.

"Hello."

"Where in the hell have you been, man?" Leon said. "Shit's been going crazy and you haven't answered your phone in a week! Your uncle's been calling me and so have his punk-ass campaign managers."

"I was out of town. Sorry I didn't tell you before I left."

"You a lie. If you had went out of town for a whole damn week your uncle would've known about it. I have my own thoughts about what happened, but I'll reserve comment. The next time you leave me holding a bag full of shit, you best let me know beforehand. Dig?"

"Why are your panties in a knot? Didn't you see the news this morning? We're in the runoff, and we're in the runoff with a four-point lead."

"True, but it sounds like you didn't see the bad news."

"Like what?"

"Like I'm getting my ass kicked up on Cleveland Road. You didn't look at the precinct-by-precinct numbers on the back page? My count ain't scientific, but Century B beat my ass. And Millbury's thrown his support behind Beckham. We're in trouble, Dean."

"But my uncle won Morse Road. Those are the only people who'll come back out for the runoff."

"See, that's where you're wrong, and that's why we've been trying to get in touch with you. Before you disappeared do you remember seeing Eva Havlicek in the paper—when she showed up at City Hall for the roofing contract?"

"Yeah," Dean said, his voice ramping down.

"Well, call it the power of the press, 'cause the next time she came up to Cleveland Road she had forty people with her. Dean, people saw her in the paper and now they're volunteering for her, not Beckham. The people up on Cleveland Road think she's famous, so when she comes around, she gets a lot of attention."

"Can't you do anything about it?"

"Not now. Hell, she's Greta Garbo. I can't get black folks to work for free, Dean, and I've run out of money. Your uncle and his people say the only way I can get campaign cash is through you. What I'm saying is, I didn't campaign with my bike brigade in the four days leading up to the election, but Century B tore it up from dawn to dusk. That's why they have the numbers and we don't."

"Motherfucker."

"That's right, Dean. Now you need to get your lazy ass out the bed and come on up to Joe's Café and give me some money right now or you can kiss this election goodbye."

"I'll meet you in twenty minutes."

"Now you're talking."

Dean didn't worry about formalities. He remained in his sweats and T-shirt, slipped into a pair of flip-flops and flew out the door. Tucked under his arm, a brown grocery bag bulging with stacks of $20 dollar bills, courtesy of J.D. Pruitt.

Despite the lingering doubts and the dripping queasiness from the binge, Dean was again vigorous with the heat and stress of the campaign. He wheeled into the parking lot at Joe's Café, seeing Leon's gleaming British cruiser parked at the back door. As Dean stepped out of the car, Leon came storming across the parking lot in a humorous air of self-importance.

"Just to calm your nerves," Leon said, "I do want to tell you that before I got broke, I rented out the VFW for five hours." He stopped and posed with his shoulders squared and his large, spidery hands fanning out to the side. "Your uncle's giving a speech tomorrow at noon. It'll be a real shindig."

"Hell yeah," Dean said.

He walked over to the bike and dropped the sack of cash in the basket.

"That's two grand. Spend it wisely."

"I always do."

"What time do you want me to be at the VFW?"

Leon shook his head and frowned.

"You can't be there. Your uncle would kill you, and we ain't gonna have no family feud at a rally I organized. Dig? In fact, why don't you let me call him today and tell him everything back on track between you and me?"

"You two have become close in my absence."

"We had no choice, Dean. Your water broke. You freaked out. We had no idea where you were at or what you were doing. I'm an old fool from the 'hood, Dean. I can tell you were up to no good, but I'll leave it at that. You got the money and that's the important thing. Maybe we can salvage your uncle's election hopes."

"What's the latest with Clovis?"

"He wants to march on Douglass Street, but to do that he needs to get paid."

"Jesus Christ. I thought he was this fucking crusader for the poor, downtrodden black man?"

Leon shrugged. "He is, but he's still a player, and players need to get paid. He's got three kids and a wife to feed."

"Well, we'll talk about that later."

"Fine with me. Oh, and Dean?"

"What?"

Leon's expression grew wise with scrutiny. He tugged at the knot of his tie.

"You freak out on me one more time and me and you is through. Dig?"

Dean composed himself.

"You're bluffing, Leon. You need me."

"Yeah I do, but not as much as you think."

He gave a wry smile and gestured toward the loot that was now his. At that instant, as if on cue, several members of Leon's bike brigade rolled into the parking lot.

"You wouldn't dare take the money and run," Dean said.

"Why not?"

"Because, there's a lot more down the road if you spend that the right way."

"Correct. But the same is true for you, too. If you don't win this election, you ain't shit."

Dean saw the logic and conceded. "You're right. I promise I'll be right on time from here on out."

Leon mounted his British cruiser. With his bike brigade behind him, he pedaled into the traffic and fury of Cleveland Road. As soon as Leon disappeared from view, Dean ceased to feel safe. Old, carnivorous junkies standing near a dumpster observed him with hungry stares. A low rider filled with youngsters wearing shades and cocked baseball caps rumbled slowly down the alley. Dean jumped into his Mercedes and sped from the parking lot. Idling at the red light, Dean thought about Leon's message. The old timer was right. If Uncle Byron didn't win the election, then he had no future as a shakedown artist. Dean knew he still had opportunities to make good decisions, but due to his weeklong binge the timeframe was uncomfortably truncated. The runoff election was in three weeks.

And someone had his blackmail notes.

Dean had no way of knowing for sure, but his gut told him Eva had the notes and that Eva had engineered the seduction. If that was the case, then Dean needed to take revenge and take it in the context of the election, where it would have its optimum impact. He thought about Eva grandstanding at City Hall when Councilman Booker tried to fire Brimhall from the roofing contract. He read an article about it in the paper the next morning. If Eva were so loyal that she would hasten to James' defense at City Hall, perhaps she would do the same if he were in danger on Douglass Street. Dean pondered the prospect of Clovis's protest and the seething angst it could engender. What would happen if Eva and Century B were to meet face to face with Clovis and his bodyguard? He beat his palm against the dashboard and howled. A stunning headline flashed through his mind. ***Beckham Volunteers Instigate Race Riot, Six Injured.*** If that were to happen, Beckham would not only lose the black vote, but would also lose the army of liberals backing his candidacy. At another time and under different circumstances the plan might be a tad absurd, Dean admitted. But the forces of love, race and greed were already in motion. All Dean had to do was spend someone else's money and those forces just might collide.

Dean tossed his cell phone onto the passenger seat as he turned south onto I-71. He merged into the slow lane as the phone started ringing. It was Uncle Byron. Dean gulped down a mouthful of courage and clicked the receive button.

"Where in the fuck have you been, Mr. Big Shot?" his uncle screamed.

"Quit your yapping, Uncle Byron. I just figured out how to win the election."

Dean whipped out from behind an 18-wheeler and punched it. The V12 engine shot the car forward until he tailgated a U-Haul. Dean banked back into the right-hand lane, passed the orange and white moving van, and slid over to the fast lane. With nothing but asphalt in front of him, Dean jammed the gas pedal and hurtled forth like a shooting star.

"How?" his uncle hollered. "'Cause you nearly lost it for me!"

"I can't tell you over the phone."

Dean heard his uncle's other campaign advisors shouting in the background. He pictured them crowded around the conference table guzzling coffee, pointing and sighing, complaining and protesting that their champion, Byron Bernadette, had lost on Cleveland Road and that the most unsightly side of District 4 might just be the linchpin in the election. Dean couldn't help but appreciate the irony. The Bernadette campaign went to Cleveland Road for an easy flanking maneuver, but it had become the center of a losing battle. Dean tried not to laugh as he awaited his uncle's reply.

"Then get your Rip Van Winkle ass down here and let me know," his uncle said. "ASAP! And if it isn't good, you're fired!"

A smile the size of a dying supernova swelled in Dean's chest. He pushed a button on the center console and the Mercedes' sunroof peeled back.

"Oh, I don't think you'll be firing me, Uncle Byron," he said, speaking over the gush of wind. "In fact, I think you'll make me chief of staff."

Dean tossed the phone onto the passenger seat and turned up the Alpine stereo—a piano cried at the end of a sonata. The wind felt good in his hair.

—

Beckham and Bernadette, as expected, garnered the most votes in the May 20 election, but neither gained the 50 percent plus-one majority needed for outright victory. Millbury and Panomorov were dropped from the ballot while Beckham and Bernadette headed into the June 12 runoff. Bernadette had cause for optimism. He had emerged from the general election with 44 percent of the vote compared to Beckham's 40 percent. His power base along Morse Road and in north Clintonville had come to the polls in droves, and it was widely expected that they would vote for him again in the runoff. Millbury, who had triumphed with black voters in the Cleveland Road precincts, had thrown his support behind Beckham. But even with Millbury's endorsement, the pundits who discussed the election on radio talk shows agreed that Beckham had a lot of work to do if he were to close that four percent gap in three weeks. Black voters didn't return to the polls in runoffs, they said, especially to vote for a white candidate.

To Bernadette's credit, his campaign did not become complacent. It poured large sums of money into every crevice of the media, promoting Bernadette as the God of economic development, while painting Beckham as the trite environmentalist intent on wrecking the city's industrial base. Beckham counter-punched with full-page color ads depicting Bernadette as the Grim Reaper using his sickle to strike down the trees on Pruitt's property. Knowing that his back was against the wall, Beckham rallied his army of volunteers and begged them for one last bare-knuckled push. He implored them to impugn Bernadette's name as often as possible rather than to address the issues. The volunteers responded with glee and returned to the streets with the sullen vigor of the underdog.

As for Leon, his marching orders didn't change. He was to remain on Cleveland Road and consolidate his base of operations around Hudson Street. As added incentive, a Bernadette aide gave Leon a firm assurance that he would be rewarded once the candidate was in office.

"Let's do this," Leon told his men, as he handed out $20 bills.

Meanwhile, Century B was ecstatic. Mingmei carefully audited the Cleveland Road precincts and found that Millbury had easily won with 60 percent of the vote. Beckham had garnered 22 percent while Bernadette came in third with

18 percent. What this meant is that Century B had somehow out-campaigned Leon in his own backyard. What the numbers also said is that Cleveland Road could offset the advantage that Bernadette enjoyed on Morse Road and in north Clintonville. Mindful that Millbury had thrown his active support behind Beckham, Mingmei rallied Century B around her and said, "We can win the whole thing right here!"

—

Leon had shocked Commander Johnson when he pulled out a thick slab of twenty-dollar bills and rented the "black" VFW hall for five hours on a Saturday.

"Damn, son," Commander Johnson had said. "You really are working for the campaign."

Leon squared his jaw as he counted the money. "If a white boy gonna win this election, it gonna be my white boy."

Leon ran announcements in the *Scioto Times* and sound bites on the soul FM stations promoting a fish fry for Bernadette. In the days leading up to the VFW rally, Leon and his men, all of them dressed in six-button pinstriped suits, stormed the old haunts along Cleveland Road. It was hard for Leon not to become drunk on the notoriety. Most of the people who were voting for Bernadette, he correctly surmised, were actually voting for him. The day of the rally, Leon and his men dressed the VFW hall with Bernadette campaign paraphernalia. They even wore old-fashioned straw boaters adorned with blue ribbons for the occasion. Before a large, enthusiastic crowd, Leon took the stage, grabbed the microphone, and introduced the candidate.

"This is the man who gonna take Cleveland Road into the next century," he proclaimed. Leon had heard applause of that magnitude before, but never after something he had said or done. Mesmerized, he nearly slipped when the broad-shouldered Bernadette clasped his hand and thanked him for all the hard work he'd done for the campaign.

"My nephew tells me you're doing a damn good job." Bernadette's wide face reddened with the crowd's adulation. "Look at all these people." He gestured magnanimously. "I can't win the election without winning Cleveland Road. When I'm in office, I won't forget what you've done."

"Thank you, sir," Leon said, keeping one eye on the crowd. "It's my honor to support the right man for the job."

For ten minutes, Bernadette pumped his fist, shook his head and rolled his shoulders. He worked his way through a speech that veered from the scripted to the improvised. All the work Leon had done seemed self-serving until he saw the sweat on Bernadette's brow and heard the rise and fall of his baritone voice. Surveying the crowd, he saw scores of folks smiling and mumbling "Amen" at Bernadette's mention of the almighty word—*jobs.*

"I want to put people to work," Bernadette said. "If we want to look at birds, we can turn on the TV and watch 'Wild Kingdom.'"

Onlookers laughed and said, "You know that's right," and "We hear you, brother." Making sure he didn't upstage the candidate, Leon pointed his finger and smiled at the familiar faces in the crowd. But in the sea of black folks, two stood out. Taking photographs, a tall redhead with the imposing girth of a draft horse. Standing next to him and scribbling on a notepad, a scrawny kid with glasses and a nest of dark curls on his head.

"I have *arrived,*" Leon muttered to himself as he recognized Dominick Van Buren, the ace metro reporter for the *Scioto Times.*

———

Bristling with campaign signs and loud with the chants of student volunteers, the Beckham rally at Huy Avenue Park was a festive affair. Scores of volunteers were bussed in from campus, but the bulk of the crowd was from the neighborhood—proof of Century B's impact in the Cleveland Road theatre. The largely black crowd was sprinkled with working-class whites and

Hispanics, a surprising sight to Eva and her cohorts. Huy Avenue Park, at one point not even a dot on the Beckham campaign's strategic map, now loomed large. Earlier that day, Bernadette had held a huge rally at the local VFW post just a few blocks down the road. The rally signaled Bernadette's momentum among veterans, who were likely to vote in the runoff. Beckham knew that Bernadette couldn't go unchecked. In a move aimed at telling voters that the battle for Cleveland Road had yet to be settled, he organized a march that culminated with lemon aide and a rally at Huy Avenue Park. Wiping sweat from his brow, Beckham rattled through his well-honed plan for turning Pruitt's land into one of the state's premier nature parks. He talked about the sales tax and the theory of sustainable development. Though he addressed other issues facing the district, such as bond issues for roadwork and the creation of a sewer improvement district, Beckham spent a lot of time on the offensive.

"Bernadette doesn't have your best interests at heart," he said. "But I do. My opponent is a callous corporate apologist, while I'm a humble member of the hoi polloi."

From her perch in the small bleachers behind where Beckham stood, Eva watched as the candidate gestured and shook and twisted and posed, deftly using vivid body language to empower his words. Beckham finished his speech with his right fist clinched and waving in the air. Sustained applause followed a respectable cheer. Waving with both hands, Beckham stuck out his tongue and feigned fatigue, a gesture that elicited a collective laugh from the crowd. Laughing himself, Beckham turned around and gestured toward the proud members of Century B, each of them clad in **BECKHAM!** baseball caps and Woodpecker T-shirts. The applause quickened for a moment, and then died down. As the gathering thinned, Beckham slid into a conversational tone, talking one-on-one and to small groups. Pushing back his wispy blond hair and smirking until his glasses lifted up from his nose, Beckham looked more like a devilish kid than a tough plaintiff's attorney seeking a seat on the City Council.

Donna Rosenbaum finally returned to Mingmei with the report she had commissioned two months ago. Donna had logged 101 precious man-hours, for which she was paid a meager $200 from Mingmei's political action committee. Mingmei graciously thanked Donna for her hard and fruitful work, collected the documents, and promptly returned to her home. She turned off the telephone, shut herself inside her bedroom, and pored over the paperwork for six hours.

Donna had culled information from the 1990 census and from the Freedom of Information requests she had filed at City Hall. Donna had located specific demographic data on the Cleveland Road corridor, including the population of Windsor Terrace, a public housing project near 11th Avenue. She had also dug through the vaults at City Hall and had unearthed 20 years-worth of election results and records on the council's appointments to city commissions and committees. The initial instincts that motivated Mingmei to hire Donna were triumphantly confirmed. In the last 20 years, not one black person had been elected to the District 4 seat. Moreover, no person with an address outside of Clintonville had ever been appointed by a District 4 councilman to serve on one of the city's commissions. And according to the information on Windsor Terrace, there were about 300 people of voting age who lived there.

Mingmei fixed herself a cup of tea, sat on the porch, and pondered how the information could be used to win the election and save the woodpeckers. Her thoughts turned to Edwina, whom she had met at City Hall the day Councilman Booker tried to fire Brimhall from the roofing contract. She recalled how Eva and Edwina had embraced when the council meeting had adjourned, and how two dozen supporters had accompanied Edwina.

Mingmei finished her tea and checked the time. It was 9 p.m., her normal bedtime. Tonight she was excited and in no way interested in going to sleep. She called Eva.

"I cannot believe I am hearing from you at such a late hour," Eva said, her voice lilting. "Did you drink too much tea today?"

"No," Mingmei said. "I have stayed up due to something much more important than a caffeine high. Are you at Larry's?"

"Yes, with Barbara. She turned twenty-one today and I am getting her legally drunk for the first time. Come down for a shot of Slivovitz."

"I will pass on the alcohol, but I need to run something by you."

Mingmei heard Barbara giggling in the background. Bar people were singing, "Happy Birthday to You," and someone was way off key.

"Come quickly," Eva said. "Barbara and I will be in disrepair in about thirty minutes."

"I will be there in ten. Do not order another drink until I arrive."

"Only for you," Eva said.

Mingmei hopped on her bike and arrived at Larry's in eight minutes. She moved quickly through the loud, crowded bar to the back booth where Eva liked to hold court. Eva, a cigarette dangling from her mouth and a green-bottled beer clutched in her left hand, stood from the booth when Mingmei arrived.

"I am honored by your presence." Eva curtsied and spread her arms into a broad gesture of welcome.

Barbara leaned out from the booth with a tipsy grin. "Did you come to have a drink with us? It's my birthday."

"I am not here for drinks and birthdays, although I am glad you lived another year."

Mingmei took a seat and flashed her serious eyes.

"I want Edwina Spurlock to join Century B and campaign for Beckham through the runoff." She pulled Donna's report from her backpack and set it on the table. "And here's why."

Eva took the report and thumbed through it. A ruddy smile gathered in her cheeks. She turned to Nicholas Staggs, the bartender, and raised a hand.

"Oh, Nick," she called, "another round, please."

Edwina knew it was important. Eva and two others from the Beckham campaign were coming over and wanted to make her an offer. This visit had something to do with the election, but exactly what, Edwina had no clue. She worked until the downstairs looked flawless. Bobby was bathed, combed and neatly clad. The coffee brewed, and a sheet of homemade oatmeal-raisin cookies sat cooling on the stove. Edwina was excited and impatient to hear what the Beckham campaign had in store for her. Edwina was also eager to see Eva again. The showdown at City Hall had proved such a thrill that everyone in the neighborhood association frequently talked about it. And they all asked about Eva, "the tall white girl," and when she was going to visit Douglass Street.

She pulled back a drape and peered through the living room window. An Acme Taxi pulled up in front of the house. Out stepped Eva and her cohort, Barbara Thurman. Close on their heels came the severe, diminutive Chinese girl whose name Edwina could not remember. She let go of the drape and made her way to the front door. She chuckled silently, and reverently, over the appearance of the unique team of women approaching her porch. Tall and exquisitely slender, Eva moved with the vibrant grace of a doe, whereas Barbara, plump and jolly, hadn't outgrown her teenage saunter. Between that dichotomy was the Chinese girl, who moved with the assurance of the servant who in truth is the master. All three of them wore **BECKHAM!** T-shirts emblazoned with the garishly charming pileated woodpecker. Beneath the froth of their appearance was the broth of confidence. Edwina took a deep breath, put her hand on the brass knob, and opened the door.

"Greetings from the Beckham campaign," Eva offered her hand and a smile.

"I'm honored," Edwina said, taking Eva's hand in her own. "Please, come in and make yourselves at home."

She led them to the kitchen where she introduced them to Bobby. He had placed a cup and saucer on each of the placemats and had arranged the cookies on a plate. The women of Century B commended him on his hospitality and took their seats at the table. The next five minutes were consumed with the awkward small talk that oftentimes precedes an important conversation. They sipped coffee and laughed about the look on Councilman Booker's face when his motion to terminate the roofing contract died for lack of support.

"We were a good team that day. And we would like to team up again."

"With that said, let's get down to business." Mingmei grabbed her backpack and hoisted it onto the table. She pulled out a thick stack of documents and pushed them across the table toward Edwina. "Those are census figures and records pertaining to council appointments to city commissions."

"Okay," Edwina said.

"If you were to go through this report you would find several things, one of which is that a person from this neighborhood has never been appointed to any city commission—at least not within the last twenty years," Mingmei said. "We and the Beckham campaign want to change all that. If Mr. Beckham is elected, he will have an appointment to the Parks Commission in September. We want you to be that appointee."

"Me?"

"The Parks Commission will be very influential when the nature preserve is being planned," reasoned Eva. "Needless to say, a seat on the Parks Commission could be your first step on the road to the City Council."

"But," Mingmei added, "we need a specific commitment in exchange for what we offer. We need you to campaign in Windsor Terrace. We think you could muster seventy-five to a hundred fifty votes there. In a runoff, that could be the difference between victory and defeat."

"Windsor Terrace?" Edwina said. "The Windsor Devils run drugs from there. And someone got shot there just three days ago. What makes you think I could do any good in the Terrace?"

"We are of the opinion that there are a lot of things you can do, and do well," Eva said. "A friend of mine at the *Scioto Times* typed your name into an archive search. You are president of the Douglass Street Neighborhood Homeowners Association. You founded the North Side Community Garden, which we looked at this morning. The rose bushes are coming in well, I might add. You won the Soul Food cook off at The Columbus Arts Festival two years in a row. And perhaps most importantly, you testified as the state's key witness in the murder trial of Antoine Lucas. Your testimony put him behind bars for life without the possibility of parole. We think you have an excellent record—and guts—and so does Mr. Beckham."

"Look, Mrs. Spurlock, how should I say this? We need a sista on this one," Barbara said. "But you won't be alone. I'll be with you, and so will Anku."

"Who's Anku?" Edwina said.

She took a sip of coffee to veil her growing interest in their offer.

"He is one of our friends in Century B," Eva said. "He is from Angola, Africa. It is my suspicion that some years ago he fought the Communists in the civil war there."

Eva paused to let that piece of information simmer. She pulled at a lock of hair that had fallen across her eye and tucked it behind her ear.

"Believe me, Mrs. Spurlock. We have walked with Anku for the last two months through these tricky streets. If he is at your side, no one will go against you. And perhaps you know some people of your own?"

"Assuming I take the offer, I think I have a few phone calls I could make."

"Mrs. Spurlock, there are strings attached, but not too many," Mingmei said. "If we win the election, we will owe you, but you will owe us nothing."

Edwina poured another round of coffee. She leaned against the counter and looked at the women sitting at her table. They were all so young, and based on the accents, two of them weren't even from the United States. How could they proffer such a well-conceived plan when their age and origin clearly distinguished them as political novices? The confidence with which they pitched the idea was enough to convince Edwina that they, and not Beckham's top brass, had hatched the Parks Commission plan. Edwina couldn't help but be impressed. Nor could she resist the lure of an appointment to the Parks Commission—even if the price was three weeks of campaigning in the gang-infested streets of Windsor Terrace. Edwina had always fended off requests from the neighborhood to seek a post in city government. She said her schedule was too busy, or that she had no interest, or that she wouldn't stand a chance against more experienced candidates. Somehow all those reservations vanished with a blink of Eva's big blue eyes.

"All this sounds good," Edwina said at last. "But I've never even met Mr. Beckham."

And then came a gentle knocking at the door. Eva cleared her throat. A blush of collusion showed on her cheeks. She traded glances with Barbara and Mingmei.

"That is about to change," Eva said.

—

Darren Bell pulled the **BECKHAM!** baseball cap down over his head so that the curled brim nearly concealed his eyes. He glanced down at the pileated woodpecker that adorned his T-shirt and shook his head with discontent. He held out his arms in a gesture of exasperation.

"Edwina, I look like a fool!"

"No you don't," she said. "You look like a nice young man who's participating in an election."

"I might look like that to you, but to me, I'm a fool."

"Come on, Darren," Barbara said. "You can't be a homeboy all the time."

"And why not?"

"Because, you need to stretch your mind every once in a while."

"And that's what you call this?"

"Yep."

"Barbara's right," Edwina said. "Think of this as a new experience that'll benefit you in the future. You might learn something in the next few days that you wouldn't learn otherwise."

"I doubt it."

He pulled the left leg of his black sweat pants up to his knee and tilted the brim of his cap ever so slightly to the left. This marked him as Old School with no gang affiliation and also provided the comfort of being ensconced in his own style. He looked over at Anku, the African bodyguard from Century B.

"Darren," he said, in his thick African-Portuguese accent, "your complaints will limit Edwina's appeal. Look."

He gestured toward the vast, grimy housing project. Old women on porches, kids on bikes and teens wearing baggy pants and bandanas stared at them. The rows of two-story, brick housing blocks stretched east of Cleveland Road and were surrounded by a trash-lined metal fence. Spray paint littered the walls. Violence and waves of bass were in the air, as was the stench from overflowing dumpsters. On parade were young women, their hips swinging in tight skirts and jeans, and their heads bobbing to a private beat. Grackles found a feast inside a fast food wrapper. A stray dog sat at the corner and scratched for fleas. Windsor Terrace could have been one of Satan's estates in hell.

"Edwina needs our undivided attention and support or we should not be here," Anku said.

Darren looked into the African's eyes. He saw the priest, the philosopher and the killer. The T-shirt with the pileated woodpecker didn't look silly on Anku. Instead, the great bird resembled military insignia. Darren and Anku clasped hands and patted each other on the shoulder.

"Yes indeed, my peoples," Edwina said.

She pushed on a pair of ghetto shades and smacked her gum. They strolled into the Terrace with fluidity.

ATTACK
AD

Brimhall downshifted into third gear and muscled the diesel dually king cab into the fast lane. He weaved with deft aggression through eastbound traffic until he arrived at the Main Street exit. A rare and gratifying sense of intrigue fueled his machismo as he rumbled into Bexley. From the tone of muzzled excitement in his attorney's voice, Brimhall figured that the meeting would prove interesting, even revelatory. His attorney, Steve Greenberg, had said nothing concrete over the phone, but Brimhall knew the call had something to do with Dean's blackmail notes. Finally. He had waited for this call since turning the notes over to his attorney a week ago, and at last, paper blood was about to be spilled.

His attorney, no friend of Byron Bernadette, wanted to run an attack ad—a double truck, in color, on Sunday—in the *Scioto Times* using Dean's blackmail notes. In particular, the notes detailing Dean's orchestration of the barroom brawl at the Brown Bag Saloon. The setting was perfect. The notes were luridly damning of Dean while they made Brimhall look like a saint for fighting a gang of skinheads in defense of an African-American woman. Most importantly, from a legal aspect that particular set of notes could be corroborated by Brimhall's hospital bills, police dispatch records, and if need be, by a sympathetic eyewitness,

Brimhall's cousin, Susie Cooper. It was easy enough to prove Dean was officially tied to his uncle's campaign. He not only had the same last name, but was also listed as a paid staff member on one of Byron Bernadette's campaign finance reports. Deliciously true and libel proof. All they needed was someone with the courage, or perhaps the naiveté, to physically bring the information to the *Scioto Times* and purchase the ad. Brimhall suggested that the proposal be pitched to Eva and Century B. His attorney agreed. The cannonade needed to come from within the campaign, not from a distance. Greenberg pledged to offer his legal services pro bono should the attack ad trigger a court case.

"I never thought it would come to this," Brimhall said.

"Nor did I, roofer man, nor did I," Greenberg said.

—

Brimhall brought the proposal to Eva. He knew through his conversations with her that she always consulted Mingmei, the brain behind Century B's successful foray into local politics. If Eva liked the plan, she could perhaps sell it to her. Without Eva's endorsement, however, Brimhall knew he'd have little or no chance to do what he wanted, the way he wanted to do it. He and Eva discussed the matter at length, and she agreed to pledge her full support.

The next day Eva told him that Mingmei would meet with him. They convened at James' kitchen table.

Brimhall felt a bit intimidated by the Chinese girl who peered at him from behind a pair of black horn-rimmed glasses. A little brass box she was, stuffed with centuries of savvy. She sipped her tea with the decorum of a diplomat, and held her chin with the sternness of a field marshal.

Brimhall nodded and took a seat. Eva served him a cup of tea.

By no stretch did he know Mingmei, but through Eva, Brimhall knew that she was worthy of his respect. She had been beaten during the pro-democracy protests on Tiananmen Square in June 1989. She had fled Beijing, surviving the treacherous journey, by freighter, to the United States. She lived for five years in the squalid quarters of San Francisco's China Town, where she worked as an indentured servant for her tycoon uncle. She hadn't seen her parents in six years and lived with the fact that she would probably never see them again. Her name, Eva had said, was probably written on a list proclaiming her an enemy of the People's Republic of China, so going home was not an option. English lessons for 10 years, yet still saddled with an impossible accent. A fulltime chemistry student, a seamstress at night and on the weekends, and now this—vice president of Century B, founder of her own political action committee, and poised to decide the outcome of the biggest Columbus City Council election in decades. All by the ripe old age of 24.

Not too long ago someone like Mingmei was nearly invisible to Brimhall. Had he seen her on the street he would have thought of her as nothing more than a non-descript international student here in the United States for a free education. He scratched his cheek and sneered at his old bigoted self.

Eva gave him a reassuring look as he reached into his scuffed brief case for the files and the money. Mingmei did not blink when he set the manila folder in the middle of the table, but did emit a slight gasp when he produced the imposing block of cash. He plunked the money down, cocked his head to the side, and served a hazel iron gaze.

"Mingmei, I hear you're the powerhouse of Century B."

"Eva must have told you that," she said. "And she is prone to hyperbole."

"But isn't she also prone to the truth?"

"She is accurate," Mingmei said.

"Good, because she said we might be able to do business."

"Perhaps." She inched up in her chair until her forearms and elbows were planted on the table. "Let's skip to the point. What is it that you bring and what is it that you want?"

Brimhall liked her already.

"That's five thousand dollars. And these here," he said, picking up the folder, "are self-incriminating notes penned by your campaign rival, Dean Bernadette. And I also have medical records that substantiate what he's written. The only way you can have the medical records is if I consent, and I do. I want you to use this information to run a two-page attack ad in the *Scioto Times*, on a Sunday, a week before the runoff election."

He handed the documents to Mingmei. He took a sip of tea and waited for a response. Her lips puckered and her brow furrowed in thought, Mingmei thumbed through the documents for 10 minutes. Brimhall saw distant lightening flashing in her eyes. Inwardly he smiled with triumph. He knew his offer was too convenient for her to reject.

"This is dirty." She set the folder on the table. "Do you agree?"

"Yeah, but it's libel proof. And I guarantee you, if this hits the papers, Byron Bernadette will lose a ton of votes."

"I have no doubt that is the truth, but there are other considerations."

"Like what?"

"My reputation."

"Please don't take this the wrong way, Mingmei, but you don't have a reputation, at least not yet."

"But if I do this, I most certainly will, and tarnished from the beginning."

She took a sip of tea.

"You'll be a villain to some and a hero to others. Mingmei, that's what it takes to really make it in politics. If there's one lesson you need to learn, it's that one."

"Fair enough, but if this is such a pressing matter, why won't you do it yourself?"

"This thing needs to have layers. It needs to have texture. It needs to come from inside the campaign, not outside."

"Surely there are others who would be willing to do your bidding."

"None that I know of. Mingmei, this is the election. This accomplishes everything you want to accomplish."

"My efforts are on Cleveland Road, Mr. Brimhall. I can strike from there."

"True, but you still might miss. This," he said, tapping his index finger on the folder, "will hit the bull's eye. Is your reputation more important than the woodpeckers and the trees? That is what you're all about, right?"

"That is correct."

"Well, it's kind of like I said earlier. Sometimes you have to get dirty for something you believe in."

"I understand, but this?"

"Mingmei, I think you're afraid of something that you don't need to be afraid of. There are powerful people in Columbus who wanna see Byron Bernadette go down—hard. If you do this, you'll have allies. Trust me."

"Who are these people?"

"First of all, me. And then there's my attorney, Steve Greenberg. He has lots of friends. All of us can spin the wheel."

Brimhall pulled one of Greenberg's business cards from his wallet and handed it to Mingmei. Her expression softened as she looked to Eva for guidance.

"Take the next step, Mingmei," Eva urged. "The information is true, so it is not really a smear campaign."

"Exactly," Brimhall said, in a tone of finality. "You'll be doing a lot of people a legitimate favor. You're in a democracy now. It's not much cleaner than Chinese Communism."

Mingmei took a sip of tea, and made a face as if it were sour.

—

Drunk.

Trey spent the evening at the Brown Bag Saloon turning his unemployment check into long necks and shots of well whiskey. After the bar closed he went to an afterhours party, drank more beer and tried to convince everyone there that he was the smartest guy in the state of Ohio. On a gush of liquid pleasure, he guided his pickup truck down the back roads to his squalid foursquare on the Hilltop. Along the way he came across a street with lawns freshly strewn with Sunday morning editions of the *Scioto Times*. He pulled over, grabbed a newspaper wrapped in dew-speckled plastic, and continued on his drunken way. The matrimonial crone would be awake and angry when he arrived home. Even if it were only worth 50 cents, the paper, Trey reasoned, was a peace offering. His wife was unemployed and needed the classified section. With paper in hand, he could honestly say he was helping her find a job.

He playfully spanked her with the paper when she confronted him at the door. Ignoring her complaints and the cries of the newborn, he staggered upstairs and fell into bed.

His slumber didn't last long. He awoke to urgent pleas from his wife, who violently shook his arm.

"Get up, Trey," she yelled. "You and Dilworth's names are in the paper and it ain't no good! Trey, get up!"

Bleary eyed and with a heavy head, he rolled out of bed and followed his wife downstairs to the kitchen. Normally he would have ignored her, but the tone in her voice was too shrill and sincere for him to deny. He poured a cup of coffee and took a seat at the kitchen table. His wife put the paper in front of him. What he saw astonished him. Laid out in the center of the A-Section was a full color, two-foot wide, thirty-inch deep double truck political ad with the words **BAD BOY BERNADETTE!** rolling across the top in banner type. On one side of the ad was a detailed account—hand-written on Byron Bernadette letterhead—of the ambush of Brimhall at the Brown Bag Saloon. On the other side were Brimhall's medical bills detailing the nature and extent of his injuries. Running beneath the bold display of documents was this message, *The brutal beating and stabbing of Eugene W. Brimhall Jr. was orchestrated by Dean Bernadette. He is the nephew of District 4 City Council candidate Byron Bernadette, and he is also a paid member of the Bernadette campaign. Ask yourself, do you want these kinds of people running our city? Vote NO to Bernadette on June 12!*

Trey plunged into the account of the days leading up to, and the night of, the brawl at the Brown Bag. Each time he arrived at his or Dilworth's name he grunted with a mix of horror and fury. His wife had already read the ad twice. She paced across the kitchen, saying, "You're goin' to jail," between nervous sips of coffee and manic drags on her cigarette.

"Stacy, you say that one more time and I'ma bust you in the lip."

Trey was certain Brimhall was behind all of this. He was the only person who had the motive, and the money, to run such an ad. But he wasn't necessarily angry with Brimhall. He understood what his ex-friend had done and why he had done it. Brimhall, after all, was the one who had been ambushed and put in the hospital with a stab wound and a severe concussion. Brimhall's only course of action was to take reprisal. His honor demanded it. Trey had known this all along. What incensed Trey to violence was that Dean Bernadette had written the notes in the first place. In Trey's mind the notes constituted probable cause for first-degree battery or aggravated assault—or even attempted murder. His hands trembled. Pieces of mental debris vanished into a vortex of paranoia. He crumpled the newspaper, tossed it across the kitchen, and slammed his fists against the table so hard that the coffee sloshed over the cup's brim.

"I told you not to mess with Brimhall," Stacy said, in the low, dour hiss of irrefutable truth. "You knew he'd win."

"Shut your mouth, Stacy." Trey's upper lip curled. "The money I got for setting up the fight bought a lot of diapers for our fuckin' kid."

"Yeah, but if you were a man, you would've worked for it."

"I said shut your mouth!"

"Make me, you sorry son-of-a-bitch."

Trey lunged to where Stacy stood and whacked her to the floor with a backhand. On her knees, she dabbed blood from her lip. With some difficulty she picked herself up from the floor.

"You let that punk Dean walk into your life and use your greed for his own ends. And look where it got you, Trey. You're still married to a fat bitch, and that shit-ass baby upstairs will one day call you daddy."

She spit out a glob of blood and proceeded to mock Trey's anger with strident, howling laughter.

He dashed up the stairs and dressed. He grabbed his revolver, shoved it into his pants and stormed out of the house. He barreled through the neighborhood and wheeled west on Broad Street and out to Dilworth's house for an impromptu emergency meeting. The pink light of dawn sparkled in his rearview mirror.

"Dean, old son," he said to himself, "if I'm a go to fuckin' prison, I'm a get my rocks off first."

———

The pager, cell phone and home phone all rang at the same time—6:30 a.m. The cacophony shattered Dean's fragile crown of solace. Leaning over from the pillow, he read the numbers posted in the message windows. Each call from Uncle Byron. Even in the hazy, early moments of awakening, Dean knew that something had happened with the blackmail notes. Muttering expletives, Dean clutched the cell phone and headed toward the bathroom. Once his urine was loud and foamy in the toilet bowl, he clicked the Receive button.

"Dean?"

"Yeah, Uncle Byron."

"Have you seen the goddamned *Scioto Times* this morning?"

"I just got up, Uncle Byron."

"Someone from the Beckham campaign took out a huge fuckin' ad talking about a fight you concocted at some shithole up on the Hilltop. The story's pretty detailed, too, Dean. It talks about skinheads and rednecks and money and some black woman from the north side. The story is written on my office letterhead, Dean. Please, tell me you didn't write this, because if you did, I'm finished. But if you didn't, we'll sue their fuckin' asses back to the Stone Ages!"

Dean shook the remaining few drops of urine from his penis and smiled.

"I didn't write those notes, Uncle Byron. I swear. Someone from the

276

Beckham campaign stole my satchel a few days ago. I confess, I had a few pieces of letterhead in my bag, but they were blank. I am, after all, one of your part-time clerks, right? Anyway, they must've written that story themselves."

Dean pulled on a pair of sweats and headed downstairs.

"Then how do you explain those medical bills and the police dispatches? They prove that some guy named Gene Brimhall got into a fight!"

"So." Dean walked across the living room to the front door. "Maybe a fight really happened, but it doesn't mean I'm the one who set it up. Right? Come on, Uncle Byron, you're a lawyer. Don't get taken in by these amateurs."

He opened the front door, headed down the porch steps to the sidewalk, and grabbed the newspaper.

"These amateurs seem pretty serious. They put that stuff in the paper, Dean. It's a nine thousand dollar ad, and it's my ass on the line!"

"Mine, too." Dean turned and headed back up the porch steps to the house. "Let's sue those motherfuckers, Uncle Byron. Let's put the Beckham campaign in a box and let it float on down the river!"

Consumed by his conversation, Dean didn't hear Trey and two skinheads sneak out from behind a hedge, fall in behind him and follow him up the steps.

As soon as Dean reached the door's threshold, Trey pushed him into the house and kicked him to the floor. While one skinhead closed and locked the front door behind them, the other reached down, grabbed Dean's cell phone, and hung up the call. The skinhead's combat boots were so close to Dean's face he could've kissed them.

"What the fuck's up, Dean?"

Standing with his feet set and his hands planted on his hips, the venom in his presence was enhanced by the fact that Trey wore a pistol tucked up front in is his jeans, the handle mashed up against his abdomen. Dean tried to speak but no words came out of his mouth. In the silence he studied the aggressors. One skinhead wore a patch over his eye from where Brimhall had poked it out. The other had no front teeth and a jagged scar above his lip because Brimhall had shattered his mouth with the butt end of a pool cue. The skinheads appeared cruel when Dean had first met them. Now, indifferent to the disfigurement of defeat, they seemed medieval. The squealing bats of fear, in a thick black gush, fluttered out from the dank cave in Dean's soul.

Then the cell phone rang again. Trey turned it off and threw it across the room, where it cracked against the wall. One of the skinheads plucked the *Scioto Times* from Dean's right hand and gave it to Trey. He held it out and shook it at Dean as if he were scolding a rambunctious puppy.

"I read your article. Hell, with a little more practice you might win the fuckin' Pulitzer Prize."

"What article?"

Trey's eyes blazed with fury. "You try and bullshit me one more time and I'ma put a bullet straight through your fuckin' skull. Why'd you write this?" He peeled through the paper until he arrived at the ad.

Dean stood up, took the paper from Trey and read the headline. **BAD BOY BERNADETTE!** He glanced over his shoulders as one of the skinheads disappeared up the stairs.

"Don't worry about him," Trey said. "Just tell me why you wrote this."

"So I could blackmail my uncle if he ever tried to cut me loose."

"You really are a sad piece of shit." Trey shook his head. "You've definitely screwed your uncle, but more importantly, you've screwed me and Dilworth."

"I'm sorry."

"Sorry don't cut it."

Dean heard the skinhead ransacking the upstairs, where Dean kept all his valuables. Trey smiled with malevolence, and then his face grew foul.

"If the cops come around, tell 'em you made all this shit up, okay. Lie like a motherfucker. Dilworth's looking at a parole violation, and I'm looking at a felony charge. If either one of us goes to prison, you'll be killed, believe me."

"This was never meant to be in the paper," Dean said. "When I wrote this, I thought the only person who would ever see it, if ever, would be my uncle."

"It's too late, yuppie."

The skinhead reappeared from upstairs with two pillowcases full of loot. He ducked into the kitchen, pulled a half-empty liter of gin from the refrigerator, and grunted with joy. At that instant, Dean realized something terrible was about to happen to him—unless he did something first. He glanced at an end table, at the lava lamp sitting there. He snatched it from its base and in one sweeping motion, brought it crashing across Trey's head. He yelped and fell to the floor, clutching at the bleeding wound. The skinheads froze, and in their moment of indecision, Dean crouched down and yanked the pistol from Trey's pants. He stood, turned to the skinhead who had looted his room, pulled the trigger and shot him in the neck. The other skinhead tried to escape, but fumbled with the front door he had locked just moments before. He turned to Dean, held out his hands for mercy, but Dean shot him anyway. Lifeless, he slumped to the floor.

"Don't shoot me, man." Trey cowered on his hands and knees.

"Fuck it, Trey. I'll count to ten."

Still reeling from being hit across the head with a lava lamp, Trey stumbled across the living room. He stepped over the dead skinhead but struggled to unlock the door. When Dean reached the count of seven, Trey finally turned the deadbolt and made for his getaway. But when Dean reached the count of ten, Trey fell down the porch steps and tumbled across the sidewalk. As he clamored to his feet, Dean came out, the pistol hot and smoking in his hand. He didn't know why, but at this moment he found clarity. With two victims behind him and a third in front, he knew this was something he had always wanted to do. The only thing remaining was to finish what he had started. He pointed the gun and squeezed the trigger. He missed, the bullet crashing through the window of a parked car. Trey started to run, so Dean stepped down to the sidewalk, and aiming at Trey's back, fired again. Trey fell to the ground, a splotch of crimson spreading across his white T-shirt.

Dean walked up to him and stood over him.

"Brimhall was too strong to kill, but you're not." He shot the redneck a second time.

As Trey lay dying, Dean dropped the gun and puked. Still, he felt better than ever.

—

Leon ordered a cup of coffee, lit a menthol, and spread the A-Section of the *Scioto Times* across the Formica tabletop. In the past he hadn't much cared about the A-section, which carried national and international news. He usually went straight to the Metro pages, where he knew the newsmakers. But by now he was interested in the homelands of his election rivals, Eva and Mingmei. Before heading to the local stories, he'd peruse *World Report* to see what was happening in the Czech Republic or China. Just last week there had been a run on the banks in Prague. Thousands of angry people were left standing in the streets with worthless vouchers in their hands. The economy, and the coalition government, had all but collapsed under the weight of the Post-Communist free market. And in China, an intellectual who criticized the government was sentenced to fifteen years of hard labor. A flood in Henan Province killed 297 people. Leon didn't read these stories with joy. Now that he had names and faces to match with the places, he read them with a burgeoning sense of sympathy. Out on the campaign he had seen sadness in the eyes of Eva and Mingmei. Reading about their countries, even if it were only in blurbs that occasionally appeared in *World Report*, he knew why.

With one hand he stirred cream into his coffee and with the other, flipped through the pages of the A-section. Before reaching *World Report*, however, he arrived at a full color, double truck political ad that consumed the entirety of pages A-6 and A-7. Running across the top of the ad were the words **BAD BOY BERNADETTE!** Leon took a long, reflective drag off his cigarette before reading the meticulous inscription on the Byron Bernadette letterhead. Flabbergasted,

Leon looked around the café to see if anyone was staring at him. A few familiar faces beckoned, but nothing out of the ordinary. Shaking his head with dismay, he returned to the attack ad and read it again. Leon experienced a hard stab of guilt because he, after all, is the one who had commissioned the work stoppage on the roofing contract at Douglass Street. Thus, he was responsible in part for Brimhall's nasty scrape with Trey Johnson, Chris Dilworth, and the skinheads. A monumental feeling of relief quickly followed the pang of guilt. His name had not appeared in Dean's studious account of how he had engineered the brawl. Had that been the case, Leon was sure he wouldn't have been welcomed at Joe's Café, or anywhere else, this morning or the next. What frightened him to chills was the certainty that his name appeared somewhere in Dean's files and that someone other than Dean possessed those files. He made a split decision—even if the decision came a few weeks too late—to never again deal with Dean. He wanted to call him and ask about this. But never meant never, and it started now.

He gestured for more coffee. A waitress was soon at his table. He slipped a five into her hand and said thanks. With the attack ad opened up in front of him, Leon propped his elbows on the tabletop and pondered the ramifications. The election was surely lost, and with it, all hopes of usurping the Douglass Street Restoration. He could still remain in cahoots with Clovis, of course, but Leon knew deep down inside that once Clovis gained a foothold on Douglass Street he'd be shoved to the side and denied his spoils. Despite his confidence throughout the campaign, Leon had always entertained the possibility that he might fail in his bid to turn Douglass Street into his playpen. Looking at the ad made him feel foolish that he had ever even tried. He thought he was supposed to feel angry over this defeat, and that he was supposed to fume over the loss of easy money. Surprisingly, he was comforted that the campaign was over and that he would no longer have to deal with people like Dean and Clovis. He longed for the simple times when he worked at the bike shop by day and sat out on north side porches by night.

Fuck it.

He leaned back in the booth. And that's when he noticed something peculiar flashing on the TV over on the countertop. Leon bolted up from his seat, and with one step stood in front of the tube. He mashed the volume button until it blared.

"District 4 candidate Byron Bernadette is reeling from the paid political ad that appeared this morning in the *Scioto Times*," the news anchor said. "He emphatically denied the allegation that his nephew, Dean Bernadette, a paid employee of his campaign, organized a brutal attack on a local roofing contractor in April. Bernadette, until now considered the frontrunner for the District 4 seat, has vowed to press a libel suit against whoever paid for the ad."

Then came footage of Bernadette and his campaign advisors pushing their way through a pack of reporters.

"His opponent, George Beckham," the anchor continued, "has not shied from the controversy."

The footage cut to Beckham, standing on the steps of City Hall. Flanked by his wife, his two children and his top political aides, Beckham wore the guarded optimism of a man on the brink of triumph.

"I demand that Byron Bernadette give a full explanation of what appeared in the paper this morning. If it's not true, then he should come out and say so. But if it is true, he needs to forget about the lawsuit, pull out of the race— immediately—and concede victory to me."

Reporters peppered Beckham with questions as cameramen jostled for the best shot. The reporters wanted to know who paid for the ad, and also asked him if he knew anything about it before it appeared in the paper.

"Yes, I have a good idea of who paid for the ad, but I refuse to mention any names," he said. "And no, I had no idea, and let me repeat, no idea, that this was going to happen. Believe me, I nearly choked on my bagel this morning when I opened the paper."

A few pundits discussed the ad and what impact it might have on the election. Leon didn't need to hear what they said because he knew the answer. Byron Bernadette was toast.

"Ain't that who you been working for?" Joe, the owner, pointed to the TV.

Leon nodded.

"Well, I guess you out of business now, huh?"

"Uh-huh," Leon muttered.

"Have a coffee on the house, Leon, and just thank God you're alive."

"Thanks, Joe."

Leon returned to his seat and took one last look at the ad. Like the reporters, he wanted to know who was behind this. He looked down at the tiny print below the ad. *Paid for by Century B for the Election of George Beckham.*

"Daaaamn. Eva strikes again!"

Leon slid a few coins into the pay phone at the corner outside the café. From memory, he dialed Edwina's number. He cleared his throat and gulped down a lump of trepidation as the phone rang—once, twice, three times.

"Hello?"

"Edwina?"

He knew she knew his voice, even if he had only spoken one word. He braced himself for scorn.

"Leon," she said, with no attempt to conceal her displeasure. "What can I do for you this morning?"

Edwina's voice was so deep with resentment and sarcasm that Leon wanted to hang up. But Edwina already knew it was him, and besides, he called to make peace, not war. He sighed with the hope that Edwina would detect a note of conciliation.

"I want to apologize for everything that's happened in the last few weeks. I'm sorry."

What followed was a low, rolling chuckle.

"You must've read the paper this morning—like everyone else in Columbus."

"It's a sad day for the Bernadette campaign," Leon said. "It's a shame what they did to that old boy named Brimhall."

"Why did you call, Leon?"

"I wanted to apologize."

"You wanna be friends now that you know Beckham's going to win the election? You tried to sell out my neighborhood, Leon, but all you managed to do was get in bed with a wannabe gangster. Did you call to admit that?"

"No, 'cause you've already figured that out. Did you know the ad was gonna be in the papers?"

"I'm not gonna tell you what I know, Leon. The bridge between us was burned the day you showed your ass down at City Hall. Why did you call, Leon?"

"Like I said, I want to apologize."

"I think it's more like damage control. And before you ask, the answer is no. I can't promise you that your name won't show up in another political ad. You've made enemies, Leon, and none of them are afraid of you and that thug you're working with."

Apologies weren't enough for street matrons like Edwina. If he were to crawl back into her good graces he needed something of value. Conveniently, he had a shiny piece of gold in his sack of information.

"How would you feel if I gave you some news you could use?"

"Like what?"

"Remember Clovis Whitfield?"

"That racist knucklehead you tried to sic on me?"

"Uh-huh."

"What about him?"

"He's supposed to be in front of your house at ten a.m. tomorrow, with his bodyguards."

"How do you know?"

"Because." He paused. "I paid him to be there."

"Why are you telling me this?"

"Like I said, I'm trying to apologize. If you won't let me do that, at least let me help you. I know you know about the element of surprise. Don't let Clovis surprise you, Edwina, or he's gonna own Douglass Street."

284

"Where are you right now?"

"At Cleveland and Hudson. Why?"

"Can you be at my house in ten minutes?"

"Yeah, why?"

"Because, if you apologize, I wanna look into your eyes when you do."

"Thanks. I'm on my way right now."

Leon stood on the pedals and muscled across Cleveland Road. Crouching aerodynamically and with the wind at his back, he sped down Hudson with moving cars just inches to the left of the handlebars, and parked cars just inches to the right. As if shot from a sling he careened around the corner onto Medina, stood on the pedals and climbed a slight incline. At the crest of the hill he mashed on the pedals even harder and slid into third gear. When he hit the decline he was moving as swiftly as the college kids who rode their bikes for sport. Then he sat up straight, took his hands off the handlebars and began to glide. Guiding the bike with his knees, he turned onto Douglass Street and coasted to his rendezvous with Edwina.

And she was waiting.

Standing on the sidewalk, she watched him arrive. He pulled to the curb. He slowly took off his shades, tucked them into the top pocket of his blazer, and looked downward in a show of subservience. When their eyes finally met, he knew without a doubt that he had not been fooled. Edwina had not asked him to come here so she could rebuff or scold him. She simply wanted a sincere apology, and for Leon to return to what he himself wanted to be, or had been—a decent, if somewhat frustrated, old man with delusions of grandeur. He glanced over her shoulder and saw Bobby and Mr. Dalrymple sitting on the porch swing. They waved.

"It's good to be back," he said.

"Is it, Leon?"

She peered into his big brown eyes.

"Yes, Edwina, it really is."

"Are you gonna be with us tomorrow at ten a.m.?"

"Wild horses, Edwina, wild horses."

They shook hands. Before Leon pedaled off, Edwina flicked out a piece of paper and handed it to him.

"Why don't you rally your bike brigade and call that number."

"Who is this?"

Edwina pursed her lips. A wild smile flashed in her eyes.

"Eva Havlicek. She's expecting you. Now that you're a member of Century B, you have work to do."

Astounded, Leon slid the number into his pants pocket. "Are you sure? We've been rivals for two months."

"Eva doesn't hold grudges, Leon. Call her and make more than amends."

"I can do that."

He stood on the pedals, raced down the block, and banked right onto Hamilton Street.

P U N K
W E L C H

L
eon and his bike brigade coasted down Hudson Street, filling the east
and westbound lanes. Leon had already told his men that they were
now campaigning for Beckham and that they were about to meet with
Eva and Century B. Far from bristling at the news, Leon's men embraced it.
The only thing they liked about campaigning for Bernadette was the money,
and Leon's men neither liked nor trusted Clovis. Eager to do whatever it
took to reclaim the good graces of Edwina and the residents of Douglass
Street, they were quick to change sides. If sabotaging Clovis's protest was
what needed to be done, then that's what they would do. Leon had no idea
what was planned for him and his men, and it was that dangling mystery that
made this trip to Larry's so exciting. All Eva had said on the phone was to
arrive there at 6:30 and to be prepared for a long evening. With that in mind,
Leon treated his men to burgers and fries along the way, slipped each of them
a twenty, and filled a thermos with stout coffee.

They entered through the back door. Leon breathed in the collegiate
admixture of beer, Parliament cigarettes, and patchouli oil. A gaggle of drunks
standing near the bar eyed him and his men with sharp curiosity. Leon ignored
them as he scanned the dim lounge for the big Czech and her entourage.

Toward the front at a cluster of tables sat a large group of students, some of whom Leon recognized. Mingmei, clipboard in hand, appeared to be checking items on a list, while Barbara Thurman, her spectacles shinning in the bar light, handed out leaflets to electioneers. Standing with her back to Leon was Eva. She gesticulated with the subdued pomp of an earnest leader. Leon could hear her but couldn't discern exactly what she said. He hadn't been this close to her since she'd made that remark about the Tour de France in the early days of the campaign. From that point onward he had seen her only from a distance—at the end of a block, on a front porch, in the papers, or in short video clips on the evening news. Yet here he was, engrossed by the deep melody in her voice and the stilted grace of her gestures.

Leon noticed that the people sitting at the tables began looking at him and his men. Eva must have noticed the disruption because she stopped speaking, took a long drink from a green bottled beer, and turned around. When their eyes met, Leon clasped his hands and nodded reverently.

"Eva," he said, in the low tone of accord.

She responded with her own beau geste.

"Leon," she said, motioning toward the few dozen electioneers sitting behind her. "We are glad you are here. The final hour will soon arrive, and we need you."

With a cursory nod of acknowledgment, Mingmei approached him. "This is a petition. Will you sign it?"

"What does it say?"

"Read it for yourself." She handed him the clipboard and a pen. "If you agree, then sign, but if not, there is no pressure."

Leon chuckled grimly as he read the petition.

"Mr. Clovis Whitfield, you don't have to go home, but you have to get the hell out of here."

Several dozen had already signed. Leon clicked the ballpoint pen and wrote his name in flowing cursive. He handed the petition to his men, and shared a grin with Eva as they signed. Leon handed the clipboard back to Mingmei and made an impulsive attempt to establish a rapport with her.

"Are you from Henan Province?"

"No. Beijing Municipality. Why do you ask?"

"There was a flood. A lot of people died. I— well, I thought about you."

"I appreciate your concern, Leon, but China is a very big place and we have many floods."

Leon was a bit crestfallen by the rude reply. Mingmei spied the disappointment in his eyes, and before she returned to her work, offered her hand in apology.

"Thank you," she said, in a much softer tone. "No one else bothered to ask about the deaths in Zhengzhou."

Finding a human connection with the steely, distant Mingmei made Leon feel as if he had accomplished something important. But he had no time to revel in his little private triumph.

"Come, come, Leon," Eva beckoned. "I want you to meet my team, Century B."

For the next ten minutes he and his men shook hands and patted shoulders with a group of bright, honest college kids the likes of whom Leon had met during his days at the bike shop. He would have felt intimidated were it not for their genuine hospitality and excitement. They wanted to know where he lived, where he was from, how old he was, how long he had been involved in politics, and thanked him for joining Century B. They complimented him on his appearance—he and his men were dressed in swap meet suits, of course—and thanked him again and again for joining them. Underneath the polite cheer bubbled the collective brooding of people who know that danger lurks. These students were about to confront Clovis, a radical and felon, and his corps of uniformed bodyguards. Leon sized up the students. With the exception of Anku, Century B's strongman, none of Eva's people were fighters. And if they served Clovis with a petition asking him to "get the hell out of here," he might just pop. Leon knew that Edwina was at home calling in favors and allies, and of both she had plenty. James and his Mexican roofers also figured to be formidable. Still, Century B would stand little chance if Clovis opted for his street game.

"So what's the plan, Miss Eva," Leon said, conveying nothing but cockiness.

He and Eva took a seat at the tables. Her eyes dimmed as she grabbed a backpack and slid it across the table. She tried to look nonchalant as she pulled a tall stack of fliers from within, but uncertainty was revealed when the left corner of her mouth curled into a frown. And then her expression grew dour. She peeled a flier from the top of the stack and pushed it over to Leon. He nearly choked on his ginger ale when he read it. The words **Say No to Clovis!** screamed across the bottom in large black print. At the top of the flier, an enlarged image of Clovis's mug shot from when he was arrested on the aggravated robbery charges. Circling his mug shot, the thick red rings of a target.

"You sure you wanna do this?" Leon said. "This is gonna make him mad, Eva."

"We know. We want him to be mad. Otherwise, he will confront us on his terms, and we can't afford to let that happen."

"But I mean *real* mad. Are you sure you wanna take that risk? He calls his bodyguards a bunch of pissed off gorillas. And I've seen them before. They're scary."

"We need to intervene, Leon, not placate." Eva lit a cigarette. "And besides, Clovis is not the only one who will see this. The entire neighborhood will. Does he really call his men a bunch of pissed off gorillas?"

"Yes, Eva, and they'll be pissed at me and you."

He studied the flier again. The boldness of the message, the starkness of the colors, and the crudeness of the design made it powerful. He knew that if he were on the receiving end of this flier he wouldn't want to trifle with the people who were brave enough to have created it. Would Clovis feel the same way? Perhaps, he thought. He set the flier down, looked at Eva and flashed a dangerous smile. The room went silent as the students awaited his response. For the sake of ego and drama, he savored the moment. "I think it works. So what do you want me to do with these?"

A muted cheer of relief arose from the members of Century B.

Eva's face brightened. "There are ten thousand of these. I want you to place them on every telephone pole, and every tree, within a five-block radius of Edwina's house. Regardless of how Clovis arrives at Douglass Street, he will have to confront the shame of his own past."

"Genius, Eva. Who came up with this?"

She grinned.

"Us," she said, and nodded toward Mingmei and Barbara. She reached into the backpack. One by one she stacked five staple guns and a couple dozen boxes of staples on the tabletop.

"Frank and Anku have bikes parked out front. They will ride with you."

"Let's do this," Leon said.

Astride fine mountain bikes, Frank and Anku coasted through a parking lot and met Leon and his men in the alley behind Larry's. Leon looked at Frank and smiled.

"You up for this white boy?" Leon said, in a friendly manner.

"White boy's up for it."

Leon and his men gave him high-fives and welcomed him into their company. The seven-man bike brigade pulled out and rolled east down Frambes Avenue. Anku, his lion's eyes sparkling in the Sunday twilight, brought up the rear.

—

Say No to Clovis! fliers papered every tree and every telephone pole from the ground up to about seven feet. So thorough was the overlay that when the wind blew, the fliers ruffled like the collective wings of a rising flock of birds. Chagrin pierced Clovis's inner aura of self-confidence. It was one thing to be angry with someone for plastering his mug shot across the neighborhood. More unnerving was the thought of how much manpower and organization it had taken to accomplish such a feat. He thought about abandoning the protest and returning another day, but he wanted to see the people who were shaming him and punish them for their arrogance.

Despite Clovis's doubts, his bodyguard, tall and thick as an old stand of mahogany, and militaristic in their combat boots, army fatigues and black berets, told him he was still the man of the hour. So he shrugged off Rasheed's strong suggestion that they turn and leave, leading his bodyguard deeper into enemy territory. En route to Edwina's house, he and his men removed as many fliers as they could. Not long into their procession, they clutched thick stacks of torn and wrinkled fliers, and their focus, so keen at the beginning of the march, was now frayed. Clovis was also unnerved by the reception from the people he saw on the porches and in the front yards of the homes lining the protest route. Instead of greeting him as a conquering hero and backing his cause, they either ignored him or greeted him with hard stares.

Clovis wasn't surprised that Leon had called earlier in the morning to say he wouldn't be participating in the march. Leon was an old man, and Clovis found it plausible that he just didn't have the heart for something like this. And if Leon didn't come to the protest, then it would be that much easier to oust him when it came time to claim the restoration grant. But this event was supposed to be a secret, a clever surprise aimed at shocking Edwina Spurlock into submission. All of it up in smoke, no doubt, and as Clovis absorbed the negativity bearing down on him, he knew he had been double-crossed.

"Don't let nothing get you down, Clovis," shouted one of his bodyguards.

"We got a bird in the hand," chimed another.

The encouragement bolstered him, but it couldn't inflate his sagging spirits. He didn't have the spark needed to convince strangers to join him. He couldn't conjure the menacing smile that always seemed to garner support from the angry and the gullible. With his thoughts focused on Leon's betrayal, Clovis's diatribes against Gene Brimhall, the target of the protest, lacked passion and zeal. So as he made his way through Linden Park, he huffed and puffed, as planned, but did so for all the wrong reasons.

"Fuck Leon," he said to Rasheed, and crammed his fist into his palm. "If he's down on Douglass Street I'ma fuck him up."

Clovis rounded the corner at Douglass Street and Loretta with his 10-man bodyguard and only a few drunks and drifters who had tagged along out of curiosity. He halted his entourage and took in the scene. Up to this point the fliers were on white paper. But the telephone poles and trees leading up to Clovis's final destination on Douglass Street were plastered with pink ones reaching up as high as 15 feet. Huge bed-sheet banners marked with black spray paint—*Say No to Clovis!*—curled from porches and makeshift flagpoles. And massed in the middle of the street in front of Edwina's house was a gang, elbow to elbow, and ten deep from gutter to gutter. A few in the crowed held up compact mirrors, catching the sun and zapping Clovis and his men with blinding rays of light, forcing them to cup their hands over their foreheads in order to see.

Peeved by the indignity, Clovis pushed forward, his bodyguards walking in step, their boots sounding in martial unison. Bombarded with lasers of light, annoying as gnats and flies, Clovis trudged on. With each step he took, the booing grew louder, and up from the noise rose a chorus, *Clovis the Bovis who stepped on a Novis. Clovis the Bovis who stepped on a Novis.* Lit emergency roadside flares and smoke bombs cascaded out from the crowd, spilling across the street to produce a hissing, scarlet cloud of confusion.

Clovis halted his bodyguard with the raising of his right hand. He peered through the smoke. He looked for Leon, but wound up counting the people who had aligned themselves against him. As he craned his neck and squinted, a tall, slender figure stepped through the ruby fumes. She planted her feet, tilted her head, and made ceremony out of sliding a little hand mirror into her pocket. Her face powdered gaunt, and her lips, where an unlit cigarette dangled, as purple as ripe plums. Her onyx hair oiled and combed tight to her scalp, and in the back, twisted into twin spikes that protruded from behind her ears like boar's tusks. She wore a black sweat suit with the left leg pushed up to the knee, and was a full six-footer in black combat boots. She peered at him from behind a pair of gangster shades. A diagonal shadow sliced across her face as she pulled the sweat suit's hood up over her head.

Punk wench, vampire, or angel of death, Clovis could not tell.

"We have waited on you," she said, in a metallic accent that further baffled Clovis. "But I should say," and she arched a brow above the rim of her shades, "that I am surprised you are here."

She lit the cigarette, exhaling from the side of her mouth.

"Are you the one who put these up?" Clovis threw his stack of fliers to the ground.

"No. That was the work of my allies. But tell me, did you not come here to ask a more important question than that?" She knelt down, grabbed one of the fliers, and stood back up. She looked at it and smirked. "After all, this silly thing would not even merit a 'C' in freshman art class."

She balled it up and threw it away.

Her brazen histrionics angered Clovis, and he ached to bully her. But he was careful to respect his adversary because he knew, and even feared, the source of her certainty. Behind her were all the pieces of chess on one square. An abundance of pawns—soft college kids who were of little consequence. But behind the foggy, flickering line of flares and bombs were the rooks, knights, and bishops—bare-chested north side blacks who formed a protective wall around their queen, Edwina.

Clovis kept his mounting sense of doom hidden behind a mask of indifference. He tipped his bowler, scanning the crowd for Leon, the traitor, and Gene Brimhall, the target, but neither could be found.

"What is it that you have come for?" She took the last drag from the cigarette and flicked it to the gutter

"I'm here for the cross burner," he said, impatient to reassert his agenda.

She shrugged. "I am sorry, Mr. Clovis, but there is no one here by that description."

"I'm here for the cross burner."

Clovis hoped the mere mention of the reviled term would strike a deep seam in the coalition arrayed against him. There were, after all, plenty of black folks present. And if there was one thing he could count on, it was their hatred of unholy white men. And among the whites, he guessed, there existed enough guilt to make at least some of them squeamish, and even resentful, about being here. He surmised that not everyone in the rival squad knew exactly what they were doing or why they were doing it. Exploitation and conquest. It was his only chance. He examined his opponents, and through the fading tails of smoke and flares, found what he hoped would be a weakness in the line. He fixed his hardest penitentiary gaze, puffed out his chest and tried to make the tall, scrawny blond kid in front of him feel like he was the only person north of the equator.

"You know why the fuck you here, son?" Clovis held out his arms in an exaggerated act of beseeching. The kid grew red in the face, hung his head, and did not respond.

"Answer me, punk! Do you know why the fuck you here? If you don't know, then I'ma tell you. You here with this freak to protect a greedy motherfuckin' redneck who burned a cross on Oakley Avenue in 1982."

"Amen, brother," one of his bodyguards said.

"And I can see you college boy. Your parents are rich. They moderate to liberal and they hate cross burners. And so do you. And so do all them niggas over there," he said, pointing toward Edwina and her host.

From the rear, a street urchin in Clovis's crew heaved a 40-ounce beer bottle. It tumbled through the air and shattered across the street, a large jagged piece skidding to the feet of the woman confronting Clovis. He crossed his arms over his chest and struck a big-man pose, hoping to regain ground in this encounter. But to Clovis's surprise, and to the arousal of his wrath, the student he'd scolded gained his composure, took hold of his gumption, and gave a response.

"Clovis, you might be right about a few things, but you're also wrong. I'm not here for the redneck. I'm here to protect her from you." He nodded toward the woman in combat boots.

"And he speaks for everyone," came Edwina's clarion voice. "Your hustler's tricks won't work here, Clovis. You're on the north side, not at City Hall."

The woman in the black sweat suit stepped on the jagged piece of broken glass, and with the heel of her boot, ground it into the pavement. Reinforced by the solidarity of her people, she crossed Clovis with a flippant sneer that warned of danger. She lifted her right hand and then dropped it. Her supporters lurched through the smoke and crowded in tight behind her. Clovis felt the heat of present combat, and sensed the growing unease within his own contingent. He knew he wasn't going to claim what he came for, and now thought only of survival. But he couldn't just turn and run, thinking it better to lose a quart of blood than an ounce of reputation.

"Bitch, you come one step closer and I'm a pimp-slap yo' ass into next week." He flashed a fist full of rings.

"I don't think you want to pimp-slap me—not today. And besides, you owe me."

"I don't owe you and your lynch mob shit."

"Oh, yes you do."

"Please, enlighten me?"

"The man who you call the cross burner has a name—Gene Brimhall. Eight men work for him. Some of them have crossed five rivers and have ridden on the tops of cargo trains just to be in this country to live and work. They send money back home to their families. And it is one of them—I cannot say his name or where he is from—who said he would destroy you if you came here and tried to take food off of his plate. It is Gene Brimhall, and I, who convinced him not to be right here, right now. I am standing in his stead, and all I want is détente."

Inside the cold, metallic folds of her intonation Clovis heard the ringing bell of truth. She spoke of the Mexicans whom he had seen a few weeks back when he had scouted out Douglass Street. He had considered them as he hatched his plan, but assessing the current situation, he realized he had not appreciated the respect they would demand, the steps they would take to protect what was theirs. And if Gene Brimhall was the one who stopped the bullet before it was fired, he had little indignation to legitimately express—at least to this crowd. Had he been able to rally the neighborhood, perhaps he would have had the muscle he needed to cause a scene, legitimacy be damned. But this woman had pilfered the trumps from his deck, and was even so bold as to play her own brand of Sportka.

With the staunch support of his bodyguard, Clovis maintained a fierce front as he pondered an exit strategy. "So who the fuck are you?"

"Me? I am Eva Havlicek, someone who knows enough to wreck your political career, and the money that goes along with it."

"How so?"

"Last night I completed a crash course in Clovis Whitfield 101," she said. "It was an interesting lesson, too. I know about your crimes, your trial, your protests, and your 'pissed off gorillas.' I even know that you had 127 tackles and five interceptions your senior year at East Side High—before you blew out your knee, that is. But most importantly, I know who you work for."

"And who is that?"

"Dean Bernadette, the biggest shitass in the city of Columbus. He is evil and he is corrupt and he is as white as virgin snow. And if you read the newspapers this morning, you would know he has been arrested on three counts of murder. Your employer. Your paycheck. And I will let everyone know about it."

Clovis emitted the pained laughter of defeat, knowing there was no way to beat this girl. He yearned to spout the lines he'd rehearsed, to go off script in a charismatic tirade and turn the tables on all these punks and bitches. But he knew his time was about to expire, and that when it did, he wouldn't be dealing with Eva, but with the growling old dogs standing in her clique. Indeed, if he wanted to make it out of Douglass Street with his snazzy bowler still on his head, he needed to make his peace, or promise war, and leave. He looked around in grudging wonderment. The large banners emblazoned with the words *Say No to Clovis!* hanging from the porches, the discarded fliers fluttering across the pavement like the ashes of a great fire, and a hill of humanity in front of him, too steep and too tall to climb. In the eyes of the silent crowd he found more than the hint of peril—a collective probity, an air of decency and resolve that Clovis hadn't expected.

"You the one who ran the attack ad in the papers?" he said.

"Of course."

"You also the one who organized the filibuster at City Hall, ain't you?"

"At four-thirty p.m. on a Friday, with short notice."

Eva pushed the shades up over her forehead and pulled back the sweat suit's hood. The sun gleamed on her oiled black hair. A brave light glimmered from a high chasm in her universe. Clovis took off his glasses, too, so that she could see the dawn of respect breaking through his scowl. It was then that she quivered, but as soon as it came is as soon as it went.

"You dyed your hair since I saw you in the papers," he said. "You used to be blonde. I like the getup, too. You look like you belong on the streets. From here on out, I'ma call you Eva the Black."

She pushed the shades back down. "Then Eva the Black it shall be."

The last roadside flare flickered out as a gust of wind blew down the street. One of the *Say No to Clovis!* fliers swept high up from the pavement and started falling back to the earth with the lazy sway of an autumn leaf. Eva the Black plucked it from the air, tore it in half and let the pieces fall to the ground. She turned out her empty palms.

"C'mon, gentlemen, let's leave these people be," Clovis said, and he and his bodyguard turned and left.

—

From atop the scaffolding at Mr. Dalrymple's house, Brimhall, James, Leon, Anku and the roofers watched Clovis and his bodyguard leave Douglass Street.

Appearing humbled yet self-satisfied, Clovis rounded the corner at Loretta Street in a full ghetto lean. He didn't notice, or pretended not to notice, Brimhall and the others in their lofty perch.

"Well," Brimhall said, "Eva was right. Had we been down there, we would've fought. She did it without us, and she did it peacefully."

"It came real close, though." James sighed. "I was about to go down there."

"We all were," Anku said. "But our patience was rewarded. Eva's plan took some time to develop."

"But when it did—damn I wish I could've heard her!" Leon said. "And she didn't even read the petition!"

The roofers talked amongst themselves in Spanglish. Their upbeat tone and jovial posturing made it clear that they were pleased with the results.

"I guess this means we don't have to find another contract," Orlando Cruz said. "And nobody's going to jail."

"You damn right, Orlando," Brimhall said. "We ain't going nowhere."

Though the drama had subsided, a thrilling scene was unfolding down below. The electioneers hoisted Eva up on their shoulders and chanted, "*E-va, E-va, E-va, E-va.*" People shook hands and hugged, laughed and danced. Eva pumped her fists and waved up toward the scaffolding as she rode over the pontoon of shoulders.

"James, you've got to marry her," Brimhall said.

"If she'll have me," James said.

A tear gathered in the corner of his eye and tumbled down his cheek. A soft breeze kissed the salty trail that ended at the base of his neck. He waved to Eva, now running toward the scaffolding.

"You feel like working today, Brimhall?" James said.

The boss peered into the bright, cloudless sky and shook his head with a mock expression of finality. "Can't work today, James. It looks like rain."

—

Tuesday nights were usually slow, but since this was Election Day in District 4, Larry's was packed by 9 p.m. That's when the roofers arrived. James, wholesome and shining with the light of the sun. Brimhall sparkling with macho studs of gold and silver. Walking with them, a noble woman as radiant as a field of autumn wheat at dawn. Behind her, a burly Latino in lizard-skin boots and a cowboy hat. Before sitting down, Brimhall looked over at the covered tub of champagne, the champagne he and James had delivered earlier in the evening, and nodded approvingly in bartender Nicholas Staggs' direction.

Then the phone rang. It was Dominick Van Buren from the *Scioto Times,* and he had the election results.

"Everybody shut up!" Nicholas yelled. "I've got the returns!"

A hungry hush enveloped the barroom.

"With one hundred percent of the precincts reporting, it's Bernadette with six thousand, one hundred and twenty three votes, and Beckham with twelve thousand, one hundred and nine! Beckham wins in a landslide!"

A loud cheer rose from the crowd. Though the energy level decreased from the outburst, it stayed higher than it had been before the announcement of the election returns. For the next 20 minutes Nicholas was swamped, as everyone wanted to celebrate the victory with a new drink. The register drawer went back and forth as he poured beer, mixed drinks, and sloshed ice into glassware pulled from the three-bay sink. His arms wet to his elbows, his apron drenched, and the tips kept rolling in. Having finally weathered the rush, Nicholas leaned back on the stainless steel cooler and dried his hands. Everyone drank, talked, gestured and laughed. He hadn't heard Larry's purr like this in quite a while. And then Eva, sunburned from campaigning up until the polls closed at 7:30 p.m., appeared through the front door with Century B. In the seasoned smile and wide eyes, Nicholas detected the sweet fatigue of her efforts. She held hands with Barbara and Mingmei, and behind them were Anku, Frank Fuller, Leon Davis, and a dozen more Americans.

Eva moved from booth to booth and table to table, shaking hands and slapping backs, stirring laughter and exchanging compliments. She had yet to wash the dye out of her hair so she was still Eva the Black. Wearing twin braids tied off with black ribbons, she appeared to relish the sobriquet. As Century B trailed her descent into the depths of the bar, Nicholas knew it was time to start passing out the champagne glasses.

He had given each of the barmaids an extra $5 on the condition that they deliver one to each and every customer. At Nicholas' command, they went to the back room and both returned to the main floor carrying a tray of plastic champagne stems. As Eva moved through the crowd, the barmaids placed glasses in front of each person sitting, and pushed them into the hands of those standing. The sound of popping corks could be heard, and the crowd's intensity grew.

Eva yelped with excitement when she saw Oxana. Everyone around them stepped to the side to give them room to express their joy. They corralled each other in their gangly arms and kissed on each cheek. They fell into deep Russian and spoke quickly and with obvious sincerity. Arriving at a point of secret humor, she and Oxana tilted back their heads and roared with laughter. Eva then hugged Edwina, Orlando and Brimhall. She slid her arm around James, planted a wet peck on his lips, and buried her head between his neck and shoulder. He pulled a white rose from the vase on the table and placed it in her hand. She gazed up at him and whispered something that made him blush.

All the glasses were full. Afoot was the collective presumption that something significant was about to be said. Nicholas grabbed his glass of Schramsberg Blanc de Blanc and walked out from behind the bar. The crowd grew quiet as he made his way to the nucleus of the gathering. Finding the ideal spot, with people stretching to his left and right, he cleared his throat.

"I'd like to propose a toast," he said, hoisting his glass.

With the eyes of many people upon him, he spoke in his deepest tenor.

"To Eva Havlicek, our American princess, and one hell of a dame."

The room grew loud with earnest concurrences, and the people drank with great decorum. Moved by the plaudits, Eva smiled. Nicholas saw it in her sporty blue eyes. She was happy in her new home.

E P I L O G U E
M O S C O W

Seven years after the Beckham-Bernadette election, the Dunn family headed to southeast Ohio for a family reunion. After the reunion, the Dunns went north and stopped for two days at one of their favorite places, the J.D. Pruitt Nature Preserve in South Columbus. Jim and Linda Dunn had met during a birding expedition on the barrier islands off the coast of South Carolina, when they were both just out of college. They had been avid birders ever since, and were now teaching their children how to keep track of all the species they had seen. The Dunns had visited the preserve twice before, as there was something magical about the pileated woodpeckers in spring, when they drilled through bark for ants and worms to feed their hungry young. What enhanced the spectacle was that the woodpeckers were not migratory birds. They mated for life and remained in one place. And they must be smart, Jim Dunn told his kids, because they had picked a good home, a place of comfort and bounty. Underneath the relentless drumming of the woodpeckers came the melodic songs of the warblers and tanagers, which fluttered in and out of the shards of errant light that pierced the high canopy.

"And to think," Jim Dunn said to his kids, "all of this was nearly bulldozed to make way for an industrial park."

The Dunns pitched their tents on the emerald field next to the handsome stand of oaks. The sun dropped below the line of royal trees and the sky turned crimson. Darkness came, and with it, millions of blinking stars.

Around the same time the Dunns crawled out from their tents the next morning, Oxana, halfway around the world, was just returning home from a long day of work at the Petroleum Ministry in Moscow. She emerged from the Mayakovskaya subway station and darted through the chaos of the Tverskaya to her posh flat in an Art Nouveau. Before taking the steps to the fourth floor she checked her mail. Bills, bills and more bills—and a surprise letter from dear Eva.

She stashed the bills in her shoulder bag but kept the letter in her hand. She ascended the stairwell and went inside. She placed the letter on the kitchen table, went to her bedroom and changed into a pair of shorts and sandals. She laughed to herself as she inexplicably went to the closet, dug deep into her strong box, and pulled out the old Beckham T-shirt emblazoned with the pileated woodpecker. She turned it over and gazed at Mingmei's fine blue embroidery across the shoulder. *LISAKOVSKYA.* Touched by the warm hand of nostalgia, she slipped into the T-shirt and went to the kitchen. She and Eva had exchanged many letters in the last five years. The latest exchange had occurred just a few weeks ago. That's why this letter, this paper visit from America, seemed ominous and strange. Oxana slid the envelope into a small purse and went to her favorite café, the Pushkinskaya, on a quiet side street near the Minsk Hotel.

She sat outside near the street, lit a cigarette and ordered tea. While the waitress retrieved her order, Oxana opened the envelope. She found a short letter and a neatly folded newspaper clip. She read the letter first.

Dear Oxana,

Nothing has changed since the last time I wrote you. James and I and the kids are fine. Things are good and status quo. Enclosed is a news article I thought you needed to read. I was skimming through the paper the other day and this story jumped out at me. I immediately thought of you and those crazy days during and after the election. I don't know how you will take this, but please, always know that it was you who had the courage to seek justice.

Love,
Eva

P.S. I will be in Prague for three weeks during Christmas and New Year's. Perhaps I can route my return flight through St. Petersburg and meet you for a day or two. If this sounds good, give me a call in the next few weeks and we can start making plans.

Oxana folded the letter and slid it back into the envelope. Then she unfolded the small piece of newsprint and read the headline. Suddenly thirsty for news, she plunged into the article.

Inmate Fatally Stabbed in Maximum Security Unit.

COLUMBUS, OHIO – *Dean Bernadette, an inmate at the Ohio State Penitentiary, was found strangled and stabbed to death in his cell Monday morning during a routine count, a prison official said. Bernadette, 35, was serving a life sentence for the June 1995 murder of 30-year-old John Johnson. Prison officials said they are still investigating Bernadette's death, the third at the prison this year. Bernadette was convicted in 1996. He unsuccessfully appealed his conviction on the grounds that certain evidence should not have been allowed at trial. Prison officials said Bernadette was being detained at the Maximum Security Unit because he had a history of attacking guards.*

Oxana went nearly breathless, but she felt no remorse. Outside of earning her double master's in environmental engineering and environmental economics—and moving to Moscow, of course—putting Dean behind bars was the best thing she had ever done.

She remembered the trial as if it had happened last week.

It was early February. The Franklin County Courthouse lawn was powdered with snow, and thick flurries danced in the dim morning light. A child of the steppes, she appeared for testimony dressed accordingly—in a mink ushanka, a black knee-length coat of Russian sable, a black sheath and black stiletto heels. She strolled through the news gantlet with the grace of a runway model, and with the dour resolve of someone intent on putting a man in prison. The camera flashes produced a galaxy of light. The reporters ran after her as if they were hounds. At the courthouse steps, beefy sheriff's deputies jostled the TV crews that blocked the front door. Strangers called her name and shoved microphones in her face. One man even stood in the courthouse lobby wildly waving the Kazakhstan flag. Oxana had never made such a grand entrance, or a more important one, as she was the state's key witness in a case that had managed to grab national headlines. The sheer intrigue of her name—Oxana Petrovna Lisakovskya—and a pilfered bag of blackmail notes, had aroused the curiosity of the coffee-stained press and the shining network media.

It was the intent of the defense to break her testimony and smear her as a whore. Fully aware that such would be the tactic, she spoke nothing but English in the year leading up to trial. By the time she took the stand she spoke million-dollar American, and not once did she use the translator provided by the state. But she didn't want to present herself as an angel or a prude. Indeed, she wanted the jury to see her and say, "Now there is a woman who can seduce a man!" And she wanted Dean to see the most beautiful woman he had ever had, and for him to feel the full venom of her sting. Hence the professional nail job, satin ruby, a new coiffure, a pearl choker, and salon quality makeup.

Oxana was on the stand for nearly four hours, and as expected, the defense tried to discredit her during cross-examination. With her head high and her jaw taut, she responded to the defense's barbed questions with the most eloquent, measured English she had ever spoken. During testimony she glanced at the jury. She gleaned from their somber faces that they were convinced by her story and that Dean was bound for the jailhouse. Her hunch was confirmed a day later when the jury issued a verdict of guilty and recommended a life sentence. The judge had warned the gallery that an outburst of any kind would merit a charge of contempt. With the exception of a muffled cry, his order was obeyed. But in the hallway just outside the courtroom, pandemonium erupted. Red-faced and screaming, members of Dean's family jeered Oxana as she trotted down the steps. The media hounds, all of them begging for an interview, were at her heels as she scampered through the rotunda. Outside in the frigid winds of dusk, John Johnson's poor, tearful mother awaited.

"God bless you, Oxana, God bless you!" she said, and kissed her on the cheek.

Oxana shook her head and sighed at the recollection.

The waitress returned with the tea. Oxana gave her a perfunctory nod and a 100-ruble note. She dipped the bag of chamomile into the cup of steaming water. Smiling, she watched a couple of young lovers meander down the street. On the other side of the café patio several intellectuals discussed the finer points of political relations among Russia, the United States, and China. From within the café came the familiar laughter of the neighborhood drunk, Ivan Sharapov, and his merry court. Oxana saw a few friends at the end of the block and waved. They headed her way. She slid the envelope back into her purse and put out her cigarette.

As the tea steeped, a pink soulful sunset crept over Moscow.

A native Texan, Richard Massey lived in New England, the Midwest, and the Deep South before settling in Northwest Arkansas in 2007. A career reporter with over a decade of experience, he cut his teeth at city hall and the courthouse. While he's been to just about every juke joint on the Mississippi Delta, he also appreciates the Rembrandt collection at the Metropolitan Museum of Art in New York. He has a bachelor's degree in history from Ohio State University, and a master's degree in journalism from Ole Miss.

CPSIA information can be obtained
at www.ICGtesting.com
Printed in the USA
FFOW02n0538050317
33020FF